# CRAZY IN BERLIN

# CRAZY
## in
# BERLIN

**THOMAS BERGER**

*CHARLES SCRIBNER'S SONS* New York

*TO JEANNE*

*Du bist verrückt, mein Kind;*
*Du musst nach Berlin . . .*

You are crazy, my child;
You must go to Berlin . . .

—Old song

# CRAZY IN BERLIN

# CHAPTER 1

IN THE twilight, the bust appeared to be that of some cocked-hat Revolutionary War hero of not the very first rank, that is, not G. Washington but perhaps one of those excellent Europeans noted in fact and apocrypha for throwing their weight on our side, Lafayette, say, or von Steuben. *Fun Shtoyben* was the right way to say it, which Reinhart knew and was certain that Marsala didn't, being his dumb but lovable buddy who was now gurgling at what was left of the bottle and would shortly hurl it away, maybe hurting someone, for a few Germans sat around in the park; he must warn him. But too late, there went the crash and narrowly missing a Kraut who merely smiled nervously and moved off, some difference from a movie Nazi who, monocled and enraged, would have spat in your face, and they were already taking a leak on Lafayette or whoever—no, "Friedrich der Grosse," the pedestal said, for Reinhart had a lighter that could be worked with one hand.

And it was a gross thing to do, he decided in one of those drifts of remorse that blow across a drunk—because he was just educated enough to recall vaguely old Frederick out at Sans Souci with Voltaire, writing in French, representing the best, or the worst, of one tradition or the other—a part of the punkhood from which he had just this day legally departed, and which he was, in fact, at this very moment celebrating.

Fastening the fly, all one hundred buttons, no zippers in the Army because you might get caught in one as the enemy crept close, he said, just as sad as he had before been exuberant: "What a way to pass your twenty-first birthday!"

"Well," answered Marsala, twenty-four, looking forty, and always fit whatever his condition, spitting, not taking out, his cigarette, and miffed, "we could of made you a party from the messhall: them cooks are all my friends. What are you, griping?"

As they turned to leave the park, a German nipped up and snatched the butt. There stood a woman by a tree. "Honey," Marsala shouted, "*schlafen mit* me, ohhh won't you *schlafen mit* me!" A kind of music the making of which was his satisfaction, for having crooned it he moved on indifferently.

On the street they encountered a Russian soldier, far from home, needless to say unkempt and weary, destination unknown most of all to himself. In the friendly light of his hound's eye they accepted, and Reinhart returned, a salute; he went on in a hopeless, probably Slavic, manner. A two-car streetcar braked to a glide and they swung aboard, paying no fare because they were Occupation; and a good thing they hadn't to, for in a moment the son of a bitch stopped and everybody detrained and walked around a bomb crater to another car waiting on the other side, Marsala all the while looking truculently hither and yon: he was amiable only to his friends.

The ride on the new car Reinhart forgot even as it was in progress, for he had now reached that secondary state of inebriation in which the mind is one vast sweep of summer sky and there is no limit to the altitude a kite may go, the condition in which one can repair intricate mechanisms at other times mysterious, solve equations, craft epigrams, make otherwise invulnerable women, and bluff formidable men, when people say, "Why, *Reinhart!*" and rivals wax bitter. Here he was in Berlin—the very name opened magic casements on the foam of seas perilous not two months since: Hitler was rumored to be still at large, the C.O. had been briefly interned by the Russians, and Art Flanders, the "crack foreign correspondent whose headquarters were in the saddle" and column in 529 dailies from Maine to the Alamo, had already called at the outfit for human-interest sketches.

Indeed, the sheer grandeur of his geographical position had overwhelmed Reinhart until this very day, for he was an irrepressible dreamer. Marsala had been out screwing and playing the black market for a week, with already a dose of crabs and a wad of Occupation marks to show for it, and at the same time bitching incessantly that they might be stuck there forever—and nonpartisan in his disinterest in any place but Home. No, he wouldn't have liked to be stuck in Calabria any better, besieged by his indigent relatives and wallowing in the dirt and backwardness for which no one could tell him of all people, his father having come from there, that Italy was not famous. "I got your Roman ruins and your art right here," he would sometimes say, grabbing his clothes in the area of the scrotum—the same place, in fact, that the Romans had had them—"You take that crap and give me the United States of America."

Now, on the car, Marsala was once again the sound of unadorned naturalism, his hard voice, the one for enemies, piercing Reinhart's shoulder, for that was all the higher he came, like a rusty blade: "You call it. I'll kick it out of you wherever you want."

His target was sealed with them in the crowd on the rear platform: an American soldier, between whom and Marsala stood, swaying with the general rhythm of the rocking car, a female citizen. Her visible part was a head of blonde hair, with a good washing probably as pale as Reinhart's own, but at present long estranged from soap and comb and as stringy as an Assyrian's beard. Notwithstanding that he had barracked with the man for two years, in whatever land, Reinhart supposed, first, a mistake, and, second, that Marsala was wronged, but these suppositions could not dwell long even in a flushed mind, for he saw the face of the other soldier charged with righteous outrage. A big man, maybe six even, with his weight from front to back, rather than in width, if one could tell from a limited view of his shoulders and fat, seedy head. He struck you right off as a lousy guy, a type who had been drafted from the driver's seat of a big-city bus, where he cursed *sotto voce* at proffered dollar bills and depressed the door-lever on latecomers; a journeyman in the Shitheels' Guild whose meanness was, after years, instinctive—but all this was irrelevant beside the fact that in a quarrel involving a woman Marsala invariably stood on the bad side. He had surely with one of his sexual instruments, voice, hands, or groin, sought an unsubtle connection—for him a crowded streetcar was as good as an alley and being caught out only a minor inconvenience soon adjusted in his favor: he had a friend, while the other man was alone.

Thus was Reinhart's euphoria wrenched away; what Marsala expected of him was by the known pattern of his friend's code so obvious as to go unstated. When the car stopped at the next bomb crater and the German passengers, all slumped and carrying bundles, duly filed around its margins to still another vehicle, the three soldiers and one girl drew apart and, out of a sudden sense of national delicacy, waited until the new car started away and the old reversed trolleys and started back. Then Marsala snarled, "Let's get him," pitching in before the other man, now manifestly regretting where amour propre had led him as he saw Reinhart's large figure on the hostile side, had got ready: he was in the act of removing his blouse, newly pressed, perhaps by the girl, and bearing the triangle of the Second Armored Division which had fought all the way from Africa—while Reinhart and Marsala were goofing off in Camp Grant, Illinois, Devonshire, and some tent city in long-liberated Normandy.

As a medic, and rear-area at that, Reinhart had no moral guts to oppose a combat man, even for cause, even when alcohol had anaesthetized his rational-young-man's disinclination to violence—and as for two setting upon one, its morality threw him into a state of shock. He stood in his tracks, feeling undue exposure, lighting a smoke, and out of a complex shame not looking at the girl, and saw Marsala imprison the opponent's arms with the half-removed jacket and call: "Okay, Carlo, in the nuts!" Saw him, not able to resist his advantage until help arrived, give the man one with the knee.

His reaction to Reinhart's coming and pulling him loose was pure astonishment, hopefully as yet unalloyed with bitterness—he must have supposed it the prelude to a more cunning mayhem—and he had just time to begin "What the fu—" before the freed adversary got a hammerlock on his throat and booted Reinhart from the field.

They fought on the site of a ruin. As Reinhart lay on the crushed-masonry ground, beneath a roof-to-basement cross section of fourteen flats, their cavities spilling tubs and bedsteads, he could not even have said where. On to two weeks in the city, and this was his first trip off base. His old buddy, for his birthday, had taken him to a black-market contact with Russian hootch to sell, his old buddy who in the grunting ranges overhead was at this moment being slaughtered. So he raised himself, hot and vital and clear, seized the traitorous and ugly bastard from the Armored by the back of the shirt-neck, turned him, and delivered two hundred three and a half pounds to the gut, to the eye and into the mouth. The man's meat broke wetly under his fists and yet retreated at one point to bulge at another, like some hateful sack of liquid, and it was for a time a joyful rage to work for a simultaneous and general recession. But where it took him was too terrible—all at once he gave it up. The enemy, in a vast cobweb of blood, still stood. Odd, he appeared old, perhaps forty; his cap had gone, showing an area of baldness pitifully made conspicuous by a strand of hair deviated to hide it. He was standing—but it was suddenly obvious that he was very dead.

Reinhart had broken both hands at the wrist. His lungs were gone, as well; his stomach was acid and his wit beclouded once more. It was so frightening that a corpse should remain upright. He watched Marsala come round and head-butt it in the midsection. It revived, and it fell, simply a beaten man, with an awful, beaten groan.

"Jesus," said Marsala. "Not a car in sight. We might have to walk all the way back just because of this prick of misery. You did good, Carlo," he went on, rubbing his sore neck, which made a rasping noise, for he had an emery-paper beard. Kept rubbing, but he was in some awe.

Reinhart had not been in a fight since early grammar school and therefore had never known how it felt to kill a man and what, when done, was the peculiar scandal. He looked to the girl, who was some distance removed in the capacity of spectator, and who in return looked at him with stupid wonderment, and commanded her to approach. Which she did with a senseless caution, as if to ask: is my turn next?

"Why don't you attend to him?"—approximately; his German was at best uncertain and now surely further corrupted by the intermittent buzzer in his skull.

"Well, yes, if you wish," she replied, still showing wonder, and speaking from a face in which the ages were so mixed that one knew not whether oldness or youth was the essence. She knelt in worn clothing more suited to that attitude than the standing and examined the felled opponent, who even at her touch was coming painfully around. Who when he arrived came up slowly and resentfully from the supine, crying: "Keep your whore off me!" With more effort he was arisen and deliberately, crazily, gone across the ruin and onto the sidewalk, where it could be found and where not, the street, where, alone, he could be seen for a great time, despite the darkness now settled.

"Hadn't you better follow him?" Reinhart asked incredulously. "If the car does come he may be hit."

"Must I?" She was nearer him now and, it struck him repugnantly, believed herself a transferred spoil of war.

"No, of course not, not if you haven't any *decency*." The last word in English; he didn't know it in German, and she didn't know it this way or, in truth, hadn't any, for she smiled.

Nothing smelled ranker than disloyalty. He had wanted so much to approve of the first German girl he met—for this was she, not counting the women seen from train and truck on the journey to Berlin or the cleaning and secretarial help—if for nothing else, as an act of anti-piety against the established faith. The very faith of which, curiously enough, he found himself at least a part-time worshiper, one of those half-agnostics who go to church without believing or stay home and believe; whatever, he had waited two weeks before going on pass, since this was the best manner in which to avoid Germans and still ache, with trepidation and even a kind of love, to see them.

"If I must go—*wiederschau'n!*" She extended her hand in the genuine enthusiasm displayed by all Europeans, not just the French, upon arrivals and departures, as if for all their hatreds they love one another, or do for a moment at making and breaking contact, and at this first touch in ten minutes not motivated by hostility, Reinhart suddenly felt drunken again and feared that he might weep—for the sore opponent vanished alone in the night, for his friend who did not understand fighting fair, for the girl now under his compulsion, and for the material things in waste all about them, all the poor, weak, assaulted and assaulting people and things, and of course for himself, isolated by a power he didn't want.

But certainly he did not cry. Instead he gave her his dizzy eyes and said:

"It's a terrible thing to desert a friend."

"*Bitte?*"

He repeated it, as near as he could come, in German, and she replied:

"There was nothing else you could do. He would have killed the small man."

*She* was granting *him* absolution! But his anger did at any rate conquer the sadness. He barked his ill will towards a woman who leaves a beaten man, and in a moment found his only ease in the thought that with luck his speech had been too bad for her full comprehension. For she had answered:

"I was not *with* the soldier! Believe me, in all my life I have never before seen him!"

So much for that. And Marsala, who had had his rest, was prepared to reassume the command so lately transferred; he might defer to Reinhart, from now on, in matters of personal combat, but surely never in affaires d'amour.

"C'mon, why mess with this one? A pig," he said without malice, perhaps kindly, if you wished to look at it that way, for there was no point in stirring up the girl's hopes, but anyhow with the candor of the unembellished man, which was just what Reinhart prized highest in Marsala and why he associated with him rather than with the refugees from college. The cruelty was an inseparable element of the greater value, a unique honesty and a kind of honor: Marsala never assumed an ethical superiority to anyone else. But he was generous in granting one, for now no sooner were his comments out than he showed with a bored jerk of the head that the girl's pigness was suddenly understood as Reinhart's precise interest.

"If the girl didn't belong to him," asked Reinhart, "what in hell was the beef?"

"How should I know?" Marsala's swarthy head revolved in unworried failure to understand the provocations constantly offered; the world was full of enemies, that was all. You watched, you took care of them, they took care of you—you did not look for a reason and you didn't actually feel any lasting grudge. "There's all kinds of bastards around." He scratched his boot-toe in the rubble. "If you really want to know, he called me a guinea."

Reinhart, missing the sly grin of mock piety and having learned Marsala's elaborate code regarding these nicknames—Marsala himself habitually used them and especially those applying to his own kind, but denied the latter to non-guineas except people like Reinhart who held an honorary card—merely said "Oh" and turned to the Kraut girl.

At close view he decided she was young and that her longitudinal lines of cheek and veteran eyes were from lifelong residence in a sanguinary country, but the darkness forbade one's being sure. She had merely come to watch a fight?

"One has to admit that it was interesting." She had moved very close to him, perhaps because of the dark, and there was enough light to see that just a chance remained to make her attractive, at least to get by. Reinhart would have liked to seize and scrub and comb and color and dress her—to straighten her out; the world was filled with people who out of simple inertia wouldn't make a move to fulfill their own promise.

"But," she went on, "you are a noncommissioned officer. Please, may I ask you: how does one get a job with the Americans?"

"There are places for such things," he disappointedly replied. He hadn't known *what*, yet had hoped for something other than the humdrum, perhaps an unexpected birthday gift. His parents' package had not arrived, very likely never would, the occasion being one on which their undependability was notable. Besides, the girl became more attractive as she talked; her voice was pitched low and had a melancholy music and her whole manner was submission to the male principle. "You want me to get you a job, is that right?" She was within a hair of contact with his belt buckle, and he had come under a compulsion at once to fuse into her body and not move his, which could be done by easing forward the belly usually, as a matter of vanity, held back.

"For Christ Almighty sake," said Marsala, in the testiness of one whose judgment has gone unheeded, "the soldier has gone horny." He was right by being wrong; he assumed their conversation to be a bargaining.

They were now touching, the girl standing firm and, madly, as if unconscious of anything strange, pursuing her first interest: "It's all so confusing. I am ready to do any kind of work—as cleaning woman if need be. . . . Do you have a *bottmann?*"

It was much too rare for his simple vocabulary. He had not learned it in two years of college where he ostensibly majored in the language but in fact moped lonely around bars and crowded, smoky places with small string combos, with no real stomach for liquor and no real courage with women, drinking much, nevertheless, and fumbling at some tail. On the margin of a flat flunk he had enlisted in the Army. At any rate, he could deliver correctly not a single long sentence in German and could translate nothing beyond very short strings of words with exact English equivalents.

*You are a bad man* was maybe what she meant; if so it was a weak remonstrance, as when you are small and exchange exposures with the neighbor girl, who coyly says "You are a bad boy," all the while pulling up her dress. He had slipped his arm into her worn coat, where a missing button made it easy, and around her narrow waist, and she came full into him, saying still, so madly!: "Is a female *bottmann* allowed?"

Suddenly and so nuttily did its sense at last arrive that he released her and retreated a step. *Lives of a Bengal Lancer, Four Feathers,* "but when it comes to slaughter you will do your work on water, an' you'll lick the bloomin' boots of 'im that's got it." When you were in the field against Mohammed Khan, Oxford-educated Pathan who returned to his mountain fastness to lead the tribes against the Crown, you had a batman; when, that is, you were a British officer serving Victoria, to whom you drank health and broke the glass, or for all he knew even at present, you had an orderly.

"Well, I'm going, *I'm on my way,*" Marsala groaned reproachfully, and hypocritically, for he scraped away only a short distance and sat down on a wasted wall, lighted a cigarette with a great flare and coughed.

Her look had no defenses: "I know just a few English words."

"That one is very rare," replied Reinhart with all his gentle forces. He added: "I am just an *Unteroffizier,* a corporal, a nobody, a silly fellow—"

She returned his smile in the exact degree of wryness with which it had been given her, aiding him, in tune with him, so that when the exchange was completed he had been purged of self-pity and satisfaction with the vision of himself as uncorrupted by efficacy; and furthermore was not made sore by its loss. He was forgiven all the way down the line, and most of all for thinking it was forgiveness—she was far beyond that, standing there before him on the mound of trash, without vanity, making no judgments, facing facts.

"*Also,*" he said. "You will have your job. You have my word."

His oath was no doubt meaningless in German; one certainty of alien languages was that each had its own way, untranslatable, for the moral expressions. But its effect was not needed by her, who it could be seen in the clearness of her eye admitted no doubt towards him.

Marsala was back, seizing Reinhart's elbow and, this time with unbelievable modesty, whispering in his ear: "You're not thinking of slipping her the tool? I mean, it's all right with me, I just wanted to get things straight, no sense for me to stand here, just gimme the sign—"

"Old buddy," said Reinhart, "friends may come and friends may go and some may peter out, I know, but I'll be yours through thick or thin."

"Yeah, I know," came Marsala's hoarse whisper, which was louder than his normal voice, "'peter out or peter in.' Well, what will it be? It's boring to stay here. I mean, for me." "Boring" was a word he had learned from Reinhart, using it with weak authority and only as a favor to his teacher. It took quite enough effort, however, to have its power.

"You must come to see me at my organization," Reinhart told the girl. "Now can you remember this? It is the 1209th—but the number doesn't matter. We are a military hospital and are in a school building in Zehlendorf, at the corner of Wilskistrasse and Hartmannsweiler Weg. Across the street in a wooden building is headquarters. You come in the door and turn left. You go all the way to the end of the hall, to the last room, and there I am."

The language became easier to use as he spoke, and he found

himself on better terms with talking than he had been in years; in German even directions were a kind of success, precise and scientific. Still in temper with him, the girl, now three feet away and in deep shadow, said: "You have a good accent!"

"Now you *will* remember?"

"Oh yes! But please, what is your name?"

He had turned to leave with Marsala, like a monarch—in all the world there are no good departures—and now, kingly, gave: "Carlo."

She was stepping towards him in an eager courtesy. "As in Monaco—I shall remember."

Marsala grinned like a possum at the traditional repast; honor was being done his old rule: give them only your first name, which cannot be traced. His lack of civilization had suddenly become repulsive.

"No—Reinhart, Carlo Reinhart. *Es ist ein deutscher Name.*"

"Certainly."

He shook hands with her and in American fashion held it too long, so that hers wilted and sought to escape.

They were still a party of three at the streetcar stop. But before one came, if ever it did, a jeep throttled up out of the blackness, bearing MPs on their eternal quest for miscreants. Like all American police, they stayed at their remove of faint hostility even after Reinhart and Marsala identified themselves and proved blameless; indeed, even after the constables took them aboard for a ride to their billeting area, which since it lay off the beat was a considerable favor, it seemed needful for the sake of an institutional pride that all pretend it was a kind of arrest and sit silent on the way. The four men, that is, for the girl had not been considered, had not, properly speaking, been seen, the non-fraternization policy being neither quite repealed nor, beyond the flagrant, enforced.

She might stay there for hours—this was a thought of Reinhart's, which he answered with the familiar indictment: so many millions of non-Germans would lie dead forever. Yet it had been so appropriate to pity her; he aggressively presented that claim to himself. "Certainly" was her answer to the characterization of his name. From birth he had been a good, sturdy *German* type, lived in a solid *German* house, on a diet of *G.* potato salad (with vinegar), *G.* cole slaw (with bacon grease), *G.* coffeecake (with butter-lakes), run on a regimen of *G.* virtue (bill-paying, bedding and rising early, melancholia), and whenever he left it was met by approving people who said: "Ah! He's going to be (or is) a big *G.* like his grandfather."

The term, however, had a double meaning, which was honored even by near-illiterates; its other use was as synonym for a kind of foulness. And now there was a third, for here he was in the ancient homeland, and he was something different.

"Home" was a compound in Zehlendorf from which the 1209th General Hospital had evicted the German residents, a block of three long apartment buildings arranged in an open rectangle around a private park. The latter, in some former time almost a university campus with green and wanton walks for rambling, had been converted at the order of the 1209th's commanding officer into a junkyard for the disposal of property the Germans left behind. The colonel was neither opposed to comfort for his men nor a partisan of pain and deprivation for the owners who after all would one day return; he was nothing, no Savonarola, no crypto-fascist symbol of the military mind, not even, because he was a medic, quite a soldier, nor, because he was commanding officer, quite a doctor—but owing to this he wished grievously to be something, if only a converter of matter from one form to another. Thus he periodically had put to the torch, had resolved into carbon and the immaterial gases, the giant cairn of objects which Reinhart and Marsala now skirted on their way to the south building: couches and loveseats, dining tables, bedsteads, chaises longues, sideboards, three pianos, fourteen wind-up victrolas and two thousand records; eight thousand books; rugs, pictures, tablecloths, postcard collections, skis, jewelry boxes, letters, diaries, journals, manuscripts, apologias, Nazi party cards, memoranda, paper, paper, paper; and one little souvenir plaque from the Western Hemisphere: an electric-pencil sketch of a pickaninny sitting in a Chic Sale, inscribed "Best wishes from Savannah, Ga." Another pile held the noncombustibles, mainly cooking utensils and fifty more or less complete china services from the royal house of an imaginary principality.

Five men had been busted in rank when caught salvaging items from the auto-da-fé. On the other hand, the colonel did not lack in a rude sense of justice: if you could make away with an overstuffed chair or an alarm clock without being seen, it was yours and beyond all future confiscation.

The tenants of Building A, first floor right, had furnished a very decent little flat, the cynosure, as Reinhart might say, of all eyes in their section. Particularly those of Buck Sergeant Tom Riley, their next-door neighbor and late technician third grade, who had made so free in their absence as not only to enter their home but also to sink his big ass into the mohair couch and fall asleep. When awakened by the crudest means they could summon on such short notice, he arose complaining, "You must of got your nose up the colonel to get to keep this furniture. Our living room looks like a Mexican cat house." He lumped fatly to the hall door. "And why only two guys here instead of three?" His swollen nose tensed with authentic peevishness, and small wonder, for he had been reduced one grade for unsuccessful pilferage from the trashpile; but more than that, he was by instinct a petulant man, with the face of an old baby.

"Don't be bitter," said Reinhart, who had followed him out. "It's my birthday."

"Oh." As might have been expected, he missed the ironic import of the non sequitur; he would be resentful, thank you, on his own time and ground; instead, he grasped Reinhart's hand in embarrassed but genuine feeling, as you could tell by his nose, which went soft, saying: "You don't mean to bird-turd me? Many happy returns of the day." And already at his own door, he turned: "Ain't it sad? Here we are, getting older by the minute." Without change of expression or girding himself for the effort, he suddenly screamed, in a voice like a jazz cornet, an obscene epithet which, though it went up the concrete stairwell like a skyrocket, made no public stir, being heard all over the 1209th so frequently that it had lost its force as description: if you ever found that fellow to whom it was originally applied, you should have to think up a new one.

Because nothing succeeded like the envy of others, Reinhart returned to the living room in a, now sober, swagger. Off the top floor of the building lay an attic stuffed with furniture—the colonel lighted the bonfire only after his space ran out—and Marsala and Reinhart had picked the lock on its door and secretly helped themselves while everybody else was away at work. As to tenants, the orders demanded three per flat; given free choice, the buddies shrewdly compacted with Doyle, who three days later left on detached service.

So they had a proper home now, Marsala, a slum boy, confessing it was the nicest he ever had and the most spacious. Parlor, kitchen, and bath were luxuries militarily undreamed of. You could, see, get some rations from a cook, have a little lunch in the kitchen, then take your broad to the couch, knock off a piece, and then wash up in the bath. Marsala had indeed gone through the series three times in recent days, failing only in the last because he could not make a swift transition from pleasure to hygiene. Hence the jar of blue ointment in the bathroom medicine chest, yet another evidence the place was truly home.

The green tiles of the corner stove were still warm from a small fire they had built just after chow; July nights were cool this far north. A fall of maroon drapery concealed the big window above the couch, which in the daytime showed their private balcony and, beyond, a green promenade between their block and the next, an *allée* in the old, European sense, banned to cars and wastecans—and to the colonel, for natives retained ownership of the adjacent buildings. The enormous sideboard on the east wall had almost ruptured them to carry, and had little utility when in place, but great authority. Central was a round table of oak and six attendant chairs. No tablecloth. Other deficiencies were: nothing matched; no pictures on the wall; no knickknacks placed around; no doilies to protect the arms of the couch; no magazine rack with *The Woman's Home Companion* and last week's *This Week* and the publication General Motors sends gratis to Chevrolet-drivers. But it was Reinhart's own home and he believed it was nice.

He seated himself at the table to brood on the folly of early-evening drinking, his close-cropped blond head propped on a red fist still tremulous from the fight, pale-blue eyes charged with red, one trouserleg loose from the knotted condom round the boot-top. Marsala, who didn't know it was not nearly time to go to bed, had ignorantly gone and tomorrow would awake extra soon and, it went without saying, loud.

Reinhart all his life had detested birthdays; they were like Sundays in the middle of the week, outlawing the ordinary by a promise of the special, never fulfilled. Until this moment, for he could never think while in motion, the twenty-first had been another of the same. But, ruminating, he saw now that it had, indeed, a touch of the exotic. He had drawn blood and spilled some of his own. He rose and went again to the hall mirror in which he had inspected himself on the route back from Riley's leaving. No, no hallucination: a nice scratch-cum-bruise on the left cheekbone, made easier to see if you tweezered your fingers about it. Riley, still sleepy, no doubt had laid it to shaving.

In addition to Marsala's salve, the bathroom cabinet held Reinhart's collection of medicines. Once every two months he had a slight complaint, each time in a different organ, never serious—whichever doctor was on duty in the 1209th dispensary would smile, prescribe, and likely as not give in to the urge to punch the tight belly and caution him jokingly not to worry, the undertaker would be a stranger to him for years.

The large merthiolate badge had dried and was almost ready to flake before he finished his final self-examination in the bathroom mirror, in the course of which his spirits curved downwards again. The pompous, pink-and-blond-faced creep who stared back at him had been endured enough for one day. He got out his rubbing alcohol, cotton, and applicator sticks, and wiped away the crimson fraud, threw the evidence out the window, went to the bedroom, kicked his clothes in the corner, fell on the bed next to Marsala's, and was immediately in sleep.

## CHAPTER 2

FIRST Lieutenant Nathan Schild, a traitor, handed a sheaf of papers to the German known as "Schatzi," a courier to—well, above all, to an impossibility, since the measure of truth is what a man will give for it and Schild would have walked to the noose to deny that this Thing had any existence outside the mind of a malignant halfwit. Schatzi himself was just barely possible, being a returned traveler from that until the twentieth century undiscovered bourne; the most efficient of men, who could answer all questions with: "I was four years in Auschwitz." Behind that, darkness, and not, according to the code of the underground, to be searched by Schild. Although Schatzi wore the garb of a petty bureaucrat—felt hat, stiff collar, briefcase—he suggested a ruin; although the night was warm, he trembled and winced, as if the whole of his skin had been sandpapered and recorded in pain the blows of the air's molecules.

"What is this stuffing?" asked Schatzi, roaming Schild's person with his free hand like a restless lover's, probing the fly-front of the blouse.

Schild extracted a folder. "I forgot it because it's more or less negligible."

"Needless remark," said Schatzi, pleasantly nasty. He struck Schild on the elbow with his finger-tips like a row of icepicks, of course hitting the nerve.

If a man could be said to have earned a broader latitude of eccentricity than most, it was Schatzi. He had once shown Schild the scars on his back, and if it had been day one could have seen the terrible commentary of his face, a kind of scorecard of the times. And that he had undergone torture and was not a Jew made it all the more criminal for Schild to detest him.

20

"Please," said Schild, with genuine, if exaggerated feeling, for, although it was not that important, neither was it of no matter, and Schatzi discounted precision, "I must have this back by to-morrow noon at the outside. Captain St. George just asked for it."

*"Er kann mich im Arsche lecken!"* Sooner or later Schatzi related everything to himself, and scatologically, which was not perverse given his late experience of life reduced to essentials. Nevertheless, while understood, the common-denominatorship of Schatzi was hardly winning. Also in character, Schatzi walked in a cloud of food odors; tonight it was herring. But who was so degraded as to gainsay his right to courtly fare, let alone such simple meals as he was no doubt issued at some Soviet mess?

They stood on a strip of Wannsee shore near a wrecked pleasure pavilion, the salient feature of which was a tin Coca-Cola sign hanging crazily in the light of Schatzi's torch, the patented slogan of its own International in German here; downtown Schild had seen the red and gold standard of Woolworth's in a similar death-agony of capitalism. Beyond the symbolism it was a remote and even foolish place to meet. Two men upon a dark bench, one a German civilian . . . it was not Schild's job to pass upon the point of rendezvous—while not forgetting for a moment that Schatzi was his superior, his mind was also wired in another circuit with the alternating current of forgetting and remembering—but he did, anyhow, make his apprehensions known, and Schatzi suggested next time bringing a girl for protective coloration. Such was Schatzi's circuit: belly-rectum-pubis. The simplest interpretation was that he lived somewhere near the lake; perhaps, like a rat, in a hole just above the water line. Sometimes, in fact, as if caught by a sudden high tide, he appeared damp at their appointments. Schild bit his mind's tongue; at least Schatzi said what Schatzi thought, suffered no internal wrestling matches with an indestructible malice like an extra organ.

In a sudden surge of self-remonstrance, Schild said: "We get a ration of candy, you know. In the American Army there are constant pressures upon the soldiers to be the same conspicuous consumers they were in civilian life. It's not enough just to fight a war."

Schatzi took the chocolate bar from his hand, undid its wrapper, scrutinized it in the light's ray with an invisible jeweler's lens, tested its friability with a thumbnail.

"I really found one last week that had all of it been shaped from brown clay. Think on that! The astonishing industriousness required, it having been a first-order job. All that work for fifty mark and you Amis are burdened with actual ones that you cannot eat till the day of doom."

He pushed five ten-mark notes, already rubber-banded into that amount—yes, the Japs held the Malay Peninsula, but his bands were pure gum—into the hand of Schild which had come forward on its own volition, on its own idiotic hand's sense that it would be shaken, just as a foot will all at once assume sovereignty and stub itself as punishment for some foot-crime or kick the girl's shoe across the way out of some foot-lust. Schild's face meanwhile was performing, in a vacuum, a squalid drama.

"But, my dear fellow, you shall not get more than this at the Tiergarten and think on the length of miles from here to there. You are an actual Greek for business, comrade!"

Schatzi returned the candy and took back the money, signifying the end of his joke.

"I know people who are pleased at your work," he resumed, "and if you are not so careful they shall give you one of these posterboards to take home to Tennessee: 'The Hitlers Come and Go Away But the German People Stay Always!'"

"If you get some pleasure from insisting that I'm from Tennessee, go ahead—" began Schild, but the flashlight quivered and sank, and Schatzi groaned from the ground: "I like the name."

"An attack of dizzy," he went on as Schild bent to aid, "brought on by four heavy suppers every day and eight hours of sleep the night, still in a warm bed. *Gemütlichkeit* is killing me.

Give me some pills in the right pocket, they will make me miserable." There was nothing in either pocket but Occupation marks. "Make all the money you canst," said Schatzi, on his feet again but breathing with a whistle and coughing bubbly.

At such moments the call of Schild's guilt echoed through the great tombs of the martyrs. Schatzi was indeed dying, yet he continued to serve. This, Schild knew in the final, serious level of the self, was why he hated him so: out of his own incapacity for a like magnitude of effort.

"You know," said Schatzi, shaking his body like a dog, blowing air from his nostrils, combing his hair, long as a woman's, with his fingers, "when Kurt brought you first, to my opinion you were a double agent. Arrived at by irrational methods, it is possible, but there was something with your eyes." He took a flask from his briefcase and tasted of it. "Ah!" He spat. "Good drink will make a cat speak! They are, isn't it true, simply myopiac? A fat small man, a little soccer ball of a man with eyes like that—and thicker spectacles—came into the K.Z. along with myself. I watched, in vainly, to see the existence there bring him down." He spat again, making a nasty sound on the sand. "Ah! Cuts the flame." Schild preferred to assume his version of "phlegm" was a portmanteau word: he must be burning inside. "One gets obsessions when you are a captive. But at the end of three months still he bounced. I never did see him on a work gang. He disappeared days somewhere but in the nights returned to the barracks. I had been convinced that he was a police spy and I am in fact yet. He lay in the bed each night end-to-end with my own bed and stared at me over his round belly and through his feet. It was terrorizing, I tell you, a man could never once find him asleep. When I awokened in the morning he looked, still; perhaps he did not close his eyes the night long. Because I do not know, you see, because I tell you I slept, I functioned as usually I do, under the watching of sixty-six devils I could do as always, because I tell you that beyond a club to my genital members there is nothing which a man can do which will touch me at all."

Schatzi's voice had taken on the authority usual to his concentration-camp reminiscences. On Schild's refusal he pocketed the flask, but not before illustrating its quality, heavy silver; its feature, a spring cap worked with the thumb. As always, he withheld the dénouement until Schild in the double dread—the tedious responsibility of the auditor to help dramatize, the terrible certitude that the small fat man, whether bona fide police spy or hero, would like all the other creatures of Schatzi's memory meet an unspeakable end—until, cold in July, he must urge him to go on.

But Schatzi had got a sudden subtlety. "Is Captain St. George the ass you take him as?" He pronounced "St." as *Sankt*: no cue for worry, a man fills out abbreviations in his native tongue.

"He's a Republican."

"Are not we all? What does this mean? I don't understand, I don't understand."

"I'm sorry, I forgot. He's nonpolitical, an aboriginal American type. I thought all the world knew. Let me explain: If I express so much as simple approval of a labor union, he will say, 'Well, I'm not against unions but you've got to admit sometimes they go too far. I understand if a light bulb burns out in a factory the place stays in darkness until an authorized member of the electrical workers' union comes to replace it.' But if he saw me leading a mob on the White House under a red flag he would lay it to money or some private passion. Do you understand now? We have billeted together for two years, he knows how I look in my underwear and that I use a soap stick instead of tube lather for shaving. He knows whatever my eyebrows do when I'm puzzled, the contents of my musette bag—"

"I understand now that *you* are the ass. How does a police agent operate if not this way? Fritz, Fritz, it is a little wonder that after four years of duty you are yet a first lieutenant!" It was not clear that Schatzi meant more than chaff. He had himself taken irresponsible risks near St. George, more than once lingering before Schild's billet on a bicycle. What was obvious now, though, was his unease at Schild's developing a point, hence the underground name, a remonstrating symbol of the overwhelming awareness and power which they both served and before which elaboration was ludicrously futile.

"With all this knowledge," Schild finished defiantly, "what could not be forgiven? He would trust a man forever whom he had watched cutting his toenails."

"*Also*," said Schatzi. "I used to swim at this place but I do not mourn it—any more than I need to play the piano again. Have I told you I once have played the piano in a splendid club where the tables were connected each to each in a system of tubes from which the air is exhausted—what do you say for them?—vacuum, *so,* vacuum tubes, through which the people in this place could communicate on little pieces of paper—this was the same place where Emil Jannings was controller of the W.C. Haha! Did you hear of this film *The Last Laugh?*" He allowed the insatiable black space over the water to swallow his light's beam for a moment, then reclaimed it to thrust into Schild's eyes. "You will never drown in the water to mock the hangman, not you. I will just as soon choke myself as to have you know my real name. Without respect for this famous naïveté, there is something sinister about an American."

"You seemed to have no worry about Kurt."

"Kurt lived until aged ten in Budapest, Paris to the age of eleven and a half, Budapest again for three years, then Rome to the age of twenty, and finally Washington. His father is in the diplomatic service, his mother is an Hungarian and the influence. Do you know Kurt's actual identity? In yesterday's *Stars and Stripes*—a queer journal, by the bye! What are these letters at the lower-left hand of page two, this so-called 'B-Bag'?"

The damp had begun an osmotic affection for Schild's feet.

"Oh," he answered in a momentary quicksand of sorrow which sucked the life from his voice but was all to the good for the present purpose: "That's supposed to be the uninhibited feelings of the enlisted men with complaints, the vox populi of ersatz democracy. The name comes from an expression, 'Blow it out your barracks bag,' let off steam, air your gripes. The enlisted men used to carry their gear in two bags, one labeled 'A,' the other, 'B.'"

"I tell you that tells nothing. I have read a letter yesterday which said"—he broke off and produced the very clipping, holding the light for Schild to read:

> You can search the whole Enclave until your goddam corns are thumping and you won't find one place where EM can get anything better to drink than flat beer that the Krauts made when Hitler was a PFC. Yet every ninety-day wonder in my outfit wallows in Haig & Haig. The chickens are getting bigger and I don't have to say what is getting deeper. Yours for World War III,
>
> T/5 P . . . . .-Off
> *Bremen*

"Yes, that's the sort of thing."

"Do you ever use it?"

"No," said Schild. "As I say, it's essentially for enlisted men. Besides," smiling in irony, his profession, place, and time's surrogate for good humor, which Schatzi could not see because he was again being nervous with the flashlight, "my complaints are not so simple."

Schatzi laughed, for a change in a pleasant tone, perhaps owing to the fact that he had nothing to gain or lose from the passage: "As to this B-Bag, obscure name still, I do not believe from a swift look that the code would be too hard to break. It is not a device without imagination, but surely American Espionage has better means for important messages. I think these are no more than general intelligences for each sector. However, it would be that one can do worse than to attempt to decode the letters signed Berlin, a damp finger to the wind, one could say."

When Schatzi spoke like a neurasthenic spinster he was not fooling, even though it was only at such times that he amused Schild, an extraordinary achievement. In good Middle European style Schatzi was most suspicious of what was most innocuous, and perhaps the reverse, although in that he had not been tested. Almost to Schild's disappointment, there was nothing dangerous, complex, or oblique in the Berlin situation. As American Intelligence analyst, he inspected confiscated Nazi correspondence files; as something else entirely, he chose interesting items for transmission to Schatzi, the jobs meshing beautifully.

But Schild was a great over-preparer, despite the persistence with which, while he stood smeared with grease, Hellesponts shriveled to birdbaths. Having been alerted for his present function since he first reported to his draft board, having been, by unseen hands, guided to and through infantry OCS and later transferred to Intelligence by like means—Schatzi could suspect American naïveté, Schild could not afford to: the Party, with all its resources, could perform the miraculous only with the aid of history's buffoons—sent to France and then to Berlin with the first Occupation troops, having on a word from X, a nod from Y, and a furtive motion of the elbow joint from Z, been put in touch with "Kurt," who conducted him twice to the presence of "Schatzi" and vanished forever; symbolizing in his very position at this juncture, this square foot of wet sand, the energy and infinite pains of the agency whose creature he was—but that was just it, what small service he rendered! Two or three sheafs of trash a week, available to anybody who would walk into a bombed building and pick up a handful of scattered papers. Not to mention that the Red Army, which had got to Berlin a month before the Western powers, had surely missed little of conse-

quence. Still, this seemed somehow his own deficiency notwithstanding the clear directions that limited him to the role, and he
was conscious, in all the weak jealousy of the impotent, that
herein lay another motive for aversion to his courier of the wide
horizons.

Schatzi left off his nonsense about the counterspies' use of the
B-Bag, or what, had it not arisen from his total dedication, would
have been nonsense and resumed his original aim. "In any rate,
in yesterday's *Stars and Stripes,* on page number three, you will
find a little item to announce the appointment of Nicholas G.
Pope, civilian military-government official, as licenser of German
newspapers in Bavaria. Kurt, Pope. The very man."

How loudly he spoke, how careless with the light. The very
fact that the beach was abandoned and dark made it more conspicuous than the stage at the Titania Palast. Schild instinctively
resisted the exposure of Kurt's identity, learned it, that is, and
didn't learn it, a technique by which information could give comfort but not be divulged even under torture.

Fortunate in all his cautions and fears, for they served, after
all, to give him a constant business that his larger function did
not, Schild arranged with Schatzi for their next assignation and
sought to move off towards the broken timbers of the pavilion
and the jeep on the forest road beyond. Schatzi's hail was very
like a shiv into the small of his back. As he turned to hear the
not-forgotten-for-a-moment fate of the soccer-ball man, between
the sound and the sense he saw in his memory Schatzi's earlier
flashlight motions. Across the water lay Kladow. Who there received his signals?

". . . so this guard made off with his cap and threw it over the
top of the wire into this area that was not permitted for the
prisoners and ordered him on the pain of death instantly to go
and bring it back. The man climbed with the strange nimbleness
of the fat, quite indifferent with the barbs going into the palms
of the hands, got this cap, made it free of the snow with his

underneath side of the arm, and then brought it down over his skull, which was of course shaven clean, down to the ears. On the climb again back, he was slow and breathed hard; on the top strand of wire, he let out some steam, for it was very cold, and at the time when just more than half of his weight was over—the guard had planned it well, you see, to ensure that the fall might be on the near side—the machine-pistol bullets released the air in him and the man did not fall as planned but shriveled and stayed on the wire like a soccer-ball bladder without the air. The wind even moved him. I think still he was a concealed police-man, shot in mistake. The guard vanished some time later."

Schild's fingers crept to the button of his holster in a parody of a poorly remembered Hoot Gibson at bay. He would not really draw his pistol on Schatzi; for one thing, in the world out-side the concentration camp this was not done, or at least not by him. If Schatzi were a double agent, the worst course was a show of violence; yet his hand would not cease its histrionism, did not indeed for some moments after Schatzi wound up the anecdote and went to the heart of the matter, for his private in-telligence system extended even to the reports of Schild's nerves.

"Look," he said and boldly morsed his light at Kladow, from which, as if ignited by his, another was briefly born, died, lived, died. "I go in a minute to Potsdam with a boat full of food from an American Army kitchen. For everything I know, this can be served to Herr Truman at Stalin's villa on the next meal-time. . . . But please do not think"—he held the torch at the point of his chin, splashing the beam up across the peaks and decliv-ities of his face, as a child might make a satan's mask in the mir-ror of a darkened room.

"Of course I didn't think—"

"—that I could do this for anything but money." Upon this summit of innocence Schatzi snapped off and withdrew. In the willows by the water he made noises of effort; and well before Schild had got to his own vehicle he heard the outboard churn off in such a splash that his courier might have been on the way to quench Hell. And above and beyond the lovely organization of the jeep in first gear, he heard the boat engine climb hysterically towards its extreme velocity and, reaching it, miss and backfire and belch and puke, and his heart worked with it in the shore man's empathy until it eventually leveled into a continuum of asymetrical impulses, like a laughter hopelessly mad, hopelessly free.

# CHAPTER 3

WHEN one was ten, nobody, least of all the boys of German stem, served willingly on the Kaiser's side in war games. The little kids and younger brothers gunned Fokkers through the back yards and crashed flaming against the garage as Rickenbacker and his hat-in-ring squadron of Spads roared overhead piloted by the big boys. Then landing at the Allied aerodrome, which was quite a different thing from an airfield, and into the flight office (again the garage) swaggered they, tightbooted, helmet straps swinging free, demanding coggnack from the Frog wench behind the bar which without transition gave onto the office; while the de-Germanized younger brothers greased the planes, for this was also a hangar.

Shortly Richthofen might pay another call in his craft painted all checkers like a taxi, pitching to the tarmac a black gauntlet, showing a brief glimpse of grim but noble face, black-goggled, over the fuselage; mocking ailerons just clearing the high-tension wires at the field's end but not the undercarriage, which was severed. Jerry now could not land; with nothing to lose, this dogfight was for keeps. Inside the glove, which a mechanic fetched in, a note in Teutonic script: "My compliments to your gallant command. I issue an open challenge." Cross of Malta. Signed, Baron R. Aloft, fabric tearing in Immelmann turns, oil-line burst spewing goggle lenses with black slime, Browning jammed, you dropped the foe with your sidearm and looked down in long salute at his incendiary spiral into the chrysanthemum bed. *Ave, atque, vale,* brave adversary! I slew you as you would have slain me, your cause was hopeless but not contemptible, we share in that community which the whey-faced civilian regardless of nation cannot enter.

To be sure, not every enemy was a Richthofen. G-8 the master spy, commuting behind German lines in the limitless disguises from his armpit cosmetic chest, was certain to meet the pigface Hun, bayoneter of Belgian babies, violator of maidens; cabbage for a head, sausage-limbed, cheeks of ass like dirigibles kissing, he waddled in cruel insolence before the helpless or groveled in fright before his master. G-8, whose trunk formed a triangle standing on its apex, was right to destroy this creature if only for aesthetic reasons.

Reinhart's paternal grandfather, who looked like one of G-8's victims, with a somewhat better distribution of weight, was more charitably described as a double for Hindenburg, a sound man. He cut meat on weekdays and on Sundays read the *Volks-Zeitung* and decanted in the cellar a thin, tasteless homebrew of which he was inordinately proud. He could support a leg of beef at full arm's length with one hand; he was a source of blutwurst slices on the sly; his place of work was floored with wood shavings and blood lay in pools on the butcher's block and dripped from the joints on the hook. He had left the Old Country to beat the draft; he had reportedly thought the Nazis were fools and was fortunate to have departed the world before they could disabuse him. These, and a small store of mispronunciations, were all Carlo could remember beyond an enormous, kindly, mustached face that smelled of beer and pipe, that was less articulate in the general tongue than himself at nine, that seemed, for all its implicit power and the massive hands that could not touch his shoulders so gently as not to bruise, a distant presence.

When in adolescence Reinhart was suddenly overwhelmed with the purposelessness of the bleak journey from pablum to embalming fluid—not for himself, but everybody else; he would somehow, alone, escape and was now investigating the various modes of exit—he once asked his father, and querulously, because the reason he alone would escape was that he alone had the guts or intelligence to ask questions rather than weakly submit, just as the power of his will would protect him, alone, from eyeglasses, baldness, false teeth, poverty, a wife: "Why didn't Grandpa ever go back to Germany?"

Could the Old Country, so remote, so rare, fail to exceed the here and now?

His father was shaving, or repairing the outside cellar door that hadn't been true to its frame for a decade, or washing the automobile, and perhaps before the answer came had done each of these tenfold, because for him a question must be repeated many times, by reason of his apathy, which was a superb thing in its way and could have been heroic if behind him Rome were burning or half of London keeling over with the plague.

Finally, as he rose from whatever job, scant of breath, with stated or implied senility of leg, he replied: "Use your head. What was there for him *there?*"

There had, of course, been so much for him *here*. He hadn't even owned his own butchershop, but was wage-slave in a native American's, a man twenty years younger. He built a brick house in an end of town that shortly thereafter suffered an encroachment of lower-class cotton-pickin' refugees from Kentucky, know locally as Briarhoppers, with their rusty cars and back-yard shacks and incestuous five-to-a-room, brought in by an absentee landlord named Horace Remington, who everyone was sure had changed his name from Levy, although they had never seen him—any more than they had seen for themselves that the earth was round. Grandma, native-born, whom he had carried off from a ten-dollar-a-week job at the pencil factory, survived him one year, and left material holdings of the house and two hundred fifty dollars. His one son, the man Carlo watched return with steel wool to the corroded hubcaps, was far from a raving success. This car, for example, was bought used with the two-fifty bequest—which showed how far back it went. And as to the house, it had gone to join its neighbors in the pocket of "Remington," who, despicable though he was, paid a third again as much as any other offerer and therefore was able to seduce even the good people into aiding his effort to destroy the respectability of such areas. Now if one passed the old homestead he heard guitar music and saw degenerate faces at the windows.

Carlo left his father at the task—he would have been glad to help on request, but would not volunteer; he received fifty cents a week in allowance, for which his obligation was to cut grass in summer and shovel snow in winter—and went indoors, to the dark cavity at the end of the basement, which was really not so much cellar-end as dead space, a kind of tomb, under the front porch. Here in a cardboard box soft with moisture were his grandfather's few effects, having for half a decade been in chemical mixture with the insatiable air: a twenty-five-cent pipe, "real bruyere" stamped on the shank; a straight razor, broken; a dollar watch, scarred chromium, its intestines locked in rust; cufflinks with the Oddfellows' paralytic eye. A letter postmarked Berlin-Something, Berlin-Smear, April 12, 1927. My God, three years after Carlo was born; he was still astonished at evidence that the world had been up and around when he was so young. Inside, handwriting that not only was in another tongue but also in an alien alphabet, even the figures were queer. Finally, a single book, the leather of which some dry past time infected with an eczema that the basement damp had treated with a salve of blue mold. *Nürnberger* something, the golden letters just visible on the granulated cover. Within, it was all pictures of that splendid medieval town of towers, castles, moats, rivers flowing through buildings, dolls' dwelling places hung over sallyports, and ironbound doors, four feet high, for dwarfs' abodes in the bottom of the city wall; labyrinthine ways among steep houses with a little extra roof sprouting over each attic window, the general roofs themselves nowhere true, everywhere splaying, overshooting, cutting back, growing dormers and log-

gias and lookouts and hexagonal capsules, restrained from soar-
ing off their timbered plaster only by the weight of these execres-
cences and a million tiles fine as the scales of a trout.

Magic and fabulous—no, it was not so much these as the Ohio
street outside his own window, with its covering of smooth tar
down which if you rolled for ten minutes you would pass a flat,
dun high school, a raw Presbyterian church without a steeple,
and fifty lawns so level and unobstructed that you could some
Sunday push a roller from one limit to the next and squash nothing but a row of homeowners trimming the edges. In Nürnberg
female angels ringed the city fountain gushing water from their
breasts, but what was extraordinary was that America could be
so ugly-dull; that was the fairy tale, along with radio programs
for the housewife, movie cowboys who never kissed a girl, public
drivel about shut-ins, mothers, flowers, the favorite prayers of
celebrities, ministers being tough guys and businessmen wise
ones, the stupid arrogance of newspaper reporters who wrote
"grass roots" and "with the arrival of spring, usually blasé New
Yorkers set aside their sophistication and frolicked gaily as children." And sports. At the end of his sophomore year in high
school he was the largest boy in the building and was invited
to come out for football by the coach, a witless man adored by
his teams apparently because he cursed them at half-time. He
took Reinhart's refusal in good grace, and was clever to do so;
Carlo had some time before sent away to York, Pa., for a set
of dumbbells and was already more muscular than the coach,
except in the head. In Europe they did such things as weight
lifting and gymnastics, although he was a touch too unwieldly
for the latter.

He thought about Harvard and Amherst, places of old stone
and vines and fireplaces in each room and tutors, as at Heidel-
berg and Leipzig, but it was revealed to him his last year in high
school that he must go to the nearest state university, on account
of the free tuition. At this institution he was permitted neither a

lodging in town nor a single in the dormitory; with the unction peculiar to the tribe, the dean of men said he must mix and placed him with a roommate who hung pennants on one side of their metal-and-concrete cell, worked a water wave in the front of his hair, and crooned popular songs in idle moments. When shortly he applied again for a single, he discovered it was already on the way: the roomie had reported that Reinhart didn't mix.

Although the architects had designed the few single rooms to be a constant punishment for the social deviates assigned them, Reinhart lived happy in his. He had loathed the college before he saw it and after a month's residence knew his prior feeling as too mild: it was in sum a flat green mall overrun with round pink faces saying "Hi!"

He had read much as a boy, but only in the literature of the imagination. Expository writing was rough, almost impossible going; he had never been easy with the language of documents and directions on packages, and was not now with that of the natural and social sciences. Philosophy was somewhat better because it didn't, and didn't really pretend to, get anywhere. English was a book of contemporary readings about, on the one hand, the underprivileged and, on the other, initially irresponsible people coming to a sense of social obligation: there was a story, in the form of a letter to her parents, about a rich girl who married a labor organizer, the compassion going all one way—inward, to the letter-writer and spouse—and no passion at all. And German, that hard and very real tongue, proved difficult and dreary, with twelve cases for each noun, insanely irregular verbs, and perverse genders that made a door a female and a maiden a neuter, defying even that principle of nature by which, according to a neighbor in psychology, projecting objects seen in dreams are male sex symbols and receptacles female, for *the pen* was in Deutsch as feminine as *the box* was not.

For these reasons he grew fond of his little room, last floor back, next to the toilets, with an air conduit passing first over the ranges in the kitchen four stories lower, and came not to hear the staccato flushings and smell the lemon sauce for the semolina pudding. He sometimes hid out there all day, cutting classes on the motive of the little ills—sinus, swollen Achilles tendon, foreign matter in the eye, etc.—for which the dispensary would write a note, eschewing meals with the aid of Oreo cookies and those stale, soap-flavored cheese-cracker sandwiches one buys at the drugstore, and reading books of his own choice.

He had now grown to six-two, still an inch below his grandfather—which he might yet attain—and as much above his father as that mark exceeds five-nine. The set of dumbbells had given way to a barbell with changeable weights; in the "clean-and-jerk" lift he could handle two hundred pounds, five more than he weighed, yet he was inclined to solid beef rather than the sharp definition of muscle permitted more wiry types; and he was clumsy, tripping over roots on tardy runs to eight-o'clock classes, tending to enter a doorway with poor aim and collide with its frame, sometimes splintering the wood. A recluse, but when he emerged, a recipient of good will and that friendly fealty paid to large men in jabs-in-the-ribs and blows-on-the-upper-body, which along with the strain of trying to better his mark in the clean and jerk every afternoon kept him always sore of skin.

The books of his choice were *The Invisible Man,* which he was at any given time rereading; a volume printed at the author's expense called *A Life in the Field,* by an Englishman who had towards the end of the nineteenth century scouted both in Matabeleland and along the Big Horn River in Montana; and Middle European short stories in English translation, in which the characters tended to live in the mountains or the valleys between them, walking to school on rutted cowpaths, sometimes getting lost in the forest—or had departed all this for the garish, quick life of the cities, which had gone to ashes in their mouths, and now yearned for the pastoral long ago forsaken; had a quiet but desperate passion for a girl who did not know they were alive or held them in sororal affection; attended day school, oppressed by a severe master and a fat bully; kept a faithful dog. Always a single sensibility, sometimes misunderstood, usually not even taken account of, by the insensate many; and in an atmosphere of mist, distant sounds, and if in the mountains, of course the silent, imperturbable snow, deceptively serene and treacherous, and on the glacier, a frozen rainbow. The stories were to be found in collections under one rubric or another but could take place in any of a variety of Central European areas at any given time under diverse political registrations: Bohemia, the Burgenland, Silesia, even Switzerland, anywhere that had a Germanic color and preferably a castle on some steep over placid water and in the foreground a cottage with a roof of straw.

Meanwhile he was almost flunking out in his course of study in German. For one thing, it was at eight o'clock, and he was most nights up till three, reading; for another, the language as taught had no relations to the tales, being at first Herr Schmidt exchanging the time of day with his neighbor and then simple scientific excerpts for the premedical students, which the instructor decided it wouldn't hurt the few general people to read, either. At the end of the year he just, but made it in German and the other courses, low C's with the exception of zoology lab, where in the interests of a moody, fitful romance a girl friend had made his dissection drawings, upping him a grade.

Simultaneous with Reinhart's entrance into junior year in high school, the Wehrmacht had invaded Poland; at the end of the term they took France; upon his graduation, entered Russia; just before his first-year college Christmas holiday, were at war with America. By one means or another, he was aware of these events although he never read the papers. He was furthermore aware that wars were wrong and foolish and the official ways of nations, always stupid and often wicked; that propaganda, regardless of side, was an absolute lie: for example, as everyone knew, the

German "atrocities" of World War I were fabrications of the British and French, who moreover did not let up in the ensuing twenty years, thereby giving Hitler some excuse for his silly ravings. Hitler held no appeal for him, having an unmistakable aroma of the tramp and no dignity, and, discounting their portrayal in Hollywood movies, the Nazis *were* preposterously vulgar; but opposed to the little, venomous, weak French and the British, thin and effeminate, they could hardly be assigned the exclusive evil in an intestine European quarrel over markets and territories.

Yet when America came into the war, it was a man's place to go soldiering, and the ideals concerned were not public ones dreamed up by journalists and pompous bores in high office but private matters. He felt himself a kind of German, yet he would cheerfully have slain the whole German army in fair combat and exposed himself to the same fate. On this principle he almost presented his person to the enlistment office early Friday morning, December 12, 1941; doubtless would have, had there been such a bureau in his little college town; but there wasn't, and the closest city, the place he crept alone every weekend to oppose his harsh weekday regimen with whiskey and coke, was eight miles off—it was impossible to hitchhike there, enlist, and get back without missing classes.

His second thoughts were confirmed three days later when the mincing dean told the assembled men that being educated people they could better serve by pursuing their studies with renewed vigor. It was not only his idea, he averred, but that of the Armed Forces, who as reward would commission every man to graduate. However, six weeks later, when the first fine fire had cooled and it was too late to volunteer from a position of enthusiasm, the male students were reconvoked. Now anyone wishing to stay *out* of the Army must *enlist*—in the reserve.

Reinhart called at the dean's office posthaste, already having been the target of remarks in bars, inarticulate grumbles by graysideburned potguts on the theme of why so much meat was not yet sacked in olive drab. The dean's secretary, one of those tight-rectumed persons whose every little motion is spite against some subject so long vanished that every other human being has taken on his-her appearance, after consulting the records told him with much satisfaction that the Enlisted Reserve Corps had a certain academic standard to which he failed to measure up. He cut classes and went to town and got stinking, which was not easy to do in an otherwise deserted tavern on Wednesday afternoon with no music. A fortyish waitress named Wanda some time in the next six hours told him *I knock off work at eleven* and at eleven-thirty, in a one-room apartment where a leaky faucet dripped a quick rhythm to which no one could have kept stride, displayed unusually kittenish ways and a pair of thick thighs marbled with blue veins. The First Time he had ever really Got In; as usual the popular consensus, which in his dormitory held that the experience was persistently overrated, was a lie; indeed, it had been in all his years the lone achievement; a pity that our society offered no male career in that direction.

In the late spring, just before the end of the year, another alteration in his university's theory of the reserves. If they limited membership to the bright students, the campus would soon be depopulated by the draft; so now a simple passing grade became a ticket of entry. Reinhart was permitted to sign up and given a little wallet-card signed by the Secretary of War as an assurance that he would do his service in the classroom. Actually, he was still ahead of time, was still not old enough to register for the draft. He had been a clever fellow in grammar school, doing eight years in seven, before the rot set in, and was yet only seventeen.

Sophomore German was *Wilhelm Tell,* tough to read, maudlin of sentiment. Reinhart now had a lodging in town and in consideration of the low rent went without maid service; a *gemütlich* sty except on those monthly occasions when his nihilism grew strong enough to annihilate itself temporarily and he borrowed the landlady's carpet sweeper. He read *The Sorrows of Werther* on his own, in English of course, and went so far as to get lent the German text by his professor, who after the fashion of the kind supposed that only good students had such ambitions and was at once wary, impressed, and all the more condescending for the pretense that he was not. But it was far too tedious to go line for line with the original; he pooped out on page two.

As to the other courses, American history was worst, debunking all the colorful legends and filling the vacuum so made with a thick Cream-of-Wheat of—as usual—economics; tariffs and taxes and indentured servants and land grants, and a general agreement that every one of the wars could have been avoided had these items not been mishandled by well-meaning but inept statesmen.

At the end of the fall term Reinhart made *I*-for-incomplete in history, as an alternative to the *F* he would have received had he not one morning in February absentmindedly cut his toenail too deep, inadvertently generating a wound which kept him from the exam. Presently the *I* stood for infinity: along about the beginning of March his gorge rose for the last time and would not come down; he went to the campus headquarters of the reserve and signed on for active duty.

His parents protested in their pallid way, finding everything a rejection of them and at a loss to see that their weak representations made self-counsel necessary; as if an impalpable father were not enough, he had a mother with whom nothing succeeded like failure. She would have preferred his staying in school, especially now that he was flunking. He tried to convince her that the Army life held promise of far more squalid drudgery than did college, that it was likely a person of his delicate constitution would collapse in training, and she was to a degree mollified.

Of course he didn't really say this; he seldom talked to his parents at all, simply, on his holiday visits home, communicating silently through the shoulder blades, a language he had learned from his father. When he was a small boy Reinhart had often wished for a temporary catastrophe from which he could rescue his folks—an unarmed burglar or minor fire—not only to show he cared but also to see if they did, if they could honor triumph as well as defeat, but the occasion never came, and just as well, for it might have come during one of his frequent illnesses—at which time, anyway, he *had* their interest.

They were German too, one generation closer than he, and celebrated the fact in their tastes—must have, because they could hardly have invented them on their own: heavy, flavorless food, limited ambitions, disapproval of the maverick, funeral-going, trust in people with broad faces, and belief in the special virtue of a dreary breed known as the German mother. "German" as a lifelong malady that was without hope but never serious; as the thin edge above want and far below plenty; as crepe-hanging; as self-pity—yet from these compounding a strange morality that regarded itself as superior to all variant modes. He had been encouraged since infancy to think of himself as an average man, but in a harshly restricted community where some were less average than others; if wealthy, had immorally taken too much from the world; if very poor, were immorally lazy; if taking pleasure in the material, ostentatious; if ascetic, holier-than-thou. But never "German" as the lofty vision, the old and exquisite manners of prince and peasant, battlements and armor, clear water splashing down from high, blue rocks, wine named for the milk of the Virgin, maleness, the noble marriage of feeling and thought.

But they sent him to college, on an insurance policy which his father, being an agent, had sold to himself, and the premiums for which, lean year in and out, had claimed all their unencumbered money, and Reinhart had first opted for Liberal Arts instead of Business Administration and now left even that. As he departed for camp he carried, along with his toilet articles and change of socks in a miniature suitcase, an acute suspicion that he would come to nothing, and . . . a marvelous sense of relief.

At the induction center an interviewer saw the B in zoology on the record and put him down for a medic, asking him first, though, for as a volunteer you had some faint choice. And he agreed, suddenly finding his bloodthirsty fancy had paled; a superior and sensitive person deplored violence; it didn't, as every retroactive commentator on past wars insisted, "settle anything." He personally had made himself so strong with the weights that no one bothered him, and if they did, he generally gave way in the conviction that not only were they probably right but that also anger and hostility were degrading. Under the Geneva Rules medical troops were all but neutral, and in recognition of this were not intentionally shot at and if captured were obliged to go on treating wounded, theirs or the enemy's, it made no difference; they were above the taking of sides.

The Germans honored this convention—that was admitted by the most rabid. For after he had been in the service a few months, Reinhart began to seek reasons why the Germans, while wrong—they warred against the U.S., for one thing, and it was probably true that Czechoslovakia and Norway and Holland, little harmless Holland!, had inoffensively not deserved invasion; true as well that, even discounting for cheap newsmen and their "copy," there had been regrettable brutalities by the extremist, Nazi units, although in view of the Belgian babies of World War I you should go cautiously here; they were surely wrong to torture Jews, who he had discovered in college were, at least in their American branch, a pretty good bunch of fellows given certain peculiarities, and who apparently had not during the German inflation of the twenties enriched themselves while gentiles starved, as alleged by Hitler & Co., although one must be careful here, too, in simple justice, for anyone who had ever traded in a Hebrew haberdashery knew the Jew as far from a naïve man—he had come under an obligation to find reasons why the Germans, though mistaken, though bullies, though bad, if you will, were yet not *bad*, were not to be allowed that case which the greatest writers assure us even Satan has.

The Army, oddly enough, was filled with superior people, the universities being then in the process of emptying to that purpose. Every barracks had its circle of cultivation, and while its membership was still outnumbered by the gross herd playing cards, shooting dice, and shouting incessantly fuck this, fuck that, it in the strength of unity read newspaper editorials, went on pass to hear the nearest city's philharmonic, and discussed international political events. At every post where Reinhart served, this circle in fact had been semi-officialized, meeting at least once a week with the authority and encouragement of an intellectual officer. Since he was channeled in that direction by cultural imperatives and nobody else seemed interested in him, Reinhart willy-nilly frequented this society, attending a few concerts, where he felt unpleasantly conspicuous as the middle-aged civilian audience beamed benevolently on the display of high-minded soldiery, and sitting in on some discussions, quaking with terror that he might be called upon to add his half-cent. If that sum were indeed low enough to symbolize the content of his head as he sat surrounded by his frighteningly articulate comrades.

The prevailing sentiment was, as one intense, red-haired, hollow-cheeked PFC (they were all privates and PFCs) put it, "just left of center, like FDR." Reinhart literally did not know what this meant, except that while in grammar and high schools, when he took his father's cue in politics, he had detested Roosevelt, had at campaign times worn little buttons against him, one for Landon pinned to a sunflower head of yellow felt, another reading simply: "We don't want Eleanor either." And still, even after he lost all interest in that sort of thing, carried a vague distaste for the man which was renewed at every picture of the teeth, the cape, the cigarette holder, the dog, the wife melting in good will, the sons drooping in false modesty, the desk ornaments, and Sarah Delano R., the grim progenitor of all these. Yet it was not subsequently hard to swallow that he had been an improvement on old Hoover, starched-collar, pickle-faced, the personified *No*. And whatever left-of-center now meant—he had always supposed it a kind of radical creed presided over by kindly-looking cranks like Norman Thomas who were understood to be not serious and a more extreme variety represented by Earl Browder with his mustache and dark shirt and faintly alien air, which might be sinister if it ever got its most improbable chance—what it meant now could only be something respectable, if somewhat strangely motivated, for these young men professed a constant concern for victims of one social outrage or another, in which company they themselves could not be counted, so that it was not a demonstration of self-interest.

Reinhart was impressed, even cowed, by their easy yet earnest assurance and disturbed by the shrinking of his hitherto supposed wide horizon. How he had wasted his faculties to date! Even if his sympathies had been all along on the right side: these people too were opposed—and from a far more intelligent point of vantage—to the double-breasted, cigar-smoking deities of business, the devotional poems in Sunday supplements, Mother's Day, Congressmen, and the suburban imagination. In college he had been too apathetic to find this out, confined in the circle of self as he was then. Beneath the surface pall there was meat in the political and economic disciplines; as approached by these acute young men, they were adventurous and splendid and, he soon saw, were far fitter areas for the mature moral effort than the gross physical projects he had earlier honored.

For example, one's build. These men, by his earlier standards, were usually physical wrecks, if small, skinny, if large, flabby, shoulders slumped, belly, if they had one, bulging, the whole man hung with garments as a point of merit shabby as the Army would allow. And no pride of carriage even in the shower, where if he met one of them Reinhart was thrown into confusion: embarrassed by his undulating biceps as he soaped the scalp, yet unwilling to loose the arm's tension if there was also present one of the common sort of soldier who didn't applaud intellect.

It was stupid, perhaps mean, to be a good soldier in any manner, although he had been right to get appointed to the medics on motives of nonviolence. All these people had been drafted, so that they had no choice, but they *would* have chosen the medical department. Some even had friends immensely admired who would not serve in anything but conscientious-objector enclosures; some others confessed that while that was going too far for them, it was a thing most noble for a man to hold fast at any sacrifice to what he believed right and true, against *the mob,* by which they certainly did not mean *the people,* who were always r. and t., but rather the crowd who ran things. Reinhart would earlier have supposed the latter meant Roosevelt and his entourage, with everything but Maine and Vermont, four terms without hindrance, no end in sight, but he soon found this a misapprehension, the situation being precisely the reverse, with all such good folk victims. Indeed, the persons to be admired were invariably victims, and the degree of their victimization was the degree of one's approval. The unfortunates even included some staggeringly rich men, who however were "liberal" and therefore smeared, earning the herohood into which poor men were enlisted at birth.

Reinhart had never used his head for much but dreams, he knew, and this new employment of the brain was exciting as well as good, for neither did it ignore the heart as it surveyed the vast panorama of the evil that men had made in the world and recommended sensible alleviations. The underfed coolies of Asia alongside the oversated warlords; the black and twisted miner deep in the earth's entrails, considered with the flabby oyster of a mineowner in his house on the hill; the poor little have-not, next to the arrogant, pudgy have. These contrasts were inexcusable in a world where education should be within everyone's reach, where it was now technically feasible for every man to be served by the machine rather than vice versa; they were wicked and what was worse, silly, most of the wrong people not wishing to be bad so much as not understanding what was good.

You take the Germans, for example, or really to test these intelligent new ethics, take Hitler. You at least had to grant that, terrible as they were, he had stuck to his ideals. If that awful energy could have been diverted into virtuous channels, if he could have stopped after solving the problem of unemployment and building the wonderful net of highways!—No, you most assuredly did not take either the Germans or Hitler; and if you did, there were strong grounds for popping you in the booby hatch. At least, so said without words the faces of the others to whom Reinhart, breaking his long silence, introduced this application of the theory they had so generously trained him to use. The trouble was that they had forgetfully omitted one clause from the grand code: no Germans need apply.

Reinhart was quick to know the justice in this, too, for, awakening from his long sleep, he had begun to see the terrible landscape of actuality. It was false to think that the Nazis were an accidental, noxious but temporary weed upon a permanently rich German ground of the essence, which might one day be cleared. No, go as far back as you would, the wars of 1914-18 and '70 against freedom-loving, culture-cradle France, the rise of brutal Prussia, way back to the war lasting thirty years and further to the razing of the magnificent Roman civilization by the tribes which Tacitus had earlier observed as being without mercy. Martin Luther overthrew the wickedness of popery; Frederick the Great sponsored the culture of the Age of Reason; Goethe was spokesman for the liberties of the heart and mind;

Schopenhauer and Nietzsche, revolted by their time's cruel and shallow materialism, drafted prescriptions for the free personality —even these were but masks for more Germanic creeds, or the same old one, of tyranny, militarism, suicide, irresponsibility, and madness.

When in the last months of the war American troops went choking through the fell streets of Buchenwald and other camps, passed the vast trenches of slack human skins, the bones inside all loose from their connections, and oven-grates of gray human ash, took in their nostrils that bouquet of burned man which for recognition it is unnecessary ever to have smelled before, and for sleep impossible to forget after—when the pictures and accounts were published, for Reinhart as usual was not there—the most malevolent indictment by the anti-Germans had not been enough, the righteous people who wished to reduce the land to a pastoral community were too mild, perhaps not even another Flood would suffice. For the outrage had been done to him, Reinhart, who had trusted in his origins.

There is no native American but the redskin; we others are something else at a slight remove, which cannot be changed; our names and looks and surely some complexion of the corpuscles themselves are to some old line peculiar, else we should blow away without identity. So he believed—his only belief, along with an idea of the possibility of simple decency—and thus, with his deep relation to what the superior, bright young men in the discussion groups were pledged to destroy, he disqualified himself from their company and took up instead—well, what was fun, booze and snatch and other pursuits generally pointless and amoral, and was forever delighting such people as Marsala with his adaptability.

His one secret was that he liked the Army, where the petty decisions were provided and the major ones ignored, and where you could live as if you had been born the day you put on the uniform.

# CHAPTER 4

JUST as it had arrived in England after the great mass of troops assembled there for the Continental assault was gone, so did the 1209th cross the Channel and proceed eastward against the stream of real soldiers returning. At the outset, the assignment to Germany was seen as punishment cruel and perverse. For a year they had run an enormous Nissen-hut hospital in Devonshire, tending casualties flown straight there from the fields of battle, wounds yet hot and reeking. They were veterans of the European Theater and should have been let to cross the water and swagger before the slobs on Stateside duty, to mix undelineated with the repatriated combat regiments, back in the frame where the greater category enveloped the smaller, overseas versus home.

Instead, the score was to stay grievously unjust: for more than a year the 1209th had had to stand holding its portable urinals while patients lay smug with honorable wounds, relating the grand experiences denied to people of the rear areas. Charging the Siegfried Line; streetcars filled with explosives rolled down the hill into Aachen; the bridge at Remagen, with its sign: "You are crossing the Rhine by courtesy of the——th Infantry Division"; the bombs falling on the ball-bearing works at Peenemünde, courtesy of the Eighth Air Force; the Ardennes, where even company clerks and cooks took up their virgin rifles and joined the defense and even a general proved a hero, courtesy of the 101st Airborne Division; and at the very end, "Germany" itself made commonplace by courtesy of the Third Army, who got to Pilsen in Czechoslovakia and burst into the famous brewery to fill their helmets with beer. By courtesy of the 1209th Gen-

49

eral Hospital, Colonel Roy Fester commanding, one passed his water, told his stories, took a pain pill, and went to sleep.

Just at the point, though, where the responsible latrine intelligence had disqualified the hysterics who insisted the 1209th would any day be shipped to the Pacific, and established beyond a peradventure that it would settle in the Helmstedt field where the unit was then resting as an alleged transient, and stay there forever—just at this point where the wailing was loudest, there being nothing else to do except peer through the single set of field glasses at the nurses' tents across the meadow, came a courier of unquestioned authority with the word.

*Berlin,* it was to be Berlin, so long as something had to be accepted, a horse of a different hue from mere Germany; considerably better, in fact, since the combat forces had never got there. It would be at the courtesy of only the Russians, and the Russians themselves, with the Germans downed, were now a kind of enemy and face to face with their allies kept weapons at port arms. Already they had sealed the Helmstedt checkpoint, and when, after a week of negotiations, the colonel was permitted to pass with jeep, driver, and one aide, he made only fifteen miles before another Soviet unit arrested and held him twenty-four hours incommunicado.

All this, not to mention Berlin of the Nazi mythos: old Hitler screaming crazy garbage; creepy little Goebbels, dark and seamed, scraping along on his twisted foot; fat, beribboned Goering, more swollen joke than menace; swastikaed bruisers maltreating gentle little Jews; the Brandenburg Gate and Unter der Linden Trees; and acres of the famous blonde pussy, whom twelve years of Nazism had made subservient to the man in uniform: one heard that an SS trooper could bend down any girl on the street and let fly. And, once in the city, little work conjoined with a peculiar honor: the crap-house spokesmen who in England had been privy to a document from higher headquarters listing the 1209th as the biggest and best hospital in the Communications Zone, saw another now which said, approximately: the

1209th, selected because it was the biggest and best in the Communications Zone, would be the only general hospital in Berlin District.

Berlin was not the worst place to end a war; better, surely, than the gooks in the islands or France where pigs lived in the same houses as people.

As Reinhart had promised the girl, he could have been found in the frame building across the street from the hospital almost any morning if the visitor came late, and any afternoon, provided the visitor came early; he put in a good four hours of daily attendance, give or take an hour either way, and had much impressed his superior, Lieutenant Harry Pound, by his drive. Pound was not properly a medical-administrative officer at all, but an infantryman, had in fact waded in on Omaha Beach on D-Day, H-Hour plus two, and shortly thereafter led a patrol into a hedge row filled with Krauts and their armament, collecting Mauser slugs and souvenirs of grenades in all four limbs and, later, the Silver Star. Under treatment by the 1209th he had healed into limited service and was transferred from bed to staff. Their job, Pound and Reinhart, was "Special Services," recreation, diversion, amusement both for patients and medics, things that had meaning in the long, pastoral days in England but which now were needless, except insofar as they satisfied the rules of organization. However, there was in the works a plan for Sunday guided tours of the Nazi ruins; Pound ostensibly was always out somewhere arranging for permission to enter with a force of sightseers into the Soviet Sector but had not yet got even an admission that he existed—if indeed he *was* really trying, for he had a girl friend in the nurses' contingent and was often seen with her when officially he was understood to be elsewhere—and besides, individuals could go across the border on their own hook without hindrance by the Russians, without the shepherding of Pound, which was to say he and Reinhart had no motive for an undue haste in consummating their project, especially since their desks were littered with schedules and itineraries and manifests and notes to show the colonel if he snooped.

Reinhart's obligation was to write up a guidepaper listing the principal Nazi monuments, their late tenants, and a fact or two, to be mimeographed and distributed to the tourists. He was not, at the outset of each period of composition, a facile writer, thinking first that here was his chance to show off, second that here was where he would be shown up, and third that it didn't matter either way because the jerks who went on the tours would immediately spiral the papers into little piccolos and toot obscenities through them at passing broads, if the experience at the Cheddar Caves and Exeter Cathedral had been representative.

However, with stage three he reached the firm ground of the professional artist and could compose with enthusiasm. The only difficulty here was that when he got fluent, he inclined towards the poetic, and when that, put aside his proper work and began a letter to a female in the States who was at once a sort of girl of his and a kind of estranged wife of another soldier on European duty, as near as he could tell no precise love existing in either relation but friendship and interest all around: he always knew where Ernie was stationed and what he was doing, and vice versa, according to Dianne, and there was even some talk, now that the war was over, for a get-together between Ernie and him, arranged through their intermediary three thousand miles off.

A week after his birthday, no more fights but a couple of drunks since—now, he thought as he looked into the bathroom mirror that morning at the pouting aftermath of dissipation, you must take it easy, greasy, and you'll slide twice as far—Reinhart sat alone in his office, with pen to foolscap, well into a new letter:

DI MY DEAR,

I certainly understand why the Princess was late with

my birthday present, and will look forward with lots of
pleasure when it arrives in Berlin after a long transatlantic
voyage, which will make it only sweeter to the undersigned.
. . . Well, I've gotten where I always wanted to be, Di, to
the heart of Europe and just wish I could be holding your
hand while we look down from the battlements of some
old palace with the peasants going along with their oxcarts
down below—Ha Ha, the real peasants I mean, not the
kind you always call me!! And I'd just as soon we left
old E. playing baseball or whatever somewhere, because
frankly Di, while I really like him, as you know, from what
you tell me I don't think he shares our tastes and maybe
that was the trouble between you. . . . .

To go from the ridiculous to the sublime—all pardons
asked—there are lots of exciting things transpiring here.
The Intelligence Officer in our outfit, who is a friend of
mine, is certain Hitler is still hiding somewhere around the
city. I met a Tyrolean Count the other day, the kind of
fellow you would love—I hope not literally! With an ascot
tie, and all. He invited me to hunt on his estate in Bavaria
which perhaps I'll get around to doing when I'm not
needed here—but that will be quite awhile. You see, no
one else in the outfit can translate the Nazi documents we
captured. I'm just attached to this medical outfit now for
eating and sleeping arrangements. I wish I could tell you
just what my job is, but even though the war is over in this
Theater, there are still plenty of secrets . . . . . . .

Oh Di, when I look at your picture I think perhaps when
I get home we won't be so platonic! Like to have your
reactions to this . . . . . . . .


He was moving along as magisterially as the Ohio River off
Cincinnati, and as impurely—but Ernie was in the paratroops
and had shot nine Germans and taken as prisoner twenty more,
and wore the Purple Heart—when a spot of color not olive-drab
came into the corner of his eye, stuck there, not moving but vital,

and since composition was the product only of solitude, his drain was corked.

The color was yellow of hair and rose of skin on a girl, just plump and no more, like a peach, who stood diffidently in the doorway. She was small, wearing spectacles with lenses large and exactly round and an abundance of drab clothing, including high woolen stockings and thick, awkward shoes that made her walk as if deformed, for under his even look she had moved gimpily into the room. Rather, was moved: the thin arm of another party could be seen as far as the elbow, at which point it disappeared round the doorframe. An inch off the arm's furthermost extension she stopped and smiling as gloriously as one can and still show no teeth, said in a high-pitched and cowardly voice:

"Razher nice vezher ve are hoffing today!"

From behind the door, a whisper, and again the disembodied arm, this time making much of its hand, after a moment of which the girl moved by the use of her own muscles. Her walk was now pleasantly normal, if prim with perhaps an aim to restrict the swinging of her long blonde braids. The latter she caught one in each hand as she halted still far enough from Reinhart's desk so that he could see her down to the round knees which the skirt did not quite reach, where although at rest she yet maintained some slight side-to-side movement as if she were still walking in the mind. The effect was curiously provocative and perverse, for she appeared to be a kind of large child rather than a small adult, and he regarded her severely.

"Tischmacher Gertrud," was her next sound. Her little fist had come loose from the right braid and was available for the shaking if he so required.

Somebody was pulling something weird. Reinhart rose and went around the desk, first going towards her to throw them off guard, and at the last minute executing a left-oblique turn of a smartness he had never been up to when in formation. Popped through the doorway, his head met that of the other girl, the one of the ruin, whose name he had not originally got and who now, though still nameless and taken in a suspicious act for which there was no apparent motive, greeted him like a friend and he had a handshake after all.

He asked her in and invited both of them, she and Fraülein Tischmacher, to chairs, of which they cornered the market, since there was only enough furniture in the shabby, rickety place to service his and Pound's narrow purposes. He even opened one of the French windows on the sand-and-crabgrass side lawn, to clear the air, for his series of cigarettes, the sine qua non for writing, had tinted the inside atmosphere gray-blue and it surely stunk to someone just entering.

The niceties owed to his guilt about not having turned a finger for her job. He had even "given his word," he remembered, whatever that was; he said such things when under the influence he became formal and constricted. In real life, as now, he was, he knew, deft, volatile, witty. Sitting on an old wooden box, his legs up on the desktop, rough-skin boots, size 11-C, murdering the papers there—oops! the letter to Dianne was ruined, but no matter—grinning easily, he lighted another cigarette and blew a process of smoke rings, each smaller than the last and spurting through it, each round as Gertrud's eyes, as she watched them with honest awe.

"I am sorry I took so long to come," said the other girl, very slow and clear so that he could understand the German. Her hair sent no message of having had a wash since the night he first saw it could stand one; similarly, her dark-green beret and gray coat with breast ornamentation of Cossack's cartridge loops. But miraculously, the fresh sunlight which marched through the open window in a brutality that made Reinhart wince, was kinder to her used face than the night had been. Something could be made of her, if you took the trouble.

Reinhart had the courage to admit that he had not yet found

the right thing for her, that he had of course been working on the problem for two weeks and would no doubt soon reach a satisfactory end. Not a day passed that he didn't arise painfully, come slowly through shaving, two portions of powdered eggs, a pint of coffee, and a lungful of Zehlendorf's pine air to health and good prospects and then feel drop over it all the shadow of his given "word." The trouble was he never knew how to get things done, how to make deals, how to "see" people who could arrange. At the same time he had no hope that anything could ever be done in a straightforward way.

The girl spoke fast, and incomprehensibly to him, to Gertrud, and Gertrud then said: "She vants—wwants you to believe she is grrateful for zis. She wwants to say sank you."

"You speak English!" Reinhart was not so astonished as he made out, but she was charming, although too young for one to admit to himself that he might find some use for the charm.

Her eyes, bluer than the high, immaculate sky revealed when he opened the window, bluer than a broken bird's egg you might find if you went behind the building and searched the pine grove, than, if you walked far enough westward you would see, the Havel; blue, the quintessence of blue, so that if the color in all its other uses had faded, Zeus might take from Gertrud's store enough to renew the blue everywhere in the world and not leave her one whit of blue the less. These remarkable eyes, surely kept behind spectacles not because they were poor of vision but rather as protection against some thief who might pluck and sell them as sapphires in Amsterdam, showed their stars to Reinhart as, below, the small pink mouth said:

"Yes, yes, I know English zo wwell, having studied it zix yearss. I sink I do not too badly, do you?"

Oh, marvelous, marvelous, he agreed, and would have preferred her over Churchill addressing Commons.

"You have acted so kindly to my cousin," she went on. "Perhaps I do not seem especi-ally rude when I ask, do you sink

there is also available for me a chob—do you sink for me—
do you sink there is also a job for me? There." Not covering her
knees when she stood, her skirt did not pretend to when she sat
but made a soft frame for the round thighs that it was no doubt
a grave evil to look at.

So he looked away quickly, looked at the other girl's sad,
sweet, and honest way, and suddenly heard his own voice saying: "*Warten Sie eine Weile*," Lovett, he would see a lieutenant
named Lovett, who was chairman of everything out of the usual
course, or if not he, then another officer named Nader, whose
duties were similar. To the girls, however, he said only "Wait,"
and in a tone which they considered too masterful to nod to, instead following his departure with heads neatly turning.

The building had no rhyme or reason. Nobody could tell what
function it had served before the Fall; it may have been the
only place in Germany where one could hide from the Gestapo,
or perhaps on the other hand was a Gestapo-designed labyrinth
through which their captives were permitted to wander free
and moaning, madly seeking a nonexistent egress. Three weeks
in Germany now, and Reinhart had yet to see his first right angle,
true line, and square space. Outside, he regularly got lost en
route to the Onkel Tom movie theater, ten minutes' walk away,
and strolling of an evening over to the Grunewald park, to the
body of water called by the Krauts "Krumme Lanke" and by the
GIs "Crummy Lake," he could not be less certain of his position
in space were he in Patagonia.

Somehow he reached the foyer and assuming the fresh soul of
one who had just entered from the street, struck out to the right,
passing the orderly room and detachment commander's office, a
treacherous area in which, although he had a certain immunity
from the worst of its menaces, it was not wise to linger. From
there on, he looked in sundry doors, sniffed up divers halls, consulted with acquaintances encountered in passing, most as be-

wildered as he, and at length spied Lovett himself, the sissy, in a large room on the northeastern corner.

The lieutenant stood willowy beside an ancient desk to which a gnarled Kraut, in a peaked Wehrmacht cap, applied cloth and a white fluid from a long brown bottle.

"I want you to bring out the highlights of the *carving*," Lovett was saying with his arbitrary, Bible-like stresses. And then, "Highlow, Reinhart," although he had not yet looked up to see him.

"I am being willfully misunderstood," he continued, in a very lowww voice indeed, which quickly rose to a kind of screech to say: "But who knows German?"

Nader, dark and thuglike, sat at another desk and relieved himself of what, asking public pardon, he called "The Return of the Swallow," by Belch. You seldom saw one without the other, and never saw either without wondering at their compact, which was surely queer and yet, on the same assurance—namely, that you simply knew it—was not *queer*.

"Well, I do, somewhat," Reinhart admitted. He was not equipped to tell the man what Lovett wished, but ordered merely: "*Polieren, polieren!*" which the fellow was doing anyway, and added "please" and "yet" and "still" and "to be sure," the little words Germans hang on everything.

Satisfied, even pleased, Lovett lowered himself into a chair in the way one might drop a length of garden hose and listened to Reinhart's requests with a crooked eyebrow, replying when they were done: "Wanna come to a party tonight?"

"Really?"

"Certainly, really. Do you *think* we are snobs? Of course we *are*, but you look civilized. A little house-warming at our billet. American *girls*—if that's what you can call our nurses. Wine—if that's what you can call this German cat-peepee. And songs. You know our place. Any time after eight."

Since there was almost no finish left, it was impossible to shine the desk. The German knew that as well as anybody, but he kept working humorlessly as a sociologist, now moving right between Reinhart and Lovett so that they could see only unimportant parts of each other, and Lovett, usually so quick to be waspish, suffered the obstruction—perhaps in the idea that any sound from him would be received by the dolt as a countermand of his previous order. Reinhart had begun to wonder about the man and what impressions he must receive, there with his bottle and rag between two aliens speaking of nothing—for two words in a foreign tongue are double too many if you don't get their drift —when Nader came over swinging his simian arms and said:

"Take off like a big-ass bird, Jack."

The German looked vulnerably from him to Reinhart, his nose long and tapered like a carrot, cheeks marred, black-brown eyes screwed in deep sockets. He was an old man, maybe fifty, commanding sympathy.

"*Er sagt, dass Sie herausgehen müssen,*" said Reinhart, shrugging the blame off himself.

"You see, Dewey, that can't be polished," said Nader to Lovett, who flipped his hand negligently and then bit at a finger. All his nails were chewed down to the nub; the fingers were long and white and maneuverable as rubber.

The German put his cleaning materials into a wooden box, the contents of which on his route to the door he stopped to re-arrange. The wine bottle, being too tall, gave him trouble; he transferred it from box to armpit, then had to lower the box to the floor for resituation. As he bent, tilting the bottle, the liquid poured off on Nader's desktop, and by the time he got his cloth to work, his head shaking stupidly, the papers thereon clung to one another in gluey fraternity.

So far as Nader went, what was done, was done. He calmly watched the man wad the papers and drop them in his box, mop up the excess fluid and then with a clean cloth rub up a high gloss, the kind Lovett had wanted on *his* desk.

"Just *look*," cried Lovett, biting his tongue.

The German crept out, and upon his heels went Nader, returning shortly with the clotted papers, which he arranged for drying across an extra chair and table near the open window.

"The only thing that burns," he said to Lovett, "is that that bastard could pull such a cheap trick and think he fooled me." He had not as yet recognized Reinhart's presence. Reinhart had no feeling towards him but distaste.

Lovett blithely ignored him and said to Reinhart: "Send this woman to me. The nurses' quarters can probably use another maid."

"Course I coulda let him take this stuff for ass-wipe," Nader went on to himself, aloud, describing one document as a report to the colonel on how many butt cans had been placed around the area.

"And what about the girl, sir? She knows English. We could use an interpreter over in our office. For one thing, we've got this tour of Berlin coming up, and neither Lieutenant Pound nor I know anything about the city. She could—"

"Oh *God!*" screamed Lovett. "Is Pound going to start that awful Cook's Tour doodoo again? Tell him to forget about it, *please!* He'll lose twenty men, just as he did at Stonehenge and I'll have to go hunt them behind every Druid altar, or here, I suppose, falling down drunk with some filthy Russian. But then I suppose nothing *I* say ever matters to that sloppy creature. All right, I'll see about the girl tomorrow, but if I ever come to your office and see you with your hands or anything else where it shouldn't be, I will know you for a deceitful person. Be at the party. Bye!" His eyes closed like the lid of a rolltop desk, and when shut were as seamed.

On the return to his own office, Reinhart crept noiselessly the last fifty steps to the door and, unobserved, studied for a few moments the backs of the girls within, who had apparently not so much as twitched in muscle-ease since he left, and not spoken, certainly, which you could tell from the long-established set of their heads. Looking at the clean pink of Gertrud's scalp-parting which ran from crown to nape without a disordered hair, he regretted the evil will that had asked Lovett for her assignment to himself; she was probably about fourteen. Under civil law it would no doubt have been a crime to employ her, but then he was under the power of no such ordinance, and besides had no criminal aims.

He entered and stopped between their chairs, saying to the older, "*Alles ist in Ordnung,* everything is arranged. You must see Lieutenant Lovett tomorrow. Ask for him at the front of this building." Her eyes were soft brown over violet shadows as she showed a gratitude that made him as uneasy as if he were wearing sweaty underwear; it was too much, in the light of his mixed motives. And still it did not make her happy, but rather more sad. Indeed, everything about her broke one's heart to see.

"I hope you don't mind being a cleaning woman for our nurses. There was nothing else available, since you have no English."

And now a kind of pride appeared for the first time, as she answered: "No, I can do that."

While he spoke, he felt near the back of his left hand the proximity of something warm and alive, not quite touching, but there: a piece of Gertrud, but whether hair, cheek, or hand he could not tell and did not wish to look. Finally, having finished his one report, he had no choice. It was her cheek, with its beautiful petal flush, extended in curiosity.

He teasingly seized the thick braid nearby and said in English: "As for you, Miss Tischmacher, how would you like to help us here, in this office, with translations?" And the soft young face moved sideways, towards a nest in his palm, but he had dropped the hand before it got there and went to sit on his box behind the desk.

There had suddenly come to him an explanation for the whole works, from start to finish, the perverse ways of this child, the other girl's melancholy poetry and strange demand on his conscience. They had successfully taken him along both roads without resistance. And the only sense it made was that they sought what could not have been gained in a direct and open appeal to the fixed authorities. Why else apply to a corporal, one lone and powerless jerk in an army of thousands? Because he looked first like a fool and second like a German, and because she, the older, was a Nazi who would have been put at picking street-rubble if she had made her appeal elsewhere. Perhaps it was even a kind of treason to get her a job under the cover of which she could hide from her proper deserts. It was what they had been warned against: the Germans did it before and would do it again if you were not vigilant, sack the world and then when beaten ask the pity for themselves, but this time we will not be duped.

Now it was done. Lovett, particularly, was not the man before whom one could change a tune and retain face. Reinhart rubbed his head, sensing he had gone white from the discovery, and two short blond hairs drifted separately down the air past his eyes. He could see them until they reached the dark floor. For an altogether different reason he was going bald: you had constantly to wear a cap in the service, the hair couldn't breathe. And then he remembered another reason why he liked the Army: no cause was ever wholly lost.

Simulating casualness, he asked: "You know, of course, that you must fill out the political questionnaire, the *Fragebogen.*"

She had arisen when he sat down, perhaps in a counterfeit respect—which, if so, failed; it made him feel like a fool to sit before a standing woman, especially one so small and shabby, and the fact that Gertrud held to her chair meant that the other was the only adult present.

But he had got her, there. In a reflex of sudden worry, she turned to Gertrud and said something in a rapid German he could not make out.

"*Das schadet nichts,*" the pretty girl replied, smiling bluely, guilelessly, at Reinhart.

No, it couldn't have mattered to her; she was luckily young enough to be disqualified from the rolls of mischief; but the other had been stirred. He knew, as she said *"Komm,* Trudchen," and walked slowly to the door, that he would not see her again. And well, in a way, it *was* sad, and because at bottom he hated to win out over any person, he finally asked her name.

"Bach Lenore." It was Trudchen who answered. "As wiss the great composer. Lori is a direct descendant."

Lori studied her in amiable suspicion. *"Was hat sie gesagt?"* she asked Reinhart, and when he told her, said: *"Es ist kein wahres Wort daran,* there's not a word of truth in it. Trudchen is a good girl, but she exaggerates too much."

"Goodbye," said Reinhart, and despite himself, "Good luck." As a pair they were at once pathetic and amusing. Now it was Trudchen who was all for going, and Lori who lingered.

*"Reinhart."* In her throat was the rich and authentic quality with which the name had been spoken two generations ago. *"Rrreinhaht,"* an old possession become new and attractive, suggesting ancient connections between them. "It is surely a German name. Have you found any relatives here?"

It was of course a new idea, to go with the name, exotic and adventurous; to find an identity in a far place, among the enemy. Yet here she was again giving him another obligation, goddamn her.

"Oh, I wouldn't know how," he said in weary helplessness. "I'm not German any nearer than my grandfather, and it must be forty years or more since he came to the States."

He got up and reclaimed his rightful chair, booting the box into a corner filled high with similar junk and obstructing a closet door which if opened would reveal more. The buildings they had inherited hardly supported the Krauts' reputation for tidiness and order. The closet boxes held ream on ream of papers carrying the letterhead of something called the National Socialist Volkswohlfahrt. Bureaucratic crap, very like the material in the 1209th's own files. He had nevertheless informed Pound, who lazily said to see the Intelligence officer. This passed on to Lovett became: "An *intelligent* officer? Don't hold your breath till I find one."

"You don't care, then," said Lori, only to establish the fact, without a hint of reproach.

Trudchen poked her arm. "*Ach,* they should be the ones to look for *him!*"

Exactly so, but his answer was: "Of course I care, but I don't even have their last address."

"Oh, then your family used to correspond with them? If you can just remember the city, you can apply to the burgomaster's office, who has records that date back, I suppose, to the Middle Ages."

Trudchen poked her again. "But if it is in the East Zone, Leipzig or Dresden, somewhere like that, he might as well forget about it." When she was serious, her little mouth puckered and extended like the jaws of a pink snapdragon.

"Yes," said Reinhart quickly. "I'm sure now it was Dresden."

Oh, goddamn her sadness! When she heard that, Lori's eyes disappeared again into the heavy violet shadows. "Then it is very likely they are dead."

Yes, he knew of the purposeless total bombing of Dresden, a nonmilitary target, and by not the barbarous Russians but the impeccable Western Allies. It was a very good place to have had relatives, and to have had them so disposed of, whatever their sins, by a crime of the righteous. Yes, if that was what she wanted, we are all depraved.

"I must get back to work," he said, and routinely added: "Shall I see you again?"

Trudchen answered, in English: "Shooly, I shall come to commence my job!" She warded off his interruption with a small hand. "After I shall have seen Lieutenant Lofatt first."

He had not really meant her, poor little instrument that she was. Besides, he realized now that she was too young to be hired, anyway. The morning which had begun so favorably with his letter to Di had ended in a thorough waste.

Lori said only *"Wiederschau'n,"* and was almost gone before he called her back.

"Why do you always say that?" he asked, irritably. "I thought it was *wiedersehen.*"

"It's the same thing!" she said in a voice bright with melody. And he wondered that such a small thing could lift her spirits.

When they had gone Reinhart sought to recover the letter he had ruined with his boots, but no luck. He should have to re-copy two whole pages, as thankless a job as sorting used laundry. Better to start all over again. He never lacked in invention, with the right audience.

He had just taken out a clean sheet of onionskin from the office supply when the old German who had made the mess over at Lovett's stopped in front of the window to light a cigarette, a miserable stub of a cigarette that he had taken from a small tin box. He fired the match in trembling fingers which brought it so slowly to the butt-end that the contact was charcoal to charred tobacco, dead to dead. He stared witlessly at both for a time, then returned the stub to the tin.

Reinhart's sudden arrival through the window took him un-awares. Scared, he hastened to leave, but his weak old legs were poor servants of his intent. His right shoe was busted out at the juncture of upper and sole, issuing a string of gray stocking.

"Don't run away," said Reinhart, jovially. "I just wanted to give you these." A five-cigarette pack of Fleetwoods, the abom-inable brand included in K rations, which had lain in his field-jacket pocket since the first day in Berlin, when the cooks had not yet been set up for hot chow.

What a shabby gift for such a wealth of gratitude! The man lost his speech, the corners of his mouth twisted in emotion, in awed delight he even forgot he was old and infirm, and disap-peared round the corner with the vigor of a stripling.

Watching him go, Reinhart thought, in satisfaction with his own courageous realism: certainly, he too could have been a Nazi, but now he was old and sick and defeated, become by the processes of cruel time himself a victim. Humanity is not the rights and wrongs of politics but a more general lottery of success and failure, and even more fundamental than those were youth and age and how one is constantly becoming the other.

If he had relatives they too would be old—for he thought of them in terms of his grandfather—and so far separated from him that the blood connections must be taken on theory . . . yet he was not a Laplander or Lestrygonian; if he had any structure beneath the meretricious American veneer, it was one he shared with them. If Nazism was a German disease of the bone, his own marrow, even at two generations' remove, could hardly be spotless. How many times had he felt within himself a black rage at existence-as-it-was and the eunuchs who prospering in it made its acceptance a standard of virtue?

Just the other Sunday he had gone with Marsala out to Wannsee to prowl the deserted mansions on the lakeside. These had already been looted by the Russians, but there remained sufficient evidences of the genteel life: sunken bathtubs in washrooms as big as stables; roofed terraces of tile, for dancing; genuine oil paintings; one home had an iron portcullis which at the instance of an electric switch ascended from the basement to guard the door. The houses were in that intermediate state of ruin asking for more. If they had been untouched, he would have looked and left. As it was, the job needed completion. The Russkies had stolen rugs and furniture, roweled the floor, spattered the walls, had multiple diarrhea in the bathtubs and washstands. But still whole were most windows, the pictures, some glassware and vases and other fragile objects prime for the breaking. He smashed everything that came to hand, assisted only feebly by Marsala, who had been a juvenile delinquent when young and in America but here and now turned delicate, as if God were watching, and occasionally said, as he witnessed a crystal goblet pulverize against the fireplace: "We maybe shoulda mailed that home instead."

Yes, that was surely Nazism, that passion to destroy simply because it could be got away with, because one had been trained all his life to respect and abide by the constraints and then found in a crisis that they held no water. Who wouldn't be a criminal if it weren't for the police?

He would find his relatives. If they were Nazis—but why suppose that? Because, although otherwise so stupid, he knew one truth, knew it so well he habitually tried to evade it—perhaps that is the definition of a dreamer, he thought, a man with an unusual sense of reality. Facts must be faced. There was such a thing as Nazism. It was a product of human beings, not some exotic heresy of the anthropoid apes that, owing to simian muteness, you must judge without ape-defense. The Nazis had first been clowns, and then almost without transition, devils. His parents, like their neighbors, had burned on sight the literature mailed by the Bund to German-sounding names, as they did the product of California box numbers which peddled data on the life-force; yet with match in one hand they might loosely say on the other that Hitler had a point when it came to the Jews. At college Klaus Greiner, a gentile refugee from Frankfurt—his father had been some kind of political writer—described his first two encounters with American strangers: a girl at a dance gave him an invidious lecture on democracy; a man in a cafeteria admired his being a national of the country that had at last settled the kikes' hash.

But whatever his relatives were, they were his. In almost every way but the accepted idea of common decency, he felt himself at odds with the world, a kind of Nazi without swastika, without revolver and gas ovens, without the specific enemies—indeed, it was a crazy feeling, an apparently motiveless identification, for although it did not include the trappings, it did comprehend the evil, as when you awoke from a nightmare of murder and for hours afterward despite the evidence of daylight and routine believed yourself an assassin; and worst of all, coexistent with the guilt, the memory of a terribly depraved yet almost romantic pride: *once, anyway, you were not a victim.*

Lori, with her quiet European authority, had no doubt known from the first that he would come to this. He must look for her again and say: I am neither pious nor indifferent—he could even, as if from outside, see himself in the attitude of gentle yet strong and manly conviction and hear his firm voice purged of boyish tenor—I will find my relatives, because no man is an island.

There remained a minor problem. His maternal grandparents, who had died when he was too small to know them and were therefore of no interest, came from what indeed was an eastern province, he was not sure just where but now in Soviet hands. His father's father had been native Berliner—but where? He vaguely recalled the old letter in the box beneath the front porch, postmarked Berlin-hyphen-blot. Ah, it was hopeless. He went, anyway, back through the window to his desk and wrote a V-mail home, although it were more sense to poke in tea leaves or consult a necromancer than ask his folks.

On the way through the labyrinth to the mailroom he thought of Lovett's party and hoped he was not the only enlisted man invited; he might be taken for a fruit. And finally, another tinge of Trudchen: how old must a girl be before you may desire her?

# CHAPTER 5

A THIN dust of talcum lay on Lieutenant Schild's sallow cheeks, notwithstanding which the beard's threat was darkly manifest. He had shaved a half-hour earlier, taking his usual care at the sharp angles of the chin and the mastoid region, peering near-sightedly, vulnerably, into the magnifying mirror, studying the giant's face which regarded him with similar scrutiny. The steel-rim, GI-issue eyeglasses were back in place now, and with them the correlative look: tranquil, remote, mathematical, self-sufficient. He buttoned himself into the blouse, which, though it corresponded at all points to the measurements of his upper body, seemed uncongenial to it, and placed upon his curly poll the cap whose forward point was subtly out of line with the rear one. Finally, he folded the tie in a knot that was lumpily gauche.

His toilet was preparation for Lovett's party, which he assumed to be well under way, the time standing at 9:30. Only slightly acquainted with his host, whom he had met the day before in official work, he had delayed his arrival until it could be unobtrusive. After checking his watch again, he strapped on the pistol that Occupation rules required—in this the medics, legally unarmed, had it better—and left the house, conscious of the housekeeper's green eyes on him. She was a comely war widow in her late thirties and slept in. He would not acknowledge her as a human being.

As he descended the outside stair, his superior, Captain Roderick St. George, came bovinely up the walk.

"Hi, Nate. Goin' out cattin'?" He had, it seemed, determined on the long ritual, not having seen Schild since just before evening chow. Schild muttered some half-audible nonsense, and it was all the same to St. George, whose low estimate of himself was necessarily transferred to his associates.

The captain withdrew a cigarette, fired his lighter and then held it aflame interminably without using it.

Squinting, Schild made known a mild complaint, and St. George forthwith snapped shut the pigskin-jacketed Ronson. He disliked giving hurt, but took a modest pleasure in being an agent of mercy.

"Oh, *I'm* sorry," he said, victoriously. "Something exciting on the string?"

Schild received a malicious impulse, gave it its head.

"Look, she has a friend, a small blonde with fine skin and breasts like lemon-halves . . ."

"Haha . . ."

"You know these Germans are unleashing the bottled-up passions of years."

"Hahahaha . . ." St. George thought this a genuine joke. He could not place himself in any kind of relation with illicit sex but the comic. Besides, he regarded all Jews as humorists.

He chuckled a stanza and then said sanctimoniously: "No, Nate, you go and have fun. I've got work to do. By the way, you haven't seen, have you, a missing folder of Kraftfahrkorps correspondence?"

"I'll look in my files tomorrow. Offhand, though, I can't remember it."

"No hurry. It was among that load I brought in today. I may have it myself."

The odd thing was that although St. George would have been a success as a civilian, he had never been one; not ever, if one didn't count his eighteen years or so as a legal infant, after which he entered the Point. He was now forty-five, with twenty-odd years of garrison and administrative duty in the States and the peacetime colonies behind him. In the war he led a small Intelligence team that during the hostile phase jeeped company to company on the Third Army front and interrogated German prisoners. At present its business was more sedentary. In many of the buildings occupied by the American forces there were great stores of abandoned Nazi correspondence. Somebody had to assemble and classify them: in the reams of paper that had fallen behind the police state like dung from a plodding horse, St. George and his little crew were put to picking straws.

The captain now reiterated his counsel about having fun and squished into the house on his crepe soles.

It had taken Schild months to accept the reality of the captain's stupidity, for despite Marx's and Lenin's examples to the contrary, Schild generally tended to overvalue people. But St. George's was far too crude a role for a double agent. And this was, in the smallest way, that is to say, personally, regrettable, providing nothing against which to sharpen the teeth.

Darkness again, lightly flavored with the smell of growing things. He resented this street which showed no mark of war. Lovett's house across the way was marked by a globed light above the door, but the window blinds were drawn—indicating, no doubt, the conservative character of a party made by medical men. At the gate, it struck him that he had no motive whatever for accepting the invitation. Lovett had rudely flung it at him as he was about to leave the office after speaking with Lieutenant Nader, a preposterous, almost illiterate officer who assured him that yes, the place was loaded with papers but he better claim them fast because the colonel had fifteen men on permanent assignment to burn all the useless trash in the building and they were already halfway through.

Next he had gone to see the colonel, to whose inner office he was conducted by an insolent sergeant-major with a border-Southern accent who announced him as "Child," and stayed to listen to his business. On his entrance the colonel, who had been sitting in deep study of the ejection device on a mechanical pencil, snatched up a huge bolo knife from beneath his desk and sprang to the open casement, screaming: "Look sharp there, private!" Handing the weapon to an unseen soldier outside: "Here's the only thing for that crabgrass—wait a minute, what are you doing with that butt? *What?* Field strip it, balls! Carry it around to the can! Wait a minute, where's Lovett? *Where?* An hour ago I saw, God damn him that nance, a lid missing from one of the garbage cans in back of the hospital. You tell Lovett to mince over there and find it. No, not you, *him*—a gold bar doesn't make him too good for that."

The colonel, Nader had told him, was scared shitless of anybody, even a corporal, from another headquarters, invariably assuming it to be a higher one that had him under surveillance for suspicion of untidiness. Schild's request to impound what remained of the enemy documents scarcely salved his nerves.

"Don't tell me Lovett hasn't been sending them to you all the while! That silly pimp!"

Schild sternly put down in himself the dirty little pleasure that it was probably not abnormal to feel at Lovett's being abused—but why does the girl-man stimulate sadism rather than pity?—and made a defense.

"That is true, colonel, today's the first time I've seen him," said the sergeant-major, neutral and hateful at the same time; he was that kind of man, just as he was the sort to turn accusingly a confession upon its maker. This worthy, it was clear, held the reins of authority; typical suburban, neat-haired, office-manager type, probably from some middle place like St. Louis or Lexington.

"I have it," said the colonel, nervously popping the eraser from his pencil, scattering across the green blotter the contents of the reserve-lead reservoir. "I'll assign Sergeant Shelby here to complete responsibility for the allocation of whatever it is you require. Shelby's your man, Lieutenant Shields, want something around here, ask the enlisted men. My officers just weren't there when the brains were passed out." He retrieved the leads one by one, a neat trick with hands sheathed in white gloves. He answered Schild's stare with a smile that vanished as quickly as oil into leather.

"Eczema," he said ruthlessly. "On all ten fingers." He tore off a glove and showed his right hand, which looked as if it were made of rusty metal. "Neurodermatitis—terrible for a man of action."

Shelby grunted "Yeah" and grandly proceeded Schild into the outer office where he imperturbably took a seat behind his desk and began to read Sad Sack in *Yank*, from time to time calling one of the clerks to witness an especially funny turn.

"Sergeant," called Schild, after a few moments had defined the insolence, "I want you to show me where the papers are stored."

"Well yes, I will." Not looking up from the page. "If you'll tell me when." But already he was weakening, that shadow of the coward was stealing across his eyes.

"Now." Schild spoke it in his smallest voice, to demonstrate to the man and his lackeys what a small, two cents' worth of force was needed to bring him to heel.

Shelby sullenly arose and led him out, smelling of after-shave lotion. In the hall Schild told him he had changed his mind, would come another day, smiled, and left almost lazily.

But the outfit was a nest of madmen and clowns, a traveling medicine show rather than a hospital. And he realized, at Lovett's gate, that this condition of comedy was what lured him to the party, that he could handle it or let it go at his pleasure, without, as it were, a tab to pay. He had already freed the latch, was stepping into the yard, when a low, evil whisper, as if from the conscience, said: "Enjoy yourself. Why not?"

He drew away in the illusion that he had collided with a kind of animate bush which, weightless and retreating, yet aggressed with whipping branches in a hundred quarters, and although he stepped to the side, off the path onto the lawn, Schatzi continued to press him. Thus, without a word, he was forced to return to the public walk, where a hand jerked his sleeve in the direction of the street corner and left off, and he followed.

At the corner, where in sound underground practice they could survey all paths of approach—or in the darkness, hear them—Schatzi spoke in a queer tone that was loud while pretending to be low, an undertone which must have been audible behind Lovett's closed door a hundred meters off.

"Yes, my good sir," he said. "I am authorized to buy from you five cartons of cigarettes. Payment on delivery."

If they were overheard, it was a black-market deal—more than that, if an enemy operative lurked behind the tree, he was forced to hear what was after all the description of a crime towards which the Allied authorities were turning severe, and might ignore it in favor of the larger, for which he had insufficient evidence, only at the cost of his clear duty. The beauty of the method was Schatzi's acting in worse and more furtive conscience than when he met Schild unmasqueraded, as at the Wannsee contacts.

However, having gone so far to establish urgency, stealth, and a suggestion of controlled hysteria, Schatzi began to talk quite banally of Lovett's party.

"I have sold them some glassware, very lovely crystal glasses which I am relying upon you to guard over. Some persons may get drunken, you see, and it will be a scandal to break these glasses which cannot be replaced all over Germany. I speak not of my own convenience, since they have paid me, but namely of the uselessness to destroy pretty objects which also have their place in the world, or don't you agree?"

This preface out of the way, he thrust himself under Schild's nose and in a passion of distrust asked: "What are your relations with Lieutenant Nader? I know yesterday you have seen him!"

It was degrading that Schatzi, with his own active assistance, managed always to take him by surprise.

"He's Intelligence officer for the 1209th General Hospital and therefore the logical man to see about the German documents in their area."

"Of course, *Intelligence officer*—does not that mean to you something odd?"

Schild regretted saying "German"; he was commonly careful to use "Nazi" or "Hitler," rather than the adjective that comprehended an entire people, not only because the distinction figured importantly in Soviet policy, but also because Schatzi was a non-Hitlerite German. And finally because he could not truly believe in the separation and clung to it all the more, in an effort towards self-mastery.

"As a matter of fact, it does." He made a joke: "He has no intelligence."

Schatzi hooked into his elbow with murderous fingers. "*Was, was?* I don't understand!" And still claimed not to on repetition. "Don't smile!" he whispered angrily. "If you do not think this is serious, something can perhaps be done about you."

He had never spoken this way before. True, he was Schild's superior, but for purposes of organization rather than discipline. And he was a German. . . . How easily vileness slips in when one is momentarily weak with indignation! Yes, Schatzi was a German, a good one, which in his time meant a hero it was a privilege to know, an honor to be rebuked by, and thus Schild accepted the onus: What error had he made with Nader?

"The responsibility of an Intelligence officer is that of an open police spy, no?" asked Schatzi. "Therefore you present yourself to him conveniently. He can simply sit in his desk and you walk into his hands. This leads a person to say there are two possibilities: you might be a fool or you might be a counter-agent." He floated an inch away, and returned to his earlier, crafty voice: "But I cannot pay more to you, since Captain Josephson of the Engineers Department has promised already to sell me all I would need for a thousand mark the carton."

Not until he finished did Schild hear the footfalls, deliberate, soft, and yet massive as a lion's on the route of his bars. As they approached, the courier grew ever more spurious, and when at last the organism that made them, in his own agonizingly good time, arrived in closeup, Schatzi sprang dramatically to the curb and found on his forehead a sweat so heavy it required both hands to dry. Now the melodrama was inflated beyond all sane proportion, and it was Schild who felt wet all over in genuine perspiration, certain, in a dread moment as the newcomer stopped before him and he saw a face as puffed and insensitive as a medicine ball, that it was an arrest.

"Lovely evening, men. May I trouble you for a light?"

A great curved pipe like Sherlock Holmes's, like Stalin's, and by the flare of the match, a golden lapel-cross. He continued to intake and expel till the flame seared Schild's fingers, and then, with one last cumulus of smoke straight into Schild's eyes, he padded on with a clabbering "good night."

"A holy man," said Schild derisively, regulating his breath as Schatzi returned. And then, as Schatzi said nothing, stood rather in silent, corrosive accusation as the minutes vibrated through the watch on Schild's wrist, up his forearm, biceps, shoulder—"*Yes. That would be the perfect disguise!*"

"Don't be ridiculouse," Schatzi answered in a very low voice. "That was the Protestant chaplain for the 1209th Hospital. He is quite likely looking for girls, the younger the better, the dirty old man. . . . You have then no explanation." It was not a question. "Among the papers of Nader was concealed a memorandum which read 'Documents—Schild.' They all go to him before you deliver them to me, yes?"

To be frightened by a fat, buttery, strolling chaplain! Schild recovered so rapidly that he all but made another small joke. "Ridiculouse," how ridiculouse it was. Schatzi was after all accusing him of treachery; of all imaginable moments it should have been the most terrible, yet he could barely withhold laughter. Nader, Lovett, the colonel, Shelby, the chaplain, and, in his own house, St. George, with their uniforms and pipes and insignia and parties and cleanup details and evening walks—who but Schatzi could envision that fat, genial toad with the gold cross pinching some German teen-ager's behind, or Nader's playing the deep game?

"I had to go to Nader, you see," he whispered. "Anything else would have been suspicious. I assure you he's a buffoon."

"Now I must not again hear you say that of anyone," said Schatzi, "or I will know you for a traitor. I have told you those are the most dangerous persons. But even so, you do not have a connection with Nader, *you say*, however, you go from him to the office of the commanding colonel and insult Sergeant Shelby."

Surely he did not presume to direct Schild's official relations with enlisted men; he was getting now clearly beyond his limits, and Schild forbore from righteous protest only because his intuition told him Schatzi had not yet reached the serious argument of which this was preface.

"Shelby?" Caution made him pretend briefly not to recall the name.

"*Shelby,* yes!" Schatzi's breath into his ear was like a long needle piercing the drum. "He is a sympatizer, but he will not forever be one with rudeness."

"How was I supposed to know that?"

"You might have smelled it—but that is not the point. A source in the very headquarters of the major American medical hospital in Berlin. If Major General Floyd Parks becomes ill, where does he go? To *1209th!* If the deputy commander, Colonel Frank Howley? *To 1209th!* Eisenhower comes to Berlin, twists his ankle—even you should see the actualities. There is no brains in making enemies of someone who has the slightest power. That is the first rule. The second is, give to a man a chance."

Give to a man a chance! It was a touching slogan of wonderful, innocent charity, like the creed of some early social reformer, some Robert Owen, now outworn but fond in memory. He had not looked for such a sentiment in Schatzi and finding it was not quite sure he got its sense, unless beneath that scarred and charred carapace there was an old idealism that had remained impervious to the arrests and tortures and the subtler ravages of the illegal life.

"I'm afraid I still don't understand. Do you wish me to identify myself to him?"

"He was told someone would come to ask his assistance."

Schild did not think it wisdom to remind Schatzi his directions had been simply to go to the 1209th, with no mention of a source; the injustice being done him stirred more caution than hurt.

"Now they must give him another carton-box of vodka."

"He is bribed?"

"To be sure, he is only a sympatizer and not under discipline. But tell me what time is it? Ah, so late! One more detail: in a room on the south front of Shelby's building is a closet filled to top with papers of the old *Winterhilfe*—this was a Nazi agency to deal with the poor, clothing and food for charitable distribution. In the last years of the war, one hears, they gave out clothing of the Jews exterminated in the camps, sometimes even forgetting to cut off the yellow badges. Haha, cynicism could not be carried farther on . . ."

How innocuous Schild's own little joke had been in contrast to this, the authentic, vintaged gallows-humor.

Schatzi continued: "Now there is a boy in that office, with some kind of entertainment service for the Ami troops. A great lout, with him you would be correct when you said clown. Just go there and get the files from him, no need to let Shelby know."

"No need to let Shelby know?" Schild could do no more than parrot the sentence.

"Certainly not! Anything you can get without him, all the better. One shouldn't wish that *Scheisskerl* to become too self-important. As I told you, he is not even a member of the Party, he cannot, in the end, be controlled—*Achtung!*" He reared back and harked with hand to ear. But it was only someone entering Lovett's door down the block.

"Isn't that a Wehrmacht cap?" asked Schild, seeking a moment's respite, for prolonged exposure to Schatzi's undiluted presence was very like being worked over with a blowtorch; one had left only short breath, and that was filled with the smell of scorching. However, Schatzi's own habit of disregarding nothing was so influential that he found himself eager for the answer, for some clue as to his frequent changes of costume, which were more likely to achieve publicity than disguise.

But Schatzi gave every notice he could, in silence and darkness, that the question was a faux pas, social and not conspiratorial, nonetheless offending.

"Go now to your party," he whispered coldly. "And for heaven's sake don't be rude to anybody. Have pleasure, dancing and drinking, show yourself to be a normal person. What there is to lose but your chains?" With the latter he moved into better humor, saying in what no doubt was a friendly way: "Here is a little gift from me to you."

He pressed a small, flat package in Schild's hand. What was it, rubbers? Schatzi didn't understand and Schild, laughing, didn't know the term of the German-in-the-street.

"Empfängnisverhütende Mittel?"

The dictionary formality got a laugh even from Schatzi. "Cigarettes of the Fleetwood brand. Also, unless emergency, the usual time and place."

He left, or rather he was no longer there. Nor was there a sound that could not have been made by a leaf crashing onto a pillow of moss. The "gift" lying uneasily in his pocket—as if it were soaked in phosphorous-water which when dry would explode—Schild went again towards Lovett's gate. Just before it he met the stout chaplain, whose pipe had once more gone out, this time, however, without appeal. A soft girl of about fifteen and in long braids stood swaying at his side.

"Good evening, men," he voiced richly. "I don't suppose—no,

I see you're busy." Peering. "Oh, just one of you! Well, to the party, eh? I may look in later, but just now I must act the Samaritan to this child, who is out all alone after curfew." He reached for a braid. "You don't suppose you—no, go on in and have fun. This is what chaplains are for. But, I say, have you any idea where Jugenheimer Weg lies?"

Telling him, Schild thought he heard a distant, hideous snicker, a passage of air through corrupted channels; and so it was, and no more: the chaplain sucked on his dead pipe.

"Sank you from zuh bottom of my hot," said the girl, with a pliant little moue very visible in the glow of Lovett's porchlight.

Were they all dead drunk or had he got the wrong night? He knocked interminably without result, and no doubt would have given up had he not received so many counsels, nay, commands, to go there and enjoy himself. At length Lovett unbarred the portal, showing a face painted by Dante Gabriel Rossetti, slightly under the weather, and donating three white fingers towards hospitality.

In the living room, which was the smaller and more airless for it, sat a number of guests in contemplation of their belt buckles. As Schild came in from the hall they looked up as one and stared ominously, hatefully, man and woman, and as quickly looked away in instant boredom. Lovett gave him a green tumbler, and Nader, who it appeared was also *en menage*, presented a hard look from beneath the one long eyebrow like a caterpillar across his forehead, and went into a corner from which presently a phonograph began to bray. The company arose to dance claustrally, the rug having been cleared away but not the furniture. A nurse or two, lacking partners, watched Schild in a hopeless expectancy which soon settled into resentment, for he had discovered a sofa in the opposite quarter where one might settle to view the passing parade.

At one end of the couch sprawled a young man, who had managed by a disorderly arrangement of large limbs to command nine-tenths of the surface that should have been free; as if this were not enough, Schild was astonished to see he wore corporal's stripes.

With a failure of consideration he immediately regretted, since the fellow on his approach made ample room, he asked: "Is this affair for enlisted men, too?"

Taking no seen offense, the young man grinned and waved his hand abroad. There were, in truth, several noncoms scattered through the crowd. A sergeant waltzed by at that moment with a bony nurse, in some danger of being impaled on her chin.

"Oh, I didn't mean anything was wrong. I've heard these medic outfits practice a good deal of democracy."

"More in the breach than in the observance." But the corporal's very impudence belied this. Schild anticipated trouble. He warily took stock of this soldier, whose olive-drab hulk slouched into the couch as if he owned it. Assuming comparable *sang-froid*, Schild without looking lifted the drink in his hand and took a modest draught. It was not a green glass at all, but a clear tumbler containing a viscous green fluid, an oleaginous, minty, sweetish ooze. His tongue curled in revulsion. While he fancied desperate measures, the liquid crawled across the palate and drained into his throat.

"God, that fool gave me a full glass of crème de menthe!"

"That's probably all he had left. They pooled the officers' liquor rations for the party, but most of it was wines and liqueurs. I got Chablis." The young man, lips parted in good humor, lifted the glass that stood between his feet. "It's awful, too, if that makes you feel better."

Strangely, it did. There was a generosity in the corporal's ease which minimized his impudence. With a wry nod at his orders, and despite a sense of imminent nausea, Schild organized himself for fun. But when the opportunity appeared, it was in the corporal's name.

"Reinhart!"

A large nurse, constructed on the plan of Rubens' second wife, stood before them offering her heroic body with a slight upthrust of the hips. High above, gigantic breasts made bold, made brutal, and threatened the poor weak seams of her olive dress. One listened for the *ping* of parting threads deep in her armpits. Very likely, said fun-loving Schild to Schild, she cocks her hips to balance the bulk of those incredible glands.

"Come on, Reinhart," she cried and rowdily assaulted the corporal's arm. "Don't be sticky." She got him on his feet and into the amplitude of her façade. From the phonograph wailed a niggardly statement of love denied. And Schild sat in his standard condition: alone.

# CHAPTER 6

NURSE Lieutenant Veronica Leary presided over the nut ward of the 1209th. Reinhart knew her by sight and name; was not, however, in the least acquainted. Were the standards of rank, which he approved, now to be swept aside?

This was his first mixed-grade party, and he had so far found it difficult to put off his snobbery, even though most of the officers were from the medical staff, which meant an amiable, unsoldierly, democratic lot whose professional view of man as viscera saved them from megalomania. The administrative officers, having got wind of the conglomerate guest-list, stayed away, victims of poor judgment. For of the enlisted personnel Lovett had invited only notorious brown-nosers whose obsequiousness no intimacy could corrupt.

With qualms about his own status, Reinhart had soon retreated to the isolation of the sofa. Now here was Leary, legitimizing him by her substantial presence, like Europa and the ox with functions reversed. But since he was, despite nature's perverse generosity, larger still than she, the issue was a push-pull in a progressively diminishing tempo, and a nettled comment, charged with liquorous and sexy odors, blown into his ear.

"Do you know, you're really a punk dancer."

"Never claimed to be a good one."

Which she went for in a large way, with a splendor of teeth and a marvel of air-blue eyes, in a demonstration of the frequently altering but at any given moment perfect dominion of her withal fragile, sentient face over the dumb classicism of that body.

"D'yuh know what?" she asked, giddy again but kindly,

"Really, when it comes right down to it, you don't have much fun, do you?"

"I'm having fun right now," he said, so pitifully that his heart cracked right through at the vibration and hung like a sundered glacier about to plunge into the sea.

"Aw, kiddy, come on and cheer up! When I used to see you I would think there's the very nicest boy in the 1209th. And also the saddest, because who knows what secrets lu-r-r-r-k in the hearts of corporals."

This was actually a horror to Reinhart: as he walked in dignity and rectitude, strange eyes had marked him, had abstracted a piece of him, as it were, that, insensitive fool that he was, he had never missed.

"All right, it was just an idea," she said then, surprisingly enough, eyes bright with the fool's-gold of ennui, mouth parodying good humor. This came from hither-and-yon; she was revolving her head, apparently surveying the room for another candidate to storm, who, not capitulating instanter, would get the same short shrift as Reinhart.

For he had her sized up, and stood enjoying bitterness confirmed. When a nurse smiles at a corporal, *caveat* would-be lover! A nurse is an ill integration of woman and officer, with one of the roles appearing wherever the ordinary lines of human deportment would ordain the other; so that you are always puckering to kiss a golden bar or saluting a breast, a stranded sycophant between sex and power.

The music having suddenly pooped out, the rest of the crowd clogged the rear of the room, where Nader gave first aid to the record player with loud frustration at the complexities of wire. No man being opposed—even the dark, nervous officer had vanished—they returned to the couch, where Lieutenant Leary announced her name-to-Reinhart as "Very," and plumped down proprietor-close. He had then, by default, been chosen.

Since high school Reinhart had made it a principle to avoid

really pretty girls, with their detestable and arrogant ignorance of the principle: they're all the same upside down. He played courtier to no one, and was gratified in college to see that the lackeys of the prom queens were to a man spectacled and pimply, usually students of science. However, although she was beautiful, Very was reclaimed by her size; it was a near-deformity, being almost divine, and made her human.

"Do you have the time?" he asked, for in spite of all, he was horribly bored.

"Sure, but who'll hold the horse?" Very answered brightly. "An old joke that if my father's said once, he's said a thousand times. But I can't tell you because yesterday I sold my watch to the Russians for two hundred and fifty dollars."

She showed a fine, empty wrist—at such narrowing places she was as slim as she was generous in the areas for expanse—and went on to add that really the watch was sold through an agent, who no doubt had kept a sizable commission since timepieces went for about five hundred; but to her it was well worth the missing half: she feared the Russians, who were reputed to prefer large women.

"And I'm not what you'd call petite." Robustly she snorted.

"The Russians like 'em fat," Reinhart said gallantly. "And that's not you.'

She looked away with a hint of pain, as if the remark were out of order, and then returned to, anyway, do best by it: "One thing I know, it's sure hard to lose it when you put on blubber. Cripes, you get so hungry, sometimes!" Her extraordinary grin over nothing, open, unafraid, witless, was more splendid than anyone else could make for cause. Trying unsuccessfully to match it, he cursed the fate that had led him early in life and from a false psychology to cultivate the impassivity of an Oriental. Now, in a time to be bravura, he found himself instead sneakily edging his knee over against hers, laying his hand on the cushion where hers, he had observed, habitually flew at punctuations in her speech, studying the rich mouth as it carved words from the adamant of the northern Midwest. If he wished to touch her, he should do it; there was a bond between large people, as among Negroes, Greek-Americans, soldiers, etc., by means of which their secrets were kept only from the outside world; thus, if he had such a wish, she already knew it and sitting there unprotestant was not offended.

But there went the music again, and since girls genuinely like to dance—so much so that they will partner another of their own sex rather than sit aside—Reinhart patiently rose and returned to the grappling, this time, however, since he was prepared, getting the initiative before she did, encircling her waist with a tensed forearm the muscle of which, though she did not complain, surely put a rope burn in the small of her back, manhandling her, on the turns raising her whole weight off the floor on just that single arm.

Coincident with her total surrender he went into tumescence and regretted that for the sake of slim hips he had worn the tight OD trousers which would show the most meager change of contour. He must hold his lower body away and cast the mind on some serene subject matter. The phonograph played "Long Ago and Far Away," from some movie faintly recalled, abominably corny yet sad and sweet. No doubt most of them here were led to thoughts of home, and he was in this mood charitable, retaining for himself an achingly beautiful sense that it was he who was far away and long ago, like someone who lingers in the theater after the performance has ended, amid the discarded programs and slowly vanishing odors and the houselights extinguishing bulb by bulb.

Thus as the hour fled, when the record player broke down and they returned to the couch, Reinhart felt nostalgia for the dance, and when it began again to revolve and they danced, he thought of the distant perfection of the time on the sofa, and was always ready to pull Very one way or the other like a great anthropomorphic balloon, for she had become incredibly light on her feet. In these activities, he got his hands on her in various quasi-legal ways: against the side of a knocker, as they went off the floor; slipping down from the waist and swooping like a swallow across the buttock-swell as they waited, swaying, between records; up her grooved back to the hard metal juncture of the strained brassiere, over which slip, shirt, and jacket provided no more cover than wallpaper over the last tenant's picture-hooks.

The society of girls is a very delightful thing, as he recalled someone had told David Copperfield, not professional, but very delightful. Reinhart had not for years, excepting café encounters and alleyway contacts with foreigners, which was something else again, had it to enjoy. Those American scents and sounds, one's own language speaking of nothing, but understood; the thousand familiar references in matter and spirit; the absence of ambiguity—Europe was suddenly squalid, skinny, crooked, and dark, he would not have taken it for *eine Mark* or *cinq francs*. With this Yankee smooth-warm cheek against his he thought of Lori and her little cousin towards whom as late as this afternoon he had had inclinations which, because he saw them now as a product of the time and place rather than himself, could be definitely labeled strange and discordant, the whole business devious and gnarled.

He decided he was in love, or that he would assume he was tonight and decide on its permanence the next morning. This, and the fact that no officer in the company looked disapproval —indeed, in the crush on the floor none could have if he would —the fragrance of cosmetics, the shadows when some excellent person turned down the lights for the dreamy songs, the warm wall of humanity around the tight little cell of their mutual interest, the yielding of his artificial will to the natural magnetism of her mass—in the strength of these he closed with her all the way to the shins, lost false modesty and with his lower-middle, that had become sensitive as the tips of both hands, could feel the very mount of Venus, while his mouth in the movement of the music slowly followed the round of her cheek to the lip-crevice and made entry.

This bliss was disrupted when some bastard inaugurated a series of hot records on the turntable. Reinhart knew as he led Very back to the sofa that it was an opportunity, even an obligation, to take her outside, perhaps in supreme audacity to make a headlong rush through the back yards to his flat just around the corner, taking the tide at its flood. Yet his feeling was more delight than desire; he wished rather to prolong this time which had come fortuitously than replace it with his own initiative, which held no surprises at all.

How marvelous it is to be singled out, and spared the tight-wire balance of establishing favor! But it also makes a man a good deal more cautious than a shy girl would believe, forwardness in small things being a fortress against large. Girls who are bold can better withhold. It is as if the tiger dug the pit, fixed the net, arranged the camouflage, and crouched laughing by while Frank Buck stumbled through and captured himself. The other side of the coin was the pleasant fantasy that you could sit very still, coining banalities when necessary, but nothing coarse or even really interested, it went without saying, sneaking through the requisite time, playing cherry, so to speak, until the girl was so wild with unrequited passion that she would positively drag you to her bed.

On still another hand, Very bore all the moldmarks of a nice girl, the sort whose intimacies were flagrant because her intentions were innocent, like some Samaritan who courts denunciation as a pickpocket by reseating your slipping watch. She could very well get you all the way to the Beautyrest only to repair a loose spring, and nothing upset him more than basing an effort on principles not understood until its miscarriage.

He again could have stood a drink, and Very had just as soon, but a difficult negotiation through the dance-floor athletes who despite their average age of thirty to forty were astonishingly spry at the fast music, discovered only a wet table of empty bottles. He returned to see Very sharing the couch with a gloomy captain whose collar caduceus bore a *D* for Dentist. He was known to Reinhart as a relatively good egg, as well as a painless practitioner, but he now wore the pious look of that partygoer who makes a fetish of his loneliness and searches grimly all evening for fellow worshipers, thus partaking in much more community than the busiest extrovert. Skinny and fuzzy, as if he had been twisted together from pipe cleaners, he sat grumbling in an undertone. However, he had dropped there only in quest of a seat, not trouble, and his scowl of greeting as Reinhart sat on the other end carried no hint of malice.

"You know," Reinhart said as she moved comfortably against his shoulder, "I used to be air-raid warden in the nurses' quarters in England. Did you ever see me there?"

"Gosh, I hope you didn't see me! I'm always a mess around the barracks, especially in England. Wasn't it awful there! The continual fog and rain, and that horrible tea all blue with milk, and fish and chips, and sausages filled with oatmeal. You know how many times I went to town? Once. Once, and I had enough."

"Weren't you ever to London?"

"Oh cripes no. That was dumb of me, wasn't it?—I should have gone to London, anyway, because as everyone says you'll never get the chance again. I bet you did, though—were the Piccadilly commandoes really pretty? Go on," she dug an unbelievably hard elbow into his side, "you can tell *me*."

At this the captain, whom he could see beyond her, ostentatiously repressed a grin and cast his eyes on the ceiling, and Reinhart was suddenly embarrassed at the public disclosure of her stupidity. A statistical friend once told him that one out of every ten girls is pretty, and one out of every ten girls is intelligent; ergo, one out of every one hundred girls is pretty and intelligent. Pooling the women he knew with those of the statistical friend made a grand total of eighty-five; they had had every expectation that somewhere in the remaining seven and a half to each man would appear the rare combination, but Reinhart had since lost track of the friend, in whose consignment the marvel would have to be, for his own quota was exhausted. As to Very, to balance the proposition she should have had to be a Mme Curie, a George Eliot, for only genius could be commensurate with her beauty, which he realized sitting there finding fault where none was appropriate, had become ever more glorious with use. She was fantastically beautiful, there was no other possible description, and comparable to nothing, lake, sky, gems, or flowers, but an until-now masturbation dream of the female essence.

So he began to lie, not grossly like a politician but subtly like a statesman, referring to his parents' street as a *road,* and to his college as *school;* spoke familiarly of dinner clothes, of riding boots, fencing, martini cocktails and the sediment of sherry wine, and of the possibility of buying oil paintings from ruined Germans for a song. He talked of love, not particularized but general, yet with a hint that behind him lay the wreckage of a hundred hearts, each keeping with it a piece of his own, for he was more passionate-impulsive than cruel. And finally, of the manly arts: boxing, judo, water polo—and creeping through the poison-gas chamber in basic training.

He was about to bear down on the last—and with justice, for it was quite true that his gas mask had sprung a leak, letting in the smell of deadly chlorine—when he reflected that since nurses had had the same training, Very was not likely to see it as exotic.

"Well, *go on,*" she screamed as the story bogged, flashing the long lashes which had some time earlier—it being, after all, a long evening after a full day's work—begun to lower.

"It wasn't really anything—" On the contrary, he sensed,

awfully, that it was the only thing for a whole half-hour that *did* interest her, and, to a degree humiliated, he determined almost vengefully for once to give the banal truth.

"Why, the instructor said if we so much as imagined we smelled chlorine to get the hell from the shed. Which I did. There was some sand in the valve of my mask, it turned out."

"But were there any toxic effects afterwards?" She pressed harder against him and seemed to study his right nostril.

"Just a little dizziness." Off on another lie.

"But you had a blood count, surely?"

"Not exactly, but—"

"How long ago was this?"

Christ, he could smell it still, that odor of laundries and swimming pools, fiercely clean, implacably antiseptic, inhuman, the same stink outer space must have beyond the farthest planet. Three years ago, when he was a punk recruit, his suntans yet shiny, his fatigues still dark green, his gas mask clotted; it gave him no pleasure to dwell on that era.

"Oh, well then, I guess it wasn't serious."

"Of course not, that's what I said."

"No mental effects?"

"Mental! You mean *crazy?* I hope not, nuts as I already am— but you can't be serious. Chlorine attacks the lungs, if it gets you, and you are so busy dying you haven't got time to go mad."

"When you've been around as many weirdies as I have, kiddy," she said in a bluff, coarse way that made him recoil, "you would know that many people don't have time for anything else."

This was a grisly turn indeed, and his feelings rumbled in his stomach as he pursued it. "Seriously, can chlorine gas—?"

"Oh, you're not worrying now, after this long? There now, I've upset you. Maybe I was joking a little. To tell the truth, I don't know anything about poison gas except what they told us." She laughed a little too violently and a touch too long, and if at its peak you had taken a still picture with a very fast camera, you might have seen that she herself for a moment looked deranged. "But are you aware that many kinds of internal medication taken to excess can produce a psychosis? Sulfa drugs, for example."

"They can!" He said it in so terrible a voice that the dentist, still there on the other side of Very, jerked in professional, hypocritical dismay, as if his drill had slipped and lacerated a tongue.

"Well, only *temporary*." Into his face she had pushed hers wide with the most glorious grin of the evening, at once splendid and grotesque, and so near that with almost no effort he could have sunk his incisors into her velvet nose. Then she drew back and laughed, laughed, laughed. "Oh, I've got you so scared! Now the next time you contract nasopharyngitis you won't take sulfa, and then you'll catch pneumonia, blaming it all on me."

He asked, somewhere between joke and real, "Does that mean I'd be put on your ward?"

"For pneumonia? No."

"I mean—the other." He deplored euphemism, but he fancied that her mirth had become briefly acid with malevolence.

"Why not get to know me off duty, instead?" She patted his hand, but it was not in the least provocative. "I'm nicer then. Besides, we don't need you, we're all filled up, got more patients now than when the war was on. Bet you thought it would be the other way around. That's because it's never the real things that crack people, but the imaginary."

The music had at last become soft. Because someone tripped over it, lightly cursing, Reinhart crossed his restless, foot-tapping leg over the quiet one; his trunk inclined in a long plastic crescent: a smooth-leather couch would have ejected him to the floor. Very when solemn was not very Very, he said to himself, and to her: "I was always in a funny position."

He was in enough of one now for her to hesitate and then produce a question he had not heard for three years, an idiotic cuteness nevertheless poignant, fragrant of Tom Collinses floating Maraschino cherries and cheeseburgers dripping catsup but with no onion, because of the necking to come, in some congested, clamorous pleasure palace on the great Midwestern plain.

And when she asked "Funny haha or funny peculiar?" he was caught, with all the force of his past, in the iron fist of love, and would inevitably have been drawn sideways in a most funny uncomfortable position to crush the charming folly against her lips with his own—had not the dentist at that moment peered ugly around her exquisite right breast and called:

"Hey, Reinhart, why don't you scout around for some hooch! That damned Lovett has some in the kitchen, I know. Do me a favor and go look."

"Why don't you go yourself?" Specialist officers would accept almost anything that was simultaneously assured and good-humored.

"That lousy skinflint faggot!" mumbled the dentist, and mixed himself again into the cushions.

Very rolled her eyes. "You were saying, when we were so r. i.?"

"That I always wanted to be in combat, but frankly, I was too cowardly to volunteer for the infantry. What I wished would happen was that I would simply be assigned there through no voluntary act of my own. Then my conscience would have been clear, as it were."

"Conscience? Who lets himself in for danger unless he has to?"

"That's it," he groaned. "I'm very sensible. I *didn't* volunteer, and I'm not sorry that I did not. My regret is that somebody else didn't make me. When I say conscience, I don't mean it bothers me now, but that it would have if I volunteered, so much so that I would probably have been killed."

"Obscure."

"Don't you get it? I would have felt I was committing suicide."

"Don't talk like that!" She manipulated his hand, as if this perversion had settled in that member, and could be worked out, like a cramp. It was only too clear that he wasn't getting through, and he understood that he very likely never would. Anyway, her failure was in itself a kind of success. Having essayed this theory with others—if you haven't heroism to bring to a woman, you have to lay your intentions at her feet—he had tasted many times the ultimate indifference most people have to the imagination's projections, especially in the hypotheses of somebody else's morality.

"I'm sometimes embarrassed at fighting the war as a kind of Broadway press agent."

"Special Services are certainly necessary, or the Army wouldn't have it. Besides, think how human it is to entertain people. Think how fine it would be if each side fought with entertainers, with the victory going to whoever made most people laugh." It was obvious from the jolly bell in her own throat, which she now tolled, who would win. And Reinhart, with this revelation of the open secret of her force—that she would always be victor, from an inability to imagine loss—knew that he must have her.

So, with mock impatience, he said: "You're not serious." And slid his arm around her splendid waist, as the captain's face hove into view once more, saying:

"You wanna dance?"

Three or four times, to Very's blind shoulder. When he eventually registered, she declined, and considering the situation, perhaps too rudely, Reinhart thought. To make up for which he grinned amenity at the man.

"I didn't ask *you*," the dentist groused, and ambled off in the half-bitter, half-stoical slump of a panhandler.

"*You* wanna dance?" she mimicked, and meant it, moving to draw Reinhart to his feet.

"How can we now, if you just refused him?"

But she didn't, genuinely, see why not.

# CHAPTER 7

IDLY, but with great care, Schild marked the room and its furnishings: solid pieces, dark; dual escutcheon lamps on the wall at various points in an academic rhythm: fireplace, for example, bracketed by a pair whose vertical members swelled like pregnant bellies to the points of the switches. A corner stove, ceramic, beige, built up of molded doughnuts of ever-diminishing circumferences, baroque welts and carvings, small black door amidships for introduction of fuel. Which was those bricks stacked neatly by.

"Compressed coal dust, very tidy," said Lovett, who had come up silently and followed the direction of Schild's eyes. "These Germans are the most technically advanced people in Europe, damn them, if that's a recommendation. The throne room upstairs has a pushbutton flusher—what I mean is, no chain!" He threw himself gingerly on the very edge of a sofa cushion, giving the impression of artificial vivacity, and staring, said: "No, I *don't* know you—you're surely new in the outfit."

"Look, Lieutenant, you invited me yesterday. Frankly, I wish you'd remember it." Schild spoke in the sharp tone of eminent reason. Yet he seldom used it for so slight a cause as this, and he wondered now at himself: whether his motive had been on Schatzi's example, or that from some hint of unconscious fear he had suddenly needed exterior proof of his identity.

"*Certainement,*" said Lovett quickly. "You're the Nazi-hunter. I'm sorry. Have you met any of these lovely people?" Upon the negative he rose, saying "How lucky you are," and snatching Schild's arm, led him through the crowd to the kitchen, which was 1920's-modern, with a gas stove up on four legs, like the one everybody's mother once had, including Schild's, and a bright, yet enclosed breakfast nook sprinkled with painted rosebuds, fir trees, and goody-goody gnomes in Lederhosen and dirndls, a sovereign little house within the house. Peering inside, Schild made out the witch, a small worn person of feminine gender, smiling bereavement, expropriation, and sycophancy.

"Atrocious old bitch of a Nazi housekeeper," said Lovett. "That's who." His attenuated index finger signaled dismissal, and the old woman trotted her carpet slippers up the back stairs to the second floor.

When they were inside the booth Lovett produced, by an elaborate act of spontaneous creation, a full bottle of Scotch and two paper cups.

"And what are *you?*" he asked without warning, lolling his head and transforming his eyes into little knife-cuts intended to symbolize high interest. "I mean, what are you *really?*"

To have reproduced exactly what Schild's mother had once asked, Lovett should have gone on: "You are still a good boy?" And should have been lying on a hospital bed, the white, segmented, cranked-and-rodded dais of pain, flanked by electrical nurse-alarms, half-filled vessels of water, folded cardboard sputum cups; should have worn magnifying glasses which projected eyes in terrible, bloated particularity, showing the iris as not a smooth round but rather an uneven burst of pigment threads darning into the void of the pupil, repeating silently the accusation so often voiced in earlier times of health: that their vision was lost in the pregnancy that engendered him. A queer, cruel, lifelong lie, that not until she was under ground did he, consulting the old schoolgirl snapshots, expose. Indeed, it was only by the spectacles that you could know her amid the anonymity of fifty middy blouses.

Come tell me the truth, they ask, of which you are manifestly a walking denial: what crimes lie concealed behind your façade, who are you to be closed when we, the rest of us, are open? And how determined they are to wonder forever, how implacable is their will to ignorance! "I am nothing that I wished to be: chronologically, not a fireman, not a cowboy, not a gentile, philosopher, lover, nor revolutionary. But what are *your* failures?"

No purpose in asking that of Lovett, who was really a kind of success, who besides had wanted only a simple statement of civilian occupation, doctor, lawyer, Indian chief, against which to set his own probably rare, surely very dear calling. He saw in no pride that Lovett had chosen him, of all the crowd, for cahoots, just as the lone Negro in a company would draw to him, or the person with a lisp or one arm, the girl with the hairlip, and it happened twice at parties for Russian war relief that he attracted the pariah of that context, the lost Republican who cornered him to trust, conspiratorially, that the aid would not strengthen communism in that forlorn country. Whatever the pariahhood, it unerringly found and clove to him: he must stink of separateness. From this final, subtlest of variations on anti-Semitism, which built its Dachau in the heart, there was no refuge, and he foresaw the day he would be assigned to infiltrate the B'nai Brith and at the first meeting be pulled aside to receive the confidence of some disguised Nazi.

"I was a teacher at a private school."

Lovett smirked triumphantly. "In New York?"

Where else? Schild felt himself capable of the accent of East Broadway and the Houston Street shrug, but was proved right in his restraint by Lovett's next question.

"Fashionable?"

Perhaps it was the Scotch which had sheared the falls and rises from the usually schizophrenic voice, leveled it into an even plain of clay, for what Schild heard was "fashionable," and he was disinclined to believe it, even of Lovett.

But a timid knock on the back door freed him from the issue, a weak knock, but followed rapidly by an entry in the opposite character, bold, brutal, hinge-torturing.

"Oh, *why* do they use the *yard?*" Lovett wailed. "We have a pretty john!"

In a moment his despair sharpened into fright. A freckled Soviet face, mounted on tunic shoulder-boards and wearing a cap awry, poked jovially into the entrance of the dinette.

And roared: *"Herr Leutnant, ich bin hier. Was für ein Haus! Schön, Schön!"*

The Russian was a little lieutenant of artillery, dressed in high-neck tunic, flared breeches like displaced wings, and boots. His good brown eyes searched for an object that did not elicit admiration, and failed. A line of dirt across his prominent Adam's apple showed how far he had washed. His hair had been shaved up to the temples, and obviously with a dull scissors, by himself and that very afternoon. He saluted Lovett, Schild, and the house. Saying *"Verzeihung,"* he stepped to the sink and took a drink of water through his hand.

Lovett had met him on a black-market mission to the Kurfürstendamm, picked him up for a souvenir, for who had ever known a *Russian?;* had written out the address—who ever thought he would *find* it? The only trouble was he only spoke *German,* who could talk to him my *Gawd!* Finding that Schild could, Lovett sniffed in pique and vanished.

In the living room the lieutenant shook off Schild's patronage and charged the cautious company with outthrust arm, announcing *"Leutnant* Lichenko!" And prevailed, pumping hands and snowing compliments, and when he had taken care of even the humblest, he turned the approbation on himself. He explained the three medals in a Venetian-blind overlap on his thin chest, the deeds of valor which they marked, and expressed curiosity that the Americans were not equipped with boots. His own, he averred, were of a superb workmanship and quality beside which the German-army issue could not dare to show its pressed-paper grain. He applied the same judgment to his tunic, breeches, belt,

and cap. The latter he removed extravagantly for the ladies but
replaced directly. He wore it as he and Schild studied the
phonograph, which by means of a small device on either side of
the turntable had knowledge of each record's duration and released new ones at the proper intervals from the stack it bore.

"Goes round, *herum*, push button to play again, to puh-lay
a-gain, pu-ush button. *Sechs* records only, will it take. Compree?
*Sechs* records," said Nader, winking stupidly at Schild.

"What's that, Dwight Fiske?" asked a thin dentist who
had joined the elbow crowd. " 'The Colonel's Tropical Bird.'
There's a sex record for you, Leek!"

Who was a plump kibitzer of a nurse that threw him a dread-
ful smile and said, dreadfully: "You're so-o-o-o gay." Pointing at
Lichenko, she asked Schild, "Suppose he'd like to dance?" But
Schild had already given her his back.

Lichenko took off his cap, scratched his head, inspected the
fingernail, replaced the cap, and begged Leek's pardon. Throughout, his left eye, which seemingly he could work independently
of the right one, was fixed towards a picture on the next wall,
and his feet were casually screwing him that way. At last he was
ready to go directly before it, to abrade its surface—in an inconspicuous corner, so that if damage were caused none would
show—and to proclaim: "A genuine oil painting. Oh, very
*schön*, indeed. Private property, yes? But roses in a bowl and
nothing else! Where can the philosophy be in something like
this?" Did Schild know Repin? Oh, *ausgezeichnet*, excellent, excellent!" "Ivan the Terrible Kills His Son." Bloody picture.
*Angst, Angst!* "This we call the *Russkaya dusha*, the Russian
soul. Or did you know that already?"

With the question, for which since he was not just making
noise he wished an answer, he gave specific notice to his benevolent patron: "You *do* know, *das ist sehr gut*: all these things
can be useful for friendship. My German is fluent, yes?—except
that it is difficult to sound the g. Let me hear you speak it. Say

'Gitler' for me. Ghitler, Ghhitler. *Ach,* it is not easy to do things the right way, but it is always possible, *ja?,* always possible, my friend."

He had said "my friend" and taken Schild's hand. Russian male friends kissed on meeting and walked hand-in-hand, yet since 1917 homosexuality had all but vanished in the Soviet Union.

His calluses torturing Schild's smooth palm, Lichenko approved: "Your German, you know, is excellent. Was this learned in the wonderful American schools?"

Oh, partly, and in part from a grandfather. Schild was pleased and apprehensive at once, the latter from questioning, any questioning.

"You are of German descent, then? Does it give you a queer feeling to return to your old motherland as an enemy? The Russian word is *rodina. Rodina*—motherland. I will teach you the Russian language in this manner, term by term, although I am Ukrainian. But Russian nowadays is more useful, yes? But you are German?"

Schild smiled lazily to let it pass, but Lichenko ripped at his fingers: "Tell me, tell me!"

Sneezes, orgasms, interrogations, their irrevocable end is ordained in their beginning.

*"Ich bin jüdisch."*

"I see, I see! Then it is not queer but pleasant!" Lichenko grinned—indeed, he had not stopped grinning: the ravines in his face were grin-grooves, his irregular nose was lumpy with grin, these along with his winged thighs making him a Mercury of mirth. It was, frankly, a private thing, which he could respect while not losing any skin from his own ass.

And he was soon away to other pictures and *objets d'art,* furniture, rugs, and the dark-blue wallpaper with its silver suggestions of flower petals dissolving in ink. He bounced into an obese chair, which bounced him halfway out. He sneaked carefully back into place, and the chair submitted to good manners. As for Schild, he sat crosslegged at its side on the floor.

Lichenko's German was very good, too, for he was an educated man, an engineer, in fact, although the war had caught him before he finished school. His intended specialty concerned dams and sluiceways, the diversion of streams, paradises from deserts, the transformation of the face of the earth, or anyway one-sixth of it. Nor was Soviet engineering a cultural Siberia. He slid easily from an apostrophe to steamshovels into American writing, where he was better than oriented.

"We read American books in the Soviet Union!" he shouted happily, digging his hard heels into the floor. "More than we do Russian. Also, more than you read in the United States. You know, of course, that American authors would starve but for the money they get from Soviet sales."

"I know," said Schild, who *did,* at that moment; did, because fact can be countermanded by wish and hope and generosity and brotherhood, else we are lost.

"Have you read Dreiser?" he asked.

"The greatest American writer," replied Lichenko. "But Upton Sinclair Lewis is *schön,* too, and Jack London's *Babbitt* and *The Iron Heel.*"

"I met Dreiser once."

"*Also,*" Lichenko mumbled, removing his cap and testing his forehead with a sweaty palm.

"He spoke at the school where I taught. A great, majestic man, a champion of humanity, and a friend of the Soviet Union, as I suppose you know."

"*Es interessiert mich das zu wissen,*" said Lichenko vaguely, but hopped to his feet positively, and bowed. For there stood Leek.

"Now, you can't keep our ally out of circulation!" she chided, and led Lichenko to the dancing area—though not before Schild was constrained to translate some small-talk, including a Soviet tribute to womanhood in an ornate German that englished as something Albert might have said to Victoria; nor before he volunteered to hold the doffed but troublesome cap, Lichenko having been at a loss for a cache where that article would be neither crushed nor stolen.

A universal sense of fun could not be withstood. The troublesome shortage of fuel reached Lichenko's apparatus, without benefit of Schild, and he laughed long and loud, tore himself from the Siamese coupling with Leek, and shot into the kitchen and out the back door. He reappeared with a shoulder sack of bottles: vodka, schnapps, whisky, and other fluids.

Glasses flowed, music tinned, everybody danced. Reinhart, Schild saw, glided about as if on figure skates with the large nurse, in the perfect attitude of the adolescent sexual captive: closed eyes, back arched *affetuoso*. A more direct confirmation of the reputed egalitarianism of medical units could not be imagined.

Schild thought about Lichenko, who had so little and so much. Throw the switch of the time machine and there he was, with his cartload of firewood, ankle-deep in mire, on his weary animal way to the sod hut, the black bread, and the cabbage; the trashy icons; the spent wife; the ravished, if pretty, the prematurely aged, if plain, daughter; swearing so vilely that if his master had the ill fortune to canter past, he might have got another crop's end for his lifelong collection of abuse. Born old, senile at twenty, dead at forty, without ever having passed through the human. A lump of dung, hating love and beauty and intelligence because he was defined by their absence. So, gorge the rotten potatoes, let the grease befoul the lips and drip from the chin, fill the gut with the stolen bottle, and when it explodes in the head, give the wife a fist to her decaying teeth and the daughter a hand between her thighs, because you are beyond judgment, beyond hope. But not beyond history, which moves not for revenge or profit or virtue, but for the negation of negation, the arrangement of disorder, above all, for an end to waste.

These things mature without ever having been formally born. Lichenko was, of a sudden, disorderly. Only a moment earlier he had displayed high, good, and legitimate spirits; now he had enrolled in that brotherhood of savage peoples from whom fire-water should be, and often is, legally withheld. His maw sagged; his eye carmined; he drank as if, oblivious to the torrent that washed his face and gummed his tunic, he hungered for glass, and proved it by incising a piece of the tumbler's rim. A pencil line of blood traced out the groove of his chin, like the after-punch make-up of movie martyr-priests who may invite their adversary to put on the gloves but never return the favor *ad hoc*.

Amidst all those medics his wound went unattended, on the theory that if he lost enough blood he might collapse peaceably. But he had just begun to play. After checking Leek in an arm-chair, he detonated into the frenzy of a solo jackknife dance. The floor quaked, for although he was small, the boards were sim-patico with his rhythm; the rolled carpet against the far wall, which was not, had its long, heavy belly rent by a boot-heel.

With such sport, with Lovett impotently aflutter, with Nader enveloping himself in the phonograph wires, with the awed company's disengagement, the room was progressively demol-ished. Lichenko's success with the carpet sent him to Leek's chair, which, after removing her, he ruined with a single jump, hard heels forward; he smashed the mantlepiece mirror, pelted coal cakes in black bursts against a carved lowboy, got a paint-ing once out of six throws with as many tumblers, and shouted *"Bezbol!"* Then, to Schild, he said: "Fascists."

"Yes," answered Schild.

"Not the Americans."

"No."

"The Germans. Why should this house be spared? If you saw what they did in my country . . ." He sank wearily into the chair and passed a hand across his face. He signaled to Leek, point-ing at his lap. She sat there submissively, bovinely, as he read her idly in Braille.

Still on the floor, Schild shifted his weight from left to right ham and adjusted his pistol belt.

"Will you permit me to see your weapon?" asked Lichenko. He ejected Leek. He looked feverish as he palmed the Colt. A vein in his forehead pumped into prominence. He worked the action, stroked the barrel, warmed it with his cheek, and peeped down the muzzle. He found the clip, extracted it, loosened a bullet, felt its slug, replaced the bullet, replaced the clip, pointed the piece at the still proximate Leek, went "Boom, boom!" or thereabouts in Russian vowels, finger on trigger guard.

Ignoring her squeak, squeaking himself in delight, he took out his own pistol and thrust it butt first at Schild.

"We'll exchange. Then we'll each have a souvenir of a time we will never forget."

It was what the Russians called a *Nagan,* a cheaply made cap-gun affair, but Schild accepted it reverently, and, though he detested firearms, gave an earnest imitation of Lichenko's ecstasy over the Colt.

"You *agree?* You will *exchange?*" shouted Lichenko. "My dear friend, I salute you!"

On his feet, he highballed with the right hand, a dwarf against the bas relief of the large Americans who had started to surge genially upon him through the dismembered furniture. Schild was rising in honor of the moment, at the very least to return the salute, when Lichenko began to discharge the .45. He perhaps intended to squeeze off only one cartridge as an additional salute to fortune, but the kick from the one convulsed his hand into another, and he was drawn *nolens volens* into a full tribute.

Below the scored ceiling and within the vermiculated walls, Lichenko, now-spent gun drooping, sniffed the atmosphere of powder, appeared about to sneeze, did not, and pushed a reproachful lower lip like a coal chute at Schild.

"Ah, my friend, this American pistol!"

He tore at his choker collar. "Excuse me, Vasya is ill . . ."

And fell prone into the plaster, which, of course, was now the common ground.

"You win the medal," said Lieutenant Leek, an unjolly snowman, to Schild.

He blew clean his glasses and inquired silently with blurred vision.

"For Number One Horse's Ass, Berlin District."

Nader touched Schild's elbow and whispered: "Look, Jack, Lovett went for the MPs. Get your ass-hole buddy out of here. We'll con them. He was just drunk." He knelt beside Lichenko and fingered back an eyelid, peered at the red orb. "Drunk as a skunk." He ordered Corporal Reinhart to lend a hand.

Reinhart lifted Lichenko by the belt and pulled him over a shoulder.

"Veronica, why don't you go along?" asked Nader. "Jesus, maybe he's dead."

"O.K. Thanks for the party," said she. "I had a lovely time anyhow."

Reinhart navigated through the rear door and into the garden. Already military-police sirens sounded in the distance. Through the back yards, having trouble at every sonbitching fence, and around the block to Schild's house was their silent way. Reinhart's calves were tired on the stairs, but he gripped the banister and made it in good shape to the room, where as his burden was lowered to the bed it came to life briefly, displaying a revolving eye, and returned to dreamland with a mouthful of bedspread.

Veronica examined the body from a distance, found it hale. Reinhart said:"You're a good fellow, sir, to do this for that Russian. If his army found out about it he'd be headed for Siberia." And Very seconded that.

"I think," said Schild, "the American Army is what we have to worry about at the moment." He took a tiny package from his pocket. "Can you use these?"

Anybody who ever opened a K ration had Fleetwood cigarettes to dispose of, yet Reinhart was sure these were his own come home. He was too weary, the evening had been too extravagant, to inquire by what route.

New relations consisting so fiercely in the precise time of day and the specific mise en scène, the sudden dislocation of these threw both Very and Reinhart into a diffidence, especially now as, their task ended, they went out of step down the sidewalk to Very's house. From the side of his eye Reinhart could see her shoulder bag swinging off the divisions of silence. An occasional officer or nurse, not breaking the peace, breathed past them in the frenetic diaspora from the party. Down the street, its siren dying like a throttled pussycat, another MP jeep arrived.

At her door, Reinhart chickened out of trying for a good-night kiss, perhaps with a view towards establishing his independence, which, in the pale simulacrum of *post coitum tristis* that was his after-party letdown, he felt had been compromised. Or perhaps it was a defense against the progressive frigidity she gave off as they approached the front step.

"Oh this is where you live?" he asked numbly.

"Haha! Were you going to charge me with breaking and entering?"

This cruel parody of his own earlier fantasies on the mansion of her person, despite the false laughter—whose spuriousness was advertised by its miraculous lack of resonance; it was as if a great bell rang so shallowly that nothing trembled—suddenly elicited his overdue response to Lichenko's rampage. To assault an entity of order, to register a spontaneous nay against the sanctioned and authorized; mean, but it were meaner than never to be so moved.

But Very skipped insouciantly inside the doorway. Shortly, her other end appeared, saying: "See you in the funny papers."

# CHAPTER 8

CAPTAIN St. George's surprise was limited. He had rapped at and opened Schild's door on his regular schedule of unnecessary morning information—"The bath is free"—and looked upon a scrawny, alien fundament. Lichenko, rump to door, was bent in a study of his big toe.

Schild's guest had awakened with a refusal to recognize his benefactor. Something Schild however took in good grace and did not sully with a word as the Russian scratched an elusive cap-a-pie itch, lip-farted at his own image in the mirror, and spat a long drizzle of saliva out the window in droll reproof of the sunlight that made him wince. Then he turned, said with ill humor: "*Da,*" and undressed for an examination of his pelt.

St. George recovered with expedition. "I thought you had a woman in here," he chortled to Schild, who was elbow-propped on the floorbound blanket that had been his bed.

Arising with the aid of the dresser corner, khaki undershirt and shorts clinging to him like old crepe paper, sallow, hairy, shivering—Berlin's air in the shadows stayed cold till noon—Schild said as St. George averted his eyes: "So what else is new?"

He watched the dull pain fill the captain's eyelids, distend his cheeks, sag the loose mouth, and lower the chin, going down like mercury in a chill. It was a kind of crying just beneath the epidermis; years of it had made his face one big bag.

St. George addressed himself to the oval mirror on the dresser. "Do you know?" His ebullience had left. "Is it necessary to have an electric shaver honed every so often? Mine is beginning to pull." He held the device towards Schild, retaining the pillbox affair which made any current American.

"Duncroft," he went on, "says it can't be done. He says the razor companies aren't going to sharpen old ones and thereby put themselves out of business. They're going to want to sell you a new one, he says. But he's always cynical."

Lichenko left off his big toe and went over the others, as if in count; midway through the left foot, he lost his sum and began again.

"Did you see a strange man as you entered this room?" asked Schild.

"A refugee from the party, I take it." St. George twisted the top of a battered tin of GI foot powder, sifted a quantity into his palm, and traced rhomboids with his fingertip.

Later, as he and Schild crossed the street towards breakfast at the 1209th officers' mess, to which St. George had got their small unit attached for rations, he said: "Strange how when you meet a man who's naked you don't get to know much about him. Maybe we all rely too much on externals, but that's the way it goes."

At the mess Schild was daily juxtaposed with many of the to him anonymous faces of the party, and occasionally received a curious but cordial nod. He was also aware, from time to time, of the regard of multiple eyes and the drone of comment at adjoining tables as he forked in his Harvard beets and masticated the grainy roast, but was conscious of no ill will, nor, in his sense of the word, suspicion. Once he saw Lovett across the tent, fragmenting bread with neurasthenic fingers and spotting the pieces individually over his tray, which could also be interpreted as evidence of placidity.

But after one lunch, Nader met him outside.

"Did you pack off the Russky? Dewey's going to make trouble, mark my words, because the Old Man's about to hang it on him."

"I'll make it good," said Schild. "It was my fault. I gave him the gun."

"Well by Jesus we'll put in a complaint through the Kommandatura," Nader said. "Just write down his name and outfit. Did you get the outfit?" He rummaged in his pockets for writing materials.

Both extremities of Nader's pencil bore chewmarks. His paper was the reverse of a snapshot carrying the pale-violet emblem of an Oklahoma developer. Schild wrote, slovenly: "Lt. Krylenko, Engrs Corps, Red Army."

"I don't have much hope this will find him." He smiled commiseration. "But you won't have to. Just let me know the amount of the damage, and I'll see you get reimbursed in full. I'll see your C.O. myself this afternoon. You'll be fully cleared."

"Now," said Nader, "I know you're oke, but you'll do best by us if you crap out early. What I mean is—" He broke off until the pencil was reseated in his breast pocket and the flap buttoned. "Let me as somebody who was soldiering when you, Dewey Lovett, and anybody else in this road show was still sucking titty. Know the Old Man since Jesus was a PFC: hates anything involved. We'll never find the Russian, but the thing will be wrapped up and Dewey will stop pissing and moaning."

"I thought it was simple decency to get him out of your place ahead of the MPs," said Schild. "That officer fought all the way from Stalingrad to Berlin. It would be outrageous if his first defeat came from blowing out some German plaster."

"As long as we're off the hook, old buddy, that's all, as long as we've got something to hand them. The phony name you wrote down here will do as well as another." He showed his chipped teeth in amiable pride. "What time I have left from being personnel officer, unit censor, permanent O.D., fire officer, postal officer, and post-exchange officer, I put to provost marshaling. You'd never make a successful crook." Nader's hairy wrist disposed of all possible demurrers, embarrassments, confusions. "Hell, I remember his name, I just don't know to spell it."

Exposure of his minor deception freed Schild to submit the whole affair to a lens, under which he saw: being caught out by such a man and in such a way was not a demerit.

Nader pushed the snapshot at him. "You still didn't look at the picture on the other side."

A ripe piece of girl in her late teens sat on the first step of a rotting porch. In the background depended the rusty chains of an old slat swing; through one link, the shaft of a raffia fan. As she cuddled a stuffed panda, her deep lower lip sat in transitory melancholia, or what may have been counterfeit desire. Pleats of voile skirt fell gradually away at the thigh on the viewer's side, as if at the border of some proscenium arch through which shortly a young man with haircut, black suit, and cascaded necktie would heel-and-toe as commencement valedictorian. She was relaxed or prepared to spring, according to which evidence had more weight: the tension of the femoral muscles or the flaccid pubis in the valley that knew no drawers.

This was an exercise to put Schild on his mettle. How to communicate in the proper measure somewhere between coarseness and patronage. For Nader, in the classic manner of such picture-passers, watched him as a bank guard observes an unshaven man; that self of his which dwelt in Nader's mind was about to acquire a habitation and a name. Schild suddenly ached with regret that he could not miraculously reduce his size and quality to the mode of the image and plunge into that seedy, sweaty, alien world of dessicated lumber, rusty metal, the treasures of shooting galleries, the failures of fabric, unshaven armpits, sagging wash-lines, off-stage radios, that universe of the enervated Sunday, and make animal love to the girl. Not having that option, he grinned wryly and said: "Choice"; watching it join the community in the wallet. "I believe the idea now is to ask who is she?"

"You don't know any less than I do," Nader replied. "This was found behind a chair after an enlisted men's dance in the service club at Camp Grant, Ill. I carry it for laughs."

Schild returned to the tent for another cup of coffee, the dregs of which he hung over until the last eater had departed and it was seemly to draw and transport Lichenko's rations. He did not know why his guest remained, but it could hardly have been for "his big brown eyes." A phrase from his father's code, applied to those business associates whose sudden appearance of friendship

logic and experience exposed as conspiracy. A "friend" dropping
into the office for a smoke was of course a spy who mentally
photographed a new button and, within half an hour after his
departure, set up machinery to reproduce the plagiarism in quantity, to steal the orders of the first party and libel *him* to the
stolen customers as a thief to confound.

He carried the laden tray towards the billet. It could hardly
have been for his big brown eyes that Lichenko lingered. This
old-Jew's suspicion would not be put down, despite his violent
attempts at negation that, as he crossed the street, became exterior, the ultimate ineffectuality. He shook his whole body as if
in a chill, and the spinach in the end compartment, having by
nature no integrity, easily lost its coherence and slipped over the
rim like a string of mucus.

Lichenko could be on furlough, on extended pass, on some perfectly uncomplicated special duty from which he had legally or
illegally gleaned four days of liberty; he may have been lost,
have searched in vain the wilderness of Berlin for his unit, temporarily have given up. He was perhaps a liaison man between
Red and American Intelligences, who—the Soviets being no fools
in these matters—could better prosecute his purpose by four or
five days' discretion, especially around an idiot like St. George,
who, it could quickly be seen by a shrewd fellow, would fly all
to pieces at the first suspicion that his outfit was to have a serious
role. There were, too, the possibilities of amnesia, outright absence without leave . . . and even, of course, desertion. Notwithstanding Schild's automatic rejection of anti-Soviet messhall
gossip that "hundreds" of Russian soldiers had decamped to the
Allied sectors, which if true would have been a lie, he was certain that it *was* true in cases. It was something that could be
faced without equivocation. Renegades ye will always have with
you.

In the middle of the street, a two-and-a-half ton truck nearly
ran him down, the driver leaning out to carp, spotting the silver

bar, recovering. A fine midsummer sun crafted suburban shadows which lay only slightly to the northeast of their objects, the time standing not far beyond one o'clock; that extreme portion of the sky that to the grounded seems at last palpable but to the winged is merely the middle distance towards another intangibility, hung unusually high even for Berlin. A soldier in fatigues lingered on the stair of one of the officers' homes, in the grip of an internal monologue that he broke off to inspect Schild with academic superiority, which indicated he was on an errand for a captain or above. Shortly such a person, wearing a khaki undershirt, appeared at the door and bellowed: "Bugger off, Wilbur!" As Wilbur without acknowledgment merged with the shrubbery, this undershirt shouted: "Bugger you, too, Rosenthal!"

One thing was certain: Schild's eyes did not improve over the years.

"Can't you see? It's Young! . . . Oh, I'm sorry, I thought you were Rosenthal. Rosenthal's a DOCTOR IN OUR OUTFIT."

College Joe type with a grin. Back to bed, my boy, the world will run very well without you, or very badly; in any case, without you. An angular girl, with hairy legs, pumped decorously past on her bicycle. It was Schatzi in transvestite disguise—of course it was not, but Schild, too, could be permitted an error of identification. In the past three days he had seen Schatzi in every bony face; he had recognized him falsely with greater assurance than he had yet seen him in actuality. It was only because the genuine article never appeared in daylight that the apparitions could be ignored.

The real Schatzi—he had left him an hour before Lichenko had come to the party. Certainly if he, Schild, were Schatzi, he would not fail to trace a connection between these events, to draw up the disjunctive proposition so favored by his courier: either . . . or; either Schatzi knew of Lichenko or he did not. If he knew, there could be no doubt that what had happened was with his connivance. If he did not, all the rules commanded that he be told. But this clause was the emergency measure, necessary now because he had ignored the first principle of the code: never to get into such a situation. Thus to obey the second was to admit a transgression of the first, and Schatzi already suspected him—or pretended to; in practical effects there was no important difference between reality and appearance—of mishandling his contact with the 1209th, either foolishly or from a motive of treason.

If, on the other hand, Lichenko had been planted on him— had *they* nothing better to do than keep him under surveillance? It was a preposterous idea. Still, since that first morning Lichenko had been sullen and unresponsive, lurking in the bathroom when Schild was home and going through his belongings when he was away: a pair of OD socks left separate in the footlocker tray had been united in a neat ball some time between breakfast and lunch. Fortunately, Schild had long been in the habit of destroying his letters—not that he received many; he had luckily cut off from Waslow when he went underground, Waslow who was not long afterwards expelled as an infantile leftist when he resisted the change of line from hard to soft vis-à-vis the bourgeois democracies; but he occasionally got communications from his sister, who typically had not only again changed husbands but again swapped gods, with the end of the war conceiving a perverse attraction towards the doctrine of Jung, whom she suggested Nathan visit, as long as he was stationed in Germany. Jung, the anti-Semite.

And then Lichenko's queer behavior over the chessboard. His visible emotions while playing could only be called ferocious; he groaned cavernously at momentary setbacks, howled at each little triumph, and upon the general victory—which he was never long in gaining, for Schild was not only an inferior player at best but would have been almost afraid in these circumstances to be a good one—Lichenko became most invidious, arrogantly shoving the board across the table like a dirty cafeteria plate and rising to swagger about the room on hard heels.

Lichenko's larger game was surely something more than chess, and unpleasant as it was to think that in this, too, they were adversaries, to that degree the mind would not accept another possibility. As to the heart: it could not endure a second enemy among the two men with whom he held a common purpose. Whatever Lichenko's menace, Schild forgave him for it.

Why should a citizen of the United States of America be a Communist?, thought Lichenko, all itchy again, a quarter-hour after his fourth bath in as many days. He felt large lice loping on his back. Off came the tunic. Spine presented to mirror. Not a beast in view. Imagination. They would leave that final place when he next wore a civilian shirt, even a dirty civilian shirt, even a lice-infested civilian shirt. Did the old holy men really wear hairshirts? What then was their lie? Surely a truth was what you gave for it. Yet everyone, and from what he could see, particularly the big-spenders of belief, had their lie. Believe in very little, said his mother, and your disappointments will be as small. This had seemed funny to him when he was ten but had grown more grave with age. Old people know more than they can tell directly. His mother then had not been old in years, but some people are born old. He had seen many a baby of whom, if you squinted your eyes, you could get a picture as an old man with cap and pipe, taking the sun in the park.

As he returned from the bathroom, the German woman moved correctly down the hall, as if on little wheels. Sluts walk so, being so large between the legs that their organs would fall out if they took long steps. You see! he grinned silently at her back, there's no need to be so grand! Next time you pass, Vasya's fingers will pinch your bottom!

He had never, in his belly, believed in the existence of foreign Communists—Communists where the Bolsheviks were not in power? No sense to that. Besides, foreign comrades were not taken seriously even by Soviet Party members, as he knew from his brother. The largest Party outside the USSR, the German C.P., had been puffed out like a match when Hitler arrived. And as to the Americans, hahaha! Who already owning an automobile, a ten-room apartment, a motion-picture projector, short-wave radio, and probably an airplane, became a Communist? Lichenko knew so much about America, had had so many fantasies about it, he oftentimes forgot that he had never been there and rather owed his data to the Soviet news agency's New York correspondent, whose dispatches he of course translated in reverse. Thus: the American worker lived like an emperor, and there was no U.S. Communist Party.

Since moving into Schild's billet Lichenko suspected he had been wrong about the latter. After all, the Bolsheviks had not always held power in his own country; everything started somewhere; if necessary, before one's own birth. The old czars, he believed despite his mother's testimony to the contrary, had not been first-rate people. The last one, he understood despite the Bolsheviks' like opinion, had no culture and was ruled by a woman herself the instrument of a corrupt monk. Therefore the Communists: who had begun as a small, weak band of, he supposed, idealists and martyrs—except that Stalin, even that early, committed armed robbery for the furtherance of *his* ideals; and no sooner had they kicked out the czar and won the Revolution than Lenin and Trotsky slaughtered the Kronstadt sailors who had helped them.

Perhaps there could be American Communists, for Nathan Schild seemed to be one: who else would consistently praise the Soviet Union while finding fault with his own country? A normal man bragged of his motherland even if he detested its superstructure, as did Lichenko, because there was a personal pride that took no account of politics. And some of the things Schild claimed to believe: that the Moscow treason trials were genuine trials and concerned with real treason—he was either a lunatic or a Communist.

More likely, both. For what Lichenko would never believe was that a gentle, generous, sweet man like Nathan could, in his right mind, give allegiance to a pack of murderers. On the counsel of his affection for him, then—the heart does not lie—he did not abandon his plan to defect to the West, but added to it a finer purpose: he would also save Nathan. It would be a finer game now, with rewards or disasters of greater magnitude, but the very irony of his situation—leave it to Vasya to choose as cover the one Communist in a division of Americans!—contributed to his courage.

Back in the room, he thought he might permit himself another tubbing. Immersed, he could cogitate better than in the liberty of the bedroom. He still had no concrete plan. Time grew no longer. The NKVD would have had his name for three days; perhaps they had already traced him as far as the house party. And as yet he had not found the propitious moment to begin his labor of truth and love with Nathan. The trouble was, these considerations made for anxiety, which was assuaged only in the bathtub's warm wet trough.

But he could not go now. There, he saw from behind the curtains, came Nathan with lunch, and an excellent lunch it was, although Nathan never gave it any importance. Indifference to the material conditions of life must be unique with American Communists. Certainly it was unknown to the Russian Party! This handsome house, for example, which Nathan treated as if it were a pigsty.

Lichenko knelt and worked out a cigarette butt embedded in a bedside circle of rug mangy with other burns. The Red Army destroyed many things but nothing that could be put to use. However, reason was a crime for which no American would ever be shot. Was it a matter of distance? Three thousand miles away. You could talk all you wanted about the universal force of gravity, the iron ball and the feather dropped from the same height hitting the ground together. Just try it: by the time the feather comes to rest the iron will be a ball of rust. So with an elephant and an ant. Density, not volume and weight. So with an American; try as you may to drop him, it will be a launching. Lichenko had been a mediocre student of physics in the Kharkov technical school and insensible at the time to its multifold uses.

## CHAPTER 9

ON HIS way to work the morning after the party, Reinhart strolled down Very's way. An irregular blob of olive-drab descending her porch was soon fashioned by his eyes into her form, but as it came towards him on the sidewalk he saw it was not Very but her antithesis: the lieutenant who took in drunken Russians.

He was rather shorter than the evening before and indefinably seedy, with dust on his glasses; yet he had a more assured address, hard and bright. He was the kind of Jew before whom Reinhart felt very vulnerable, as if somewhere back he had done him a dirtiness which he, himself, did not remember but the Jew never forgot. He felt this while knowing it was not true, for not only had he not done them wrong: he had never done them anything one way or the other. None of his best friends were Jews. The species was unknown in his home town, which had no foreigners—just another reason for its unspeakable dreariness. At college there were some, who had their own fraternity and seemed to go around en bloc, occasionally sitting next to one in classes, where they were usually witty and always clever; and some girls as well, who were either remarkably beautiful or characteristically ugly, never plain, and it was a pity the lovely ones were off-limits—there had been a girl, forever enrolled on his list of classics, with sable hair, alabaster nose, cheeks of white iris, and an exquisite name, Esther Rosewater, which he used to say underbreath when she passed oblivious, *Esther Rosewater, how I love you, Esther Rosewater;* she made him weak in the knees, and never knew it. For that was the other thing about Jews; when they weren't eying you with suspicion, they never saw you at all.

*118*

As to this lieutenant, Reinhart thought: I could break him in two. At the same time, he was vaguely afraid of him.

Badly returning Reinhart's salute—his fingertips not quite making it to the inferior rim of his spectacles—the lieutenant referred briefly to their mission of the night before. He had found upon awakening that Miss Leary had dropped a comb in his rooms, and he had just returned it. Palpably of small value but it was her property and women care about such things, don't they?, smiling in the condescending conspiracy of the males. He could have been lying. Reinhart, who was unusually observant, remembered no loss. Yet losses remembered are hardly losses; moreover, an officer, unlike a noncom, had little reason to dissemble in courting a nurse.

"Was Miss Leary in?"

"No, I left it with her roommate."

"What's her name, by the way?"

But Schild didn't know and cared enough only to ask: "Don't you know? Isn't Lieutenant Leary your girl?"

Reinhart had a tendency to toss the ball to his superiors, to tell an excess of truth that would confront them with the damning fact of their authority. When he said sorrowfully "How can she be?" the lieutenant's response confirmed him. He, the officer, showed not only understanding but sympathy.

"*I* have no objections, certainly."

Now it was his apparent approbation that made Reinhart uneasy. He would have preferred to leave while he was ahead, but the lieutenant hung on, walking with him towards the administration building.

"The Russian—did he recover all right? He was a crazy little fellow. Sometimes I think all Russians are mad, or is that Communism in action? Have you seen what they did in Wannsee?"

He fancied that with his first word the lieutenant had shot an angry look: of course, one's big mouth had not considered that he might be a Russian Jew. Then, too, he had earlier observed that any mention of Russians not obvious praise never sat well with "liberals," and he would have bet his duffel bag, with all its souvenirs, that his companion belonged to that breed. He had, therefore, found his weakness; he no longer felt gauche; he could not help falling before the temptation.

"No one who hasn't seen them would believe what a bunch of dirty tramps the Russians are. When we came in on the autobahn and met that crew, we thought first they were slave laborers for the Germans, and then service forces, maybe. But no, they were the cream of the combat troops."

He saw pure hate through the lieutenant's glasses—or was it agony?—the eyes were all watery.

The hell with him. He was not an officer in the 1209th, and you couldn't be court-martialed for an honest description of what you, and no doubt he as well, had seen. Everyone had his own chauvinism, the sacred affiliation that he would not suffer to be questioned, let alone criticized. And how disgustingly stupid, for, in this case, was it not their very uncouthness that made the Russians' victory all the more remarkable?

So he said something to that effect, but even then the lieutenant's manner did not improve, and since by that time they had arrived in the front hall of headquarters, they parted coolly, no salute being necessary under a roof.

"Goot morning, a very nice day ve are hoffing!"

Trudchen sat blooming behind Pound's big, messy desk against the forward wall, except that it was not messy but rather a place of truly stacked papers, dustless, and with a little bouquet of yellow pansies in a jam jar. On his own desk, similarly impeccable, was a pink rose. She was already flying her own colors.

"You are *sur*prised, yes?"

Right, but his habit was never to show it. He thought, for the first time, that she might be uncomfortable to have around.

She arose and came towards him, the thick sweater, unbuttoned, swaying in its two parts equivalent to the braids.

"You see, I work for no payment until the opplication is officially opproved. But I also cannot eat at the mess until that time. Perhaps you can bring me somesing at lunchtime."

Reinhart tucked his cap under the belt and drifted into his chair.

"What age did you put down?"

"Eighteen."

"And they believed it?"

"Oh, vy not. It is only two years a lie!"

Sixteen—even those tender years seemed too many, but they did put her under the wire. Through her sweater halves he saw soft little breasts, very round, under the crocheted shirt. She was the kind of girl who in a movie would be asked by the hero, do you really need those glasses? No, she would say and fling them away forever. But Reinhart rather liked spectacles on a pretty girl; they were vulnerable-making, sexy.

"Let's see now, what can we find for you to do?" He fished through the desk drawers, coming first upon the last letter from Di, which when he had put it away yesterday, having finished the answer, was open, with its envelope paperclipped to the back. Now the former was inserted in the latter, as if it had just arrived; for a moment, until he saw the slit in the envelope top, he thought it had: the outside of all her letters looked the same, with "Mrs. Ernest Cooley" in bright-purple ink in the return-address space. Ah well, Trudchen had made it neat, which reminded him to write the customary "Ans." and the date on the face of the envelope. He reached for the fountain pen habitually kept in the righthand corner of the central drawer, and felt nothing. Nor was it elsewhere in the desk or in his pocket, and Trudchen had not seen it when she policed up.

The loss was serious. What with the black market, the PX stock of pens was exhausted, and it was not seemly to sign correspondence with a pencil. Reinhart felt an ill mood come down over him like a sack. The worst thing was that he could not, with depressed senses, find any work for Trudchen. The map of Berlin, on which she could have been employed to trace a route for the tour of the Nazi ruins, had also vanished. And he dreaded the coming of Pound, whom he had not told of their new employee, for the excellent reason that he himself had not believed she would be hired.

As if his nerves had created him prematurely, for it was only eleven o'clock, he heard Pound's footsteps in the hall.

"Quick!" he said to Trudchen, "start straightening out those boxes." He pointed, without looking, to the chaos in front of the closet, and grabbing a fistful of papers from his now-tidy "out" basket, fell on them with knitted brow and deliberative forefinger.

Pound sounded two feet from the door when Reinhart realized that Trudchen had moved not to the ordered task but rather closer to him. She had removed her sweater and was flexing her arms in a most provocative, catlike manner, her pink shirt everywhere in undulation.

"What are you doing!'" he said furiously.

"But you see, already I have arranged those boxes this morning before you arrived."

How irrefutably true, now that the eyes were turned in that direction: rank on rank, they pyramided almost to the ceiling, with not a loose paper showing, not a cartonflap awry. Impossible that one small girl could have done all that in a week, but there they were.

And here also was—not Pound. The liberal lieutenant, with an ingratiating smile, stood in the doorway.

"Too bad I didn't know when we came in that you were the fellow," he said.

"For what?" Reinhart stood up.

"Yes, and here they are." The lieutenant pulled a box from the left slope of the pyramid, weakening the whole organization so that if Trudchen had not sprung to the gap the work of her morning would have been at naught.

"You must replace that at once!" she shouted, and the lieutenant, walking from the pile with his box, showed her a look he might have given some vermin too ripe to crush.

Christ, didn't he even know the simple principles of stress and strain? thought Reinhart, whose height permitted him to get the topmost carton and fill the hole.

"Okay, this one is small enough to carry with me now. I'll send a detail over for the rest."

He was halfway to the door when Reinhart, standing high and wide, blocked the route.

"I'm afraid, *sir*, that you'll have to tell me what this is all about." He weighted the title with deliberate provocation—for one thing, because he was wholly in the right; for another, to break the officer's damnable insolence.

For a moment, and for all his natural, seedy weakness and his fake amenity, the lieutenant's eyes were hostile.

"Get out of my way—" This at once calm, masterful, and most persuasive, and Reinhart would have complied had not Trudchen rushed up desperately to add her small person to the barrier. Not even the lieutenant could resist this preposterous event. He smiled, albeit in somewhat ill grace, and set his box on the floor.

"Schild is my name, Army Intelligence. Would you like a receipt?"

No wonder now at his sang-froid. Army Intelligence! The very title had a splendid, piercing authority, far grander, because including brains, than even the paratroops, Rangers, or fighter squadrons: keen, intrepid operators in the very camp of the enemy, many-faced, anonymous; if caught, standing before the wall with a contemptuous smirk towards the rifles; if successful, only the gratification of knowing oneself supreme; no vulgar show, whatever medals were due must wait perhaps ten years hence, and perhaps not even then, for the secrets of the bureau can never be revealed.

"I'm sorry," said Reinhart with a mouth of contrition. "You

see, I didn't understand. I couldn't just let anyone take these things in the absence of Lieutenant Pound. He's in charge here. Actually I don't care about the stuff at all, and neither does he. What is it, or are we allowed to ask?"

Intelligence. No sooner had he got in the medics on his own request than Reinhart sought to escape. It was humiliating to be the one kind of soldier denied a gun. Intelligence. He even knew German, or enough for a start anyway, the rest he could pick up quickly in a training program. Psychologically he had probably all his life been a kind of undercover agent. In high school he used to follow certain girls in their Friday-evening walks, trail them from nine to midnight, at a distance, in and out of candy-store doorways, and, with the aid of evergreen bushes, right to their front steps, all unbeknownst to them, sometimes forever, sometimes only until the next morning's study-hall revelation. Intelligence. Its operations turned out to be very secret indeed; in three years of service he had never so much as learned where to apply.

"Just routine correspondence of some German agency, I should think," said Lieutenant Schild, staring grimly at Trudchen, who kept leaning into Reinhart and kept getting pushed away. "It's pretty tedious to have to go through it, but we must."

Trudchen leaned against Reinhart again and said, with great, solemn lashes, "Anyvay, ve should vait for Lieutenant Pound!"

"Truchen, I want you to do something for me. Go over and sit in that chair behind my desk and *schweigen Sie.*"

"Vy so *formal?*" she asked pouting, but did it.

Just as he had hoped, Schild's interest was caught.

"You are fluent?"

"Not really, but I have enough for a good base. I'd like to have an opportunity to brush up my German."

Schild leaned close and said in an undertone, jerking his thumb towards Trudchen: "Where did you get that little tot?"

For a moment Reinhart thought: oh, but she's not that young;

then he realized that what Schild had said, in his Eastern accent, was "tart," a term out of old plays, meaning "whore" or thereabouts, perhaps not so strong; what he always saw when he read it was a circular piece of pastry with strawberry jam in the center, and hence, a girl whose person might symbolize such a sweet. That was Trudchen all right. Yet he was responsible for her, in a way, and although it was funny it was also nasty.

His remonstrance was lost before he found it, for Schild, very certain, proceeded.

"Take my word and get rid of her before she gets you in trouble."

"But she's just a kid!" He said it too loud and dared not look towards her. "I swear I haven't touched her, Lieutenant, I haven't even thought of her in that way—"

"Don't be foolish," said Schild, sharply, "I'm not concerned about her welfare but yours."

So he had made an impression on him! Reinhart was almost ready to say: I'll trade Trudchen for a transfer to Intelligence; perhaps now the war was over, some of Schild's men would go home on points and there would be openings.

"She was peddling her little ass up and down the officers' street last night. Finally she got her prey, that fat—, well, it's better not to say. . . . One of these days she'll turn up pregnant and I don't think you'll want to be made the goat."

Hurt, Reinhart grunted thanks; the lieutenant clearly thought him naïveté incarnate; the trouble was, his complexion was too fair, there were no shadows on his face, no lines of character, and his eyes being pale blue looked stupid; he had labored his life long under the prejudice of his appearance. He was like a big, bland baseball bat; Schild on the other hand resembled a pair of scissors, ugly, black, incisive. How he envied him, even to the tarnish on his silver bar, the dried fog at the edge of his glasses, and the bulge in the flyfront of his ETO jacket that betrayed an undone button. And, as he watched him leave, perhaps even his dirty mind, which was a symbol of freedom.

A sob from Trudchen drew him to her, more in curiosity than pity.

"What are you doing!"

She was crying, had her spectacles off for that purpose, was flushed and dripping, and presented so much misery that, despite himself, he gave her his olive-drab handkerchief, which luckily was clean.

"He has told you somesing evil about me, that—" Whatever followed went into the handkerchief. One braid had got twisted about her neck like a noose, and Reinhart, leaning across the desk, returned it to order. The flushed face came briefly out of the cloth to say "Sank you."

"Trudchen, where were you last night?"

"Wiss my cousin Lori in her cellar. This is all the place we have to live, in a cellar which is all cold and wet and without light. The dampness comes into one's bones and most nights one cannot sleep because of the pain . . ."

Suddenly arthritic and conscious that the sun had some moments before left the big window, he sat down on the desktop.

"No," he said gently, "I mean earlier, before you went to bed— were you in this area last evening?"

"Most absolutely n—" She started to speak into the handkerchief but emerged to study him narrowly. "You won't think that I must be a foolish or superstitious person? . . . I consulted with your priest."

Priest. By chance he knew that the Catholic priest of the 1209th was away on leave to Rome; his assistant, Joe Para, who was one of Tom Riley's roommates across the hall, had taken a shower that morning in Reinhart's bathroom. Yet there was surely an unintentional error here.

"Well, then," said Trudchen when he explained, "this was the Protestant priest, a very large man, do you know him?"

Of course, Schild's "fat—"; things were linking up in sweet reason.

"I wished to see him for guidance," she went on. "I am alone in the world, without father and mother, sometimes it is all so confusing. Do you believe in God?"

"I haven't made my mind up," said Reinhart. "But I don't hold anything against someone who does." It were cruel, if Chaplain Peggott gave her comfort, to abuse that great, grinning, flabby sententious ass, and it certainly had nothing to do with God, who if He existed at all, Reinhart was sure, was an It rather than a He and altogether neutral. As for himself, who had been as infant a Lutheran and then, when a schism developed within that congregation over whether or not the Ladies Aid should amortize the church mortgage by serving public suppers and his parents left with the progressive element, a Presbyterian. He believed that Protestantism was deadly mediocrity, Catholicism weak-minded, and Judaism alien—and all harmless. He was incapable of bigotry, on the ground that it was a massive bore—like the convictions from which it sprang. On the other hand, if it were carried to fanaticism, to that ultimate degree in which to advance his cause the believer was willing to destroy himself rather than other people: gone this far, it was, as with a Joan of Arc, a heroism to which the original motive was irrelevant.

Gertrud of Berlin—it was scandalous to be with the force which compelled a small girl towards martyrdom.

"Look, I'll see if I can get you a better place to live. I think they have rooms around this area for civilian employees, maybe right in this building, God knows there's room enough." He revolved his head in disgust at a vision of a thousand rooms unoccupied while girls slept in wet cellars. "And for Lori, too."

"Oh, but there is a reason that she cannot," said Trudchen, and immediately began again to weep softly. "But your priest is not a good man. He tried to have his vay viss me." She reached to Reinhart's hand. "He touched me—here." She cupped his hand very neatly around one of her breasts and, even though the illustration was clear, kept it there infinitely. " 'I just must see if you are wearing your medal,' he said. 'But perhaps it slipped down.' And then, so quick as one could think of it, he—" In the quickness she described, Trudchen had stretched open the neck of her shirt and inserted Reinhart's hand on the bare skin underneath. " 'Vair is it?' he asked, with a very horrible smile. 'This must be it—' "

Withdrawing so swiftly that he unraveled a strand of pink crochet, he shouted: "It's a lie, Trudchen, it's a contemptible lie!"

Piggy Peggott—he had many sins, but they were of another kind of gluttony: he was famous in the officers' mess for seconds, thirds, and fourths; but all one had to do was look at him to see that somewhere back home he had the inevitable preacher's wife in dowdy, unkempt clothing and disorderly hair, to whom he was flagrantly faithful; it was simply a matter of definition.

Not to mention that: "Protestants don't wear medals!"

If she had earlier cried in soft self-pity, she howled now in the most violent hatred, her face red and ugly, swinish.

"It vas this Jew who turned your feelings against me!"

He felt himself tremble fearfully, thought for a second that he had hit her; indeed, his big hand hung tremulously in the air between them as if it had bounced there off her small face. But it had not—at the instant it would have struck, the fist had been seized by the mind, for Trudchen, in her temper, was not silent.

"They have no respect. Of course none of this did happen, but that was what he told you, was it not?—only he made me the bad person, that dirty, filthy creature, that foul—"

"Don't say it, Trudchen, it simply is not said. He must have made a mistake, anybody could do that. You have to admit that there are German girls who might—well, anyway, it had nothing to do with his being of the Hebrew faith."

"But it does have something to be connected to that I am a German. At least for him it does. Because the Nazis do not like the Jews, I am made to suffer. In 1933 I am four yearss old; in 1938, nine yearss. They did not permit children to operate the concentration camps."

Reinhart had a weakness in the small of his back, which standing up did not relieve. He wished he had a grievance; being without one in the modern world was disabling. How gratifying to be the lowliest Negro in Alabama, with no person alive who was not in your debt. How satisfying to be a Jew, with a two-thousand-year claim or, now, a German who had got his medicine unjustly. He should have been in combat and had his foot shot off, so that when he was brought a complaint he could point to the stump and say: obviously, I can do nothing about it, I can't even walk.

He produced a roll of peppermint Lifesavers and, thumbnailing back the tinfoil, offered the first segment to Trudchen. Shortly it could be heard clicking against her little rabbit-teeth.

"This is very sweet and not at all—what do you say?"

" 'Hot,' I guess."

"It is 'not so hot'? But that means 'no good,' yes? That is not what I mean. I like it better than ours, which are more—"

" 'Hot.' That's another usage—the word is good for almost anything."

Such as her face, which now, with glossy lines of tear, was cooling. He should have liked to stroke it. She was so helpless, yet at the same time, if that were possible, indomitable. It was the same combination of contraries he had seen in Lieutenant Schild.

In the afternoon a PFC sent by Schild began to remove the cartons, antlike—with small burdens and many trips. Pound slopped in at two o'clock, looking for his sunglasses, which after a moment's search he remembered he had sold, listened to Reinhart's explanation of Trudchen and account of Schild's mission, saying to the first, "Why not?" and to the second, "Good deal," punched Reinhart in the belly, and left at two-ten.

Neither Lovett nor Nader was in their office, owing, Reinhart assumed, to the catastrophic finale to the party; the colonel no doubt was grinding them into powder. About which even if he had liked them Reinhart would have felt rather more pleasure than pain, he being an enlisted man to the core.

Since, then, official authority could not be consulted, he prowled through the empty rooms in the furthermost reaches of his own wing and found a little closetlike chamber that would meet Trudchen's want. It was already outfitted with a tiny stove and a naked steel bedstead and spring; from the 1209th supply room he fought a mattress and sleeping bag out of the sergeant in charge.

Delighted, Trudchen threw her arms about him when she saw the new quarters.

"Do you need some help to get your things from Lori's?"

"Oh no, you must not bother!" A brief crease flew through her clear brow. "I have almost nothing. You will not go there?"

"Not if you don't want me to."

"Ah, not I. But Lori would be *aim*borrossed."

"By the way, did she get her job?"

Trudchen showed a sly look. "Do you know, she did not tell me! She is a very odd human being. One must accustom oneself to her strangeness, but she is very nice."

Leaving her there, he returned to the office. Four o'clock. The PFC had disappeared, after having taken away all of three cartons. On the point of calling it a day, himself, he saw the heavy sweater that Trudchen had left behind. He carried it to her room, but already she had gone, either by the window or some secret back door off the hall, whose existence he knew not of. Folding the sweater, with a view to placing it on the bed, he felt a hard, cylindrical object somewhere in the weave. It was his missing pen, along the bottom seam of a pocket. So funny: she could hardly have stolen it and then permitted so simple a discovery. Must, rather, first have borrowed and then retained in a slip of the hand. Yet if he reclaimed it now, she might remember, look, find it again with him, think he had caught her in a theft but for reasons of his own would not protest, be discomfited. He placed the sweater on her pillow and left.

He was inclined to visit Veronica, but rather than search the hospital building for her ward, which in his imagination had acquired a sinister aura, he strolled again down the street of her billet on the chance that her duty, too, was done.

The salmon-colored gauze had been removed from the glass of the front door; on the inside surface an unseen agency, swift and sure, manipulated a cleaning rag. Its movements were mesmerizing; he had an impulse to throw himself on the grass and watch it as the warm-cool late afternoon relaxed into calm evening. Beside the door grew a bush bearing round, white berries like small versions of those pure-sugar jawbreakers with a nut in the center. There was a bush like that in his parents' front yard, and next to it a weeping willow high in which he had once established an outpost for General Custer. Alone among the men of the 1209th he had been in no hurry to get back to the States, had in fact long planned to ask, in rakish defiance, for permanent assignment to the Occupation forces, was waiting only until it could be more than an empty, sour-grape gesture— for, without combat points, he was more or less permanent as it stood. Now, just now, watching the rag fly across the pane, seeing the bush, recalling General Custer, and with the sudden, almost unbearably dear smell of grass—he had not at first marked that the lawn was newly cut—he ached for home.

The door opened just as the general bliss had given into the deadly specificities. He had come far since his first year in the Army when he frequently had such seizures; yes, he had enlisted to escape, but there was forever another present to flee from; in the summertime, especially, one craved elsewhere. But he had nothing to get back to. In the most literal sense: already in September 1943 his parents had let his room to a man who worked an electric drill in the local defense plant, a man who had remained, had settled down, who surely had dispensed with the arrowhead collection and the stuffed bass's head on the bookcase. And college: he simply could not face that again after three years of the expansive life.

The door had opened and a figure in head-handkerchief and apron came onto the step, saying: "*Sind Sie nicht wohl?*"

It was not unreasonable, since he had, after all, fallen on the lawn—an event thus called to his own attention. The person was Lori.

"No, I'm quite well," he said in German. "It is pleasant to sit here. I see you have your job, come tell me about it. Sit down here with me."

"I cannot sit on the grass!" she said incredulously. "I am the maid."

At any rate, if she looked no happier now, she was no sadder. Since he was on their level, he noticed that her legs, though dressed in coarse cotton, were finely turned and rather long for her height. But there was also something terribly competent in her appearance now that she wore working clothes, a hint of hard strength that reminded him of his suspicions.

"There were no difficulties about the *Fragebogen?*"

"What you wish to ask is whether I was a Nazi, isn't it? You are more shy than your fellow Americans. . . . There was no such thing as a Nazi—you should know that if you have asked any other Germans. In all this great country there were no Nazis; not even Hitler, as you would hear if you could find him."

He sat up, aghast at her change from suppliance to this arrogant self-possession. It was the famous German alternation from serf to lord, no doubt, and he felt it cruelly there on the fresh grass.

Getting to his feet, he said braggingly in English: "What the hell do I care?"

"*Bitte?*"

"*Mit mir macht es nichts.*"

"I know," she said. "That is why—" She took a deep breath and suddenly finished it in English: "—I love you."

You couldn't stay angry when that was said to you, but you could look insane.

"Have I said something wrong?" She took off her dusting cap, and a wealth of hair came forth, and golden it was and clean.

"You do not know English," he said in a voice full of augury— as if he were to go on with: you can say awful things in it. "What you mean is that you like me."

"It is not the same as in French?"

"I think not."

"*Also.*"

In the distance he heard a laugh like a great bronze chime. Unmistakable. He felt criminally that he didn't wish Very to see him with this girl. But Lori, too, had heard and was even more anxious to flee from him.

"There comes one of my mistresses," she whispered, already in backward motion. "I must go."

"Veronica Leary? Lieutenant Leary?"

"I do not know the name, but the laugh cannot be mistaken."

It was heard again, turning the corner only a few yards away, and Reinhart audaciously pushed into the house after Lori.

"Ah, what are you doing here, you mad fellow?" she asked in confusion.

"I'm going into the kitchen." And so he did, and sat silently until Very and what sounded like a roommate entered the door and went upstairs.

"Where is Miss Leary's room—the laughing one?" he whispered.

In frightful wonder Lori answered: "In the rear. You will go there?"

"Certainly not. Then I can leave by the front and she won't see me out the window."

But instead of moving on that plan, he looked at Lori and said: "You've washed your hair. It is very *schön*."

"Thank you. I didn't have any soap until I started this work. . . . But please go now."

Didn't have any soap—he was terribly touched by that fact. One thought of the bombings and fires and loss of loved ones, the *Götterdämmerung,* but not to be able to wash your socks or bathe, that was degrading and mean.

"And where you live, I understand, is in some wet cellar. Let me get you a better place—"

"All right, but now you must go." She took his hand in her small but very strong one and pulled him from the chair.

"Tonight, as soon as you leave work, we'll get you a new room. I won't leave now until you promise."

"*Ach, was kann ich tun!*" she breathed in despair. "I cannot."

"Why not?" He tightened his hand on hers.

"For reasons too long to explain now—"

"Promise! After work. What time do you finish?"

"Ah, what can I do?" she repeated. "I'll lose my job if you do not go."

"Come with me!" Now it was he who impelled her, through the hall to the foot of the stair.

"Hey Very, are you decent?" he shouted in a tremendous voice which agitated a small vase on the foyer table. And in no time his large friend appeared at the top, blooming lavishly in a powder-blue dressing gown, a dea ex machina about to catch the next elevator down from Olympus.

"Kiddy!" she screamed jovially. "Did you break in here to violate me? You-all ain't supposed to be in nurses' quarters!"

"That's what your maid insisted."

"Well, get out then, you fiend. I'll see you after chow—outside."

"I can't, I've gotta work tonight." He turned to Lori, who looked very grave, and said as quickly as he could in German: "Unless you meet me this evening I shall cause you trouble. What time?"

"*Um sechs Uhr.* I eat at your mess after the soldiers are finished." She turned away in shame.

"Okay then," shouted Very. "Don't go away mad. Hey, where did you learn German? Wait a minute." She disappeared, and returned with a piece of olive-colored apparel, pitched it downstairs, it taking the air like a parachute and falling to rest at Lori's feet.

"Would you tell her to press it and be careful not to use too hot an iron?"

Which he did, adding: "*Um sechs Uhr,* outside the mess tent."

Chow was SOS, shit-on-a-shingle, ground beef and gravy slopped across a slice of bread, diced carrots and canned peas, rice pudding filled with raisins resembling dead flies. Reinhart ate a grimacing spoonful of each and then smoked two consecutive cigarettes, his only pleasure the dropping of their butts into the swill.

"Anyone ever tell you you eat like a goat?" he asked Marsala, who was stuffing down seconds.

"I've got a right to, I worked all day," his roommate answered on a rising, plaintive note, missing the point.

At the garbage cans were two small boys who had temporarily ducked the guard. As Reinhart prepared to empty his full messkit, one of them, saying "Pleasse," took it from him, with a spoon flipped out the cigarette-ends, poured the contents in a tin with jagged rim, and began ravenously to feed.

Marsala pushed his boy roughly aside. "Go on, you goddam Krauthead." But there was nothing in his kit but three drops of gravy, and when the guard appeared, sweating and worried, with his switch at the ready, Marsala stared into his bland face and threatened: "Go on, you fuck, or I'll take ya apart. How do you like that," he went on to Reinhart, "those kids belong to his own country."

"Well, we hired him to keep them away."

"Yeah, but who would really do it except a German?"

Their natural anarchism saved Italians. They were, after all, the original fascists, but even Mussolini had inspired more laughter than hatred. Someone should take the guard aside and say: Sit down, Hans, have a smoke. Now I'll give you the run-down on life. People are worth more than things, and abstractions have almost no worth at all. When you get an order your sole responsibility is to *act* as if you are carrying it out. Hypocrisy is the better part of competence. It is foolish, I know, and defies everything you and I were taught; but in the degree to which you serve others and not yourself, the others will forsake you. However, comprehending neither Marsala's threat nor Reinhart's interior monologue, "Hans" had driven the children out of range, lashing their meager shins in the most dispassionate manner.

Reinhart had delayed taking his meal, and Marsala with him, until the tent was almost empty of soldiers and the queue of civilian workers had begun to form at the front flap, and en route to and at the apartment he dawdled for twenty minutes, part of which was aimed to bore Marsala with his company. It worked: the buddy at last drifted across the hall to needle Riley, and Reinhart returned to the mess area. Almost too late: the Army trucks used for workers' transport idled at the curb. He spotted Lori, carrying a small, lidded pail, about to mount a tailgate.

"*Also, Sie sind falsch!*" he accused.

"I looked for you," she stoically replied. "I have either to ride this truck or walk many kilometers."

Within, the side benches were loaded with women who gave off chattering to stare at Reinhart.

"Go on." He lifted her up in one strong action, getting on his jacket a bit of splash as the cover jarred from her can, and vaulted himself in with a terrible noise on the metal floor.

Which prompted the driver to peer through his spy-window and call: "Haul ass, kid. No riders."

"The Lover sent me, Eberhard. I have to get new quarters for this woman."

"Lovett never told me about it."

"All right, all you have to do is tell him when you get back."

"*You* tell him, for Jesus' sake," grunted Eberhard, dropping the isinglass trapdoor.

They had squeezed onto the bench between a very fat girl and a very skinny woman, so that Lori was compressed and Reinhart slashed by sharp elbows.

"Tell me now," he asked. "Why all the strange reactions? I think you should want to have a better place to live. Trudchen told me this afternoon about your cellar—how she couldn't sleep there for the wet—"

"Trudchen? She doesn't live with me! . . . I warned you about her untruths, but I suppose not enough. She lives with her parents in a pleasant flat, not bombed, near the hospital."

"And I got her a room in headquarters building! What game is she playing?"

"That's just it, you see, a game. She is very young and willful. It is not easy to be an adolescent girl in the present time."

No, he supposed not; for that matter, it had not been easy for him to be an adolescent boy, five years and three thousand miles back, in a smooth place where the only craters were excavations for new bungalows. At least Trudchen had no pimples.

"And then, too, perhaps her family are not all that could be desired—but that's another story. As to me, well, frankly, I have a husband."

"Oh, that's all right. You see, I'm not—" He had intended to say: interested in you in that way. But it would have been insulting.

"He is very strange—as now it seems I am helpless to prevent your seeing for yourself."

The truck was under way, clanking, creaking, and in clouds of blue exhaust, which defying the principles was drawn stinking into their compartment. Under cover of his conversation in the other direction, Bony Elbows waxed friendly, cutting her sharp patella into the outer surface of his thigh. She was, he had seen on entering, at least forty-five years of age.

"Was he in the war?"

"He had an odd role." That was her last word until a half hour later when, after various stops, one of which freed them of Fat and Thin at the same time, the vehicle came to rest at what seemed to him a purely arbitrary point in nowhere and she and he detrucked.

They stood before a hill of waste whose farthest margin must have, spilling over Asia's width, been forever eroding into the Pacific. The sun, elsewhere on this day so rich, voided this dark field, and the sweet air had long ago sold out to its competitor gases. On this range figures thin and slumped roamed crumbling through its Brenners, sack-bearing, searching, genitors of no sound. But on the summit a small girl, a ragged head above a cotton bag, called shrill and disconsolate to nobody below: *"Wo is der Heinrich?"*

"Behold," said Lori. "Nürnberger Strasse."

Five minutes' impossible trek and they teetered on the powdered brick at the entrance to a subterranean passage. Reinhart fired his lighter, but Lori hastily lowered its cap. "There may be escaping gas." She drew him, now blind, down the prairie-dog way.

# CHAPTER 10

On the sofa lay an amorphous lump to which was appended a great pale ham. Lori slammed the door. A hollow groan issued from the ham, and two apertures appeared in its wan surface. After a time a mouth revealed itself, as if in one of those motion-picture cartoons where inanimate objects come to life through lines from nowhere, with the breezy implication that humanity is some sleight-of-hand. However, the present process was not flippant, but ponderous and awesome.

Lori put down her pail and fired more oil lamps, and in the richer light the great object rose gradually and with tremendous deliberation, like a sinking ship preparing for the final and irrevocable plunge, to an attitude of sitting.

"*Herr Reinhart, mein Mann,*" Lori waved loosely at the hulk.

"*Sehr angenehm.*" The voice was full, sonorous, making a grand thing of the words, and the eyes which the light showed to be as large and ripe as purple-black plums honored Reinhart directly and briefly, then shifted within the largesse of lid to Lori, who stood before the table, one hand at the base of a lamp, her left side from flank to hair bright in its refulgence.

"Here is your dinner."

He ignored her to revolve his head to Reinhart, saying in English without accent: "Ah, this is your corporal!"

As Reinhart closed on the cold sponginess of the extended hand, he felt with surprise that his own was not being shaken in acquaintance but rather used as a purchase whereby this large figure was lifting itself from the couch, and the weight was such as to compel him to throw his rear feet wide, lest he be toppled forward.

"*S'il vous plait,*" his burden wheezed with difficulty on the way up, and then, all at once, was upright before him, or rather looming over him, for the man was a good seven feet tall and bulky as the great Kodiak bear. Reinhart was cast into the, for him, rare feeling of slightness. The pull left the hand, but it stayed clammily and, oddly, weightless, in his own, until he opened his fingers and gravity, not its parent body, moved it to fall slowly away.

Using that language, Lori's man noted that he could speak English, and would, as a courtesy. Swaying a bit, he said that it was all but impossible for him to stay erect, but that he insisted on doing so until his guest was seated. Lori having furnished a chair, he sank again to the sofa, and drew the dressing gown that was his lone garment more snugly about him.

Lying still, pale, and full, like a sack of mozzarella, he tasted of the air with porcine nostrils, and began:

"Now we can converse at our ease. My name is Bach, which as you perhaps know, signifies 'brook' in German, and, naturally, to every German, and very likely to others as well, simply to utter the name is to conjure up the image of the master of the Thomasschule and the three most eminent of his twenty offspring—for his loins were apparently as prolific as his brain—who were also composers of a high rank, but not quite so well known outside their own land. So far as I know, I am not a descendant of that noble line. And you are called . . . ?"

"Reinhart."

"The name, of course, means 'pure of heart,' *Hart* being the Low German variant of *Herz*. But I have a feeling that you, like so many Americans, have no great interest in etymology. Unfortunately, it is one of my many weaknesses. And I do have more than my share." He indicated his body with a sweep of the hand. "The main among them being a physical impuissance, if you'll permit the word, in spite of a monstrous size. This misfortune has caused my energy to be diverted directly to my brain, which as a result is extraordinarily active and frequently denies me sleep, occupied as it forever is with a thousand and one theories, ideas, and bits of information which it should like to synthesize. I speak of this brain as if it acts of its own volition, has a life, as it were, of its own. For indeed it seems to have such an independent existence—awe-inspiring, to say the least. I—it is ridiculous, is it not, to speak of an 'I' separate from one's brain? but it really seems that way to me—I conceive of my own identity as relating more closely to the emotions, for I am their creature and toil under the dominion of the harsh ambassadors they send to the external world, the senses." Here he snorted: "Smell!" Poked a pair of spread fingers into his eyes: "Sight!" Extended a fat, pink tongue, swollen as a bladder: "Taste! And so on. Do I make myself clear?" He stared for a while at Reinhart, as if he had forgotten him, then asked, shyly: "I say, do you smoke?"

Reinhart offered the cigarettes, saying, "Please keep them all. I have many."

"Oh, kind, kind. I cannot thank you enough." He seemed about to rise, but decided against it. He dropped a tear. Wiping his nose on his dressing gown of dirty-orange cotton, he reverently chose a cigarette from the pack, called for a light from Lori, and getting it puffed luxuriously, his huge bald skull reflecting light like a mirrored ball upon a lawn.

"Now where were we? Oh yes, I believe some biography may be in order. Perhaps you would like to hear of my term of years in the Orient, where I served as cultural attaché in the Embassy in Tokyo. A strange people, the Japanese, rather stolid, in spite of their reputation for wit. Their art is curiously constipated. Nevertheless, it has a kind of mordant humor all its own, in its juxtaposition of human limitation and the infinity of nature. But perhaps I'm doing them an injustice. They have, like all peoples, much to recommend them. Good clear skins, for example; one never finds them shriveling up in later years, and scrupulously clean. Absolutely no odor! This may owe to their arriving at puberty earlier than we. Our Western pubescence, which, although we think it consonant with some divine ordinance, is the slave of social, rather than natural, imperatives, has certain unpleasant concomitants: the foul stink of perspiration, for example. Children, you will note, never stink, even in the heat of strenuous play. The Japanese, arriving at adulthood still in the vigor of extreme youth, consume the life-stuff *in toto,* while in us a certain excess accrues which maturates. Your excellent English verb, by the way, expresses beautifully both aspects of this process: the fructification and the rot. Orientals maintain that white men smell like corpses."

The slight movement of Bach's trunk, as he pitched the cigarette butt to the cracked concrete floor, where Lori stamped it dead, communicated a tremor to his lower extremities; the robe slipped away, exposing a view of verdigrised leg braces, complex in rods, wires, and articulations.

"The Japanese have an unusual poetry, which resists qualitative judgement. So long as a *haiku* is written in accordance with the traditional seventeen-syllable form, it is the peer of every other constructed in the past, or to be constructed in the future. If it violates the form, it is not a *haiku.* A Westerner at his first exposure is nearly driven mad by the question as to whether this is the beginning or the end of art, not to mention morality and history. Of course, this question is of no concern to the Japanese: it simply *is,* without qualification. They are wise and courageous enough to accept the given. Westerners can approach this knowledge only by burlesque, as when the Englishman says the great thing about the Order of the Garter is that no damned merit's involved."

Bach repeated the phrase, fondling it word by word, with the lust of a gourmand measuring off the links of a sausage, and developing an amusement which terminated in a high-pressure giggle, half-audible; the remainder being in the upper, silent-dog-whistle ranges, where it worked a secret violance on Reinhart's nerves, so that forboding ballooned the membranes of his heart as might a seizure of gas.

Bach gasped and grunted a tongue which Reinhart took for Japanese. "Let me translate:

> The snow crowns pale Fuji
> Here below, it is spring.

That is of my own authorship, but it will do."

He spoke Orientally again, in an altered voice.

"Chinese. Their verse is considerably different, but I am too exhausted to explore the subtleties of the difference at this time."

Despite his growing nausea, Reinhart asked for a translation. He was determined not to permit this strange man to elude fact, believing that the secret of power lay in its mystery.

"Oh, yes, that is Meng Hsien-Wong.

> Like a shimmer of bird calls
> The petals of the pear-flower drift
> Through the late clear air;
> Already since the morning rain
> The blossoms have grown older.
> So does the pear-branch, snow-perfumed,
> Hold a bright mirror up to man.

"You can see right off that this is not so pure as the *haiku*, being corrupted with morality. You perceived the moral, of course?"

Reinhart did not attend to this bit of malice. He had, at the mention of the "pear-flower," discovered a primary cause of his illness: the room stank of rotten fruit.

"The latter was a tributory verse to an incomparable thirteenth-century painting by Chien Hsuan which I once owned but was confiscated, supposedly for some use in the advancement of the war, but how such an item could be used for such a purpose, I have no idea."

"No, Bach," said Lori, still standing by the table. "You sold it, don't you remember?"

He narrowed his eyes at Reinhart, and his massive face became mean, piggish, as he spoke to Lori in German: "Manners, manners! We here speak the language of our guest."

"But I have no English, as you know."

Reinhart, working at a piece of gum, felt slightly relieved. He explained that he knew German and suggested that it be spoken for Lori's benefit.

"To be sure," said Bach, "I am at your command. Yet, I am about to tell you something in confidence. However, I wonder if I dare? She understood enough of my comments on the painting to correct me."

"You probably have told the story before," observed Reinhart, in a schoolmasterish voice.

"Of course! That's exactly it." He peered sagely at Reinhart. "You look like quite a decent fellow. Tell me, how many Germans have you shot?"

Reinhart enjoyed a brief daydream of cutting down rank upon rank of blond men with a Thompson submachine gun. But he lacked in nerve to carry it off. He sheepishly admitted:

"I've never fired a gun since I put on the uniform. I'm a medic, a sort of half a soldier. Geneva Convention . . ."

Bach made the best of it. "An appropriate office for an American, really; an exemplary role." With a beatific smile, "A marvelous people: one-hundred thirty millions of decent chaps spread out across that strange Siberia. I have been there, of course, so I will not amuse you by asking if you know my friend Smith in New York."

"My home is in Ohio," said Reinhart, dolefully.

"Quite so. Very near Chicago. You see, I do know. I once, with a friend, took a motor trip from that city to Michigan. We passed a number of persons who hailed us with leafy stalks, and felt like Christ entering Jerusalem through the palm branches.

However, when we were eventually brought to halt by an exceptionally violent signal, we were asked to purchase celery. But excuse me for a moment, won't you?"

He called Lori, and with the same kind of help Reinhart had rendered earlier, performed the impressive ritual of rising. By a tottering, brink-of-disaster, Humpty-Dumpty locomotion he arrived at the door, where he leaned briefly against the jamb, while that frail member moaned at the weight, and then went out. The door stood open. His voice boomed in the hall in a complaint about the lack of light, and another door could be heard to open, but not afterwards to close. The rich rush of his water was audible.

Lori sat on the edge of the couch, extending both hands in supplication. "I fear he's been drinking. It's horribly embarrassing, you must forgive me."

Reinhart was also embarrassed—for his own membership in the sex that made noise at the toilet. To cover up, he said, "It's true, then, that he knows Chinese, and so on."

"Yes," said Lori, smiling wearily. "For some years he was assistant curator of Oriental art at the museum. I am sorry we have no paintings or china left for him to show you. He can be very illuminating. But most of our own collection had to be sold and what few things remained went to the incendiary bombs."

"You sold them to pay for his medical treatment?"

"Oh no—it is another long story."

"You have so many."

"Yes, life is merely several long stories laid end to end." She reached across and patted his knee maternally. "They must not trouble you."

Although they should have, at that moment they did not. His distress owed rather to the dreadful odor, which was on the point of laying him low. Life takes precedence over courtesy.

Lori shook her head at his apologetic question. "That is one of Bach's conceits. He read in Eckermann that Schiller was stimulated by the aroma of rotting apples." She opened a drawer in the table. *"Voila!"* Exposing, sure enough, three blackened, scabrous fruits.

Bach was missing for a long time after he could no longer be heard. When he reappeared he stated that, having taken the air, he was much refreshed, which claim was supported by his looking a shade stronger on his pins, though still not by any means competent.

Reinhart was not sure as to what proportion of Bach's weakness could be attributed to gigantism and what to drink. Indeed, the drunkenness referred to by Lori had taken Reinhart by surprise, for Bach, given his odd body, had not spoken in a way that would have seemed, to Reinhart, out of consonance with it had Bach been sober.

At any rate, Bach swayed in, regained the sofa, where now with his new-found strength he sat rather than reclined, and confessed to copious draughts of potato schnapps; had, in truth, drained the bottle, otherwise he would have offered some to his guest. A pity, grievously hard to get; for the past few years in Germany, there were few potatoes to eat, let alone drink. He gauged the present state of his inebriation to be at the half-saturation point, but rapidly clearing.

"If you stay with me throughout the period of sobering, you will no doubt see the engine run diminuendo and eventually cough dead, so I had better make the most of what articulate time's left.

"Now I am not unconscious of my failure to ask you of yourself, but your status is not in question. I have reason to believe that the American Intelligence, when it finds time, will be unusually interested in mine. You see in me one whose only engagement for the future is with Judgment Day, for, frankly, I was a National Socialist."

Reinhart straightened in his chair, crossed his legs the other way, tugged at the margin of his jacket, and checked his buttons. How seldom we meet the real thing!

"It would be silly for me to do anything else, my record being readily available. For I was no more tepid in my political convictions than in anything else. In short, if I was a Nazi, I was an absolute one. My only wish is to tell my story without rancor, without extenuation, and submit myself to your mercy. Will you, as a matter of simple humanity, grant me this favor? *Hier stehe ich—*"

"Only you are reclining, Bach," interrupted Lori, with a foolish giggle which made Bach frown and even Reinhart to turn his head in impatience. She had brought up another chair when dispossessed of the sofa, and slumped there like a discarded rag doll.

"Please, please," Bach replied in German, "none of your *Quatsch*. This is a sober affair."

"How can I hide it?" asked Bach. "What is done is done. Nazism might be defined as an extreme attempt to alter the relations of Jews and gentiles, in the latter's favor. All the other involvements start from this, and this is one of those sublime simplicities that achieve the miracle of fecundity in reduction, like the Cartesian *cogito*. It requires the utmost in intellectual courage to accept the proposition that all human beings are either Jews or non-Jews; with anything less, the whole thing collapses into absurdity.

"Yes, exactly, you smile. So should have I genuinely, not too many years ago, and so do I now, with the hypocrisy of courtesy, and also with real sympathy, for I can deny myself no indulgence in my present state. But I did not begin life as an anti-Semite. There were no Jews in my birthplace, a small village in Bavaria, and it was not until I entered the Gymnasium at ten years old that I ever saw a Jew, and not until I entered the university that I ever, to my knowledge, heard Jews remarked on in a special way. In short, for many years I thought of Jews as simply Germans of a religious persuasion different from my own. Such hostile attitudes towards the Israelites as I came across from time to time, I believed to be the by-products of doctrinal differences of the sort that obtain between Catholics and Protestants—of which I was thoroughly aware, as a Protestant Bavarian.

"I continued in my naïve tolerance throughout the university years. A force to support it was my personal status as an aesthete. I avoided the drinking and the fraternal societies and the other nonsense, and consequently did not escape being marked as an odd one. Finding myself in the same category as the Jews, I went so far as to make some friends among their ranks. They were, naturally, excellent scholars, and their scholarship was conditioned with the sort of finesse that is so sadly lacking among the Germans. In my reaction against *Spiessbürgertum*, I shortly became infatuated with the Jews, and with their culture. And surely no culture is more attractive to the young man than the Jewish, just as there is no more repugnant than the German. Besides, Orientalism was my pursuit, and the Jew was the earliest flowering of the East. I gradually became aware of the indictment brought against my pets by the Germans, in all of its ramifications, but I still was not be moved. Indeed, I became more pro-Jewish than before. And I did this in an unusual mode. I accepted the accusations as truth, taking issue only with the interpretation. That is to say if the charge was that Jews owed allegiance only to their international Jewish state, I agreed and approved. For, thought I, what else could they do, when throughout history they have been rejected from the Christian society they sought innocently and sincerely to join? In the Twenties, as you may know, the Germans were in narrow straits, while the Jews allegedly flourished. Now it took some nerve to hold, as I did, that it was natural and just that they should tighten the screws against the gentile, for would not the latter have done so had the situation been reversed? I could never see anything peculiarly evil in the Jew's economic behavior. Should the executioner be blamed for the practice of hanging?

"As for the arguments on racial grounds, they were sheer

foolishness, only to be believed in by the kind of people who take up vegetarianism, Rosicrucianism, and other crackbrained schemes to evade paying the piper. I paid little attention to them, and I think this was also true of most convinced anti-Semites, whatever certain loudmouths said. This phase of Nazism was sheer spectacle; this was the Nazis' analogy to Christianity's graven images, saints' relics, etc., and a central vulgarity on which Protestants and Catholics could agree. Never since Luther, whose nationalistic fury vis-à-vis Rome withered his sense of psychology, had the national appetite for histrionics been so appeased.

"Well, then, in the light of all this, why did I eventually reverse myself and become ineluctably anti-Semitic, even to the extent of joining the National Socialist party, which I had from the first abominated as an unholy alliance of gangsters and buffoons? I became an anti-Semite, not for the usual reason—because of the anti-Semites—but because of the Jews, and I joined the united front against the Jews because there was nowhere else to go.

"When I emerged from the university into the great world, moved to Berlin and entered its intellectual life—which in that time was almost uniformly Jewish—I did not change my stand. I still baited the anti-Semites, and, as one will when in the grip of a self-righteous obsession, in the absence of suitable adversaries engaged in dialogues with myself, acting first as *advocatus diaboli* in the presentation of the strongest possible case against the Jew, then demolishing it with my better arguments. I would probably never have had cause to change had I kept company only with gentiles, and certainly never, had my associates been anti-Semites. But I found myself in ever-closer relationships with Jews, whom I attracted as my philo-Judaic position became known, and whom I of course sought out. And thus the foundation came to be built, stone by stone, for the mansion of knowledge. For I found that no matter how well disposed a gentile is towards a Jew it can never be sufficient, for the Jew will not stop short of the total debasement of his friends. The Jew does not want, and does not ask for simple understanding. He craves only total victory, and rewards anything less with corrosive hatred.

"I was not permitted by the Jews to deplore the persecutions they had suffered at Christian hands. In their arrogance they asserted that this very act of deploring was a form of anti-Semitism because it credited their enemies with efficacy, and no matter how superficially well-intentioned the gentile who entertained such sentiments, he could not avoid unconscious *Schadenfreude,* no more than can the athlete who sympathizes with the cripple.

"This is an excellent example of the Jew's ability to pursue his end by contradictory means. Sometimes he will object to the very designation of 'the Jews,' maintaining that no such racial, cultural, religious, ethnic, or whatnot entity exists, that it is the sheerest invention, the most fantastic lie. If you point out that if this were so, anti-Semitism would also be nonexistent, he will say, "Exactly, that supports my claim that the whole affair is simply the eternal struggle between the mob and the elite, with no relation to Jewishness." At other times, and under other guises, he will present the argument that only the Jews exist, and no other people, because of all the peoples of the earth, only the Jews have been able to preserve their identity in every milieu. He can disclaim Jewish influence on any culture, or assert that the Jew is the *Ernährer* of our heritage, and cite Abraham, Moses, and Jesus. Yes, he will cite Jesus with the composure which is his forte! The modern world is, for him, a theater in which the Jews are anonymous members of the cast—unless the situation requires the reverse strategy, in which case he produces a list of leading performers beside whom the gentiles are relegated to the beer-hall stage: Marx, Freud, Einstein.

"He can assume any position at will, for he believes in none. And he hates the sympathizer because sympathy implies melioration, and melioration is change. The Jew's real aim is to bring

Time to a stop. Like all Asiatics, he has a horror of motion, process, becoming—whatever name you like—for us Occidentals, the superior Deity. When *is* replaces *to be,* he will have won. Humanitarianism, liberalism, evolution, tolerance, understanding, these he rightly sees as temporal devices to frustrate him, whereas he delights in the antagonism of fanatics. The anti-Semite is his darling, just as the atheist is the theist's sweetheart, the murderer the victim's beloved. The Jew would be a god. How near to success is he then when called a devil! And how he writhes in hatred when a slobbering, mealy-mouthed humanitarian addresses him as Man!

"Totalitarianism provides his most congenial society, with its stupid calls and alarms, its aping of the Jew's own tricks, such as the obliteration of time and the fierce attack on moderates, and—*its persecution of the Jew!* When he becomes an obsession, he is on the threshold of victory."

Bach retracted his big head into layers of neck-flesh, recovered, then began again, right forefinger extended:

"I do not mean to claim that I quickly saw the light. Young and innocent as I was, I determined after each rejection to re-double my efforts at understanding, feeling still that it was *our* responsibility that this strange people faced the world in a crabbed, distorted way. How very close was I to the truth! A human being if thrown into water at birth can swim. A few years of growth and this talent is gone, to be regained only by artifice. Yet, this is as it should be. Artifice is what makes us human. It is morally necessary to withhold this function from a child until he has lived long enough to learn the properties of water and the human body, and to experience a sense of achievement in placing them in a new relationship. So with me. By the heart, I had arrived at the proper relationship with the Jews, the masterly one, but I was condemned to tread the earth for some years in ignorance before returning to it by ratiocination.

"But, to proceed. I told myself again that the Jews had no

reason to think kindly on their oppressors, and that it was only natural they would out of pride decline any aid that tended to imply a lack of self-competency on their part. I summoned up my resources of love, decency, intelligence. They might deny me, but I would not deny them. I suddenly took on, through the force of my commitment, the identity of a Jew; and the soma reflected the psyche: the cartilaginous tissue of my nose thinned, my eyebrows thickened, and my shoulders developed a nervous twinge.

"At first, my gentile friends derived much fun from this state of affairs, and would jokingly call upon me for the Jewish point of view on every question (this "Jewish opinion" is a favorite delusion of gentiles, and one which while ostensibly deploring, Jews enjoy enormously). But it did not take long for them to discover that what was an idle jest to them, was deadly serious to me. As my philo-Semitism became firmer and firmer, I felt a wall rising between us. The last brick fell into place when a story began to go around that I was really half-Jewish, and had thrown my lot with the alien part of my heritage. This fiction, I realized, was only their defense against accepting the terrible fact that I had, in free will, abdicated from the gentile's estate.

"But, of course, neither was I received as a fellow by the Israelites. Here there existed no solid wall—this people could not have survived all those agonizing centuries by material means. (The Jew, by the way, has always deluded his enemies into thinking he is materialistic. Nothing could be farther from the truth, which you can appreciate when you observe that he has flourished in the West under capitalism, a philosophy which above all others is abstract and visionary, and based on the intangibles of faith and spirit. He is, however, naturally opposed to the recent developments of capitalism. If it becomes humane, that is to say, evolves into true socialism—which is absolute materialism—we have a chance of conquering him. Vain thought!)

"So I was with and around the Jews without being of them. Oh, they don't hold secret meetings, like the mythical Elders of Zion (that wonderful legend, which is far too gross to be of Jewish origin—you know they, themselves, 'plant' most of the anti-Semitic fairy tales—is an example of the gratuitous aid they are often rendered by moronic gentiles), they have no arcane signs or handgrips, no insigne. How they communicate their identity to each other is so mysterious that it exceeds mystery, as does the manner in which a single spermatazoon out of ten thousand penetrates the egg. The important thing is that it happens. And, if *we* cannot grasp it, no Jew can fail to. Which is why no Jew can truly forsake his people, and why the Jews display that odd combination of mockery and pity towards those of their fellows who vainly toy with religious 'conversions' and facial surgery.

"The great reversal (from philo- to anti-Semitism) came, as those things do, all at once. I was in the habit at that time of spending the evenings with my Jews in a cellar-café where over a single glass of beer or cheap wine we would exhaust hours talking art, literature, philosophy, and those other diversions of the young, including politics, of which ours was, in that day—1927—communism. All in what I cherished, despite numerous disillusionments, as the intimate atmosphere of brotherhood. One evening a newcomer appeared at our table, a fierce, hideous, wooly-headed young Israelite, looking like the pictures one sees of Trotsky as a youth. He was discoursing passionately on some topic, political I should imagine, but as I took a seat, he terminated abruptly. 'It's all right,' one of the others told him, 'Bach is all right.' He nodded amiably at me, and rather transparently began to comment on inconsequential matters. Later, when I had left the table briefly to speak with a friend across the room, I saw on returning that he and Schwartz, whom I regarded as my closest comrade, had their heads together, snickering. The object of their amusement was obvious. Now, lest you think me hypersensitive, I must explain to you that the Jew's humor is concerned solely with satire; he does not laugh at things, but always at people. That is to say, he finds funny not what occurs by chance, such as a stout man's tumble on the ice, but what has taken place by human will, and the involvements therefrom, such as, say, a gentile posing as a Jew. This temper stems first from the Jews themselves having suffered too much from chance to find comedy in the fortuitous, and, second, from their great reverence for the given, the inanimate, the timeless. One might almost say the Jew would see the ice mocked by the stout man's hindquarters.

"I felt a rush of loathing at that moment, as one about to vomit feels the bile-bitter fluid rise in his throat, and not at the Jews, but at myself. For a moment I had seen in those mirrors of degradation that dreadful, abominable specter that no one can face with composure: my naked self. But I choked it down and took my seat, for the deepest self-knowledge bears with it the deepest cowardice. The impulse to action was to come almost an hour later. The conversation had continued in the same silly direction the newcomer had indicated: tastes in wine, the beasts at the Zoo, a job a friend had lately got on one of the Ullstein papers—B.Z. am Mittag, I believe—and so on. Finally, the group began, only half-seriously, to plan an outing in the next week. Half-seriously, I say, because we were all unemployed, and could not have raised the money for the elaborate refreshments listed as the minimum fare. 'Where shall we go?' cried Schwartz. Someone named a favorite section of the Grunewald. The eternal dupe, I had been swept up again into the warmth of the fraternity, and was adding my bit. I noted with good humor that we should avoid the spot named, because on a recent Sunday stroll I had marked that it was uncomfortably crowded.

"'Yes,' said the young Trotsky, 'too many Jews.' I think now that he was merely passing a harmless, if masochistic jest, as Jews often do, but, then, it struck the spot that had been worked raw by the earlier incident. I broke down and wept. God, there is nothing more terrible than a young man's sorrow! But not even that will move a Jew! I sprang to my feet. 'Yes,' I sobbed, 'just as here,' and fled from the café. From that moment on, the battle was joined.

"I had been a fool, but my greater folly was yet to come. I fell prey to the subtlest device of this devil, and joined the ranks of his greatest ally, the National Socialist Party.

"To war on decency, love, truth, freedom, is to permit the Jew to mask himself with the Good, and thus to embrace him. Through our aid, the Jew was able to achieve what in all the anguished millenia before he was not. *Si monumentum requiris, circumspice!* We weeded out his weaklings, while increasing his moral capital with every one we destroyed. We hardened him with our tortures. *We* tempered him, refined him in our fires, *we* polished him down to the indestructible core. Today you can see the results of our craftsmanship: he is pure hard diamond, and his radiant leer sparkles in triumph over his fallen forge-slave."

In conclusion Bach reached over and dropped his hand on Reinhart's knee with a startling weight. Startling because when he had held it earlier in greeting, it was light, and since it was clammy as well, reminiscent of a damp sponge. Now it hit with a *plop* like a waterlogged sponge, and, sure enough, when Reinhart looked down he saw a faint wet stain melting the crease from his trouser-knee. This oddity was as full of liquid, it occurred to Reinhart, who remembered both the tears of gratitude at the cigarettes and the weeping in the story, as a cheese is full of "whey" in all the best fairy tales. As the first occasion on which he had come across anyone whose hands genuinely dripped with perspiration, it was worthy of cataloguing. Then too, in this damp cellar nothing dried. His own sweat, while not as plentiful as Bach's, sheathed him like a trout's mucous envelope. A strip of stagnant water lined the base of the wall; the concrete blocks above had sieved out a patina of mineral salts.

Bach's rhetoric had made poor Reinhart's head reel, from amusement through indignation to logical vertigo. He repeated the process, this time at greater cost, that he had undergone in Philosophy 100, where the splendid promise of the fall catalogue—"The major traditions of European thought"—was blighted by the inevitable petty-Machiavelli of a lecturer with his *cul-de-sacs:* "Epimenides, a Cretan, said all Cretans are liars. Was he telling the truth?" And even if he understood, he was lost, and guilty, guilty.

At last, in desperation, he said: "Just let me get hold of this. You want to kill the Jews with kindness?"

Bach made his giggle, and the hairs rose on Reinhart's neck.

"Leave it to the American to put things without equivocation!"

Reinhart took his advantage to steer into the congenial area of behaviorism. "But all this is in terms of *feelings* and *ideas*. What exactly did you *do*, as a Nazi?"

Bach withdrew the sponge to his own knee, his eyes bagging in disappointment.

"I should have thought the intellectual history to be the more valuable. Well, then, if you insist, I can produce a few crumbs of physical activity. Humiliating, but perhaps useful as an index to the nightmare from which it took me so long to awaken.

"I joined the Party in November, 1938. I shan't dwell on the scruples the conquering of which took me an entire decade from the aforementioned events. I placed the button under my lapel a few days before the celebrated *Kristallnacht* when, in retaliation for the murder by the Polish Jew Grynszpan of an attaché at the German Embassy in Paris, the Nazis instituted an action against Jews and Jewish property throughout the Reich. It may sound queer to you that I participated in some of the raids in Berlin. Yes, I the aesthete! My request for a role was most suspiciously received, the storm troops being constituted of the most ungodly scum you can imagine, whose motivation was not a holy passion against Jews but a simple nihilistic lust for destruction. However, a fanatical eye is an effective persuader. I managed to win a position on one of the flying squads that swooped on the Jewish shops in the Kurfürstendamm. You cannot understand, nor can I describe the exultation with which I plied my axe, even astonishing the thugs whom I accompanied, so that by the end of the night there was a tacit agreement among these canaille that I was their leader.

"In a china shop, where we had done a job worthy of your proverbial wild bull and were ready to depart, one of my companions came upon a hidden safe, buried in the rear wall. We had to send out for explosives to open it, it being impervious to the pick, and I was all for abandoning the project for better work elsewhere. But the cupidity of these swine was aroused; they were convinced the Jew had cached his treasure there. The door was eventually burst, revealing an empty chamber save for a single object, a small vase, which on examination I determined to be a piece of thirty-pfennig trash from Woolworth's.

"Now why the Jew would have placed such a thing in his vault I could not at first explain, and, indeed, was about to pitch it aside, when the thought struck me that the scoundrel had got intelligence of the raid, and, lacking anything better, had employed this means of retaliation, with a sense that Nazis of the common stripe would be certain to think it valuable and demonstrate their idiocy by confiscating it unbroken. A very deep joke, typically Jewish. But I knew, with the penultimate hatred which is, as I now know, stupidity, but which then seemed wisdom, that at last I had in my hands an instrument to enable me to top the Jew at his own game. I led my men in another diligent round of razing. When we had done, the showcases were flinders, the walls demolished to the lath, the woodwork a pile of faggots for the stove, the wiring ripped out—in short, a reduction that could have qualified us journeymen house-wreckers. A tiny table was spared, and placed in the center of the room. On it, I centered the vase, filled to the rim with my ordure."

For all the foliage, thought Reinhart, he is a clown at the core. "That was sort of childish, wasn't it?"

Bach could not be conned. "No, with gratitude, if you mean 'and therefore not responsible.'" And, not seeing Reinhart's grin grow dim, he struggled to his feet without assistance; swaying over him, face contorted, arms rising and falling like a crazy windmill, he screamed in the voice of his giggle, piercing, forceful, but not loud: *"Oh no, no. Can't you understand? In Auschwitz we of the SS could kill two thousand head in half an hour, but it was burning the bodies that took time."*

He produced a cavernous belch that shook him to the fundament, and toppled backwards, ever so slowly, onto the couch, which recoiled to the floor and recovered. Massively he slept.

Lori, too, slept in the chair, but the absence of sound as Reinhart rose and prepared to creep away, awakened her.

"No, are you leaving?"

Reinhart pointed to the sofa.

"He is spent, poor man!"

At the purity of her look, Reinhart seized her bony shoulders and shook them violently as he might have washed his overcoat with air. When he had exhausted the brutality of his violated virtue and summarized Bach's dissertation, she tossed back her head and laughed extravagantly.

"Bach in the SS! Pardon my rudeness. Perhaps one must be German to see the joke. The SS had most severe physical requirements."

"Why would he tell such a story?" asked Reinhart, aloud but to himself, as the chair again received his mass. "If he concocts this out of the thin air the man is surely mad."

"No, he is not insane. The minds of the insane run in straight lines, not always Euclidean, but always straight. The job there is to find the geometrical system by which to measure them.

Here, if you insist, we have something eccentric, twisted but normal. In fact," she added, "normal is twisted."

"But why evil?" he wailed. "When people lie they make themselves better, not worse."

"No, you foolish boy!" She thrust her face up at him. "No, they first make themselves something, whether good or bad, but something. A man cannot live without a function. Can you understand that, you *American?*"

He had never in all his life heard the national adjective pronounced with contempt. *Amerikaner:* he loathed it for a moment himself, but there was yet one more hateful.

"You *German!*" he ranted. "Can you understand this: I am ashamed to be of German descent! It makes me sick to my stomach. I might lie to make myself worse, as you say, but not to claim I hurt defenseless people. You once asked about my relatives—I hope they were killed in the bombing! And if they weren't, they are dead anyway in their souls. Do you know what you did when you murdered the Jews? You committed suicide, all of you!" Of course, no sooner was it out than he realized he echoed Bach to the letter, and was ashamed.

"Don't talk of things you cannot understand." She turned her back.

He reclaimed from the table the pack of cigarettes he had given Bach and made for the door. Lori pursued him. In the dank passageway, in the pale light that reached there from the lamps within, they grappled, she shrilling: "I must make you understand about Bach. It is simply an overactive anterior pituitary. Not only does this outlaw of a gland produce great size, but it also eliminates the sexual urge!"

"I don't care, I don't care." Saying which again and again, he nevertheless permitted her to pull him back inside. He knew now of his own impotence: his great moral address had been delivered, every word, in English.

Lori drew him to the chair and notwithstanding their differences in size, literally knocked him into it, all that was necessary being one good push in the midsection.

"Now," she cried, standing militantly before him. "It was you who insisted on coming here. You forced me to bring you against my will. Therefore you will stay until I finish. Bach has done as much for me as one human being can do for another. He has saved my life, my very life!, every single day for three years."

"You were anti-Nazi?" asked Reinhart in rapturous awe, but she paid him no mind.

"And it involved more than simply not turning me in to the Gestapo—you perhaps think in your naïve way that that much could be expected of a husband; you have not lived in Germany —and more than concealing me, too, although that at the daily risk of his own life."

Beneath the vast, important feelings Reinhart had a little tickle of pride, no less important, at her ceasing to speak so as to favor his imperfect knowledge of the tongue. She spoke swiftly and with the full resources of idiom and construction, and he did not miss a word.

"The long story of his art collection is pitifully short. He sold it, piece by piece, to pay for day by day of my life."

"The Gestapo then could be bribed." The idea made that dread agency less terrible.

"The money went elsewhere. Who got it does not matter."

"Excuse me, I am so stupid, foolish as you say—if you don't wish to answer you don't have to. Why, when he has this to tell, does Bach pretend to be the reverse?"

"Because the meaningful things are never said. Because he is infected with the Berliner's disease, irony and gallows-humor. Because—" She moved intensely near, and he was afraid she might call him *American* again, with all that scorn. "No, *I* shall not lie to you. . . . Because the time when he could do something for me has now passed."

He found that, idiotically, he had replaced the wretched cigarettes on the table.

"I came here tonight to take pity on you," he said. "I have to ask it instead for myself. Believe me, it is not easy to be a fool. You have to work hard at it." He went again to the door, this time unaccompanied, from which distance he looked long at her minor, crumpled figure, and said: "You are a Jew."

Bach groaned lightly in his sleep while Lori with careful hands arranged a quilt on his recumbent hulk. Then, extinguishing all the lamps but the one on the central table, she came once more to Reinhart.

"That saves me, *nicht wahr?* That one-half Jewishness, that mongrel portion which so short a time ago condemned me, is now my salvation. And enlightened people no longer believe in miracles! Yet within oneself, one is always just a person. Even Hitler. Do you know, his favorite meal was corn-on-the-cob and jelly omelet. Think of that: there were moments when his sole concern was to retain a bit of slippery jam on a fork."

He opened the door and stared forlornly into the gloomy passage.

"Shall I light you out?"

"No thanks. I'll try to manage that much on my own. May I come again?"

Briefly she was against him, her small head in the hollow of his rib cage.

"You are a fool, a good fool, a kind fool."

She gave his hand the short, one-shot European shake and said no more as he began the tortuous ascent to the mid-world.

# CHAPTER 11

ONE had his choice in the officers' liquor ration, but one could not command what was not available. The fifth of gin represented an impressive trial of even Captain St. George's noted patience, not to mention the vermouth.

"Eleven months, Nate, it took me to assemble the ingredients of a martini, with the olives still to come. And the funny part is that I never eat the olives. Still, a drink looks naked without it, and I think, don't you, that an olive adds a certain essential something. And the ice! There's something, where can a fellow get ice in this stricken city?"

No, pickled onions would never do, and although the fashion was passing to lemon peel, St. George had read, he held with the olive.

"Besides, the question is academic: I haven't seen pearl onions or lemons, either."

The captain was therapeutic, a plump, well-padded bandage. Why the medics did not use him as resident healer in some recuperation camp was beyond Schild's reason.

Sunset in the back yard with St. George, an awful thought as recent as two weeks ago, now was Schild's hope. He had fallen into an attendance on the captain's problems as one tormented by the rash might lower himself into a pool of warm oil and, comforted, in debt to the oil, so to speak, take up its study. A new approach for Schild, who hitherto might instead have gone into dermatology. But he had at once lost his strength, not by a slow erosion but at once, as if someone had opened a valve.

Last night, undoing his tie before the mirror—an atypical incident; Schild was so little concerned with his appearance that he rarely stood before the glass to put on his necktie, let alone remove it—standing, then, at the dresser, the room's interior precisely reversed from the real, he was overcome by a quick delight, like some small-flat resident with his persistent discovery in dreams of a door behind the bookshelf that opens into another room no one knew about. Admiring the new figure in the wallpaper, all the fresh textures, the dimensions not yet contemptible by use, his eye swept to Lichenko and arrest. He had not, in the farthest reach of the new landscape, forgotten his guest; indeed, deliberately he had sought him out, as if, since the mirror worked a comprehensive reversal, it would also reverse Lichenko; as if from a novel aspect he would be seen again as he had entered Schild's affairs, the subsequent devious patterns now revealed as a foible of the stale vision.

Instead, on Lichenko's face reigned a supreme and splendid peace, a glutton's on arising from the board, a sadist's on hanging up his whip, a drunkard's on counting his corks. He looked not at all at Schild but into the obesity of the featherbed that collapsed and reasserted itself under his experimental hand as if in breathing. His own serene breaths followed suit. He had got heavier in fourteen days, a fact that his reversed image stated with a kind of hostile assurance not apparent right side front. The German woman did up his clothes: his blouse a thing of smooth planes, his boots another mirror, the trouser crease a lethal edge. His eyes hung heavy, as if he could not bear the weight of the lids. Give him six months and he would be a little fat man, a fat little tradesman, retaining his cheek-furrows but in the discontent of prosperity. The fact was that an agent provocateur satisfied, however that surfeit sat upon his features, was an agent whose mission went well. To watch him was like looking into the mouth of a clogged toilet.

The violence remained in the glass, as, turning away, he began to measure his position, he, Schild, the man of limited ambitions, commonplace talents, one who served, a rational man, mistaken now by who knew what compound of humanity and history and place for the reverse of these qualities; for although he may have been guilty it was not of the transgression for which he was now under surveillance, could not be, for it was precisely his crime that he was incapable of a crime, and unfortunately no secret police or central committee was yet in search of that kind of deviation.

As a boy he had developed a feat of controlled consciousness, a triumph over what was initially a disability, almost, he had feared at the time, a madness. Under duress of his parents, who were tyrants for the communal life—at least in theory, at least for the children; when it came to themselves it was another thing: "when you grow up you got to work don't forget it"— expelled from home, he had gone with a children's group, Jewish, always and forever Jewish, to Coney Island for "fun"; always and again "fun," a separate and distinct endeavor from one's other pursuits, to be sought only by congress with, in this case, a million other organisms who had not forgotten to leave behind their flesh and sweat glands. Despite the sun's inability to plumb the floor of this forest of skin where he lay, he had, impossibly, got a bad burn. He did not tan and therefore unless forced avoided the sun; once in it by necessity, however, he tested that familiar theory that stern resolution overcomes all, arriving at the invariable and, for one with dark hair and eyes, peculiarly shameful rebuttal of scorched hide. The end of this day found the flames mounting to his head; he was lost for an hour and when found was sick enough to warrant being taken all the way to Manhattan in a taxi—for which when he was well he heard "somebody had to pay guess who?"—and, home, was in a half-delirium for three days while his pelt grew leprous.

Only half a delirium, because he knew what he was about and didn't, simultaneously; or did but suspected he shouldn't; feeling so queer in the head one hadn't the right, so to speak, to be on the same terms with reality as other people. Lying on the sofa whose brown plush marked with patches of psoriasis the points

of humanity too often stated—head, hips, and heels—watching
his mother drop the wooden egg into the stocking toe, beneath
the bridge lamp whose transverse member had long ago been
separated from its upright by nervous readjustments and now
bore its oiled-paper shade on the frayed cord alone, he felt a
dread that she might not look up on schedule and carp.
People don't read on the flat of their backs holding the book
over them like a sunshade, it blinds them at twenty. He yearned
to receive the admonition that in normal times would have driven
him out to the library and its public privacy; now to assure himself of actuality, it was a value from the past that he
would have given even his assent to establish. His sister, in bed
fifteen minutes, failed once to call for water; for once his father,
who rarely left the house after dark, was out for cigars, which
he rarely smoked. Across the airshaft from the kitchen, the
Kaminskys were anaesthetized, for the first time in history they
forbore to exchange insults in heavy Polish accents.

In his three days of partial coma Schild learned what his
twelve years of comparative clarity had not laid clear: in the
degree of one's need, one's companions and surroundings become negative, fail to comply. One seizes the bathroom in a quiet
hour and instantly sets a fashion for the others, who appear at
the door in force; one goes to the movies on Monday night and
cannot win a seat from the horde of people who will miss work
next morning to perform this natural service of denial; one is
hungriest the evening the rest of the familly, ill, dine on rye and
cream cheese and admire each other's lack of appetite. These
schemes are seen with the semiconsciousness as colors are more
vivid and distances overcome with squinted eyes. In health, we
are tormented by reality's presence; sick, by its loss.

When well, Schild commanded this partial coma as it had in
illness mastered him, for when the prisoner holds the key, a cell
changes from a proscription to a defense of liberty. It later became his obsession that experience in the large could be con-

trolled—nay, must be, which had no regard for could—the alternative was fascism. But experience in the small, in the disparate grooves where the larger powers, so to speak, lacked elbow room, what could not be ordered could at least be converted.

In the present circumstance, Schild looked at Schild from a distance, finding him not small but different, as if in dramatic irony he knew something that his double did not. One Schild was doomed; the other could stand here invisible and invulnerable, if necessary watch from asylum the first go to the noose.

Schatzi had not appeared in ages. Schild had made two fruitless trips to Wannsee on consecutive nights; on the third he had posted a note on a tree in the Fasanenstrasse, in Wilmersdorf, used as a bulletin board by bombed-out persons seeking their families. This schedule, to be put into effect in case of emergency, had been ready for use since his first engagement with Schatzi. The note read: "Seek whereabouts of Oskar Reichel, formerly of Ludwigkirchstrasse 32. His wife is alive and well. Apply Bauer, Weddingweg 8, Lichterfelde."

In theory, contact having been broken, Schatzi was thus directed to come to Schild, at the former's discretion. In practice, he did not: clearly, because Schild had all at once acquired a bad odor. That Schatzi had himself fallen afoul of one power or another was unlikely, if not impossible; further, it could not be imagined. If for no other reason, fate would keep him free to taunt Schild, whatever the extremity.

Schild felt comfortably like a corpse, with Captain St. George droning on as sole mourner at the wake. The evening lurked in the population of leaves overhead, pandering for nightfall, which in Berlin appeared later than elsewhere and then only after extensive preliminaries, leaving early: at half-past three you could read your watch without a flashlight. St. George's cigar-end periodically bloomed with fire, drooled a thin bouquet. His voice, deficient in resonance, permitted the transmission of noises from small live things rustling in the bush.

"Even the lizards, or whatever that is, are going, as our British friends say, to Bedfordshire. That's my idea, too. I am so [yawn] sleepy. Must be the [yawn] air. Goo[yawn]night."

The captain rose and snapped-to his folding camp stool, tonight with satisfaction. He liked smooth-snapping things, as being both easy and smart; but his taste was often impeded by the stool, for which he frequently cursed Aberfitch & Crombie: the extra ten dollars they added to every item had no justification when things stuck.

Schild sorely wished him to stay, should have liked to make the brief sound which would have accomplished that, for it was no great or difficult feat to convince St. George his presence was wanted. Yet he could not, as it were, solemnize his conversion to the invertebrate. Assuming Schild was asleep or, more likely, forgetting him simultaneously with his decision to retire, the captain stumbled into the rear door of the house.

The night chill found Schild's marrow. A bulky insect dropped into the hair of his forearm and was entangled to frenzy. Fool that it was, it interpreted his humane efforts as malicious and died shortly of its false assumption. He sat alone within the limitations of the fence; a small yard, smaller still without St. George; a corral with like squares on either side, extending on to the ends of the block: multiple petty-bourgeois cells. A creeper rose embraced the pickets. He once knew an Eagle Scout who was born and raised five stories above the sidewalk on 191st Street but could identify every plant within a ten-mile radius of the camp at Alpine, New Jersey.

Their landlady slept on two biscuit mattresses on the floor of the kitchen. The easiest thing in the world, if she had not been German, would be to walk right in and have her. If she had not been German, however, it would not be the easiest thing. He fancied his contempt had some sexual attraction for her. The angles of her face sharpened as he passed, and he sensed furtive movements behind doors when St. George was out of the house. But he had already had his gentile, and of the classic kind, complete with rabbit nose, soap-and-water cheeks, and anti-Semitic Daddy and Mother, and he had no strong sadism even towards Germans.

He turned his slat chair, property of the house, squealing rustfully in the joints, so that he could not see the kitchen window. A dog whined in the distance; a Southerner or a Negro, passing on the sidewalk out front, described to a mute companion a succession of events that were invariably *mothafuhn;* the faint odor of pine, which was everywhere at night in the western quarter of Berlin, was superseded by the sudden smell of candy, moreover, a precise candy: Mary Janes, nut-flavored, tallowlike caramel on the outside, peanut butter in the center. Mrs. Grossman gave you one less for a penny than her competitors; Milton, when she took ten minutes off for raspberry soda and plain cake, gave one more. Amazing so shrewd a woman never knew this for fifteen years. It was after Milton had been killed in Spain that she received this knowledge, along with the other things that had to be said, fat and old and bitter, knotting a cord end from the drawer of saved string. "Better they were poison!" Although she should have known that her son was his master, and not vice versa. A boy, buying some candy, slipped a nickel underneath a newspaper on the counter, for it was Sabbath and Mrs. Grossman would not touch money until the sun had set. "Go read your books!" she shouted to Schild in Yiddish, the language, it struck him suddenly, for many things but, above all, humor; he could feel nothing beyond a terrible impulse to laugh and a sense of how terrible was his impulse. In the doorway, he bumped into the boy, who had been delayed a moment, stripping the wrapper from his bit of sweet; it was a Mary Jane. Schild's teeth clogged in empathy, he could almost taste the peanut butter, it had always been very like putty.

All this in the second before he knew, like a bat, that a human being stood in the darkness behind his chair. He sat easy, who else could it be but Schatzi?

"And here we have Herr Schild, *zu Hause* like any merchant."

Where had he been? was an obvious question, but could not be asked. Schatzi made succulent sounds over his candy, offering some to Schild which when taken was a disappointment not living up to its odor: so much for the memory. He was called back to the present; the atmosphere was less charged at once. There sat Schatzi, renewing the link. He had been a fool to concoct an elaborate, sinister design from meaningless coincidence, for it was through Schatzi that his line of authority led. How could a simple lieutenant in the Red Army be concerned? One must face it that Lichenko was even rather pitiful. It was no disrespect, it took nothing from his honor, was no adverse implication on the triumph of the society that had given him his chance for manliness and heroism, that Lichenko was—he almost thought, was no Milton Grossman; but Lichenko, too, had charged the fascist guns.

"I suppose you wonder where have I been," said Schatzi, careful to keep it low. It was so dark now that he was seen as black on black, improbable but not impossible, which could not have been more appropriate to him. His voice, his rustlings, the thump of his butt-bones to the ground—all expressed an unusual geniality. In his own way, he apparently felt it good to see Schild again. He refused an offer of the chair, although it must have been uncomfortable for an ill man to sit on the cold earth.

"I saw your note some days ago; although, I was otherwise preoccupied . . . no, really, I am just pleased, stay where you are sitting. The ground is not unpleasant. Beneath the grass you know is sand, it does not hold the water. Berlin is one single great island of sand on the Brandenburg plain, yet it permits a lush growth of plant life, no? In spite of its architecture, Berlin is a beautiful city, but so few foreigners know it and that is sorrowful."

Schild assumed the cynicism of his answer would be *de rigueur:* "There is little left to see now."

"So much the worse for all," said Schatzi, not shouting but giving the illusion he was and with the kind of conviction that Schild recognized as having originated in higher chancelleries than either of them would ever subordinate. "It was senseless of the Americans to destroy the city. The most unfortunate way to win the German people away from fascism."

Lichenko had assured Schild that Russian artillery, particularly that multibarreled weapon known by the Germans as Stalin's Organ, had leveled more of Berlin than the Eighth and Royal Air Forces together, and he had agreed then as he did now, yet neither time in hypocrisy.

Schatzi, making liquid, furry, catlike noises, swabbed his gums with his tongue, and then went with the keen tip of his smallest finger for a molar in the recalcitrant love of caramel. Actually he could not be seen with such precision: his ring flashed in transit, his cuff rustled, and Schild supplied the other details from memory.

"Not to speak of reconstruction," continued Schatzi. "The Soviet Union has been given the most horrible section of the city." To go any farther would be to imply that Stalin had been hoodwinked by Churchill and Roosevelt. Indeed, he had already gone too far. "You must indulge me in my English. Certainly I did not intend to say 'horrible' except in regard to the bombing there. It is, on one's other hand, the sector most worth for rehabilitation."

They had from the first always spoken English together, although Schild had often sought to turn to German, partly from a masochistic pride in his fluency—and partly from the vicarious nostalgia in which he looked back on the time before his majority: the tongue of the old International had been German. But Schatzi had resisted, not so much from a pride of his own, Schild thought, as from his sixth sense for conspiracy, which told him that obscurity had as great a role as precision in underground technique. In one's second language, facts are never finally established; when blame must be cast, it can thus fall on the vocabulary and not the man, or if the man, then first on him who by birth qualifies for absolute comprehension. There is at any rate a possibility for such miscarriage, and the professional asks for no more, from his own side or the foe.

Exploiting, to himself, his ambivalent pleasure with the present confirmation of the hypothesis, he received another notice—as he often did and as often was unarmed against, for it was his constant failure that though he had the imagination of disaster, he had not the mind. His suspicions rose the faster for his inability to believe in them. Not only had Schatzi never before transmitted the "line"; he had never been so generally obliging. His manner asked for forbearance, as if, getting that, he would go on to request ten dollars, repayable on demand. He was not, for once, in haste: he had never before sat at an interview; he had never before come to Schild's billet; *he had never before been pleasant.*

He continued to be, despite his theme, which was the occasion for neither grace nor evil but the neutrality of fact. And the first fact laid in Schild's head by Schatzi multiplied within the minute; in the same minute that his heart multiplied its reasons for foreboding, his reason produced offspring, like some woman in Asia, or what-have-you *mise-en-scène* for the current classic instance of futile misery, who continues to reproduce like a mink notwithstanding the famine.

"In the Western zones," Schild said, "all the ex-Nazis are getting jobs with the Military Government."

This cut off Schatzi for a moment of aggrieved silence. Now Schild had perhaps gone too far. His question was put in a voice that suggested this was the first time he had ever been brought to this turn of the road, one nearer the hairpin than was comfortable, and unless Schild could produce Automobile Association sanction he would drag his feet.

The sudden caution, standard operating procedure for anyone

else to be met in Schild's professional circles, was unusual for
Schatzi, a piece with the rest of his tonight unique demeanor.
But that this was the norm and Schatzi's usual manner the
oddity, had no force, for the ordinary Schatzi, who was extraordinary, was precisely what Schild had been prepared to meet
in Europe. He had hated him, true, and he had just now begun
to like him, but these nervous reactions were beside the point
that Schatzi had been absolutely authentic.

Or perhaps so directly to the point that they were invisible,
integrated in the drama of hatred and fear and fascination of
which Schatzi was a walking précis. Whatever his temporary
odors, to Schild he stank of the concentration camp; he had
acquired there a beastliness which but for the final morality
could not be separated from that of his captors. Hideous to think
so; but only moral realism to know that the difference between
saint and devil was frequently never revealed until the last
judgment.

"By the way," Schild said at last, when Schatzi's moment of
silence had lengthened into an evident volition not to speak at
all, "I saw the 'big lout' and have begun to go through the papers
from his office. Only the top two or three cartons have Winterhilfe files. The rest is material from the Bund Deutscher Mädel."

"A female division of the Hitler Youth."

"Yes, I know that." Schild was as usual irritated at being told
what he already knew. "At any rate, I have filtered out some
things for you."

No answer. The sounds of Schatzi's breathing became quickly
like the aspiration of a rubber pillow crushed by a thigh, and
died. The crickets sang madly below the fence—or wherever; if
you went there to find them, they would instead be at the place
you had left, and back there again only to hear their song in the
bush. Behind Schild, a casement had its fastenings undone,
its halves slithering open in slow provocation, followed swiftly
by a broad drift of light that created a visible Schatzi but did

not animate him. He wore bicycle cuff-guards resembling money clips. His shoes were swarthy, pebble-grained, and had long Italian points. The sole of one, showing a medallion of chewing gum in the arch, hung directly before Schild; danced to a rhythm that owed more to emaciation and senility than tacit music; the leg within its frayed sheath of woolen underwear was surely bare tibia and fibula and a snarl of ancient sinews. Long underwear in the middle of summer: for his pants cuff had ridden high, one bicycle clip, being sprung, failing; and he lay on his back in the grass, with one leg arched high, the other looped over it. Had he suffered a seizure? Schild rose to see beyond the bridge of legs, saw Schatzi's eyes wide open, bland and insensitive as two bottle caps, paralytic. Dread had just put down his immediate, instinctive disbelief, he had just received the full import of the underwear shroud, when Schatzi belched like a cannon and with a sudden effort of overbearing vitality raised to the sitting position.

"Queer person who lives in your quarters," he said.

Schild turned expecting that the German woman, *déshabillé*, could be seen framed in the window—not in concupiscence of his own but in amused anticipation of Schatzi's; he was captivated by the sudden transition from imagined death to carnality. Instead he saw Lichenko, in undress rightly enough, but Lichenko! Who, bent at the waist, lips funneled and eyes squinted in bestial ill humor, swung one arm apelike. He was naked. The other arm crooked in menace. In his paw was, again, Schild's .45.

In the haste to the door Schild yet had attention for the nimble Schatzi, who had sprung up beside him and maintained the pace at his elbow. He saw in his courier's action that which relieved his greater worry: would Schatzi, knowing of Lichenko, show the innocent curiosity of a boy chasing a ladder wagon?

They symbolically broke into the kitchen, for its door was open and only the oppressive light of the interior barred entry. The German woman lay stiff and still on her mattress in the corner, frozen in contempt, not fear, her handsome face fierce, free, and remote as an eagle's. She had, it was clear, cowed Lichenko with no more than her moral advantage.

Lichenko had jumped behind a high cabinet at the first sound of intrusion, where he thrust the pistol, or sought to thrust it, into the space between cabinet and wall. He was apprehended before this was managed. But, as if in that brief moment with himself he had taken a realistic account of his project's miscarriage, seen it, that is, as a mere limited venture gone awry with no permanent blot on the amour propre, he met Schild straight on, handing him the pistol butt-first—to show, by its empty slot, that it was not loaded—and offering his guileless face, open and unafraid.

Was he drunk again? Schild had taken care to keep whiskey from his own room and Lichenko without direction had set a personal off-limits on St. George's quarters; he had in fact developed an unusual delicacy towards the house in general, which Schild found more difficult to excuse than the expected barbarism. Yet here was the return of the barbaric, and he, Schild, had run to brook it, in his reflexes one with the scared calves at Lovett's party.

Schatzi, temporarily forgotten, spoke to the woman—had been speaking to her and was now heard reacting to her consistent silence: "*Keine Antwort is auch eine Antwort.*" No answer is also an answer: for what reason was she working with Schild?

But Lichenko was not drunk. He began to shiver from the cold and adjusted the cinch in the towel about his waist, for neither was he wholly nude. He was, indeed, suddenly nothing he had been, neither victim nor captor nor naïve nor sinister, and as he prepared to speak from this new person, Schild struck him in the mouth. He had meant to knock him unconscious, so that Schatzi could not hear the Russian accent, but he had never before struck a person with this intent; he had never, since boyhood, struck any person for any reason, even comedy. He now punched too high and tore his third knuckle on Lichenko's teeth.

It had been as hard a blow as he could summon in cold blood, but with only the free-swinging arm and no body behind it, did no physical damage. Lichenko, however, was whipped, all the more for his initial show of dignity. He grasped again at his towel, grinned in coy brutishness, rolled his head like a fawning dog. And then he whined, in German, and all was lost: "My friend, this whore tempted me!" In his accent the first letter of *Hure* was a great and obvious *G*.

From the other corner Schatzi burst into his aspirant snigger, and an oxlike plodding at the door announced St. George, who, in maroon robe with white piping, slippers with elastic inserts, and pajamas a continuum of pale-blue hounds-teeth, after some deliberation had formulated his amiable comment.

"This looks like Grand Central Station!"

The pistol in his right fist, Schild furiously cut its barrel into Lichenko's cheek and, as he went to the floor, followed him down, hacking him down, not ceasing his awful work until St. George, whose cries had gone unheeded, fell on him and stilled him with his bulk.

# CHAPTER 12

"CAN'T find any letters of Grandpa's you asked for—stuff all cleaned out from under the porch to provide place for screens years ago," wrote Reinhart's father. "Maybe you even did it yourself—if you were paid for it. If my advice means anything, tho, I'd drop the idea—your just asking for trouble—as soon as you find any German relations they will want to borrow money from you . . . ," etc., typed on a V-mail blank, small as the Lord's Prayer engraved on the head of a pin.

Ask a stupid man, get a stupid answer. When he told Trudchen about it—for, despite her peculiarities, she was still around, still without pay, reporting to the office every morning long before he arrived—she said: "Ah, vy bozzuh! I will be your relative."

That was all he had told her. He did not seek to expose her pitiful lies; he let stand the assumption that she lived, orphaned, in the little back room in the office building, where indeed she did report at the end of each workday. Above all, he remained silent on the visit to Lori's. What he had learned there was for adults only, and he was not at all certain he could stand to think of it himself.

He at last understood that the complement to his long self-identification with Germanness had been a resolve never to know the German actuality. Knowledge had exhausted his options; he now had no choice but to seek out, if still they existed, his links to what, a brief half-century after Siegfried Reinhardt took ship for the New World, had disintegrated in murder and betrayal.

He had not really believed the witness of the Buchenwald photographs; mass exterminations were incredible. Real deaths

176

were your friend Bill, one moment live, the next run down by a drunken driver; Al killed by pneumonia; Roy, his heart full of Jap metal, taking the Iwo Jima bastion and expiring a hero; or someone's brother, well known, electrocuted by the state for the crime of homicide, and his victim; these corpses were believable in sight and mind; despite the mortician's garish art, beyond the mystery of any death, were the concrete memories of impediments of speech, casts of eye, a rolling gait, a red Ford with a two-tone horn, and the only four-button suit in southern Ohio.

Similarly with the violet shadows under Lori's eyes. Whoever had sold her safety from incineration had seen them upon every payment, must have had the queer guts to imagine their transformation into white ash and his own agency in the burning. And the man who would have fired the oven, dressed in his black SS-suit, with his blond crown and his blue eyes, the model to which every boy aspires, the handsome soldier fearless before the enemy, gentle with women. . . . These types were not explained by the simple, pious indignation of: two kinds of man, one good and one bad; we of course are the first; they, the second.

Nor by the lack of a democratic tradition: was this what men did when denied the vote? Nor militarism: you mean that the great Frederick mounted his stallion and rode down women and children and unarmed men, and that the old knights of Nürnberg swung their blades against little ghetto-tailors?

Reinhart had been reared in what he assumed to be (since everything else was) the German code; there are two kinds of cowards: one who will not fight a man his own size or larger, and one who will fight only someone weaker; sometimes, but by no means always, the same person. But the validity of this, too, was here outmoded, for the SSman, fresh from his ravages on the helpless, stood fast against the superior enemy; was, to be sure, the fiercest soldier met by the Allied troops.

As to the anonymous blackmailer, Reinhart insisted that his, too, was a strange, mad kind of courage, for beyond gentleness and humanitarianism and a deficiency of passion, what stays the normal man from murder or even its threat is fear, not of the godly or human law or vengeance or nightmares, but of the suggestion of his own mortality.

Here all the known qualities of humanity had been united with their contradictions. This was what Bach dramatized in his monstrous monologue of truth in falsehood, that guilt could be confessed to only in a lie of the guiltless, that the first loss of the criminals had been in their human imaginations. Where Reinhart had looked in Germany for life, first in dreams of ancient glory and then, after the Nazis, for a vitality at least of evil, he saw only a horror of deadness, of which the literal corpses, the loose skins of Dachau, were but the minor part.

Yet more important than this moribund nation were the good people, those "good Germans" on whom the sanctimonious propaganda of Our Side did its work of slaughter, the mature ones like Bach who by conscious volition stayed decent and sought no fanfare for it now, and children like Trudchen who willy-nilly were clean. Were his relatives to be counted with them?

Even in his duty of conscience, however, he was balked by the same ineptness which characterized his dealings in the humdrum; when fountain pens were hard to get, people like Marsala had pocketsful; similarly with liquor, broads, and passes; he, Reinhart, so damned special, one of the ought-ought per cent of the American population to go to college, a member of the owning and stable class, could manage nothing.

It was very well to say loosely, as Lori had, to go to the burgomaster's office. He tried just that, visited the town hall in Schöneberg, which he was astonished to see employed as many bureaucratic flunkies as it were an American city untouched by war, who notwithstanding that he was Occupation showed much the same bored insolence and then when pressed claimed a search of the birth records back to 1850 turned up no Siegfried Reinhart. Of course, there was always the Russian Sector, which the eyeglassed clerk recommended snottily-reproachful, as if to say: that's what you get for dividing our city. There was what Reinhart would earlier have identified as certainly a Nazi; now he thought it more likely the man might turn out to be an unsung hero of the anti-Hitler opposition and this job his reward.

He got aid from an unconsidered quarter. Although when he had first revealed it to Trudchen his project left her cold, she greeted him one morning with sudden interest and suggestion.

"You must have a *dett*-ek-tive! And I have just your person. The man who makes some work about here—he with the scarred face. He is called—so silly!—Schatzi, that means 'sweetheart,' did you know? Do you know which I intend?" She had her own table now, a jittery-jointed piece which swayed like a drunken spider when she assaulted the old Underwood. "He is very active in the black market. This takes him everywhere and in consequence to that he knows everyone."

"Not the old man in the Wehrmacht cap?"

A regrettable concomitant of Trudchen's employment was false tint laid on thickly over her natural color, and Reinhart also bore the guilt of that. He had bought her lipstick and rouge from the PX, on her request for the "raddest of the rad."

"Oh, he has worn it, yes, but also many other costumes. When he sells one thing, he attires himself in another."

"You don't mean that old man who works in Lovett's office?"

"Not regularly. He makes much money on the black market—why should he vorry?"

And he had thought the old fellow pitiful; it was a true instance of what one, disinclined to contribute, says of street cripples with their tin cups: they could probably buy and sell any of us poor working stiffs.

"I don't suppose he was a National Socialist?" Reinhart could no longer use "Nazi"; with the passing of each German day the term became more like the name of a soap powder, some slick and vulgar "Rinso" invented by Americans, who eventually re-

duce everything to that level: "Nazi," the cute name for a pack
of buffoons, played always by the same actors, regularly thwarted
by some clean-shaven Beverly Hills Boy Scout whom a ruptured
eardrum disqualified from the real war.

However, he was not wholly serious even in putting it the
long way, since in this area Trudchen's unreliability was massive.
Perhaps understandably, to her the history of modern times was
a catalogue of her own losses and the responsible instrument,
fate in general.

She lifted her little painted clown's-face, the freshness obscured by the rouge but the innocence still there, and said: "Not
he! He was a prisoner in a concentration camp."

Which was a flat lie—although perhaps not hers but the old
man's; the surviving martyrs of the camps were hardly thrown
into menial jobs and black-marketeering.

"*Ausgezeichnet! Prima!* Then he should be just the man to
find *die Familie* Reinhart," he said in an irony that she did not
receive. "Of course it isn't likely he'll find anybody. There's a
separation of fifty years. Think of that, Trudchen, the last time
I was German my father hadn't yet been born."

"Please?"

Instead of clarifying it, he fell to work with his pencil—which
was blunt and unpleasant to use; if she didn't soon return his
pen he must come right out and ask her to—on the long-delayed
Guide to the Ruins for the sightseeing tour.

The Olympic Stadium, built for the Olympic Games in
1936, has a seating capacity—

Or was it more graceful to say "seats"? Or "seats" as a noun:
"stadium, etc., has 124,000 seats." "Capacity" of course had a
more serious tone. This was one of those days when nothing
sounded right, which unluckily had begun to outnumber those
on which nothing sounded wrong.

"You do not wish to hire this man?" asked Trudchen, starting to type the stencil for Page One, which, for Pound had decided on a grandiose project that would impress the colonel, was to stand as title sheet.

He had to grin. All European girls spoke with an animation at once funny and delightful, an excess of feminine vitality that juiced each word. If this held even in a sadness like Lori's, with Trudchen, who was never less than gay, who was young and unmarred and in a perpetual celebration of ripeness, it was the very model of unalloyed girlship; you never, as sometimes at Home, suspected that you confronted a transvestite boy.

"Ah," she went on, "how hoppy you will make zem! In these timess to have an American cowsin!"

In mock grimness he answered: *"Our American Cowsin.* I hope for better luck. That's the name of the play Lincoln was watching when he was shot."

"By Chon Vil-kes Boat, yes?" This in an eagerness which threw a tremble into her physical establishment. "And the year, 1864, yes? The day I do not know."

"Don't ask me!" He ambled to the French window to look on as perfect weather as the earth offered, the life-enhancing air of the Brandenburg plain, full of golden light and green smells. "My family wasn't in the country at the time. They were here."

Could Jews have been killed on such a day, or had they waited for rain?

The great pines stood high in the adjacent grove, and seeing down among their feet he recognized the steel-gray, crosshatched shadows from old German engravings, which were not artist's strategy but the true lay of the land. He could have watched without doubt a delegation of trolls emerge from some root-home and bear away the Nibelungs' lode, but impossible to the mind's eye were the long sallow lines of victims.

"This man, this good German, how can I get in touch?"

Trudchen giggled like a spring: "Tahch—this is very vivid and so clear that no explanation is needed—baht he vill come here some time. I have taken the freedom to ask him that you might . . . vould . . . could—oh well, that you want to see him."

Along with the cosmetics she wore a peek-a-boo white blouse disclosing an eyelet-margin slip and, beyond, the rim of a brassiere which carried larger burdens than formerly had hung upon her chest, and the pigtails no longer swung free but were entwined about her head in a yellow cocoon. In the aggregate, this was also a lie: that she was a mature girl.

"If he was in a camp, then he must be a Jew?"

Asking which he returned to his desk and fell into the chair with the noise of a beef haunch flung onto a butcher's block.

"Oh no!" cried Trudchen with candid enthusiasm. "You are incorrect when you think only Jews were mistreated. You do not know of the Resistance?"

Sure, the plot to kill Hitler of 20 July 1944. This had already been exposed in his discussion groups as a conspiracy of re-actionary generals, scarcely better than der Führer himself, whose motives were suspect and results, a failure; and who were eleven years late.

Of course there was that—she took no notice of the negating conditions, perhaps because he lost his nerve while talking to her, who was blameless, and presented them weakly—but what she meant was something of a greater scope and duration, embracing all of the non-Nazi population: a total rejection of Hitler and all of his works, dating back to 1933 and earlier. She as a German could tell him that, even though she took no interest in politics, being young and silly.

"And what did they do about it?"

"Ah, what can anybody do against beasts who are ruthless? The SS and the Gestapo, their first job was to control Germans, not Jews."

He sat upright and brought down his fist upon the desk, not in anger but rather a kind of pleading.

"That is understood. But it is over now. National Socialism turned out to be nothing. You couldn't find one German today who would say a good word about it. Yet it was a *German* thing, wasn't it? I don't mean the war, or the Axis, but what went on here: a horrible, dreadful thing that was completely new. Old Genghis Khan and Attila the Hun were saints alongside of this. The whole history of man is disgusting, I grant you, but why would the Germans try to set a new record? But no, I don't even want to ask that. God knows if I had been a German what I would have been. *But why can't someone at least say he is sorry?*" He looked into space, for he had no wish or reason to make it personal.

He was an idiot to speak of this to Trudchen, and she was quite right to look calfly insensate and say: "One cannot be sorry for what one has not done."

"You must pay me no attention," she went on, "because I am not clever, but what I can see is that God makes people suffer." Her mouth and eyes went into round wonder, which made her, there behind the crazy lines of lopsided table and old typing machine, a complex of circles: head, eyes, glasses, mouth, breasts, hips. "At eleven o'clock in the morning of 3 February, this year, I had the fortune to be in the Bayerischer Platz Underground station when your planes came over making a direct strike with an aerial mine that blew a thirty-feet hole out of the bottom of the tube. So suddenly I did not feel anysing, no wownd, and knew only what occurred when this baby in the arms of the vo-man in front of me, now, with the blast, on top of me, this baby stared down and tried to cry at me but instead of the cry this string of blood dripped quietly from its mouth. It was alive, but dead, also; both at the same time—how can I explain this terrible sing that I mean! Your planes had come to kill Nazis, but the bombs cannot tell good from bad. A little chilt of eight months old, it had to suffer. Is it not the same way with God's vengeance for the murder of Jesus Christ?"

It was wackily, harmlessly funny, as when the village crank says of the cyclone-torn bungalow: this is what they get for all that drinking. But she was growing into a big girl, and it was time to be set straight—which no one had bothered to do for him when he was on that level.

"You don't—" he began, when Lieutenant Pound appeared in the doorway and Trudchen hurriedly flung back into her story.

"So when this blood began to descend upon me I reached towards my sleeve for the handkerchief but my hand could not go far, being halted by a soft, varm, cling-ging mass such as one's hair after washing it, and I thought: so I have lost an arm, how easier in the fact than in the worry. Limbs, limbs, I have always feared losing them most."

"Don't bullshit, Trudchen," said Pound, patiently genial, closing the door which was in his absence never closed, demonstrating his talent for violently hurling it to without its latching: he "pulled" it, as one does a punch in a false fight. "You've got two bigfat white arms today."

Although his monastery was now neat, this abbot had stayed slovenly; as he went briskly to his desk below the little window, his loose shoelaces clicked, his tie end flapped over his shoulder, his bowlegs like two lips endlessly yawned away from each other and gulped shut.

Perhaps it was Pound's own experience in violence: he never believed anything she said. And by his example, Reinhart, too, invariably lost belief. Although, given her time and place, the tale had been credible enough at the outset, with the introduction of self it became fiction like all the others. She was, he had to face it, the most incredible liar he had ever met.

With a significant look at Pound, who was too bored to register it, Reinhart said: "Go on, Trudchen. What happened then?"

"Well, it was really an arm, but blown off from someone other and lodged between mine and my ripps, as if it were robbing my pocket." She placed a rolled-up stencil in the position described;

buff backing to the outside, it was a painfully authentic replica.

Her attention was now directed exclusively towards Pound, and Reinhart, in half-conscious jealousy, went to block her line of vision.

"You know what? You are a prevaricator!"

Silently, Trudchen unrolled the third arm in the enormous self-confidence the mythomaniac shares with the artist, while at the same time her round nose sharpened as if in death, as if for a moment she really tested that condition the truthful call life, and rounded again as quickly; she had been there before and did not like it.

"Stop pissing around with the kid," Pound ordered irritably. He was in a rare short mood, probably connected with the miscarriage of certain affairs of money, towards which these days he had developed an obsession. The black market had denuded him of watch, pen, pocket knife, cigarette case, lighter, ring, identification bracelet, all bedding but one blanket, all ties, shirts, drawers, undershirts, socks, and caps beyond one each, towels, writing paper, the leather frame of his wife's picture, and his musette bag. Three days earlier he had received by mail a new pipe and pouch: the latter had already metamorphosed into a paper envelope. Which he rustled in now, spilling much, but onto a page of *Yank,* which when done he coned to funnel back the overflow, his narrow eyebrows shimmering ever upwards like heat waves fleeing a summer pavement.

"Haven't you finished that guidebook yet?" he went on, with querulous twitchings. "The colonel has a wild hair in his asshole ever since Lovett's Folly. He might put us on cleaning butt cans any minute."

Because he was properly a cigarette man, he smoked a pipe the wrong way, inhaling great mortifying draughts which after a time in his innards came back through every superior aperture, mouth, nose, ears, eyes, suggesting that his head was afire.

"I'll finish it today," Reinhart answered sullenly, not unmindful of Trudchen's spectacular show of industry; she socked so loudly at the typewriter you couldn't hear the clearing of your own throat. No sooner did a third person come than he felt odd man out; his maximum for rapport was one being at a time. Thus it was fine with Pound alone, or alone with Trudchen, but with three people he invariably sensed a conspiracy against him.

"Oh good," said Pound. "If you are that close to the end, you can put the fucker aside for fifteen minutes and write me a letter to the wife. You know, this and that, etc., and I'm short on dough because we had to buy new winter uniforms this month."

"*You* short on dough?"

Pound made a sighing descent into his swivel chair. "Come over here," he said confidentially. "I don't know why I can't tell you, since you know all my other chicken-shit business. The thought of going back to that woman—the one you write for me—is more than I can stomach. You know, when I was wounded I made kind of an agreement with Fate that if I didn't die I would be somebody new. I never told this before to anybody in the service, but I used to be, before I was drafted, a bank teller for thirty-seven fifty a week, a creepy little rectum-kissing rabbit with two snot-nosed kids and a dog with some kinda skin rash that made his hair fall out in pink spots—he also used to sit around on the rug in the evening and fart all the time—and this woman, see. Well, she isn't the worst person in the world, but she is set on making a man a coward. She even wanted to scare me out of using a blowtorch to take off the old paint on the outside of the house—which I was only doing cause who can afford those prick union painters and if you hire scabs the others will come by and bomb your house—you'll start a fire, she said. And by Christ I went ahead and did it anyway, and you guessed it, it did start a fire that burned off one wall. I never missed Bob Hope's radio show on Thursday nights for five years—Professor Colonna: 'that's what I keep telling them down at the office'; Brenda and Cobina, and the rest of them. Think of that: 259 straight; once they were off because of a special news feature, something about that fucking shitbum Hitler. I tell you I was yellow as they come, but after basic they sent me to OCS where they thought that was just being cautious, I guess, a good quality for a officer. Well, we were pinned down along this hedge row in Normandy and I was dumping in my pants for fear, but still I noticed my top fly button was loose and I fastened it. And then I thought what a dirty little turd I was: with your ass about to be blown off and you button the barn door—do you get the picture? I was more afraid of my dong showing than of the German 88s. So I thought all of a sudden: World, you got twenty-eight years from me, you can keep all the rest and stick them up your giggy, and I jumped up and went across there and took that Kraut platoon, and I don't mean to say I wasn't scared, but anyway for once there was a reason. Shit."

He had puffed so hard on his pipe that already its tobacco was exhausted and the air made noxious.

"You know what I made so far on the black market? Thirteen thousand, two hundred and twenty-two dollars, and it's all gone back to the States to a bank in L.A., California. That's where my nurse Anne Lightner is from, L.A., where they go in for the beach living. I'm going to get sprung from this woman as soon as I get home, and then I'm going out there and buy a used-car lot. That's the kind of thing they go big for out there, with all that beach living. Everybody drives a car, that's what Anne says."

So was another idea exploded. It was sad, in a way, that nobody, simply nobody was what he seemed. To Reinhart, Pound had been the classic type of swashbuckler. Now he saw the late bank-clerk lines of worry and doubt, faded but still visible, at the corners of mouth and eyes, and he even liked him better for them—for daring has no unusual moral worth if you have lived with it from the cradle—yet there was no discounting the loss of something rare.

"But I have to play it cool with Alice till I get back and can defend myself," said Pound, refilling his pipe. "So write her nice. I don't have to tell you what to say, you have enough crap to snow anybody." This was admiringly put, with the quick wink he must have learned in his new life, but looking sharply Reinhart saw the hint of a quaver in it, as if, in at least the most minor part, there was still a tinge of bluff.

All the while Trudchen had been typing with fanatic energy—faking madly, for the guidebook manuscript lay on Reinhart's desk.

As he passed her on the return route, a doorknock sounded, and notwithstanding his shouted "Enter!" she leaped up and teetered to the knob—high heels, yet!

It was a soldier, for Pound. She made him wait while she proceeded to the lieutenant with a formal announcement, working her body in a queer movement which Reinhart first believed was an effort to balance on the high spikes and then recognized as an amateur version of a whore's undulations. Her breasts were hard metallic cones, yet she still wore the thin, little-girl's skirt ending an inch above the knees, and still the owlish, juvenile spectacles. Involuntarily he burst into a loud, barking laugh, which hideous though it was nobody but himself seemed to hear.

Lieutenant Schild's judgment had been correct, only a bit premature (as an Intelligence man, of course, he was expected to be one jump ahead of events); if she was not on her way to tartdom, then Reinhart was an orangutan.

"Dearest Alice," he scrawled on the yellow pad, taking in return a warm thrill of fancy that this unseen proxy wife was really his own, that he had entered her in the connubial bed and that she had borne him two small resemblances of himself, albeit snot-nosed.

On Pound's indifferent grunt Trudchen wobbled back to her table. Reinhart had also purchased the mascara which gave her an appearance of sore, fire-tinged eyes, but the high heels were from another protector, he now had no doubt.

The soldier had gone. In his stead, in the hall shadows beyond the half-open doorway stood a shrouded representation of a human figure, crepuscular, mysterious. Upon Reinhart's look it slid noiselessly out of range. Sauntering, Pound took Trudchen's typewriter from beneath her very pounding fingers, ripped out and discarded the paper, and saying "At last I found the Kraut who can fix this old machine," left.

"Darling Alice: Sweetheart, I—" Reinhart began again.

"You try alvays to hoomiliate me . . ." Trudchen's lips were fashioned into a little red crossbow, through which slid the pink bolt of her tongue, in and out, tasting the lipstick.

He threw down the pencil in disgust, said malevolently: "How about returning my pen?"

"Vy do you always do this? Because I am only this little German girl?"

He strode massively across and bruised his fist on her table: "Right now, I want that pen!"

"Oh, Gee whiz!"

Find who taught her that and you had the whoremaster: Reinhart had never said "Gee whiz" in all his life long. But the tears were her own. He had last seen them when she cursed that poor Jew for telling the truth.

"Well, Gee, take it beck again, and don't say I vas shtealing it." Engulfed by the mixture of water and words, dissolving mascara, smeared rouge, falling hairpins—for in the grief she tore her hair down into the old pigtails—she opened the middle drawer and drew away.

Reinhart came round behind her. There it lay, the old black Parker, that gallant, veteran instrument of romance and adventure on two continents, vicarious cannon, sceptre, phallus. He seized it, already feeling the brute, and when her blue eyes peeped sideways at him over their scorched rims and she said "I *opp*ologize"—by this time he had long forgotten what the beef was and took the pen merely so as to return it to her formally, as a permanent gift.

"So kind," she cried, smiling-through-tears. "Do you care for my shoes? I have yesterday traded them with the chocolate you gave me."

"*Fabelhaft!*" He stood behind her, hands lightly riding her narrow shoulders, eyes descending into the sweet crevasse of the pectoral range, very clear through the thin cloud of blouse.

"And I have somesing for you," she said, "so you will not think so bad of this little Germany."

From the drawer she withdrew a handbill of cheap European paper, weightless, the color and grain of whole-wheat bread, infamously inked. All he could read from where he stood was a headline: ES LEBE MENSCHLICHKEIT!

"Proclamation of the Resistance," she crooned victoriously. "I have found it in this very room, in the carton-boxes. Perhaps this selfsame room in which we sit was nothing but head-qvarters!"

*Long Live Humanity!,* no doubt to be understood in the sense of Hitler's Peace, a peculiar German cruelty. He received her greatest whopper with an enervation so profound as to be almost pity.

"Trudchen, I can read German . . ." he groaned, his hands rising heavily from her shoulders and more heavily returning.

"Then read!" she screamed, turning in frenzy, and his left hand traveled into her blouse at the open neck and down the breasts' warm canyon. Her mouth, open throughout the quick trans-formations of fury, fear, awe, and finally, madness, rose to his neck like the sucker of a great vampire fish surfacing from the depths of the sea, fastening to the elbow of his windpipe, so that, prohibited from breathing he fisted a tail of blonde hair and pulled as if to sever her head from the shoulders. In a mo-ment his large right arm proved stronger than small-girl lips; he had her loose and held her gaping, an interval for bullying mastery, and then turned her, brought her forward and up, the nether hand taking a purchase within her fat furrow, hot beneath cool cloth, and carried her to cover the light snow of tobacco grains on Pound's clean desk.

He had come so far in what had seemed desperate comedy, as in school when the kids steal your cap and you tolerate their passing it just out of reach until the smallest boy is the bearer and you engulf and batter him to the point at which his incipient grief takes the laugh off you. But Trudchen now had fear least of all, and laughed, herself, as one does whose will is consonant with the world's; the little witch's face in a garish disorder of evil, yet her odor was childlike, of soap.

In endless pursuit of pride, then, he became fastidious, working his way through the jungle of queer fasteners and ribbons, and the three buttons which at the crucial junction of her parts secured the last guardian triangle of doveskin fabric, beaching finally upon a little round belly incapable of further discovery.

The key in the devil's lock, *entrez monsieur, enchanté de faire votre connaissance,* excruciating, pain, pain, pleasure—well into that groove of unification where the senses are harnessed towards a single fanatical end, his suddenly lost purpose. Ah, it was all so crazy. A small window broke the wall above Pound's desk, high above—standing at full height Reinhart could just frame his face in it—and absurd, fit only for some lazy postman on stilts to pass a parcel in from the outside, to save a trip through the labyrinth. It was from this glass that he got an immaterial signal into the corner of the eye, and as if to breathe and moisten the throat, he straightened and turned his head, saw close up to the pane the feathered neck of a man who wanted a barber, Pound's; beyond and lower, a face like a contour map of an asteroid, ripped and pitted by hot chips flying off Jupiter; two had by accident embedded collaterally and, still smoking, were eyes: ostensibly directed at Pound, but seeing him, knowing him and what he was at, not caring, not even amused, but knowing. The old German, now named: Sweetheart. In exchange for the typewriter he presented a thick wad of notes. Pound buttoned them in an upper pocket and, one-breasted like an Amazon, vanished.

"*Mein Tiger!*" whispered Trudchen. Looking down, melting, Reinhart felt rather than saw he had unwittingly been a success. He had also forgotten all precautions, and swift through his mind like an Army documentary ran the series of awful upshots.

"*Ach,*" said Trudchen, yet hypersensitive, opposing partition, "I have taken care . . ." Not knowing to what she referred, he accepted her assurance.

Crumpled in her fist, the old handbill, taken in surprise like everything else, was still their partner. He tore it from her and read the first line below the bold title, read it twice as with his unoccupied hand he returned himself to order. It did not change: "The appeal of Hitlerism is to the eternal *Schweinhund* in man." Of course it was anti-Nazi; no matter by whom or where, it had been produced in honor and conscience and at cost, and its anonymous author, if he had eluded his compatriot enemies, had lived perhaps only to drown in the same foreign flood that swamped them.

He kissed her, long and exploratory, for the first time, and saying "Ah, I must be crazy, anyone could have walked in," he burst away, she moaning in the sudden isolation. He ran through the French window and around the corner, and saw that Schatzi had not, because of his heavy burden, got farther than the public sidewalk.

Schatzi accepted the inevitable cigarette and slipped it between his ear and the drooping rim of the workman's cap that with neckerchief and soiled jacket and weary trousers formed his present costume, which he would surely have had trouble in selling to a naked man.

"Do you need some conversation?" he asked, with a tremble of his nose, "or is it simply generosity? Excuse my lack of strength."

He placed the typewriter upon the octagonal stones of the sidewalk. No sooner was it done than a woman rode by on the adjacent bicycle path and they felt the slipstream of her passing.

"Into the mechanism no doubt this blew some sand," said Schatzi, his voice like a dumping of gravel. "So much longer to clean!" He elevated his hands in a Jewish shrug, and while the right one was up, put out a finger and ran it across his upper lip, making a gargoyle mouth.

Seeing him now in reality and close-up, Reinhart could not doubt his girl friends' tales were true: if Schatzi were not from the concentration camp, then that establishment was illusion. True, he was more than mere skin, but give an unfilled pelt a few months' meals and you would have Schatzi. He lived, but just lived and no more, with not one breath beyond the essential. His face was dreadful, romantically hideous, in the ugliness only supreme virtue permits, perhaps creates, as with the old saints; and though his angles were sharp, his constant tremble blurred and made them remote.

Confronted with this overwhelming authenticity, Reinhart on the instant forgot his purpose and, instead of speaking, sent a grin. He watched Schatzi catch it, warp it with the secret they shared, and send it back.

"Your breathing is labored," he said. "Exercise shortens the span of life. He lives most long who lies in one place without movement, like a piece of warm bacon, all his life long, *ja?*"

"I never thought of that," answered Reinhart. It seemed so marvelously reasonable; he put from his mind the obvious reference to the tumble with Trudchen and worried about the years gone in nailing down his coffin with a barbell. He had never before talked with an authority on mortality—who yet, he saw with a happy loss of trepidation, was also a human being, whose smile was only superficially diabolic.

For a great sweetness was exuded by Schatzi's hard person as he suddenly stared into Reinhart's face and said: "You wish to send me on a qvest, *ja?* She told me, this little piece of sausage, this Gretchen—"

"Trudchen."

"*So.* You search for your kinfolk—this is correct, 'kinfolk' or simply 'kin'?"

So close was he, perhaps by reason of defective hearing, he almost climbed Reinhart's frame. It was disconcerting, especially since Reinhart judged from his clothing that he must stink and drew always away, until on the fifth circle of their patch of walk he envisioned how from a distance their two figures must look in revolution and permitted himself to be captured. He had been quite wrong: Schatzi put forth the distinct odor of eau-de-cologne.

"Wwwwell," said Schatzi, "you have come to the right potty. "Ve vill"—successful pronunciation of the first *w* satisfied him in perpetuity—"simply look for all the Reinharts who are not yet dead and there you are!" He actually winked, which is to say one eye was swallowed whole by the lids, like a ravenous bird ingesting a black cherry.

Impossible to think the concentration camps had not been serious; therefore what Reinhart saw before him now was the human triumph, a wit which had faced the dreadful and survived, no cloistered humor like his own. He himself was suffering depression, feeling wet and dirty and unusually exposed, and indeed, since Schatzi had taken the initiative he was no longer interested in his own mission.

"I don't want to remind you of your troubles," he said, though of course he did, "but would you say the concentration camp was the worst thing that could be imagined?"

If Schatzi had earlier been ebullient, he now went into a positive delight that Reinhart, because he had no experience of the world, found very grisly.

"Ah, no, no, not the worst! The worst, my young friend, is to die. Just that simple. Two added to two makes four, always. The living and the dying, and nothing else, makes ray-oll-ity."

So Reinhart, conscious it was asinine but getting no other suggestions, gave him another cigarette. Which went behind the other ear.

"Now you must tell me an answer," Schatzi said. "Why must you find these relatives? Of course," he went on before Reinhart could speak, "to help them. You Amis are a decent lot. You do not become happy to see anyone starve, let by themselves relations of blood, *ja?* This gives one faith for the future of the world in your hands."

Hard as Reinhart looked among the rocks which clicked together in Schatzi's voice, he could find no insincerity, therefore he stifled the impulse to say "Horseshit!" He had at last, there could be no mistake this time, found the man with a right to say anything and it be valid. Not even Bach and not even Lori, not even when he had learned their truth, had so impressed him.

"I'd think you would hate the Germans."

"I hate them? My friend, *I am myself a German.*" Saying which Schatzi bent to the typewriter, on the way down adjusting his cap, the crown of which was dark with oil. Someone had borrowed his tie to hang a felon and returned it with a frozen knot that would never undo; no doubt he had it wired to his collar or to that frail armature on which his pennyworth of skin was hung.

A marvel that he could pick up such a weight. Reinhart moved to aid him but was waved off.

"But one detail—"

"Of course." In this regard Reinhart never admitted another as master. He produced his wallet and counted off five hundred-mark notes, fifty dollars, from the wad of five thousand which Marsala had got from a Russian soldier for Reinhart's graduation watch.

"I didn't mean you to do this for nothing."

"Now," said Schatzi, "you have shamed me with your generosity. Ray-olly, I cannot—" He drew from his pocket a brilliant blue handkerchief and snorted into it, thin and airy like a fife badly played. He took the money. "This is not what I purposed to say—which at any pace, I have now forgotten."

Reinhart watched him go down the walk with his burden. Twenty feet away, he turned and shouted, "You shall hear of me!" And then he moved off the pavement into the trees, where he spat fiercely and vanished.

Reinhart had neglected to give him his grandfather's name! Hot on the trail he ran, through the patch of forest to the wide prospect of Argentinische Allee, and surveyed the feasible directions. But Schatzi was gone.

# CHAPTER 13

SCHILD's father's business was concerned with buttons—well, you know how capitalism works on the petty levels, he neither made them nor used them, but stood in the middle between maker and user, collecting a profit.

Lichenko, however, did not know these things, which was why he asked. He was especially interested in the money: were the earnings large from such a trade?

"He never thought so," said Schild. "But they were considerably better than working-class wages." His smile was both bitter and genial—the first towards the distasteful topic; the second for Lichenko, to whose will he was now committed.

"Oh, but the workers, we will not speak of them," Lichenko said contemptuously. "You surely are of a superior class." This was the kind of thing he had been saying, in one way or another, for three days, and Schild could not yet gauge the degree of its subtlety.

Lichenko closed his eyes now and breathed profoundly, as if he were falling off. Sometimes he did; sometimes, after the same indications, not. The game hinged on whether or not Schild rose to go: if he did, Lichenko awakened; if he did not, Lichenko slept.

The bed was a chaos of stale sheets decorated with brown blood and streaks of St. George's iodine salve. Lichenko had not left it since they laid him there on the night of the beating. Not that he had been seriously hurt: his actual wounds—a slash of the cheek, an abrasion of the lower lip—had, after the excitement was done, proved superficial. The rest were bruises, ugly, indigo-and-lavender, but bruises, and had already begun to pale under the application of St. George's paste. And he had been

197

struck only in the face, so that his body was as sound as ever and could have no special need for this perpetual pillowing.

Yet there he lay, sometimes straight and stiff as a corpse, suppressing breath; sometimes curled like a foetus, in which position he made bubbly noises; sometimes with limbs wanton and torn mouth wearing a wan, roguish smile, as if he had dropped there exhausted from a saturnalia.

Schild felt towards him a strange, new emotion: not, as in the case of Schatzi, loathing compounded of fear and envy, and certainly not the fierce hatred which was the sudden motive for the beating—indeed, the latter had been transformed in his memory to a distant episode involving two strangers who bore no resemblance to the Lichenko and the self he knew. Rather, this strange new feeling was the sad, sour regret of a father towards an offspring he can neither endure nor discard. He would have liked, in a moment when his own back was turned, to have had him obliterated in some bloodless, painless fashion, with no noise.

His blows had pierced the mask. He at last faced that issue he had hitherto obscured with romantic moralizing. Lichenko had originally stayed on at the billet to grovel in comfort like a pig in a slough, although admittedly deserved. But the fact of his second breach of peace indicated not all of him had yet gone soft. The fine, progressive elements in his conscience had rebelled against the ease, not with sufficient force to carry him back to duty, but at least enough to generate a protest, which appropriately had been directed towards the German woman. At that point a deft understanding might have restored him to manhood. Instead, Schild had pushed him back again, perhaps forever beyond redemption.

But in destroying him, he had also cemented Lichenko to himself. If his earlier hosthood, which he recognized as having been too permissive, owed to simple courtesy, it had since the beating become a nurseship, bonded by the obligations of guilt and limited by nothing. He found it ethically impossible even to object when Lichenko, who certainly could walk as well as ever, preferred the bedpan to the bathroom, and that only when transported by Schild—he would not suffer the *Hausfrau* in the room. Although at other times he showed great facility in bed-positions—the ass mountain, the pretzel, the scissors, the beached fish, the dismembered Osiris, the solipsist ostrich—at mealtime Lichenko would not elevate from absolute supine, so that there was nothing to do but spoon-feed him like an infant. His back itched fiercely every quarter-hour and would admit no cure but the application of Schild's hairbrush, wielded by Schild, to the trough of his spine.

The problem of washing, which offended Schild most, even more than the bedpan, had been rather more simply resolved: Lichenko left it behind when he took to invalidism. A person, he believed, did not get dirty in bed. With the passing of the days, his decision seemed less fortunate. After three, in a room from which Lichenko also had decided to bar fresh air on the ground that in his weakened condition he might contract a disease of the lungs, Schild had ceased to dread, might even in two more days have come to yearn, the call for soap and water.

Naturally, a man in sickbed needed recreation. Lichenko required an oral reading of each day's *Stars and Stripes*, first in the original—so that he could "study English"—and then in German translation. The comics were to be read with full gesture and if possible in voices simulating the spirit and sex of each character, especially the female ones, like Miss Lace and Daisy Mae, to whom it was impossible to give credence if they spoke in baritone. Furthermore, it was cruelly difficult to understand the narrative without a sense of what had gone before—before, that is, Lichenko had come West—synopses must be furnished, and definitions. For example, who really was Skeezix? A typical American? A character to identify with, or one to hold in *secret* contempt? He insisted grimly on *secret*: one was not so stupid as to think you could sneer openly at a feature of an official Army publication.

After the reading came the cards—he claimed to be too weak nowadays for chess—which Lichenko scattered across the foul sheets in Russian arrangements, for games that three hours hence Schild would savvy no better than at the outset except to know he was loser and must pay, the fee being invariably fifty marks, arrived at by a computation as exotic as the game.

Nursing his patient of course demanded more time than Schild's Army duties would allow, and no one was quicker to see this than St. George, as soon as the morning after the beating.

"Oh Nate," he said, looking away, for he could not have met Schild's eye with anything but reproach, and he was the soul of tolerance, "Nate, take a few days off to look after the little fellow."

Conjure with this: a captain of Intelligence, the commanding officer of a unit of the United States Army, a career officer—he still had never inquired why Lichenko was a guest in the first place. One kind of charge placed against the revolutionary by the voices of petrifaction, was arrogance: 'He asks us to believe that he, and he alone, knows the Way, and if we do not admit this, he will not admit that we are fellow human beings.' Schild had read that somewhere long ago, had banned its source from his memory—very likely some renegade, they were always eloquent; of course if he wished he read them, too, he was no Catholic with an Index—but afterwards carried its indictment with him, like a pocket rule, speaking to it on occasion: You talk of arrogance, you, in your arrogant assumption that we suppress all doubt; we at least have the humility to abandon our selves.

He asked it now: And what of St. George, *l'homme moyen sensual,* could there be a more ruthless overbearing than that on which his bovine assurance was fixed? In his mood Schild held it outrageous that St. George had not that first morning after Lovett's party turned in Lichenko to the MPs as a deserter from the Red Army. Which was his clear duty, the Yalta Agreement standing as witness. Indeed, St. George could be court-martialed for malfeasance of office, were it known, and reduced to his permanent rank of PFC or whatever was the breath-taking altitude to which he had mounted in the fifteen years before Pearl Harbor.

Thus as always, Schild in his deliberations surrendered to irony, the only weapon whose victories were won exclusively from its wielder, the sword with which the Jews, like Samurai, disembowel themselves to spite their enemies. He knew now, in retroactive projection, that he had always known Lichenko was a deserter, even as early as that first rap on Lovett's door, and in full cognizance encouraged him in the defection. He, Schild, was a traitor; he denounced himself in the dock, took himself to the cellar, shot a revolver into the base of his own skull, and did not weep over the loss of one more counterrevolutionary.

Who wept for a Jew? He derived from the question a brutal, hurting pleasure, of the kind one feels as a child, scratching an itch till it bleeds. And whether it was the pain, the pleasure, or the warmth of blood that gave him courage to press on, on he went with sharp nails through the soft flesh and webbed sinews to the nerve core. In twenty-eight years, among the regiments of shadows which had come and gone, wearing whatever badge of unit—no matter whether Star-of-David or even hammer and sickle; no matter whether in love or hatred, sympathy or suspicion—he had met one man alone who did not treat him as a Jew.

Who would weep for a Jew? *Lichenko would not.* Deserter, drunkard, schnorrer, leech, to the undeluded eye he was a compound of the baser failings—indeed he was what Schild's father had always predicted Schild himself would grow up to be—and very likely a liar as well, for when a man is one thing, it is natural to suppose he completes the series, and it seemed appropriate to Schild, perhaps desirable, that Lichenko had not been a valiant warrior, either, but was rather a coward wearing counterfeit or stolen medals. If he would grant him all, he must begin by giving him nothing.

The final solution will have arrived that day on which one man admits to another that he is a Jew and the second neither laughs nor draws his revolver nor melts in feigned, or more dreadful yet, authentic sympathy, but rather collapses in boredom—as Lichenko at the party indicated he might if Schild said another word on the subject. In Lichenko's egocentric vision he knew now that he had never been more, or less, than a host fat for the parasiting, a mere object, a thing to be used, not comrade nor ally, not even a man—*and therefore not a Jew.*

Lichenko was the new man who had sprung, unarmed, from the forehead of the Idea, with no chains, no history, and a concern only for himself, the product of a proposition that worked. Never say that new kinds of creation are impossible; if you can build a bridge, you can make a man with the sensibility of a bridge, without debts, incapable of guilt, and lacking all purpose beyond his immediate function—and therefore neither a Jew nor interested in one. It had been worth the effort, was Schild's thought, and the thought was also new: for not one moment of his service had he sought any manner of payment, any proximate hope.

One day in August 1939, Ribbentrop's plane descended on Moscow, where the airport building flew the swastika and the band played the Horst Wessel Song, Molotov called fascism a matter of taste, and Stalin signed the pact with Hitler. In New York, Schild straightaway joined the Party. Truth is never literal: he was already a member for some months, and his first response to the Pact was a suicide of all that was not his body.

'If a universal proposition is true, the particular which stands under it is also true; but if the universal is false, the particular may or may not be true.' The merciless clarity of the Greek logic; before it, the Hebraic superstitions were quaintly impotent.

If you say A, you must also say B. Those who are not with us
are against us. What does it matter, said Lenin, how the chicken
is carved, so long as it is finally in pieces?

Alternatives to these were the Munich Agreement; Roosevelt
in his wheel chair; the furniture of the Seder—roasted egg, bitter
herbs, piece of bone, eye of newt and toe of frog, wool of bat
and tongue of dog, presided over by Schild's father, an unbe-
liever; and millions of weak little Jews chanting the *Kaddish* for
the dead. Now they could pray for the latest corpses, those "antifascists" who fled this Party and its compact with the devil.

Schild would stay. And he did not simply stay but joined,
took that second breath to which all earlier belonging was mere
apprenticeship. For a cause, a real cause, a man first forsakes all
others to become one; and then, if he has the true vocation,
denies the one to become many. First gives up women, if he is
a monk, and then gives up the desire for women; if a Nazi, first
tolerates the murder of the Jews, and then after that second
breath, himself shoots the revolver.

If a Communist . . . the only virtue Schild would grant himself
was that in his internal dialogues he never lied: that was for the
liberals. Certainly the NKVD, like the Gestapo, pays its call
without warning, in the small hours; surely "we" have our concentration camps, our dictator, our elite, our peculiar truth
which denies the witness of the uninstructed eye, and if your
métier is opposition to the regime, you did no better to migrate
to the Worker's Homeland than had you tried it with Hitler. We
wish to hear no exotic points of view; we will not suffer variety;
our conscience, too, is corporate. Now we have entered into a
pact with what we so much resemble in our means that the
cowards and opportunists can cry: all enemies of "decency" are
together in one basket.

We do not cavil: it is precisely your "decency," a world in
chains, that we would destroy, and if Hitler can hasten its end,
he will be used until history is ready to fling him aside. The

difference between us and you is that we will do anything to prevail; between us and Hitler, that *we are right*.

Thus had Schild accepted reality. In the destructive element, immerse! To create that future life in which there will be no separations of one man from another, which is to say that time when no one is a Jew real or symbolic, when all the old rises and falls are planed away and men are simply man and he a stranger to passion, one must first, in the now, act upon the reverse of that vision, be separate—be a Jew, that is, in extremis; if necessary, as it was, ally with an anti-Semite.

Schild's progress had not been easy, or of short duration, and whether the end was serene he did not know, to date not having reached it. In particular, he was corrupted by a special feeling towards the Germans, throughout and in spite of the ideological transformations. With Hitler's invasion of the USSR the pact of course fell from memory. From then until the final victory was apparent, the eye was shifted from sharp focus on fascism-versus-the-Socialist-ideal to the less demanding *Gestalt* of Germans-against-humanity, the latter represented most crucially by the Russian people, who incidentally had a government which tried new things but was essentially a Slavic branch of that general democracy now menaced by barbarism.

True, to the professionals Nazism was still finance capital in the last terrible flush before death, and the Western Powers, temporarily useful, were the same thing not yet so far advanced that they themselves knew it. Nazism was fascism and fascism, capitalism; nowhere was the specific quality of Germanness material. And no sooner did the Red Army take Berlin than it erected its billboards: The Hitlers Come and Go, But the German People Remain.

Insofar as the populace had connived with the Nazis they had seriously erred and must not now resent their rightful punishment by the Soviet troops. But more important, what was past was past and the future stretched out bright and grand, offering that great opportunity which so seldom comes to a people: to start out new, from nothing. Crushed and smoking lay everywhere at foot the best evidence of the failure of all hitherto existing societies. The Germans were wrong, and guilty—guilty of following an extreme reactionary in his mad-dog assault on the Socialist homeland—but were neither fundamentally maddog themselves (for peoples can be misguided but are never bad) nor in any way hopeless of reclamation; indeed, by so simple a measure as prompt adherence to the correct ideology they could enter immediate partnership with the Soviet Union itself, as magnanimous in victory as it was invincible in war.

A historical crisis, admittedly, capitalism being done in by its inherent contradictions—yet why Germany? No, excuse me, that is of course understood: the most advanced capitalist country of Europe; inevitably the agony would there have its nucleus. But why the one peculiar feature. Why the Jews?

To answer the first question is not to need the second: in its desperation, crumbling capitalism will seek a scapegoat on whom to hang its failure. As simple as that, comrade, nothing Dostoyevskian—unless you will admit that Dostoyevsky, too, was a by-product of the social decay preceding the Revolution—and above all do not quote me Heine: "It is indeed striking, the deep affinity between these two ethical nations, Jews and old Germans. This affinity has no historical origin . . . basically the two people are so similar that one might regard the Palestine of the past as an Oriental Germany . . ."

With full respect to all cultures and races, comrade—after all, it was Lenin who with the brilliant collaboration of Stalin, always the foremost of his colleagues, drew up that system by which for the first time in history Russia's many and diverse subnational cultures live today in peace and harmony, each with its own autonomous state, including even the Volga Germans (unfortunately the presence of certain fascist agents provocateurs and counterrevolutionaries concealed among the predominantly loyal mass of the latter made necessary certain rearrangements when the area was threatened by the Hitlerite invasion, and the patriotic Volga Germans themselves requested to be transported elsewhere in the Soviet Union, which plea was granted; a far cry from the concentration camps to which the Nisei were sent in America). With full respect to all cultures, comrade, and to their interesting and colorful traditions each of which symbolizes some old socio-economic thesis or antithesis, it is fruitless and perhaps heretical to stagnate with the past. Not what peoples have been but what they will be, is our sole concern.

Hatred of the Germans, therefore, is not valid, and if persisted in might become a dangerous malady. Similarly with the obsession that one is a Jew, which incorrectly puts too much stress on two delusions: (1) that Jews are that important, and (2) that oneself is.

By the Central Committee in his own skull, then, the first, the last, and the most ruthless of the Party's disciplinary boards, Schild had long before the arrival of Lichenko been granted only one more chance to rectify his errors. Had there been a thousand, he now realized, he would have spoiled them all, because he was not, and could never be, pure, adamant, resolute, unilateral; that is, could not be a Lenin. Lenin was not a Jew.

But Trotsky—yes, regard that classic example, that bright needle of a Jewish mind and its corrosion from pride, which is a Christian sin. And Milton Grossman, who at twenty-five had collected no excess in his passage through the world, who had seemed only a disembodied conscience and a pair of black eyes fixed on a morning horizon. He was to leave for Spain on a tramp merchantman of which he would say no more than that it sailed soon from Halifax. In his room behind the shop he had packed the knapsack which yet bore the symbol of the Boy Scouts of America. The irony of this had been funny, and Schild laughed, but then seeing that Milton did not, he knew it was no irony, which is the tension between the way things are and the way they are imagined, but rather another marker on Milton's undeviating and dedicated road.

Schild, too, had been a scout, in the same troop. It had of course degenerated by his time—bullying by the patrol leaders, petty thefts in the tents at the Alpine camp, obscene language and practices—Milton, with his thirty-six merit badges, was by then only a distant legend, and it meant nothing to the others that Schild was his friend. Not until years later did Schild come to know that at the arrival of the Miltons, too, the *grosse Männer,* the troop is always in decay—and falls again upon their passing from the scene, because without a constant image of strength before their eyes men, or boys, see nothing.

At nineteen, Schild was big enough to go to Spain himself, that is, old enough and large enough in size to be in his first year at City College, to sit through purposeless lectures, to sign petitions and stand with a claque at anti-fascist rallies and peace movements and enlist in involved conspiracies to stop the Socialist candidates for student council, to study the terrain of the essential American ground: folk songs, baseball, comic strips— and to report at four o'clock each afternoon to the squalid office which his father kept on Broadway just above the northern boundary of Union Square, there to involve himself for two and a half hours in the commerce of buttons.

But he was not big enough to go to Spain. It was characteristic of his friend that Milton did not suggest it. What we admire in those who stand above us is their assurance that they do, truly, see over our heads. He had similarly never suggested that Schild join the Young Communist League, never indeed that he so much as become intellectually a Marxist. Milton went towards the truth, the true was the necessary, follow if you will. Of the pre-Marxian thinkers Milton's favorites were the Stoics, whom he had read as a college freshman and shared with Schild, then on the bottom rung of high school and still a simple idolator of athletes and a noisy drinker of cokes at Mrs. Grossman's counter.

"Fate leads the willing and drags the unwilling by the neck. *But they both go.*"

It was the first genuine idea that Schild had ever heard, and its function in his *Bildung* was that upon its movement he had twice passed from adolescence into maturity. The second time—and not a piece with his second breath of commitment to the Party, because it both pre- and post-dated that event, had really no fixed duration, continued still—his second transformation began when he understood its heresy.

Milton Grossman died in Spain, in July 1937. As to the means of his death there could be no question; this was one of the rare times the fact followed from the simple conditions of time, place, character. He had achieved the herohood for which his progress through twenty-five years, from Washington Heights to a Catalan field, had been apprenticeship. And so it was assumed, without the spelling out, for reports were necessarily fragmentary and cryptic, the Lincoln Brigade was outside the law of the country of its origin, and Spain under its cumulus of gunsmoke lay three thousand miles across the sea.

Another year, and someone was returned, or someone knew someone who had come back, who knew someone in Valencia who had seen Milton in the hospital, felled by tetanus, and since the shortage of serum was notorious. . . . Yet the achievement was not diminished; Byron, who had gone to fight for Greek liberty, died of meningitis, and the shorter literary dictionaries, with no space for elaboration, read: "died, for the freedom of Greece, Missolonghi, 1824."

. . . but what did those rarer reference books on the shelf of some terrible agency tell of Grossman, Milton? "Found guilty of Trotskyist wrecking. Liquidated." "Executed after investigation uncovered his role in the conspiracy of the Fascist gang known as P.O.U.M." "Agent provocateur in the pay of Franco. Sentence carried out, July 1937." Or perhaps only a sparrow-track of cypher. The world had not become more cruel since

Byron, but its truths were more devious, less capable of proof, yet, for all that, truer. The real story of Byron, the *concrete* one—a term of Milton's for a quality he always sought beneath the capitalist veil of lies—might be of another order, the mission to Greece a shabby quest of ego, a Trotskyism of that time, and who knew but what the meningitis were some Aesopian code-name for the 'control of disorderly elements'?

But surely it was unprecedented that at home a friend dare not speak his name. For Schild naturally had gone with his questions to those who returned. The cause had been lost and they were weary and older than their years, but they were also proud and illuminated with what could only be called the sad joy of men who have wet their comradeship in blood. They sang fierce, exuberant songs, were curt, succinct, yet eloquent in a language which was properly half-alien to the beneficiaries of their sacrifice.

But for Milton Grossman not even Spanish idiom would serve. There had not, to their memory, ever been such a person, or if there had, no doubt he was overlooked in the terrible struggle against the open fascists on the other side of no-man's-land and the *fifth columnists behind our own lines.*

Of course Schild knew of the wreckers, the anarchists, the hirelings of Trotsky, those worst of all enemies because they are one's own kind, who extend a hand as comrades and with the other clasp their dagger. The greatness of a cause can be measured by the decadence of its adversaries; we can be proud of the very rottenness of those we have cast out. For all their mumbo-jumbo, and all matters of clerical fascism aside, the Catholics have a valid principle: he who embraces the incorrect faith in ignorance may be saved; only he who knows the true faith and rejects it is certain to be damned. It could never be said that Milton Grossman was ignorant; like Trotsky he was all mind, his mind all blade, and that all edge, the Jewish edge . . . and behind it, the abysmal weakness.

To continue the inquiry was to make oneself suspect. And needlessly—for Schild asked the questions only to test the answers already in his possession. No doubt the flaw had always been there, waiting for the day when the force of concrete, historical events would burst it wide. But it had been the earlier Milton in whom Schild had seen the Way, who had armed him with the weapons. There was ironical justice, but justice, in turning them now against the too-competent teacher. And his oddest feeling was that in so doing he did Milton an honor greater than he deserved; that in the measure of its being undeserved, Milton would be pleased; that, finally, he deserved to be pleased.

It was then, when he thought of Milton, though dead, though discredited, though renegade, as someone still to be taken into account, that Schild realized his sole defense against insanity was the Party. The acceptance of one's own complicity in the Party's crimes was the only escape from knowing oneself a criminal. Fate leads the willing and drags the unwilling by the neck: ostensibly Greek, but how much closer to the long, moaning servitude of the Jews, with whom in the end Milton chose to identify.

For he had written Schild one letter from Spain, a strange letter, in the early spring of '37. Strange even for Milton, who was more talker than writer—"like Sophocles, Jesus of Nazareth, and Hitler," as he used to say in his Bren-gun voice and then stop to catch breath before throwing it away again, eyes rising through an atmosphere of mixed slyness and purity, "all seekers of oral gratification; you will notice none of us smoked. *O vanitas!*"—and hence never wrote proper letters but rather short scrawls discontinuous in thought and calligraphy, on whatever surface lay at hand and could be mailed, cigarette packages, cereal boxtops, the reverse of one's own note to him; and in Spain, until now, no letters at all.

This one was pencil, on an unbleached, glazed strip, serrated across the midsection, of—Spanish toilet paper. "If I should not be at large by next Yom Kippur, read this." On the religious holidays in New York, Milton's observance was, dragging Schild along, to go to some lunch counter and stuff himself with pork; his ambition at twenty had been to lay a girl between afternoon and evening prayers on the Day of Atonement; he had never yet done this, he said, because he could not determine which was the greater sin, to screw a Jewish girl or to commit racial shame with a shiksah, for which he used the Nazi term *Rassenschande*. Once on that day, sitting on a bench in the middle island of Broadway, watching the promenaders in their best clothes, he said: "When at last the Messiah comes, he will be an anti-Semite."

The letter therefore fell within the known context, had besides the familiar mordant-shading-into-mortuary wit, the *Galgenhumorische* pun like Mercutio's: if I should not be *at large,* that is, if I should not be a *gross Mann;* he anticipated his death. Then followed a translated quotation from a Hebrew religious poem of the eleventh century. He had returned to God. Small wonder he could not have made that candid.

But an old mutual admiration of theirs had been Poe's "Purloined Letter" and Dupin's theory of deception, which he explains by a game of puzzles played upon a map. One player requires his opponent to find the name of a certain town. A novice will invariably choose the "most minutely lettered names; but the adept selects such words as stretch, in large characters, from one end of the chart to the other. These, like the over-largely lettered signs and placards of the street, escape observation by being excessively obvious."

It was a faith that Milton spoke of, but rather one lost than another gained:

> . . . thou didst vouchsafe to give me a perfect creed, to believe that thou art the God of Truth and thy prophets are true, and when thou didst not place my portion among

those who rise up and rebel against thee; among the foolish
people who blaspheme thy name; who deride thy law;
chide thy servants, and deny the truth of thy prophets.
They assume innocence, but underneath is deceit; they
make a show of a pure and clean soul, whilst the bright
spots of the leper are concealed underneath . . . SOLOMON
BEN GABIROL, *died Valencia, c. 1057*

Lichenko stayed. To keep him was to abet a desertion from
the Soviet Union. To turn him in was an admission that the
hideous sacrifices which had gone into his making were not
finally criminal, but useless. Milton had never been able to forgive a confusion of the two.

# CHAPTER *14*

LICHENKO stayed. And in that staying Schild ironically discovered a focus for that energy he had ever kept on call against the grand mission. For he was, or had been, a romantic, a man to whom time now and past were ancillary to time's end, and while he saw history as a continuous process and within that process himself as nothing, with the other eye he looked on the personal life as a series of choices culminating in an absolute, a supreme of either victory or martyrdom, a storming of some Winter Palace or a fell day like that in 1933 when the Gestapo was unleashed on the German Communist Party.

Instead, his future had arrived in the form of—Lichenko; and time had stopped. Schatzi, who for all his shrewdness had not known of Lichenko until the beating, for all his eccentricity was a good Communist and had made his report; and what he, for all his hatefulness yet a hero of the camps, thought of the newest traitor did not figure in Schild's reveries so markedly as that Schatzi's long-held, unjust, fantastic suspicions of him had been confirmed and, finally, that, for the first time personally liable for an actual crime, he felt less guilt than serenity and lacked absolutely the sense of being hunted.

And most corrupt, his sense of humor had despite his efforts to brook it begun to prevail over the conscience. Lichenko's invalidism had required only his attendance to be supremely ludicrous—to be, in fact, lunatic. Objectively the situation was simply a Russian slob nursed by a nervous Jew; the first was not ill, but the second was; and since each in his present arrangement was necessary to the other in just that condition, both were mad.

Or perhaps only Schild was, for he noticed that Lichenko

these days never laughed; indeed, since entering into permanent
bed, and despite his abominable appearance, he had developed a
dignified gravity which one who knew only the earlier Lichenko
would have believed impossible. One lunchtime when, carrying
the loaded tray and an under-arm burden of newspapers and
magazines, Schild had difficulty at the door, Lichenko sprang
from the sheets to his relief, showing not only vigor but incredible strength for so small a man: he took the heavy tray in one
hand and the papers in the other and, studying *Life's* cover tit-
girl as he went, walked silently, stately, to the bed as if it were
the high altar in St. Basil's and he Patriarch; and immediately
upon reclining was again the man so infirm that Schild must
needs not only spoon the mashed potatoes into his mouth but
also support his head simultaneously. Lunacy, to be sure, but
Lichenko's were not so much the doings of a lunatic—Schild
realized, as he heard himself laughing without accompaniment
from his patient—as those of a sane man who is humoring a
lunatic.

Similarly, Lichenko of an evening had invented a new amusement. He had fallen off his taste for public reading and even for
cards. As to the former, he had been disillusioned by the knowledge that Skeezix lived in time, more or less relative to the
limited days of actual people, had years ago at the beginning of
the story been a baby, was now in his twenties, would grow old.
Since fictional persons are a lie to begin with, he said, they are
only interesting if they stick to it and do not pretend to have the
dull troubles of real people; otherwise you did better to have
true stories, which of course are always boring but then don't
pretend not to be. Like—he broke off to peer at Schild in a kind
of suspicion and remark that it was possible he, Schild, would
not agree, and immediately launched an attack on L'il Abner
from the opposing ground: nobody could tell him an American
peasant acted in that fashion.

As to the cards, it was immoral to win from a man ignorant of
the game; had he known that at the outset he would not have

played; he might even return the winnings, as he was not a *gengster*, unless—again he stopped abruptly as if to give prominence to his expression, which was this time a sneer; one so broad, however, that surely its purpose was rather mock than serious. And again Schild laughed, and again Lichenko's face returned to wood.

Conversation appeared as the new entertainment. It was hardly more, being Lichenko's questions and Schild's answers; but it was not less, and since Schild had never known speech could be employed for amusement, at least not by him—he had listened to Milton; in both the Party and the Army the human sound was used only to assent to orders from above and command what lay below; to St. George it was the minimum of small-talk to get rid of him; his parents and sister had been great talkers in disregard of the defenseless tympanum, which was why he was not—since his voice had no resonance in this small room with the peaked ceiling which in the corners joined the wall a scant five feet above the floor, crowded with furniture and now with the warm congestion of dependent humanity; although Lichenko was not ill, it *did* make a difference to him that Schild was there to serve—these were reasons enough, if still morally inadmissible, why he should enjoy their mutual discourse.

But more important was the fact that after the initial ten minutes at Lovett's they had never really talked. An ordinary citizen of the Soviet Union, that person who to an American existed only in theory, he had had one under his roof for three weeks and never yet found the propitious moment to ask: what is it like, the experience of that citizenship? Indeed, to place the query was not only an opportunity but, in the present context, an obligation, just as in Party circles in America one was under the reverse imperative *not* to question the mysterious figures who were manifestly Russian but carried passports bearing names like T. Smith.

Before the beating, Lichenko had obviously never been in the mood for talk; he had been eating, or sleeping, or washing, or scratching, or hanging over magazines or the chessboard; and that was the answer to the question never asked: there was no question about life in the USSR, it was life with incessant activity and without doubt, and even a deserter from it, one who could not meet its demands, yet carried with him its energy. In his very exploitation of Schild, Lichenko honored his society: a bourgeois gone bad would not have had the guts to go so far.

As to the other question—why had he deserted?—the science of dialectics admitted no such concern; Schild was not permitted to receive it into his mind; a person was either this or that; if that, he should either be ignored or destroyed; the alternative, if one did neither of these, was to relate it to the fact that oneself was lost. And this Schild had already done.

Now that conversation had finally come, it was appropriately on the theme of, not Lichenko, but Schild; not on the simple deserter but on the more complex; and Lichenko's half of it was so shrewd that Schild briefly considered whether after all he had not been wrong about him.

According to Schild's wristwatch—which was strapped to Lichenko's bony arm, having been the stake in one last game of cards before the no-gaming resolution went into effect—the time measured seven in the evening. The tray had been washed and lay gleaming on the dressertop, against next morning's breakfast time when it would vanish briefly to reappear heavy with eggs, melting yellow in the centers, and oatmeal porridge slushed with milk and sugar; in the end compartment, two pieces of white bread, thick as bricks, coated so lavishly with golden butter you could not lift them without smearing your fingers, which was as pleasant a sensation as running your hands over a woman, and though he knew that with this abundance the Americans had developed a culture of eating—it was some old law or another that when there was overproduction on the one hand and a shortage of markets on the other, a society tried to fill the gap with elaborate manners—and while he approved of this whole lovely ensemble of errors, he could not forbear from licking his hands. And Nathan made no objection.

That, indeed, was Schild's reaction to all of life, so far as Lichenko could see, and he wondered again why a man with such tolerance would join a band of evil thugs whose only difference from the other group just defeated lay in the latter's being German. Although there were German Communists, too, and surely many among them who were but lately Nazis, and wait and see if it was not exactly those who were raised to power in the East Sector. Ah, Nathan, you fool!, you who were rightly so quick to act when Vasya disgraced your house, in the big things you are truly like the silly comic strips you so dearly love to read. Look into the mirror and you will see the living Small Abner.

Though not hurt (and it was an awful strain to continue to pretend he had been; actors justly earned higher wages than a fellow who operated a lathe); although in fantastically better physical condition than he had ever before enjoyed (for the first time he had hopes of one day becoming handsomely stout), the kind it was shameful to have to hide under a mock illness rather than announce with much noise and movement; in spite of the great rewards at hand and the greater ones in promise (if the United States proved but a vain dream, then perhaps merely some sleepy hamlet in the Black Forest and a German woman with a nice round ass and a little craft like decorating Christmas-tree ornaments, and a garden of cabbage and beets—if one lived too high he got only boils and the gout) . . . despite every reason for being up and about, for seizing life and making it groan, he had instead chosen to play the sick hog. And it had begun to work.

Nathan was a queer fish. For some reason he had buried his humanness so deep that one could bring it to the surface only by outraging him. Yet Lichenko had always known it was there, else he would not have taken the trouble to find it—and it *was* trouble, and Nathan was very lucky to have him. For now he had, at who could tell what final cost, at last established the conditions for that intimacy in which the truth could be aired.

Seven o'clock, the good air outside the closed window, which he had not had in his nose for weeks, still bright and full of August. But Nathan had turned on the dresser lamp like the indoor man he was, and come to sit by the bed to await his, Vasya's, pleasure. The room which had on first sight looked so grand that he assumed Nathan must share it with a regiment had truly become a home. With use, the very bedsheets, so white and hard when first entered, had softened and lost their harsh odor of bleach. Even Nathan's sloppiness, which until the "illness" intervened he had constantly opposed, had worked to the homely purpose, the rug dark with scorchings, the rent in the curtains, the deep scratches of footboard and dresser-front catching the shadows like old scars on the faces of your loved ones. . . .

With a scissor-kick, as if in the water, he shot himself backwards, conking his skull on the headboard, which was not intentional but certainly claimed Nathan's attention. Instantly his friend was up and arranging the pillow.

"Are you hurt?"

Could Nathan truly be as pained as he looked, at the possible hurt of another?

"Ah, no!" Lichenko tried to joke. "The bedstead is undamaged!"

He had got him there: Nathan fell back laughing. He himself of course did not, it being a kind of vulgarity to laugh at one's own jokes, and instead, with serious mien, fixed the pillow from which Schild had puffed out all the good head-hollows.

"*Was für Knöpfe macht Ihr Vater?*" he asked.

Nathan could sit in a straight chair for hours without so much as crossing his legs, and he was thin, too, so that this ability owed nothing to the padding on his rump.

"Oh, he doesn't make the buttons. He buys them from a buttonmaker and sells them to a manufacturer of women's dresses. If that's confusing, don't bother with it. Your country is mercifully free of the middleman."

Again Lichenko shot himself backward, but this time the pillow dulled the thud of his head hitting oak, and this time Schild did not rise, for simultaneously with the action away, Lichenko had shot his hand forward and asked: "What is that you say, free . . .?"

"From the middleman."

"*So.*" The olive-drab undershirt, which with drawers of the same cloth, on loan from Schild, was his costume of illness, had with the movements ridden up and constricted about his narrow chest like a dog harness. "I should have told you earlier, my dear friend, I hear what is said, but between the words sometimes comes the *swoosh* of the rockets: 'free'—*swoosh*—'from the middleman'—*swoosh*, so that what goes into my mind is often different from what has been spoken. For example, I thought just now I heard you say someone was free in the Middle Ages."

"Haha," laughed Nathan, but wryly. "Not being a Jesuit, I could hardly say that."

"Ah, again, another example: what I heard then was something about Jesus Christ! . . . You see what I mean." He threw his feet about under the bedclothes, which commotion looked as if a small animal were trapped there, and smiled helplessly.

Just the thing to replace Nathan's nervousness with the responsibility of a job; he could never endure being misunderstood. It was a relief to see him break the stiff column of his spine as he leaned forward and said very slowly and with the enunciation of him who speaks into an ear trumpet: "Je-su-it—a religious order which invented a kind of fascism four hundred years before Mussolini."

"Of course I knew it was something old," Lichenko answered. "But you see a hydraulic engineer does not have time to learn much beyond the principles of his science. I . . . , my dear friend, should you be angry if I confessed to a dishonesty?"

Behind Schild's genial façade he saw an emotion begin at the throat and descend—a giraffe would look like that if it swallowed a melon—either hatred or fear, since these were the only feelings a person might find politic not always to reveal, but which of these was here operative Lichenko could not say, there being no apparent reason for either. Wishing no lies to stand between them, he had prepared merely to admit he had not read the American books they discussed at Lovett's party, so long as the truth was out that an engineering student had no spare time.

Instead, he said quickly: "I borrowed another of your handkerchiefs while you were gone to the dining hall. I shall send you a dozen when I go—" For a moment he imagined he had heard himself continue with: "to America," for suddenly that was where his fancy had fled, in just that wink of the eye he had seen himself at the handkerchief stall in a store big as a sports arena, had gone back further to park his yellow Ford at the curb outside. He wore a tight blue suit of narrow gray stripes and a black felt hat low over his brow; the woman at the counter believed him a suave but dangerous racketeer, a pearl-handled revolver encased in a silk glove, as he smiled with sharp white teeth and said "Enchanted," or whatever was proper at such a moment, which he would know.

"—a dozen. Tell me which color do you prefer? Always this olive, or should you like some of blue with narrow gray stripes?"

This was what he really said while Nathan loosened, sat back, and finally crossed his legs, one trouser riding up to uncover a pale shin whipped with dark hair.

"You know you may take anything of mine," said Schild, "and I'll be disturbed only if you try to pay me back."

His incredible generosity! It had, more than any other single thing, been the cause of Lichenko's delay. He understood that far back around the time of Jesus Christ the first Communists worked on that motive and no other, when, that is to say, they were weak and victims rather than victimizers, and it must have been splendid to live then, when good and bad were easy to isolate. Some time since, they had become so mixed that one could no longer take the sayings of one's mother as a serious guide to life. For example, of Schild his mother would first make some old-peasant observation such as that a man with a high bridge to his nose was untrustworthy, or that ears set at that angle caught only evil wisdom. But if he showed his manners she would think him fine as a "nobleman," which in her lexicon took on ever more precious connotations as she grew older and had further to look to see the lovely time of her youth when her father had one hundred per cent more land than her husband had now, since the latter owned none at all, and when the fields were the property of a handsome count who never cursed rather than a gang of rude bullies who stole nine-tenths of every harvest in the name of some swindler they called "the people."

Lichenko's mother had been illiterate. She had gone under orders to night school and learned to read and write, but she had still been illiterate—according to his brother, who belonged to the Party and, being very literate, wrote articles on agricultural matters for a newspaper in Kiev, which Lichenko, perhaps because he himself was only moderately literate, could never read beyond the first paragraph: "The representative liaison committee from the Stalin Collective Farm at Rusovo yesterday presented to the Central Organization of Rural Co-operative Societies a voluntary petition from the Third Link of field workers on the Stalin Collective Farm that it be permitted to raise its quota in regard to the harvest of wheat. Now, what does this mean relative to the development of large-scale socialist production in the sphere of agriculture? This means . . ."

Or take his brother—now you would assume he and Schild,

being political comrades, would hit it off. But, ah no, his brother had no respect for foreigners, Communists or not, as he had once admitted to Vasya; indeed, he placed little value on any people but the Great Russian and had got so that just before the war he would speak Ukrainian only with the greatest distaste.

No, to understand Nathan one must regard him with one's own eyes: it was the generosity, not the Communism, that was native to him, and if you said well, the Americans have so much they can afford to give some away, you had only to compare him with another like Captain St. George to see the difference. Nathan lived like a holy man of yore.

"I suppose your dearest wish is to return to your family now the fighting is over," he said, straightening the undershirt. "Tell me of them. Your sister—is she beautiful? Is she so slender? You have a photograph, of course."

"No—well, I did have," Schild spoke in concern, "but in the area of Metz my belongings were stolen."

"And your mother—can she read and write? No, don't answer. How silly of me to ask! A fine, cultivated noble—gentleman like you! Besides, certainly everybody in the United States is literate."

This seemed to soothe Schild, and his black eyes glowed behind the lenses as he protested happily: "Not at all. There are about ten or twelve million Americans who cannot read and write. We are not speaking now of the Soviet Union, Vasili Niko-laievitch."

"But then it is not necessary for everyone to read and write," said Lichenko, shrugging with his voice. "All one really needs is something to eat and wear—protection from the *golod* and *kholod,* as one says in Russian—girls to love, maybe a drink of spirits now and again, and the policeman not on your tail. I mean, if one belongs to the common people."

Schild assented by his silence.

"The uncommon ones," Lichenko went on, "take care of themselves. Then there are the ones between, who don't know what they want, *nicht wahr?* Something different, anyway; this is not right and that is not right. Nothing is right for them!" he exclaimed in a kind of joyful hopelessness, pedaling his legs rapidly as if riding a bicycle. "But look at a big oak tree: it loves no girls, drinks only water, does not eat at all, lasts longer than the oldest man, and is satisfied throughout."

"And is chopped down by the first fellow who needs wood," said Schild, nodding pleasantly. His shirt pocket might be unbuttoned, but his tie and collar were fast and most uncomfortable to see through the heavy, still air. Keeping the windows shut had been a phase of Lichenko's scheme of absolute pressure to the body as well as the spirit, and while no effect could be discerned in Schild, he himself was sweating like a plowhorse.

"Yet," Nathan continued, not so much as a gloss on his steep forehead, "isn't even that oak better than a worker under capitalism?, who is chopped down when he is *not* needed."

"Stupid!"

"Yes, stupid is a better word for it than evil."

Stupid Nathan! He saw even a tree politically, and no doubt would be the first to cut down an oak, to make paper for pamphlets to celebrate someone else's sowing of the reclaimed ground, or to denounce them for seeding the wrong thing, whichever would be most bleak and deadly and contradictory of his generous heart. There was a difference of thousands of meters, in more than land and sea, between him and Lichenko's brother, in spite of their similar faiths. His brother had, all to himself, a four-room apartment with a refrigerator and a private bathroom, but what had Schild to gain? He even disapproved of his father's wealth.

"It would be better, I think, if the window were open." Lichenko scrubbed his face with the undershirt tail, which when he pulled it down again was wet as a swimming suit, and since by that time Schild had opened one half of the casement and the evening air made chill entry, his belly was shortly cramped with cold.

"Good, that is just enough. Now please close it."

"You haven't a fever?" asked Schild as he came back to his chair softly as a cat.

"Frankly, I don't know. I feel very strange. Perhaps I should take a bath. . . . Of course you have a bathroom in your home in the U.S.A. And with hot water, no? *Schön!*"

"But there are many people who have not. My grandparents lived in the working-class quarter of New York City, in unbelievable slums. They had nothing but a cold-water flat, one room for living and sleeping, and the other a combination kitchen-bath. The tub had a wooden cover that served as dining table."

"*Wundervoll!*" Lichenko chortled. "I knew it! They were workers and yet had a private bath, and their son grew up to be a great industrialist of buttons and *his* son became a fine intellectual." He saw a cruel angle develop in the corner of Schild's mouth, at odds with a sad cast of the eye. He, Vasya, had been carried away as usual: fact, fact was wanted and not his opinions, which only irked his friend in the proportion they were genuine.

He writhed about until his feet hung over one side of the bed and his head, the other. In upside-down vision Schild looked like a baldheaded man with a beard—indeed, somewhat like a Lenin with glasses. He had played this game as a boy: if you frowned, the lines of the forehead resembled a mouth; the real mouth you must ignore, and also that the nose opens in the wrong direction; with the remainder you had a fairly credible face which gave to the expressions what the Moscow radio gave to the truth—an odd twist, both human and not. It was years since he had played it, however, and he had lost his old proficiency in interpretation.

"What are you doing now?"

The mouth in the center of Schild's head answered: "I'm smiling."

"Forgive me, one gets restless in bed. To entertain myself while you are gone I have remembered certain boyhood amusements." He righted himself, all hot above the neck, and sighed. "When I was sick as a child my mother sang little songs to me.

They were always about food. For the life of me I cannot now recall a note, or I should sing one. They only come back when I am hungry."

Schild bathed in a pond of jocularity as he said: "Then we shall have to starve you."

"No," Lichenko answered, "that has already been done, and believe me, my friend, just for the singing it is not worth it."

It was aired, his first open attack on the regime of his country; he felt excellent well for having made it, and he stared fearlessly at Schild, who appropriately cast his eyes aside in deep embarrassment. Which meant he knew, then, of the Kremlin-made famine of 1933, and it meant as well that he was not so corrupt as to try to defend it. Yet if Nathan did know and, regardless of a disapproval however sincere, continued to work for those devils who had not only created the famine but standing on two million corpses denied they were there . . . Lichenko lost the path as all at once he found he wanted Schild to be both innocent and guilty, for only in that combination could he forgive him.

But Nathan was neither. So solemnly eloquent he almost cracked one's heart, yet with a peculiar elation that seemed to swell his own, he spoke of Hitler's assault on the USSR and the scorched-earth tactics and withdrawals which, because of the treacherous surprise, had been at first the Soviets' only defense. He spoke well; indeed, so well that Lichenko almost believed the hunger here at issue was rather that of 1941 than 1933. No question that the invasion by the Germans had been worse than living under Stalin: they were foreigners. Yet, although the data was of course suppressed, hundreds of thousands of his compatriots had had another opinion, hung garlands on the invaders and enlisted in General Vlasov's anti-Kremlin army or even in the Wehrmacht. They were wrong. If you must have a tyrant, why not keep your own?

He could not help it, he still had scruples about disabusing

Schild. The Red Army, as Nathan was saying, *had* done a magnificent job; they *were* heroes; he, Vasya, was a hero and it was just and proper to hear someone say so. The Soviet Union was the greatest country in the world: there lay no contradiction between believing that and fleeing to America, or the Black Forest, or some southern land where dark-complexioned people drank wine and slept all day in the shade. And it was very probable that the Party elite represented a new and superior kind of man. He even believed Bolshevism would triumph in the long run, everywhere, because he could see in it no weaknesses and knew by experience it would stop at nothing. Even Hitler had a limit: the Germanic "race," by which he measured everything, including his Ukrainian allies, and in the end this folly brought down his house. He was wrong.

The Communists, however, were right—oh yes, no doubt even the famine was correct from the high point of vantage, the Kremlin had its eye always on the main chance, for there in the grave lay Lichenko's father and mother, who starved, yet there was he, son and heir, fewer than ten years later at the breech of the rocket gun, fighting loyally to save Moscow, and Stalin, from the enemy.

Communism, Nathan, is never wrong—as you would immediately agree but not understand—because its only principle is success. Just as yours is failure; what you really love is not the Red Army's victories but the sacrifices and agony required to achieve them. How you would have approved of the famine! . . . But the point I wish to make is that Stalin and his gang neither liked nor disliked starving two million people. They saw it as necessary to their plan that they requisition more foodstuffs than the peasants produced. If as a result the peasants died, they simply did not care. Communism is never wrong, Nathan, because it has no feelings at all, certainly no good ones, but no bad ones either—none at all. It is difficult to tell you that, because I have and you have, and furthermore I am a man without ambition and thus discredited.

The unspoken rang so loudly against his frontal bone that Lichenko could hardly believe Schild had not heard it, too; crystalline, cold, and true it was, like the sound of a gong made of glass. And he had never been a great one for thinking, which was his brother's talent.

Once before the war his brother in a literary phase had read a book called *The Idiot* by a writer towards whom his brother had mixed feelings—saying on the one hand he did show a consciousness of something, although on the other he was of course hopelessly something and you could not look to him for something else—at any rate, in an unusually amiable mood he quoted to Vasya the very kernel of what in this writer he thoroughly disapproved: this Idiot, who if that were not enough was also a prince, appropriately found everything strange; but one evening in Switzerland, where typical of the decadent Russian nobility having nothing else to do he went to drink sulfur-water or whatnot, he heard the bray of an ass in the marketplace: "I was immensely struck with the ass, and for some reason extraordinarily pleased with it, and suddenly everything seemed to clear up in my head."

Following the quotation his brother observed that heavy silence which means such nonsense speaks for itself. To Vasya it had said nothing until this moment more than five years later when, without the ass's aid, he found himself in the princely condition. Everything seemed to clear up. . . . He had stayed on not to save Schild but to understand him, not because Schild was good but rather because he was interesting. It was the game of the Communists, who were never wrong, to save people. For an ordinary man, an idiot, it was enough to know how the next fellow used the privilege and obligation of life, which was not the best thing imaginable, but we none of us—his brother, Stalin, Hitler, the Americans, the prince—had anything else.

Naturally, Nathan had not heard. That inner ear through which the rest of humanity hears the most important sounds is confiscated when one joins the Communists. He had often confirmed this by speaking silently to his brother: "You bastard, the only reason I wouldn't shoot you if I had the chance is that we have the same blood." Results always negative, despite his brother's noted gift for smelling out heresy.

However, Schild had picked up a subtler noise which Lichenko missed. His voice became furtive as he left the siege of Stalingrad to warn: "St. George is coming upstairs."

At last Lichenko heard the footsteps, which being both heavy and soft like those of any large animal but the horse, were unmistakable: those shoes which he so coveted, with their fat soles of yellow gum rubber; shod so, a man could run right up a smooth wall. Why Schild should think St. George a menace, however, was far from clear—if at the same time, as Nathan insisted, and Lichenko had to agree, the captain was also a fool. But a good fool, a jovial one, at least wise enough not to try to be clever. He did not even suspect he had a political as second-in-command, and was the happier for it. In a Russian company the most harmless-looking boob was invariably the secret-police informer. The wonderful American invention was a man who looked his role.

He lay badly in need now of just the neutrality that St. George dispensed. He readied his mouth to call "Kom een!" his pronunciation of which the captain never failed to approve; he was already enmired in St. George's warm sludge, that secure, absolute, fool's medium in which all was forever orderly—when, just as the footfalls reached the door, darkness smothered him in its close sheet.

Outside the window night had come unnoticed, but the room was blacker still, for even a night swollen and dim with cloud has its suggestions of distant fire. Damn you, Nathan, for extinguishing the lamp on a friend! Now what had been merely necessary became imperative. He called to St. George and could not hear his own voice; he strove to rise but lost the first fall to inertia, the second to his knotted bedclothes, and won the third only to hear his quarry pad beyond the bend of the hall. Nevertheless he got to the lamp, eerily not meeting Schild on the way, choked the button in its narrow throat, making light—of which he had the conviction it would reveal nothing but a chamber enclosing only himself.

Yet there sat Nathan on his hard chair, on his cast-iron behind, and looking not at all guilty, when for once he should have, but rather self-righteous.

"Yes, it's all right now," he said. "He's gone to his room."

In the interval of darkness the lamp had prepared for a success, developing its weak yellow into a splendid flare—only to lose the contest to Schild's face, which like unpolished bone claimed all the light and gave none back. He had never looked more saintly.

"But come," he said, rising to Lichenko's aid and fading quickly into his old contrition. "You shouldn't be up—you'll take a chill." He offered to support him and, when that was spurned, walked before, as if he were clearing a channel through some invisible marsh between the dresser and bed; alone and unwitting he went, and no one followed.

For Lichenko had turned to the big clothes cabinet in the corner next the window, turned the key, and peered into its cavern which gave the illusion of a vaster space than the surrounding room. At one end of the rod Schild's uniforms hung unruly, as if rifled by a thief. At the other, his own, which seemed unusually small upon its hanger; and his boots, bow-legged, slumped, wanting straight heels.

"My cap, I do not see my cap, and I cannot go without it," he said, into the depths but to Schild.

"Oh yes," Schild answered, in a strangely strong voice. "You will want your cap. Isn't it there on the shelf?"

Surely it was; he had forgotten the single shelf across the top of the cabinet, perhaps because he was too short to use it, but the edge of the cap's shiny visor poked an inch beyond the board, like the nose of a midget peeking down from hiding, and he seized it. Upon his head the cap was tight, since he had not had a real haircut for three weeks, only Nathan's trim-job around the ears with a little sewing scissors. He also got into his boots, balancing badly on one leg at a time—you cannot live abed for more than a day, even faking, and not feel giddy on your feet— and then seeing in the mirror a soldier on tropics-duty, for he wore cap, olive-drab shorts and undershirt, and boots, he groaned at his stupidity and sat upon the floor.

Schild came to him and, bending over, grasped his left heel and toe.

"I'll pull and you pull, and off it comes. Ready?" Before he could answer, Nathan did his part unaccompanied; off it came and then the other.

"Now," said Schild, "we'll just put these back into the cabinet where they can't be scuffed. And the cap, too. You won't want to get it full of lint." He plucked it from Lichenko's head and ran his elbow across it twice.

"Don't crush my cap," Lichenko shouted.

"Ah no, this is how they brush hats in the fine American stores."

"How am I to know that?"

Seizing his hand, Schild brought him upright.

"What you do know is that I have no reason to ruin it, *nicht wahr*? Therefore what I do must be to its advantage." He looked very scholarly as he replaced the cap on the shelf. At the angle Lichenko saw that his glasses were covered with a film of dust and at least one fingerprint, distinct in oil.

"Why don't you clean your spectacles?" he shouted angrily. "You can't see out of your own head!"

Carefully, Schild unhooked the temple pieces from behind his ears, and painstakingly shined the lenses with the small end of his straw-colored necktie, which tonight as usual was twisted ahead of the larger.

Lichenko turned aside, embarrassed by the naked face, saying: "You should not have done that to the captain."

"Then come," Schild offered, the glasses yet in his fingers, "we shall go and apologize to him; I mean, we'll go and I will apologize, and you can see his feelings haven't been hurt."

"Oh, I'm sure of that." He reached up under the tunic and drew his breeches from the crossbar of the hanger. No matter where he wandered hence he would never find another man so alert to his moods and purposes, but was that not the trouble?

"Yes," Schild reassured, "he is just a person. . . . But whatever are you doing? You are ill, my friend, and must not worry about your uniform. As you can see I have taken good care of it. Look at the blouse—as clean and pressed as new, eh? And the medals —only yesterday I sponged the ribbons with gasoline. How bright their colors are! See the Order of the Red Banner—"

Lichenko sidestepped him and struggled into the breeches. After the fly was fastened he could hardly get a hand into his pocket, so American had been three weeks of meals—and that, too, was the trouble. He withdrew a wad of marks and thrust them at Schild.

"Here is payment for the underwear and handkerchiefs and whatever else I have taken, and also the winnings from the cards. You see, I cheated in those games—silly, no?, since I could have beaten you anyway, still I could not resist when it was so easy. But there you have it all back again." He threw the bills upon the dresser.

"Yes, the cards!" Schild said, desperately exuberant. "We'll have a three-handed game of something and get old St. George —you'll see he isn't hurt in any way—and take his money. He'll like that, he'll do anything for company."

"As to your personal kindness," Lichenko continued, reaching for his blouse, "there is no repaying that, not when one understands what kindness is, a thing which should make the giver feel good or he should not do it." He said more as he crumpled the blouse over his head, but could not hear it, himself. He was so sick of himself he feared he might vomit on the very uniform whose smartness he also owed to Schild. He had learned in fifty seconds that cowardice may be a slow disease but is felt as an instant affliction, and comes more violently in rooms than on the fields of battle; at Kursk, when a Tiger tank broke rumbling and malignant through to their artillery position, he had leaped upon the deck and dropped a grenade down its throat; in *gemütlich* Zehlendorf he could not even stave off the insulting of a fool, much less tell the cold truth to a friend.

"Come," said Schild, who looked now as if he were drunk or, rather, pretending to be drunk and wild, in the manner of some honor student ostentatiously letting down his hair at the end of term. "St. George has a bottle . . ." He rolled his eyes in what he surely meant as license, but to Lichenko they suggested those of a horse gone mad with fright.

Fright? Why should *he* be afraid, the one who wasn't taking a risk? Or did his odd sympathy even extend to Lichenko's future troubles in the great world outside?, where, after all, most people had had to struggle all their lives without his help. For the first time he was struck by Nathan's incredible arrogance.

He buckled on the wide dress belt and strung the breast strap through the epaulette on his right shoulder, and reached again for the boots, which Nathan still held.

But Schild swung them behind his back, like a child, saying: "First let's have that drink."

"No, Nathan, I am not fooling any more." He took the boots from him and this time sat down upon the bed to pull them on. "I shall say goodbye to the captain but I want no drink." He needed only three drops of spirits to fall unconscious; his head already felt like an electric-light bulb, hot, light, empty, fragile, and loose where it screwed onto his neck; a moment somewhere back he had discovered he was ironically and genuinely ill.

"Goodbye?" asked Schild, his voice very ugly, so nasty it caught him up a bit, himself, and he pressed it out sweeter for the rest: "Where can *you* go?" He did not wait for a reply—being already in possession of all answers to all questions; indeed, it was mere courtesy that he had put the statement in the interrogative.

"Almost anywhere but home," said Lichenko, grinning weakly, trying to, at any rate, as his head slowly unscrewed and Schild's image kaleidoscoped with the vivid colors of the hair-lotion bottles on the dressertop. Nevertheless his mind stayed clear.

*"You son of a bitch."*

Nathan had spoken in English, that flat, nasal language in which nothing sounded either interesting or important; and so far as he could see him through the spinning, his expression followed suit. Lichenko grinned again, hard and acid, but this time within his own heart and on the terms of his own failure. In the end, how he had conducted himself did not matter, that was the funniness of it and also the horror; in the end, the great truths could not pass through the neck of the smallest one: you cannot stir the curiosity of a corpse.

He would leave in a moment. As soon as he recovered his balance he would get his cap from the cabinet and walk through the door, down the stairs—the German woman, he reflected, handsome if too thin, would continue to go to seed—and stand upon the threshold, facing outward. One could hope the night was not windy; the world seemed larger when the wind blew, especially if the sky was dark and you could see so little that was permanent. Other persons feared lighting bolts, sunstroke, drowning, snakebites—he had always had fantasies of being blown away in a gale.

In a moment . . . already he could feel the strength rising from somewhere down about his ankles, which were firm in the good old boots. You couldn't beat boots, which would hold you erect when you were limp with exhaustion. He could not believe that the Americans, in their low shoes, had much endurance.

After looking at him a long time in the same blank way, Nathan had suddenly turned towards the dresser lamp, seized the wad of Occupation marks, and begun to count. It would be an impressive sum, for what Lichenko had won in the cards from Schild were just a few negligible leaves around the fat core of the bonus he had been paid on the day of Lovett's party. The regular pay, in rubles, was allegedly deposited at home against one's return; these marks, intended to be spent in Germany, had on some guarantee of the Americans been printed wholesale and cost the Red Army nothing. They also, if he knew his bureaucrats and their ingenious scheme of allotments, were very likely all one would ever get in his hand. For him, of course, the matter was now academic.

He would face the world with empty pockets and without a plan. This, he realized, in a chill about the kneecaps which was closer to a falling nerve than a rising strength, was absolute freedom.

"Yes, Nathan, all of it is yours," he said faintly, for part of him was in that state of freedom while the rest held tenaciously to the here-and-now, and his voice was not strong enough to sound both places with the same volume. "Count it, keep it, spend it. Money is a good thing, *especially for a person of your type.*" He meant: it may not be grand or powerful, but it is human to know the price of beans.

As if he had arrived at the total, Schild nodded to himself and rerolled the bills.

"Thank you," he said quietly. "We are quits. And now if you can spare a minute I must get St. George to come and say his *Lebewohl.*"

"*Lassen Sie sich Zeit,*" Lichenko answered, "take your own good time." He lay back across the bed and closed his eyes; he felt a small object drop upon his chest and separate like a broken egg; he heard Nathan leave the room. He would sleep a minute.

"Well," St. George had said to Schild, "I did wonder if he had permission to stay this long away from his company. I did think it was funny." In his pajamas—his alternate set, of vertical green and white stripes—lipping an unlighted pipe, smelling of mouthwash, he stood sagging near his window just opened over the black-quiet yard. "But desertion! I hope you're certain about that. Or rather, I hope you are wrong, because he is a nice fellow." He anyway had to sleep the night on it.

Schild neither slept nor tried to, nor could have said how he passed the hours of darkness, for they were too grievous small: a turn of the corridor and already the bathroom window was mother-of-pearl; another, and five o'clock had surely come. Silently he crept into St. George's room and took up the wrist-watch from the bedside table, held the cold snake of its expansion bracelet: only four o'clock in Berlin's delusive and too-early light. Nevertheless he woke the captain, who took his warnings with a face like a stale onion roll and at last rose, puffing and aged, to stuff himself into the uniform.

"Boy oh boy," said St. George when he was dressed. "Here's a time I would give these bars to anyone who would take them. This is a lousy business I have to do, Nate. You should be glad you're out of it." He made a pot of his overseas cap and drew it on. "God knows what they'll do to him. I don't think Russia's much of a place."

"But then you didn't make the regulations, did you?" asked Schild, as he pressured him, without touching, to the door.

"I guess that's how to look at it." With a foot into the hall, though, he recoiled and, whispering, brushed Schild's ear with his earnest, bulbous nose: "But does he know yet?"

Schild answered harsh: "Now I would hardly tell him."

He ate this thought like a caramel and, swallowing it, grimaced, and then going into a profound melancholy moved with heavy hump of shoulders towards the staircase.

Within the hour two military policemen—Americans: Schild had somehow believed they would be Russian—came in tall, thin, and bored from the street, mounted the stair with drawn pistols on white lanyards . . . and soon descended supporting Lichenko between them, for, still in half-sleep, he could not walk erect and would not try to see with his eyes. Yet at the threshold he straightened, jerked his arms from captivity to fix his cap, said *"Ladno!"* the Russian okay, and walked unassisted in the new, barren day.

St. George had not returned. His mouth metallic with want of rest, Schild mounted to the room which he had not seen since the evening before and in which he had not been alone for three weeks. Scattered across the bed he saw the roll of marks in the pattern in which it had burst when he threw it. He believed that he should burn them straightaway, but as he stooped to the gathering the door downstairs made its sound and he was hailed by a raucous American voice.

The taller MP stood wide-legged and screamed up the stairwell: "Lootenant, did that fuckin' Communist steal your wristwatch? He's wearing a gold Bulova."

"No," said Schild, after a moment. "I sold it to him."

He thought: I will never know how long it might have gone on if he had not made that crack about Jews and money.

# CHAPTER 15

CONSIDERED as a unit, Reinhart and Very were some twelve feet, three hundred and forty pounds of person, and, as the beast with two backs, would have ranked in the hierarchy of animal size just after the whale, the Indian elephant, and the hippopotamus. Their coupling, however, was apparently not to come —unless it was she who overwhelmed Reinhart—for all day now he ached with the surfeit obtained in another quarter. Discretion ruled out any further sport at the office, but immediately after work each afternoon he had been calling at Trudchen's little room down the hall, to vault between her soft legs in a ferocity which, though it had long left reason behind, never stayed her call for more and worse. Indeed, it had become S.O.P. for her, just before the climax, to scream into his ear: "You don't hurt me enough!" and drive her small fangs into the lobe, which, while it is that portion of the human surface with the fewest nerve endings and correspondingly insensitive, still feels pressure and can swell fat and red with mistreatment and make you look odd as you go about your other business.

But all in all Reinhart felt very natural and right about the arrangement, as one can only when he so adjusts his life as to be dirty on the one hand and clean on the other—a sort of Renaissance ideal—and therefore hypocritical on neither. With Trudchen there was no pretense of love; with Very, very little of sex; although, not being a brute or a pervert, with the former he did not withhold "love"—he was very kind to Trudchen—and with Very his imagination was not so barren as to exclude "sex" —he after all kissed her rather more than he did Trudchen, if not in so French a style, and who knew what random transport might seize her in some propitious time and place? Meanwhile, it was

237

satisfaction of a kind of lust merely to be with her, to have her seen at his side by resentful others. Though they were not flagrant: in public they never held hands.

And usually they were in public: for one, because even in Berlin, with its acres of forests and ruins, even if you could drag a respectable girl through stocking-snagging jungles, people abounded—Germans of course did not count, but Americans were behind each tree and in the hollow of every bomb crater—for another, having no strong need to tumble her, a man had to find public amusements with his woman.

For example, the Nazi monuments. Pound's and his tour had at last moved from paper to actuality. One Sunday shortly past noon two of the small vehicles termed "weapons carriers," the parallel benches in their roofless beds creaking with packed behinds in olive drab, tooled from Zehlendorf to the now deranged nerve center of Hitler Germany.

Very's turn was like the stately movement of a world-ball on its axis—not a petty soccer-sized globe, mind you, but the grand sphere that dominates some centennial exposition—as she descended from the truck on the same helpful hand that Reinhart, as official guide, had granted the other nurses in the party. Her other difference was that she gave his fingers a pronounced squeeze, which not only brought pain to his knuckles but also impatience to his heart: there they were, in the great chaotic plaza before the ruined Chancellery and she was obviously unmoved. Not to mention that she had given, he had seen—for on general grounds it was a pleasure to watch her—only perfunctory notice to the legend incarnate of the series: Brandenburg Gate, Unter den Linden, entrance to the Wilhelmstrasse, Hotel Adlon, Foreign Office, Propaganda Ministry; had instead touched her cap, flicked her lapel, straightened her skirt, and coughed ladylike behind satiny nails.

Now she nicely picked, with the others in the party of fourteen, across the center island nasty with torn Volkswagens and an Opel, on its side, showing naked steel supports for a roof long gone, and a lamppost twisted and wilting like a licorice whip on end; in her turn presented the long red pass to the inevitable tommygun Russians at the Chancellery door and was, with stupid, mammary ogling, admitted.

Reinhart clove to her side, and the others, officers, nurses, and enlisted men, clung to his; shortly they were all lost together in a choppy surf of crushed marble through which black wires squirmed like sea-snakes. And as quickly were again found, in a vast chamber of pale-gray mosaic, where a skylight of ten thousand broken panes still dribbled glass fragments down the golden incline of sun that met the shrapnel-pitted wall. They stood there, the fourteen, in a noisy, echoing silence of rubber heels abrading marble, inhaling the sour white dust which floated on the air like steam in winter, in their awe daring nothing but to take this polluted breath and give it back at the proper intervals. Over the doorway, a mile down a runway of litter fifty feet wide and to the depth of a horse, the Nazi eagle of stone-and-gilded-bronze. Besides themselves, no man.

Naturally, thoughts of a mighty morality spilled into Reinhart's mind, through, as it were, the skylight: if you seek his monument, look around you; Ozymandias, king of kings, etc.; living and dying with and by the sword. And PFC Farnsworth T. Cronin, who had majored in political science, in Massachusetts, and who at this moment subtly wedged himself between Reinhart and Veronica, intoned softly: "Power corrupts, and absolute power corrupts absolutely."

Sidestepping, Reinhart eased over to Very. "Can you imagine him walking down the middle of this vault, his bootheels echoing for ten minutes before you could see him? He must have looked pretty insignificant in his own house."

"Who?" asked Very, throwing highlights off the undercushion of her scarlet lip. "Oh you mean Hitler. But did he live right here in the Reichstag? Must have been drafty, haha."

If you were careless you might identify as imbecility that which was rather inattentiveness; before penetrating the Brandenburg Gate, they had swung left up the squalid lane to the old Reichstag ruin, a long, columned cinder surmounted by a dome burned to chicken wire and facing a park of weeds. In his cicerone remarks Reinhart attributed its burns to a fire set by the Nazis in 1933. Cronin corrected in a voice flat with certainty: "No, it was restored after that. What you see here came from the bombings and the Russian assault this spring"—he had apparently snooped in all these places before the tour got under way, while the real men in the outfit were out getting tail. Anyway, perhaps it was just as well this all had eluded Veronica, who also probably failed to notice that thereupon Reinhart suppressed the remainder of his own commentary, not only for the Reichstag but the succeeding buildings as well.

"My fault," he said now, manfully. "This is the Chancellery."

"The What-cellery?" But he saw in her blue eyes a candid fooling.

"Of course," said Cronin, studying the mosaics with his bland face, "we are in the New Chancellery which Hitler built circa 1938-39. The Old one, dating from the time of the Hohenzollerns, is next door." Cronin never put his eyes on a person; meeting one on the arctic tundra, with nothing else to look at, he no doubt would try to inspect the wind. A tedious creep, yet you could tell by the measure of his tediousness that he did know whereof he spoke; it were destructive vanity not to use him for what he could provide.

"If you know the place, Farnie, tell us what else is worth seeing."

"Well, the terrace and garden are certainly *there*," Cronin answered, almost, in his pleasure, giving one a fair shot at his face, but not quite.

"Then lead on, McSnerd, and make a trail through the swamp!" said Very, sending her chime like a bowling ball down the marble gallery. And this time Cronin looked full face, demonstrating above it a dun-colored scalp parted dead center, like a statesman of the Harding era, and wondering, Amherst eyes: wondering not only who she was but why.

Eventually they crossed a hall of massive pillars, where Russian names, in their queer letters sometimes just eluding comprehension by a hair, were scratched into the bomb-sprayed walls and from a ceiling of bare girders loose power cables swung like thin pythons anxious to drop upon a meal. And, as a thick, sifting carpet, the usual litter of broken stone, plaster powder, splintered wood, and piecemeal metal, in a quantity which if reassembled, by divine act or motion-picture film run backwards, into its original forms would twice exceed them, for no fecundity can match disintegration's.

Reinhart thought about this, but it was Very, with her fine intuition, who said: "Why when things are broken do they seem like more than when they're together?"

"Dunno," answered Cronin, who had apparently determined her quality and was peculiarly intrigued by it—he was breaking a trail through the trash, as she had asked, and just for her, while the others mushed ankle-deep—"no doubt the air between the pieces."

"I don't read you." She stepped to the French window, of which Cronin opened and held the shutter and then caught her arm: beyond its threshold was a two-foot drop to the terrace floor.

Meanwhile, Reinhart bulled on through and nearly broke both ankles but recovered with the gay veldt-bound of a springbok. Coming back, he raised his hands under Very's elbows and lowered her like a light barbell, effortlessly, then in malice offered the same to less-than-average-size Cronin, who took it!, being indecently beyond that kind of vanity.

As the others tumbled through each in his own fashion, a nurse named Lieutenant Leek despite support turning her foot, the trio of leaders waded across the terrace and into the junkyard garden of sand, dismembered trees, disjunctive wheels and pipes and tin air ducts, disjected planks; blooming out of these, in the dirty fungus-white of sunless growths, two concrete structures, pocked by shot, seared by flame, sprouting excrescences of scaffold and webbed iron, yet squatted conditionally whole.

On the left—they had come round to the far side—was Hitler's bunker, according to Cronin, who named the other, a cylinder with conical roof, as a sentry blockhouse manned by the SS until the eleventh hour. In the deep embrasure of the bunker entrance a detached steel door stood angled; next to it at the same degree slouched a Mongol guard, who at their appearance sullenly presented his shoulder blades and a view of trousers-rear seemingly heavy with a load.

"Slav slob," wittily noted Reinhart.

"Yes," said Cronin to a length of corroded pipe lying at his feet, "he should be wearing a J. Press jacket and white bucks." Although his statement was cryptic, his emotion was not: when he looked towards the guard his eyes were filmy with approval. Then, in the self-congratulatory manner of a white man extending common courtesy to a Negro, he plunged across the debris to the doorway, open pack of cigarettes at the ready position, loudly saying: "Z-DRAHST-voo-ee-tee, ta-VA-reesch, KAHK pa-jee-VA-yee-tee?" You could hear all the stresses of the little Russian phrasebook distributed a month earlier by Reinhart's department.

The Mongol revolved instantly and gave him the submachine-gun muzzle big as a megaphone and all perforated with dime-sized air vents, more death-ray than gun, and if a man ever meant to squeeze the trigger, it was he. But Cronin was a stranger to cowardice; with inexorable good will he advanced, and the Mongol, though snarling imprecations in a tongue that sounded nothing like Russian and never lowering his equalizer, gave ground. Reaching the entrance, Cronin pressed the smokes at him as one might a cross upon a devil, engaged him in a going-and-coming, frustrating inquiry, and was at last driven by him into the waste of loose planks before the SS turret, where Reinhart and Very waited.

"I'm afraid it's forbidden to enter the bunker," he said pridefully, stepping up, as if myopic, so near that Reinhart, always uncomfortable in close approach, backed off, caught his heel in the fork of a grounded tree-branch, and freeing it too violently threw away his balance and fell backwards into a shallow trench which till then no one had marked.

"But that's the next best thing," said Cronin, pretending not to see, or perhaps really, in his odd way, not noticing, as Very howled vulgarly and the rest of the party, clattering through the ventilating ducts, joined her in sadistic mirth, "that's the ditch where they burned the bodies of Hitler and Eva Braun."

Reinhart's back-skin bubbled in gooseflesh, more historical than personal, as he scrambled slowly upwards: he had felt a distinct and depraved wish to continue lying there for a while.

"Ostensibly," Cronin went on.

On the bank now, Reinhart saw in the trench's sandy gutter only an ambiguous rubbish of dead leaves, board-ends, and fragments of paper coarsened and grayed by dried rain. Already he had become as reluctant to kneel and rummage in it as he had been, a moment earlier, to leave its placid bed.

"Here, in this ditch?" No, it was too much, along with the imperial chaos inside the Chancellery, to believe; was rather lock, stock, and barrel a vast hoax of propaganda and journalism; normal people like himself not only did not make history but did not see its leavings firsthand.

"I said ostensibly," Cronin answered. "In my opinion it was a not too ingenious device to cover his escape to South America."

"Oh you don't think so?" asked Veronica, the corners of her mouth yet remembering the laugh on Reinhart, as did her wet eyes, life-blue in this landscape of neutral tones canescing into time past.

"If so, it worked." Said by a newcomer to the area of the

three, a stout captain in green trenchcoat, his shirt collar wearing the doctor's bare caduceus, and Lieutenant Leek hobbled up, and in another moment the others, too, lining round the pseudo grave.

"Unfortunately yes," said Cronin, although the captain had not properly addressed the comment to him, "anything German always succeeds famously with us. Give Hitler a year and we'll welcome him back to defend us against the 'Reds.' "

Reinhart had got interested in watching the captain, whom he did not know, whose face was manifestly German-American, wide-cheeked, beer-florid, piggishly nostriled, stupid and good— what had it to say in defense of that old seed sprung from this ground and carried across the ocean to form it?

"Do you think the Reds are a real danger now?" the captain asked in utter innocence, coloring more, for to see Cronin he had to send his eyes across Very's Himalayan front.

"Only the American Legion and the vigilantes can save us from them. First, the unions must be stamped out . . ." Cronin's face became a mask of crafty evil, apparently mimicking a memory of Goebbels'. "FDR has already been got rid of, thank God."

How much of the sarcasm, which Cronin injected with real ferocity, astonishing Reinhart who had not believed he could show much feeling towards anything, how much of it reached the captain it was difficult to say. Too little, Reinhart feared, and he hastened to spread it abroad that Cronin spoke in jest.

"Well," the captain answered, humorlessly shaking his thick jowls, "I don't know it's anything to kid about, if these Reds are going to make trouble just as soon as we get rid of this fellow." He pointed into the depression. "If he means the Communists, I don't think in the end they'd be much better than Hitler. Didn't they make a pact with him which gave him a green light to start the war? And then proceeded to divvy up poor old Poland, even though they later became our allies. Killing people is all any of those fellows know, robbing people and killing them, year in and year out, for no reason at all. I've been a physician for seventeen years but I've never been able to figure out what makes fellows like that—because that's what they are, aren't they, just fellows, people like anybody else in the beginning."

Excellent fat captain, with your wide, honest, Nordic face: you have come through! Reinhart watched him kneel like a barrage balloon folding, ever threatening to burst upwards again, and poke into the trench with graceful, doctor-sensitive hands that bore not an ounce of the excess flesh he carried elsewhere. Soon he discovered nothing and rose, despite his weight, easily, saying: "The American Legion stamping out the unions? I have five or six patients at home who belong to both and I also think they were good Roosevelt-Truman men, and so you've got me all confused."

"Truman, ha!" snorted Cronin and suddenly gave Reinhart a knowing eye; in this matter he was willing to grant that they shared a community, and what was shameful was that Reinhart had no courage to indicate him nay, from a combination of guilt and vanity was yellow to reveal he stood with the doctor, two dense and heavy light-complexioned oafs who saw the mellow where the bright boys detected the sinister. On the other hand, he, Reinhart, would as soon cut his throat as join the American Legion or a union or the Communists or the Republicans or the New Deal, or any other outfit the joining of which prohibited one the next day from being malignantly anti-Legion, anti-union, etc., which alternation, irresponsible as it might be, to him signified, as nothing else, the precious quality of humanness.

The others by now had lost interest—in the trench; towards Cronin and the doctor they had shown none to start with or end —and broke their ring, meandering into the rubbish towards the Chancellery terrace and the wall through which they had earlier issued, a series of high windows, shutters in all degrees of angle and caries, above each its own *oeil-de-boeuf* like the dot to an exclamation.

"We can split up, if you want," Reinhart cried before the dispersal had gone absolute. "Everybody meet in one hour at the truck outside!" Two persons made a noise of despair. "All right, forty-five minutes then. There's lots more to see inside: you won't be bored for a moment." Nevertheless he again heard the groans.

"If little Harry Truman's all that will stand in his way, expect Hitler back next month from Argentina," said Cronin, "and back in the saddle."

"No," the captain answered, not looking into the ditch now and not with corny, self-conscious moral majesty, but with majesty nonetheless, the placebo-prescription majesty of the American general practitioner, famed source of the basic wisdom. "No," he said, looking directly and honestly at Cronin, the punk kid yet with downy lip, probably still with Onan as his model, "no, *he must never happen again.*"

From the exodus one figure lingered back, a first lieutenant who held his doffed cap and scratched a graying sideburn with the same hand. He studied something in the litter on which he stood and called, without raising his head: "Hey Bernstein!"

Cronin's captain was named Bernstein. He joined his friend, who had found a Wehrmacht belt buckle in the sand, translated for him its inscription, *Gott mit uns,* and with him, two men whose race was half run, walked out of sight beyond the SS tower.

*Bernstein:* his forebears, like so many Jews, forced by the census takers to assume cognomens, had gone to gems, precious metals, and flowers for their names, had chosen that crystallized juice of ancient trees on the Baltic coast of Prussia, the sherry-golden amber, for theirs, and, fortune's dupes, brought it to America where its sound was more rasping than lovely on the air, if not downright comic, signifying bagels and upthrust hands. But it was another crime to be laid at the German door and not against the Jews, whose old desert tongue contained no word like "Bernstein"—or "Reinhart," which in Reinhart's sudden view was scarcely better and only different from the doctor's in that no one owed it apology—or "Schicklgruber-Hitler," the funniest and ugliest of the lot.

What could a man called Cronin say to Bernstein, Reinhart & Schicklgruber, attorneys at law, delicatessen owners, or what have you, who fell out over the fratricide practiced by the last-named? Germans, Hitler's first victims were Germans!, for that's what German Jews were, no mistake; else, observing no loyalty but to their own tribe everywhere alien, they would better have defended themselves. Nay, might have taken the offensive, their noted acumen more than compensating for deficiency in numbers, and launched their own Hitler. But no, they had been too trusting, too naïve, too German and not Jewish enough. Jews shrewd? They were rather the rubes and boobs of history; after two thousand years they were still fresh from the sticks, assuming booblike that even in the city men were men and life was what you made it.

Such innocence was almost wicked. Watching Bernstein's shoulders too heavy to be moved by the effort of walking, Bernstein's too-solid flesh which, if some ambitious or perhaps merely desperate forebear had not shipped the Atlantic, would have by his fellow Germans been resolved into a dew, still hearing oxlike Bernstein's simple, hateless statement that Hitler must not happen again—Reinhart himself, pure Teuton, on the margin of this ditch would have condemned German, no, the world's gentiles to eternal fire and thought it too cool—considering Bernstein the good, the innocent, the Jew, obsessed by Bernstein, Reinhart hated him.

Jews really were the chosen, the superior people. This had been Bach's final meaning, only put in the queer, inside-out logic with which the truth was approached by Middle-Europeans, who really were sapient and deep and lived on an old ground ever fertilized by fresh gore. Poor cloistered Cronin, poor dear Veronica, they could not understand irony, that means to confront the ideal with the actual and not go mad, that whip which produced the pain that hurts-so-good, so that in the measure to which it hurt it was also funny. Finally, having flogged and laughed yourself to the rim of death's trench, you looked within and saw irony's own irony: the last truth was the first.

Poor Cronin's hitherto mobile mouth fell open, static and silent at the incantatory syllables of "Bernstein." He could be read like a highway poster: 'Can a Jew, vis-à-vis Hitler's ghost, be wrong?' Far easier to accept that oneself is an ass. When he closed his lips again he wore a smile bespeaking relief; when he returned to the ivy he would switch his major to natural science.

"Politics," said Very, pressing her bosom like an armload of soccer balls against Reinhart's arm—accidentally?: to study that was Reinhart's own relief—"thank God that's an Irish trait I don't have! Find a politician, find a crook, as the man says." Poutingly she flung away from his side, as if he were sure to hold the opposing view, swinging capelike her soft fall of hair which, seining the sun, caught a sudden amber shaming old Prussia with its clarity and fire.

In the combination of Very and Trudchen, Reinhart's needs were met. Such a thing was thereby proved possible, contrary to the popular wisdom which crepe-hangingly warned that man, the questing beast, was never satisfied, that worse than not achieving your aim was getting it. Indeed, he was living high off the hog in Berlin. He was rich: Marsala had sold all his gadgets in the black market and, each week, the candy ration. He did even less work than before: now that the tour was set it ran itself and Pound was gone off on leave to Switzerland, of course in the company of Nurse Lightner, where he intended to buy and transport to Berlin as personal luggage a footlocker full of wrist-watches.

Organize your sex life and all else followed, the phallus being the key to the general metropolis of manhood, which most of the grand old civilizations knew but we in America had forgotten. For example, in Ohio carnal knowledge of a sixteen-year-old girl was a prelude to the penitentiary; they could stick their pointed tits like crayon-ends in your face, wag their sloping little behinds, in summer wear shorts to the junction of belly and thigh, but if you rolled an eyeball towards them you were a pervert. He never entered Trudchen without tremors of retroactive revenge.

With Very, on the other hand, he was getting back at Germany and all its exoticism gone nasty. That was the great thing about women: with one, you had a place in a context. He had begun to think of himself as the kind of fellow who might one day get married; at least he detected the future inclination. Writing to Pound's wife he had felt vicariously that peculiar pleasure of having an attachment one owed to and was owed by. Love as a mutual debt—certainly it was new to him as he grew old.

No longer did he spring from bed at Marsala's eight-o'clock clarion, but lingered for a second and a third and then the thrust of a hard hand against his head, at which, still unconscious—which was his excuse—he punched out wildly at his disturber, and even though he usually missed, Marsala stayed sullen all day at these thanks. A mature man should not live with another, but with a woman from whose soft lump beside him under the steaming, odorous blankets he can take a motive to rise, the sooner to be off to honest work, the sooner to be home again as evening falls to meet this sweet dependent, now the smiling presence of the succulent table, prepared for two and not five hundred.

Yet what honest work? Had the war not come he would now have been for a year and a quarter a Bachelor of—what? A process beginning in Central Europe in 1933 (Carlo had a popgun, wanted an air rifle), or 1924, then: Hitler, having failed to capture Bavaria with his private army of cranks and loafers, sits in the prison of Landsberg am Lech dictating to Hess a lunatic statement of aims which two decades later when they have been realized to the letter are still unbelievable (umbilical cord severed and tied, Doctor slaps Carlo's bare bottom, Carlo wails, he is human and alive), a process whose origins are in the mists of the past, whose products are millions of dead and a continent made garbage—this same process, the blowing of an ill wind, solves for one young man a dilemma, what to do with himself?, but only for the nonce.

Insurance? His father could get him in at Ecumenical Indemnity (Laughter). The campus again?; this time indebted to nobody: "they" were going to make it free for veterans, no selling apples this postwar. Which meant either of two: either everybody would go to college, and being mass it would be mean; or none of the ex-servicemen would go, leaving the same old collection of pubescent punks he had got his fill of long before coming to occupy Berlin. Germany itself. Take out papers, if you could find a government to become a national of. Pose as a mustered-out SSman, for which you had the proper appearance, make a living in chocolate bars and Lucky Strikes, pimping for Trudchen. Or merely sit in some congenial ruin and weep away to a skeleton, for what as a German you did, as an American you did not do, and as a man you saw no fit atonement for.

Since his needs were met—women, riches, life of leisure, *gemütlich* flat, loyal friend (who else but a true-life Horatio would dodge punches to do one a favor?), his connection with history (American news correspondents staged a spontaneous demonstration of Berlin GIs celebrating the Japanese surrender; photographed it; Reinhart stood upper left dutifully tossing his cap towards the sky)—since all these holdings were verifiable to the senses, euphoria must, by definition, ensue.

Yet, within the very seed of comfort he detected an inimical, corrosive juice which like the acid in a hand grenade waited tirelessly on the pulling of a pin to begin incendiary mixture. Satisfaction was his, but so also was a growing conviction it should not be: why should he alone be rewarded when the rest of the world was taxed? Even the other Americans had their troubles, wanted grievously to go home, suffered in what he so grossly enjoyed.

He began to fear his own compulsions; if he did not hurt Trudchen enough, neither did she him, and it was not because each did not try. Violent as it was, that plunging to explosion only suggested a damage he could imagine but never yet achieve, that catastrophic end the reaching of which he came, in a kind of pride of horror, to believe was his true vocation. Truly, Trudchen was too depraved to defile and too small a mount to ride to victory.

Virtually unused went his murderous-muscled body, the welted hands with one of which he could have lifted Hitler and cracked off that weak neck like a sparrow's, penetrated Goering's breadbasket as a thumb would sink into a rotten pear. Where was the game worth the candle, where now, standing in the empty stadium, too late, alone, a lackey groundskeeper amid discarded programs and ticket stubs, where now to find another contest?

Time had fled. *Berlin bleibt doch Berlin,* as the natives said, but for the original occupiers—the 82nd Airborne having replaced the 2nd Armored, Reinhart's medics were seniors in service and disenchantment—as September approached, it was a different city from that Newfoundland into which their trucks had rolled on a sun-swept afternoon in July. The aftermath of war had shaded into the onset of peacetime. Regiments of women in kerchiefs and dark stockings labored to clear the bombsites and reclaim sound bricks. The Russians freed and dumped into the Allied sectors some thousands of Wehrmacht prisoners, who staggered along the main thoroughfares tattered, holloweyed, embarrassing civilians, panhandling American passersby. The black market shrank from too-flagrant spectacle. The newest currency regulations were difficult to evade: Pound converted his Swiss watches into Occupation marks—and because the going price had fallen with the replacement of Soviet combat troops by a more conservative element, nonrapists, small spenders, of a dour respectability, got only half as much as he would have in July—but could not get them into dollars and home. "Here I sit," he said to Reinhart, once for every hour they spent together, "with my finger in my ass and one hundred thousand marks."

With the new Russians came fewer explosions from their sector, although incidents, frequently mortal, continued. Earlier they had shot Allies and one another in jest; now the motive had changed to a solemn dislike. Americans were counseled to avoid the eastern quarters of the city, were seduced to remain on home ground by a grandiose Red Cross Club on the Kronprinzenallee, where in the stately dining room a string ensemble in threadbare tuxedoes ingratiatingly whined and the fare was sinkers and coffee in individual silver pots; by the Uncle Tom movie theater on Onkel-Tom-Strasse which led to a structure called Uncle Tom's Hut in the Grunewald Forest, the name German-given, long before VE-Day, for a reason no GI could grasp; by the Berlin Philharmonic, at concerts in the Titania Palast in Steglitz, though soon its conductor, out legally one night after curfew, was misunderstood by an American sentry and shot dead.

Personnel who numbered their years in the late thirties or more were shipped back to the States as senile. So went Reinhart's friend Ben Pluck, in civil life a lawyer; in the Army, having declined to serve, eternal PFC. Others left on longevity points; thus transported was Tom Riley, from across the hall, saddening everyone whose flat lay adjacent to the stairwell; no more would the iron treads echo his jovial filth.

In the latrines they predicted the 1209th would go to Osaka, Japan, where the bearded clam ran crosswise, or the Azores, as in the limerick about sores, or as a kind of liaison force to the Turks in Istanbul. On the wards were one hundred twenty complainants of nasopharyngitis, all on the light diet. The colonel ate out the assembled officers and nurses on the subject of fourteen spent contraceptives spiked off the hospital grounds on the lances of his sanitation crew, directing his remarks principally to Chaplain Peggott and Major Clementine Monroe, the superannuated chief nurse.

Everybody in Reinhart's apartment building had a local mistress save two ethereal privates from Supply, who had each other. Don Mestrovicz, technician fourth grade of the EENT clinic, had two in the same family: a mother still young enough, a daughter just old enough, to whom he was the filling in their sandwich. Corporal Toole from the motor pool owned a big round woman with a behind like the belly of a lute. Bruce Freeman, of X-Ray, had an ash-blonde named Mimi Hammerschlag who played bit parts in Ufa pictures; Jack Eberhard, company clerk, a dishwater blonde who like him made strange noises when drunk. Sergeant Deventer's girl could do a take-off on Hitler with a comb for a mustache; Bill Castel's woman, an artist, cut out his silhouette in orange paper. Ernie Wilson's piece was three weeks pregnant; Roy Savery's, one month; five others professed falsely to the condition, three of whom named the same sire, T-3 "Plumber" Cobb—he laid a lot of pipe—but were duly unmasked. And Farnsworth Cronin was sometimes seen with a boyish girl whose name was spelled *Irene* and pronounced *Ee-ray-nuh;* he, however, called her *Boo.*

Supply outfitted everyone with short jackets, like Eisenhower's, calling in the old skirted blouses. All noncommissioned officers in the ETO were granted a liquor and beer ration; in the 1209th these were consumed on the rear balconies, feet on ledge, cigars in jaw, and in the company of the girls, who giggled much and sometimes sang in English. No Werewolves having turned up, the district order that US personnel carry arms when off compound—the medics, their red-cross sleeve bands—was rescinded. Under the authority of the Information and Education Program, Gerald Gest was sent to Paris for a month to study

French civilization at the Sore-bone, and a class in basic psychology, meeting once a week in an empty storeroom in headquarters, was offered to qualified enlisted men, which meant everybody; in its chair, PFC Harvey Rappaport, MA from NYU.

A sandy-haired corporal named Gladstone, who worked in the post exchange, blew out his brains there one night after closing, leaving no note. Veronica's neuropsychiatric ward, already so crowded that three patients bunked in a supply room, somehow stuffed in five more beds. Walking past its door you never heard a sound, although by her account half a dozen patients wept all day and another man made squealing noises with a finger against his teeth. A paratrooper, under observation for persistent bedwetting, was discovered to be a poseur—in the wee hours he did not really wee-wee but soaked his mattress with $H_2O$ from the bedside glass—and sent back to his outfit on charges of malingering. A tentatively diagnosed schiz struck Lieutenant Llewellyn, assistant psychiatrist, in the nape, knocking off his glasses, then sought to crush them but couldn't with bare feet. Another patient, a brawny man with the hair of a goat, incessantly planned to become a novice in the Carmelite nuns.

No doubt it owed to such spectacular persons and events that Veronica by the fourth week of their acquaintance had lost her bloom, or rather that part of it which was rosy towards Reinhart, who suspected that being normal he bored her. And he could not very well divulge the doings of that other self who lodged with Trudchen, the mad one, the one with passions which, being there resolved, freed this one, the front man, to be so smooth and bland. Back there, Himmler did his dreadful work; up here was elegant Ribbentrop, kissing hands.

For years he had cultivated the art of surrender to women to offset his bulk, which sometimes on its approach caused, particularly small, girls to look for cover. The brute tamed by gentility, the handsome and moral equilibrium of opposites. No, its validity consisted only in the abstract, never in practice. For in-

stance with Very: he cared little about the destination of a date,
so long as it was not an official Army entertainment where they
must be separated by rank. But Very had for the movies the insatiable hunger with which it was said expectant mothers went
to dill pickles—a touch of madness for them, really, Western,
gangster, comical, historical, pastoral, pastoral-comical, histor-
ical-pastoral, any passage of arc light through celluloid into
minuscule glass beads generating counterfeit life, but especially
Dramas in which any one of those actresses with big eyes and
hard white jaws, dressed in jodhpurs, carrying whips, riding stal-
lions, of course gelded, consummated a union with the scion of
a swell family of old Virginia and ate for breakfast grapefruit
in a bed of ice, her nostrils flaring.

In the absence of an enlisted boy friend this taste would have
carried Very every evening to the Onkel Tom Kino, to that
roped-off centrally situated block of seats exclusive to officers,
there for two hours to shuffle off the coil of banal mortality.

Now if this was her pleasure, and as a gentleman his was in
seeing she received hers, why now admit obstruction? "Look,
honey, don't worry about me. I'll sit back in the enlisted section
and meet you outside somewhere when the show's over." "Now
you're sore." Of course he was not angry, just piqued at her resistance to civility. With the best intent in the world she went on:
"No, tonight we'll do what you want." "I want to see the movie."
and usually they did, segregated for two hours and when afterwards they met, Veronica, and not he, looked miffed.

At other times when there had been no conflict of wishes,
when they had taken long night strolls sometimes as far as the
walled villas of Dahlem's tree-murmuring walks (almost the only
alternative he could offer to the movie-show, which was another
reason for his reluctance to prevail), necessarily avoiding society, when they should have formed not two but one, in a sealed
capsule of mutual affection, Veronica had lately seemed, not
exactly withdrawn, but at least preoccupied. Working with these

lunatics all day—apparently her thesis that they got worse in peacetime was daily confirmed—what could you expect? At first he tried to jolly her out of it, but in itself it is a morbid thing to have to cheer a woman, a transposition of the proper roles, she being by nature equipped to bring joy, while man is the rightful brooder.

And considering the precise Very, unfortunately her physical design was not for melancholy. When not in the mobile oval of laughter, her mouth formed a horizontal too broad; her chin appeared square and somewhat virile; when not quivering, her nose was a mere cartilaginous organ, not altogether true, for the induction of breath, and one could understand that it might turn crimson with the grippe. Her eyes when solemn were too pale a blue, the little skeins of iris-color patchily breaking unity, and was not the right one a lash-breadth off the zero aim? Not stimulated, her blood declined to flood her cheeks, and once, at the corner of Max-Eyth-Strasse, in the side apron of his flashlight beam he saw her face was ashen.

Vaguely desperate—for he *was* extremely fond of Very; not in love, actually: that was just something he had thought—Reinhart conceived a plan to get her into the fresh daylight air with a view of water and woods, away from minds, anyway, for one afternoon. He organized some hardboiled eggs, canned meat, and other junk from the mess sergeant, even borrowed the still half-full jars of mustard pickle and mayonnaise Bruce Freeman's mother had mailed that gourmet, and one Wednesday, which that week was Very's day off, with her set out for a picnic on the shore of the Havel.

From the beginning, from the moment Corporal Toole let them out of his jeep at the woodland corner of Pfaueninsel-chaussee and Koenigstrasse, everything went right. The better part of an hour went before they gained the shore, but Very's color improved with each brisk step. At intervals Reinhart hopped off the road into the forest, to bring back talismans: a spray of lace fern, pine cones, a root like the trunk of an elf-woman, a stone resembling an eye, and of course, even out there, a clip of rifle cartridges. Excepting the latter, he gave them one by one to Very, who by the fourth presentation complained of loaded hands, twitted him for his idiocy, and, at last, laughed—perhaps only a snicker, but her first in a week. He was rapidly bringing her back.

On the beach, of which, wandering to the right from the spit pointing towards Peacock Island, they found a length unoccupied by military wreckage, Reinhart brought the goodies from his musette bag. In a messkit bottom Very mashed the eggs with mayo. When Reinhart bit into the first sandwich a fragment of shell cracked between his teeth, just as if he were home. He ate two, and then one of Spam, and then three pairs of saltines enclosing a hard cheese the color and taste of GI soap, and then an orange—for he had brought nothing else for thirst—and Veronica joked about his capacity. The scorings he had lately noticed in her cheeks were but night shadows, already dispersed by the sun.

He lowered his head against a massive log half-buried in the sand and extended his legs luxuriously, out, out, out, toes towards the lake, taking the pleasure of a prolonged stretch, rather like that of a mild orgasm, grunting, eyes narrowed, arms going back over the log. Five yards away the water munched quietly on the sand. Across against its far margin, the dark horizontal of the Kladow shore, a white sail quivered. On the left, and so near that in his view it seemed not an island but rather the other side of an unbroken bay, lay the Pfaueninsel. A suspicion of autumn, a certain chill filament woven into the otherwise still very warm fabric of sunlight, rather imagined than felt, and as yet too thin to penetrate vegetable nature, was felt by Reinhart, in whom it engendered a sad, sweet deliberation on the coming death of the year; and since the end of anything is peace, his heart, too, like Very's, fell placid.

"Ah," he cried suddenly, sitting up, "we forgot the mustard pickles!" He unscrewed the jar and offered it.

Very, while he had unfeelingly stuffed himself, had not eaten a bite, he now noticed retroactively; and the flush in her cheek was nearer the introduction of illness than health returned, as she stared with terrible white eyes into the jar and said, feebly: "They look like alligators in the mud."

She raised her stare to him, and he saw in it a catastrophe from which he would fain have run, had it not been intermixed with a beautiful weakness towards which his manhood inexorably flowed as all streams to the sea. She had essayed a joke, but tears caught her hard upon the last word. Against his chest he brought her weeping, fragrant head, and told close into her ear the platitudes of comfort.

She shortly pushed him off in a kind of anger and, with eyes still melting, assigned all guilt to him.

"If this isn't anything, nothing ever was: I am pregnant."

At the edge of the beach, a fish, or a frog, or some other animate and lonely thing, loudly slapped the water and sank through a necklace of air bubbles.

# CHAPTER 16

NEXT came the insectal hum of a far-off engine, in perfect rhythm with the prickling of Reinhart's hide. Unless nocturnal fancies could inseminate, his tremors belonged to another man, for he, Reinhart, had been no closer to Very's reproductive area than the line of her belt. To put down the guilt, he developed a fury: And I, he raged in secret, I have always acted as if she didn't have a —— (the good old bare word from the honest Anglo-Saxon culture of artisans and farmers, dating from a time before the mincing French crossed the Channel, before the eunuch scholars began to drone in tedious Latin, and eons before small Reinhart belatedly learned from a schoolmate that females are not smooth between their legs and do not produce young by unwinding at the navel).

And by extension, the term applied not only to the orifice but also to that woman who made free with hers. In love with a— but he would not think it again, this short, blunt syllable which in barracks was aired as frequently as exhausted breath: he would not because ——ness was not here at issue. Suddenly he envied her her achievement, lusted not for her body but for her trouble; wished he could weep for having committed a grand foolishness and be comforted by a big disinterested horse's ass who never took a chance; began himself to grieve for all the errors he never made, all the disasters that all at once he strickenly knew would never ruin him—except that, so far as was apparent to the outside eye, he stayed slick and bland. Control. How detestable it was, control; how uncontrollable. How selfish!

Wildly he seized her again, this woman attractively defiled with adventure, for the first time his hand went where the eye's fingers had so often dawdled, to the great hemisphere of her right breast and then to the left, circumnavigating like a Renaissance explorer. Licensed, it was a disappointment; and indeed he knew not why he toyed there, since his purpose was, with lump in throat, self-sacrifice.

His one hand still mobile and encountering more brass button than pendulous woman—at least, that must be what was cutting him—with his other Reinhart lifted her rinsing face, now of a more poignant beauty, pale, implying the sanctity of a plaster, Hibernian-featured Virgin, so much more moving than must have been the real one, dark and muttering in guttural Hebrew. Deep into her eyes he was careful not to look, as he said: "Very, I will marry you!"

What did he expect?: at minimum that the rivulets would cease to flow? Rather were they renewed, as like the heat of summer reaching the highest snow, a brilliant flush mounted to her forehead and a greater rush of water came down.

"How can you!" she wailed. "You are not Catholic!" Repeatedly she struck his chest with her balled fist, no doubt leaving bruises.

Jesus Christ. Like a mongoloid he stared expressionlessly at the lake. The hum of the engine had grown to a still-distant roar.

"Isn't there anything I can do?" He heard himself say it and was astonished by the mousiness of his tenor.

"Hold me."

He did, with static hands, and squeezed her, and pushed his nose into her soft hair and breathed relief that he had not really loved her but only thought so for a while.

"But Him, what about Him?"

Because he had clearly pronounced the capital, she germanely asked: "God?"

"Christ sakes, I mean the guy, who certainly wasn't me! The Invisible Man, because I was under the impression I saw you in all your off-time—unless of course it was one of your psychopaths during duty hours. Is that now part of the therapy?"

In more abandonment than she ever showed while necking, Veronica snuggled into him. "Go on," she whispered, "say anything, I deserve it."

No, with just that quantity of censure he was done. Reinhart on the judicial bench would have freed all malefactors who pleaded guilty, for what could subsequent punishment do but incriminate the judge? Besides, he recognized in his coarseness the tedious old suburban lie that the sexual life was to be regulated by a middle-aged housewife's sense of right and wrong. Screw, screw, screw, if you wanted to, he was proud to think was his credo; and that his own girl friend sported on that plan was the sincerest form of tribute.

Still, if that were her taste, why had she to look elsewhere from him? He was not repulsive to women; time past, he had actually spurned unsolicited advances.

"Who am I to say anything?" he asked, now looking into her eyes. "I'm nobody—as you have proved." He attempted to loosen their connection, but she had clasped her arms about his waist and locked her fingers, as in that test of strength in which you try to crack the other fellow's spine.

"You're the best friend I've ever had. Do you think I could tell anyone else?" Her mouth with its liberal lipstick was crushed against his blousefront; on the journey home he would look as if he had been shotgunned in the chest. In her rich hair, which was no longer his property, was caught a fragment of twig, which, nevertheless, he plucked out. That dear fragrance which in the old days clung to his cheek for hours after leaving her, which during a night of sleep transferred to the hood of his sleeping bag, where he could smell it next bleak morning, now penetrated his nostrils as he supposed a sister's might, stirring mild affection but also thoughts of silly stench.

"I know, I'm like a brother to you—but God damn it, Very, I never knew that till now. You've made a fool of me."

The chopped-egg sandwich Very had made for herself and not eaten, already slightly wilted, lay upon the green canvas of the musette bag. Still holding her, he took it and began to bite off the valances of squeezed-out filling. He did this theatrically, playing the conscious role of a person who vulgarly stuffs himself at high moments, learned from the motion pictures.

"Well, now what are your plans?" he asked. A bit of egg fell, narrowly missing the gold bar on Very's right epaulet, the tracking of which brought his glance to a side view of her cheek and his attention, since her eyes were closed, to the matter of whether or not she had gone to sleep. "Hey," he said, striking her roughly with the blunt of his palm, "recover! What are you going to do now? Look, first, are you dead sure? You know swimming will delay it, and an illness too, I think. Didn't you have a cold last week?" Without physical intimacy he yet knew very well the schedule of her menses: the laugh was not so broad in that quartet of days, and she sometimes complained of headaches. It was just, or should have been, over.

"I've had the Curse enough years to know all its tricks," she answered wryly, cocking up a brow that suggested the old, witty Very's—and he would have liked to catch her there, saying That's it, hold it right at that point and nothing is lost, but she was seized sooner by her own voice, which wavered and ended brokenly: "This time it's for real."

Ah, Reinhart thought, means business, does it?; isn't kidding around; no joke; on the level; for real. Perhaps he believed that nothing ever happened to him because when it did, its effects were stated in barbarous language. Once in Piccadilly talking to a streetwalker he heard overhead the Model T chatter of a buzz-bomb and thought he might die, there in the thronging black street, while a whore said "Coo, ain't it a loud one? Four pounds for awnight, I'm no bawgen basement." His apprehension proved baseless; the bomb sailed on to detonate in some working-class quarter, where the survivors climbed from the smoking ruins to say "Gor, that wasn't 'alf close." Poets are never bombed and, if women, never knocked up.

"Well, what am I to do about it, since you so nicely included me in? I don't want in—you might say, I never *got* in."

Obviously with Very it had been love; and hardly the kind he talked of to himself in his childish way—never again! Very in love, a victim of the conquistador passion; what would ten minutes earlier have been impossible to accept was now only difficult. At least she displayed one requisite of the authentic state: sorrow.

"You?" she answered. "It isn't your trouble, Carlo. You could just get up and walk away from me—you ought to. I can't ask anything of you." She finished crying and sat stolidly in that neutral condition which precedes the return of vanity; unlike Trudchen she looked older without make-up. She *was* older than Reinhart by three years; his girls always, saving Trudchen, were; one's elders are kinder than his juniors and peers. Maureen Veronica Leary, from a suburb of Milwaukee fittingly named St. Francis, graduate of a grade school, high school, and hospital (on the three-year wartime crash program) each under the rubric of another saint. She had a brother and three sisters, all older, and her father, a retired street-railway motorman, told stories of Galway, where the supernatural was commonplace, although he hailed from a town near Dublin named Blackrock. By the time toys and clothing had come down to Very, stuffing leaked from the dollbabies and the stocking-toes were lumpy with darning; but once when she was twelve her father, drunk, brought home a pair of rollerskates her very own. Her mother stood five-ten and her number two sister, just under six and was unmarried at thirty.

So much had Reinhart, in the normal course of events, learned. But who was the real, the essential Very?, to the exterior of which he had been attracted by its air of simpleminded jolly Catholic health. Perhaps a pagan. Not only did he usually go for older girls, he also had a weakness for Roman Catholics, who even when Irish remembered the Latin basis of their persuasion and were very feminine, seldom prudes even when they would not submit: to them a man's appetites, being natural, being God's splendid trick to ensure the race's continuance, were never, even when illicit, loathsome. Now he realized he probably could have, with Very; too late he remembered her constant surrender; indeed, she at the outset had chosen him and then waited in vain.

"You're in love with this guy, is that it? I suppose you don't want to tell me who he is." She still sat within the enclosure of his right arm, while his left, propped against the ground, suffered a slow paralysis. The sand worked up under his fingernails and shortly into a small, smarting cut on the first joint of his thumb, on which he had forgotten to put a new Band-Aid after removing the old one that morning. He had damaged himself on the clip of Trudchen's brassiere, which lousy German thing was not a simple hook-and-eye but a pronged buckle with criminal tines. Since in his subsequent lust he had not taken care, if she had VD he with his open wound was a goner. Ah, accept it, we are all submerged in filth up to our heads. Accepting which, he saw the one man who was exempt emerge from the high thicket of marsh grass thirty yards down the beach.

Preceding this, the engine noise he had unregisteringly heard earlier, had grown loud, identifying itself as an outboard motor; had come so thundrous close to their position that Reinhart expected momentarily to be swamped but didn't care; had, just as it must either become visible or explode, shut itself off with two loud farts in the marsh, yet unseen. Within the minute, this person in black beret and bulky coat appeared, stamping down the last few rushes which denied him clearance to the beach and, that done, seeing them—not necessarily looking towards them, but seeing. By the man's use of this unusual faculty Reinhart recognized, despite the altered outline, Schatzi; who surveyed the four points of the world and approached.

Fearfully Reinhart promised Very they would return to her business later and ruthlessly withdrew his arm. Not adjusting to the new arrangement, Very stayed numbly huddled, leaning against—nothing, for Reinhart was already on his feet, obstreperous in greeting.

"*Guten Tag! Wie befinden Sie sich? Wir machen ein—wie sagt man 'picnic'?*"

"Just so," replied Schatzi, ten yards away and apprehensively halting there as if he foresaw an attack. "*Picknick,* one and same." He winced obsequiously. "Do I receive your permission to come there?"

"*Wo?*" Reinhart was still yelling as though his auditor were in Kladow.

"In the vicinity of you and your lady."

"*Warum nicht?*"

Schatzi came, still cautious, shoulders thrown high and hands buried in the pockets of the great overcoat, which was a dirty teddy-bear plush and fell to his ankles; scarred face contorted below the beret like a withered acorn in its cap; feet, of which only the neat little brown toes were visible, scuttling forward, one-two, pause, one-two—his overcoat fell past his ankles to brush between his footprints the spoor of a tired fox that drags its tail.

"Fancy occurring here with you," he said when he arrived, gauging on the balances of his eyes a specimen of flesh from both the large lumps before him: the one on the ground and Reinhart.

"Whatever are you doing here—way out here?" asked Reinhart, altering to superiority. At the same time his unease grew more severe: he was certain Schatzi thought he had again caught him in a screw, or just after; for a crazy moment he suspected Schatzi trailed him for just that purpose.

"*Ach,* business, always business—your gentle lady, she is ill?" At last Veronica acknowledged his arrival, looking up with forlorn-beagle visage, saying naught. He removed his beret.

"Just tired," said Reinhart. "We had a long—" he lost his voice as he watched Schatzi prepare and deliver a massive, obscene, hideous wink. However offensive, it was mesmeric: the lid flattened and then went concave, seeming to close upon a hole rather than a ball. More horrible yet, Reinhart helplessly felt his own eye return the favor.

"We had a long walk," he said quickly.

"Exercise, ceaseless exercise," said Schatzi benignly. "Well, why not?, as you say. You are yet too young for a *Herzschlag, ja? Auf Englisch heisst das* 'failure of the heart,' am I correct?" With fingers like wire-clippers he pinched a bit of jacket, shirt, and skin on Reinhart's forearm. "Your lady as well, though. Whatever will be her difficulty? Paleness! Ah, right in the pocket I have this brandy which will make the trick."

Ignoring Reinhart's weak verbal opposition, he withdrew a silver flask, unscrewed the cap and let it dangle upon its little chain, hitting the body of the vessel *tok-tok,* and stared down onto Veronica's crown.

"She doesn't want any," said Reinhart, but so as not to offend Schatzi he offered to take a draught himself.

"Who doesn't?" Very, who had been playing no heed, now with violent interest seized the same forearm that had been pinched and pulled herself up. Daintily accepting the flask, she arched her neck like an old grad under the stadium and drained off quite a large slug, then paused to take air and would have returned to kill what was left had not Schatzi, deft as a mongoose, leaped into the breach between her movements and reclaimed his property, saying: "Already better, *ja?*"

"Whew!" whistled Very towards Reinhart. "That went down like a whole loaf of bread." She gulped five times and smoothed the sitting-wrinkles from her skirt; lingeringly, with some evident pleasure in the touch of her own belly and thighs. Schatzi averted his face, as if offended.

If so, how right he was to be. "At least thank the man," Reinhart muttered low.

"I don't know Kraut."

"Haven't you just heard him speaking English?"

"I'll take your word for it." Turning to Schatzi, she asked, naturally very loud: "Hey, didn't I spot you hanging around in front of Lieutenant Schild's place the other night?"

Schatzi twisted his neck to favor the left ear. "Spot? Hanging?"

"On the level now, weren't you? Oh, you weren't in that getup. You had on a cap with a beak and you sat on a bike. Well what I mean is, it was you, I know. Come clean, I won't blow the whistle on you for being out after curfew."

Reinhart made the sound of a bellows. "Damn it, Veronica, what do you think our friend will be able to understand of that?"

By way of answer she simply smirked: drunk, apparently, or pretending to be from the moment her lips had kissed the flask. It was a way out of her difficulties.

"She thanks you very much," said Reinhart to Schatzi, who was confusedly repeating under his breath, 'cap with a beak, sat on a bike.' "And she thinks she saw you last night in front of the house where—where lives an officer she knows."

Where lived, indeed, to admit to himself the complete data, Lieutenant Schild. *Lieutenant Schild.* Which, admitted to the mind, was instantly transformed to: *that Jew.* Who hath usurped my office twixt the sheets? The Jew, the Jew . . .

"Lieutenant Schild," repeated Schatzi, wonderingly, pointing his ridged carrot-nose towards the lake, high; meanwhile his eyes went everywhere else. "Lieutena—wait a moment, I think —no. *Also!* A great fat beast of a man, with a mustache like a broom, and an implement to his speech, so that when he says something he makes this sound between the words: *shicksh, shicksh.* Now tell me am I right?"

"He is thin and dark," Reinhart said evenly.

"Yes, an Italian," Schatzi smiled his recognition. "Yes, I was able to obtain for him—you will pardon me, Madame—some items of which we shall only say they are worn by the ladies and cannot be seen unless one is—please pardon me, Madame—in a relationship of intimacy." He laughed quaintly: "Hahahaheehee-hee," colored, and said: "Now I have gone too far."

"That isn't possible in the present company," Reinhart answered hatefully.

"Oh, he speaks English all right, but I don't get a word," said Veronica to herself, and then to Reinhart: "Ask him if I can have another drink of that radiator fluid." She threw up her hand. "I'll pay him for it, don't look so ghoulish."

"Nonsense," said Schatzi, already presenting the flask. "My compliments. You are a friend of Lieutenant Schilda? Please, I do not mean to offend." Again he laughed, this time in a very horsy manner with open, serrated mouth. "Herr Unteroffizier Reinhart, please tell the lady what is the joke."

"I wish I knew it myself," Reinhart said sullenly. "I wish I knew what was so goddamned funny."

"*Also,* Schilda is the town where the fools live. What is it in the States?"

"Reinhartville," said its exclusive inhabitant, watching Very swallow the rest of the brandy. With gelid courtesy he accepted the weightless flask and gave it to Schatzi. "Well," he said, turning to her, "your troubles are solved. Since Schild is Italian, he is also Catholic. He can marry you, and may I say no one would be more appropriate."

She failed to answer. Already her eyes were distorted, as if one saw them under water.

"You will mah-ree Lieutenant Schild? How lovely," crooned Schatzi, moving in upon her, thin jowls tremulous, as an ambitious chihuahua might approach a mastiff bitch. "I can furnish food and drink for the feast. But you must both soon go back to the U.S. When?"

"See what I mean?" murmured Very. "If that's English, I'll eat it." Now her eyes looked as though a hair were drawn across each retina. By age thirty her figure would be throughout, like a Balkan peasant woman's, the diameter of her chest; her abdomen in permanent pregnancy; thighs, like jodhpurs. The catalogue of Reinhart's malice continued through her parts, which in the here and now were flawless . . . and the receptacle for a Jew. Evil, evil, evil—with evil he flagellated himself while there was still time. For of course he had this deep feeling about Jews, deeper than any he had had for Very; indeed, he recognized now, in the core of his hatred, that it was love. He loved the dead of the camps, and Bernstein, and half of Lori, and . . . Schild; and the dearer the possession, the dearer it was to lose it to them; nay, the dearest were not enough. Thus had Schild been in his presence then, he might have killed him as his wedding gift: Jews were too good to live.

"With all my resources am I trying to be understandable," said Schatzi to Reinhart, pathetically. "*So*, you tell me please, Herr Reinhart, when is this mar-ee-ahzh?" He replaced the beret which he whipped off whenever he spoke to Very and drew Reinhart aside. In an undertone he asked: "And is not this queer?, this little *fête champêtre* without the fiancé? You rogue! The little Trudl is not sufficient for your capacity. And then the Bach woman, too, I believe, as well. Extraordinary. Soon you will have exceeded the Swiss Ambassador, Herr Vögli von Mögli Tägli." As a period to his joke he again whinnied. "Did you grab it? *Vögle von moglich täglich.* Ah, no matter."

"I had nothing to do with Lori," Reinhart stated gravely, "at least not in that way." Nevertheless he was grateful for the accusation. He might have resented another man's combining the disparate ideas of sensuality and Frau Bach and projecting them upon him; but he saw at this juncture that rather than the deed it is the nature of the doer that rules moral judgment. Schatzi, the good German, the gentile, the witness that martyrdom was not exclusively Jewish; was it not a glorious truth of humanity that one virtuous man reclaimed a multitude of sinners? Looking at Schatzi—this twisted, blackened wire, never again to charge chandeliers, to make possible the splendors of filament or the shrewdness of connection; but *wire it still was; honor cannot be annihilated*—looking at him in homage, Reinhart said: "Why were you sent to Auschwitz?"

"Because I was a criminal," Schatzi said mercilessly. "But now as concerning this present matter: who actually—he switched to German—"Who is this female lieutenant? Is she really going to marry this Schild? And, if so, when? Pardon my unusual curiosity, but the man owes me a considerable amount of money—enough, let us say, to give me an interest in any major activity of his. I suspect he's a slippery customer. You know these Italians."

How unfeeling of Reinhart to have stimulated these unpleasant memories! With an agitation painful to see, Schatzi babbled on in rapid and incomprehensible German, blinking, panting, wiping his nose.

"My friend," said Reinhart, placing his big hand on Schatzi's shoulder cap, encountering nothing there but bunched teddy-bear plush, withdrawing it lest the weight fell the poor ill person, "my friend, I did not mean to disturb you. I just want to say: is it not tragic that in our time it came to pass that a man had to be a criminal to remain decent?"

"No, please, I'm not—"

"No," said Reinhart, "I won't say anything more about it, I promise." He sat down on the log he had earlier used as headstop. "Here, have a cigarette with me." He took one himself and pressed the remainder of the pack upon Schatzi, who, still upset, struck it away. "Go on, you can keep them, I mean it," Reinhart said and with sweet exasperation looked to Very for support, and saw her ambling drunkenly up the trail off the beach.

Schatzi marked her too and in a kind of fear choked: "She leaves!"

"Yes," Reinhart answered dully. "And I don't think she knows the way back." Aware of his responsibility, he nevertheless took his own good time in mounting a pursuit, so that when at last he arose she had for some moments been out of vision, beyond a bristling turn of bush. And then the essential sadness struck him like an instant fever: a woman abandoned, unloved, stumbling off alone. In this matter he could be of some use, all the more because of the late harm done his vanity: for once put aside your goddamned self!

Pelting round the bush, squashing pine cones, whipped by green streamers, he spied her moving particularly, whoopsily up a bank of firs ten yards from the path where stood motionless a substantial animal showing the outline of a wolf, as well as its immediate difference: a tiny twig between its monster jaws. Seeing Reinhart, the dog spat out and as soon recaptured the twig, danced, made as if at him then away, and suddenly losing guts and idea, dropped the stick and with lifted leg discharged a high stream of urine against a sapling.

"Come back, Veronica," Reinhart called. "The dog is harmless."

But first to respond was the animal. Kicking back a spray of sand and leaves, it advanced on him sportively, threw great paws upon his blouse, and sought to lave his face with a tongue big as a towel.

"Down, boy!" By a mistake of tactics he was drawn into the game of shove-return; the more forcefully he flung the heavy body back, the more joyfully did it thrust in again, with salivary grin and mock-ferocious tusks. From her place among the firs Very peeped through the hairy branches and screamed.

"Cut it out!" Reinhart yelled. "I told you he was harmless. Down, you fool! Get down, damn you. Oh, damn you. *Heraus!*"

But nothing served till Schatzi, coming up silently behind, barked: *"Pfui!"* Midway in its spring, the dog at once closed in upon itself like a jackknife and folded to the ground.

"What we call a German shepherd," said Reinhart, brushing himself clean. "Does he belong to you?" The dog looked from Schatzi to him in the quick, simple changes of canine emotion, from a loyal shame to a disloyal expectation, and slunk its great head forward in a neutral direction.

"Oh my goodness gracious!" Schatzi said in exasperation. "It follows me about—but swiftly now before she returns back . . ."

It appeared he had taken as an expression of fact Reinhart's wry remark that this Schild should marry Veronica; was concerned about the money Schild owed him: "married men have spare marks" were his words. "But if they marry they must leave soon for the States, *ja*? Married couples are not permitted by the military laws to exist while giving service into the American Army—do I make this clear?"

Reinhart backed away a step: in the high emotion of his interest Schatzi had begun to spray a mist of spit. Curious fellow; but then if Schild, whom it seemed everybody had a case against, was in his debt, no wonder. Owing money to an alumnus of Auschwitz was a good deal rottener than any sexual transgression. He decided it was impeccable to detest Schild, and since that detestation had no intercourse with anti-Semitism, it was generative of power.

"Look," he said in a strong, new voice. "I will get your money back. *I* will. Just don't you worry. You shall have it." He seized the man's birdlike right hand and crushed it in pledge. Then seeing Schatzi's emotion rise rather than fall and not wishing the embarrassment of maudlin thank-you's, he slipped away to fetch Very, who while they talked had gingerly emerged from her green shelter and reached the trail.

"*Pfui teufel!*" said Schatzi, behind him, and the dog, who had presumably offered to be out of order, whined like the slow splitting of a board.

Picking the briars from Very's uniform, brushing her with disinterested, whisked hands, he counseled her not to brood upon and surrender to misfortune; for his promise to retrieve Schatzi's money had been but a prefatory resolution to the main, to the one with which he assumed the obligation of her rescue.

"Don't tell me what to do," said Very, as a drunk does, *de haut en bas*. "And watch your hands." Since he was at that moment in the region of her shoulder blades and had not gone lower, this could hardly be the complaint of modesty outraged.

So he laughed and smacked her full on the bum and repeated: "Don't worry!"

"You're vulgar," she said with dignity and marched on to the log, and sat, and coolly went a-fishing in her bag.

Reinhart threw up his hands in light despair, for the benefit of Schatzi, who was looking the very devil. The dog leaped to its feet; Schatzi cried: "*Pfui!*" It subsided.

"Why does he keep making that hideous sound?" asked Very, pinching her face into a tiny looking glass while her other hand screwed a scarlet bullet of lipstick from its golden shell.

"Madame," he answered, instantly restored, definitely bowing. "This ahneemal is an undisciplined rahscal without a code of ethical manners. One feels that one must give apologies."

"I think," said Reinhart as he saw her face sour, "that she wants to know why you say 'Fooey.' Is that the dog's name?"

"Ah! Ohhohoho, *jetzt verstehe ich*. But no, this is how in German we speak to docks. What must you say? We say *Pfui!* This means 'stop what you do!' 'dezist!' and so forth."

"It seems to work very well," said Reinhart. "I've never seen a dog trained so well."

"Why not?" Very said to her mirror in weary disgust. "That's the way the people are here, except that instead of 'Fooey' it was Der Fooey. Heil, Der Fooey!" She fascist-armed her lipstick.

"Knock it off, Veronica. You don't know what you're saying."

"Heil Reinhart," she cried, playing on him the sun's little spotlight off the mirror.

"Ignore her," he told Schatzi, only to see the man vastly amused and himself raise a flat palm and say: "Heil Reinhart!" and laugh with stained teeth.

"Excuse me," said Schatzi, repeating the salute but this time only mouthing the address. "However, it is very funny to see Americans do this." He clapped himself upon the skull. "Of course! I am forgetting! Soon I may find your relatives, dear boy."

Reinhart counterfeited an excitement he did not feel: "You don't mean it."

"Most surely I do." Schatzi shrugged in his coat, cast an ominous glance upon the dog, and grimaced at the lapping margin of the water unclean with minor driftwood. "I am on the tracks, it is as much as to say." He inspected Reinhart to see what he had aroused, put a finger in the aperture of his own ear, and said: "Ah well, perhaps I am interfering with your afternoon."

"Not at all! Sit down on this log and tell me about it. What could be more important!" Or more inconvenient? He sat down, himself, a weariness having caught him in the reins. He envisioned his kin as tattered, hungry, and cellar-dwelling, that much responsibility added to his present chores. Arrange an abortion for a Catholic, retrieve money from a Jew, accept as family a tribe of Germans, go and catch a falling star, get with child a mandrake root—here at last were things to do, God wot. The dog, he noticed, was inching towards him on its belly, great gray lout of a thing, beseeching.

"Well," said Schatzi, continuing to stand. "I have my look upon a certain family right there in Zehlendorf, who I know had had some great-uncle go to America many years ago."

"But is their name Reinhart?"

"That is simply the whole point. No. But could not have your grandfather a sister?—who would quite naturally change her name when she married a husband?"

In relief, Reinhart said: "Now you're joking." Behind Schatzi's back the dog had crept forward two feet; now it paused and slavered amiably. "No doubt thousands of Germans have relatives in America, and none of them named Reinhart. But it's my fault. I never gave you my grandfather's first name and date of birth."

"*Also*," Schatzi reacted. "You had better do that, so that we can put to shame the false persons who will try to claim your blood." Jamming his fists deep into his pockets, he shuddered.

"I'll write it down," said Reinhart, "—are you cold in the sunlight?"

"Mere *Angst*," Schatzi smiled. "Freedom is difficult to endure. But you must use my pen." He brought forth one of those American fountain pens that profess to last a lifetime—Reinhart wondered if he had owned it in Auschwitz: "Mr. Schatzi of Berlin, Germany, used this Superba Everlasting Masterwriter for three years in the living death of a concentration camp. Yet when he was liberated *it still wrote good as new!*" He also produced a writing surface: a matchbook cover, also Yankee, on the outside a riot of yellow and red exhortation; within, a cooler plea terminating in a tiny coupon one could, if his name were no longer than Li Po's, mail in with ten cents for a sample of accessories to shaving.

Under the salutation provided by the advertiser—*Dear Allah Shavecream Folks: Yes, I want to take advantage of your generous offer. Please rush sample kit to:*—Reinhart had no alternative but to write:

> Gottfr. Rein-
> hart, b. Aug
> 14, '61.

"Thus!" said Schatzi, reading the script close to his face. "An old man."

"He died more than ten years ago."

"Therefore one can die in America just as anywhere else, *ja?* This is sometimes doubted in Europe, and then it is too suggested you stuff your dead as hunting trophies and mount them round the parlor, but I am sure this is peculiar to Kah-lee-for-nia, if there."

Quick to catch his mood of levity, Reinhart jokingly commiserated: "Too bad, I spoiled your coupon."

Schatzi reclaimed his pen so quickly that Reinhart's fingers felt as if struck by the beak of a carnivorous bird. "Whatever do you mean?" he cried, reading the matchbook, then slyly cocked his head: "This is a swindle, *ja?* The persons at this postal box will still keep your ten cents and send you nothing, *ja?* Hahaha . . ."

No doubt it lay very deep, but Reinhart was never hindered by such a concern when it would be mean and ill-mannered to withhold a reply in kind. He made laughter, too, and as Schatzi's increased in volume his own increased in racket, sobbing for breath, and was joined in the second chorus by Very's golden instrument—how healthy it was to hear her!

Screaming with laughter as one does when he finds the joke is that there is none, Reinhart watched the dog worm in under the clamorous cover and, taking from the general amusement a fool's license, roll upon its spine and wave great ludicrous paws.

Expecting Schatzi to begin laughing all over again, he saw him instead hide the matchbook in a fastness of his coat and, stooping, attempt to take the dog unawares with a hook of fingers to its upside-down head. To scratch was apparently his intent; but the dog held to the first appearance, rolled upright, and fell back snarling into the fence of Reinhart's legs.

"I offer to this thing love," Schatzi said, "and receive back only ill humor. *Was kann man tun?* Worse than a human woman." He stared at Very. "I must be about to my business, now. What did you say Madame's name is?"

Since in her present state Very would no doubt take unkindly an oral answer; since her head was at the moment turned away, Reinhart picked up a stick and scratched VERONICA LEARY in the sand, feeling somehow, against his better judgment, as if he were selling her to a white-slaver; and in atonement to Schatzi— for how wickedly misguided was a heart which was queasy towards *him*—offered another five hundred marks to finance his assignment.

"You must not at all times be so ready with your purse,"

Schatzi adjured. "What have I done for you as yet? Besides, do you know, there could be only a single payment if I give you satisfaction. Namely, that when you return back to the Oo Ess Ah you find my kinsfolk there."

"*You* have American relatives?" Reinhart wished instantly he had not sounded incredulous.

"That is my only trouble. But I should accept some, nonetheless, and they could be gangsters or anything, I would not care."

Little, wistful man, he shook goodbye with Reinhart and then with Very—yes, she too put out her hand—and ambled up the trail. With no more clowning, with frequent backward faces of reproach, the dog followed.

# CHAPTER 17

IT WAS a fallacy to confuse animals with human beings. Schatzi thought for a moment, as if he were counting seconds on his fingers, then gave the dog another taste of the stick. He had a technique of whipping refined to maximum sting, minimum bruise. The dog was his property and to disable it were no sense. Simultaneously with the blow, he said soberly and with no great volume:

"Guard the boat."

The beast cried out, as was to be expected, and, as Schatzi knew, far in excess of what the pain would require, for it was not without a limited intelligence. Its chief want was constancy: a singular defect in one of a breed noted for just that virtue. But then, in justice to the dog, it had come into his possession no longer than a fortnight ago, and there was reason to believe its primary loyalty was still fastened to the former owner, a fellow countryman who had reciprocated to the extent that he recoiled from an offer of two packs of cigarettes but sold him for three.

He, Schatzi, had fed it well, had made obvious a capacity for return affection relative to what the beast showed him, had shown tolerance to the first few miscarriages of the dog's assignments, was now nearing the margin of estrangement. When the disobedience could be interpreted as willful, he understood, even approved: the finest organisms are those with a recalcitrant substance which when tamed by its master does not dissolve but compounds with his own. Thus Russian cavalrymen he had seen who were one with their horses, not so much riders as centaurs. This in fact was the timeless sense of the ancient myth. But he had begun to think otherwise of the dog, to see in it a fundamental baseness which said not: "I refuse to guard your cursed boat until you associate it with my being." But rather, "What boat? I chase hares and sport in the sand, and you beat me for your pleasure."

The latter it was saying now, with the voice of its large craven eyes, its great back hunched against the forward seat; and with the repugnant knowledge that it had duped him, that he had given it what it most wished and so confirmed its appraisal of him, he in fury threw the stick far across the water. The dog went over the side and into the surf with a sudden displacement of weight that put the deck awash, and before Schatzi could work with the bilge can, was back and rearing its wet snout to the gunwale, the dripping stick between its jaws. Yes, it was not without intelligence, he admitted, reluctantly amused, but see what it could make of this! He spun the flywheel and the motor caught, and gunned away full throttle. Looking behind, he saw the dog strike out valiantly in pursuit, in a violent battle with the water, which as the distance grew between them it slowly lost but would not admit. Halfway across the Havel and far enough, he assumed, to make his point—he could no longer see its commotion—Schatzi bent back towards the Tiefehorn, the apex of the Wannsee peninsula.

Two hundred yards from shore he stilled the motor and rowed in, an eye on the woods. Which after a time satisfied him that they were deserted, and he beached and concealed the craft. Ten minutes' walk through the forest brought him to a compound of four brick buildings around a garden: a peacetime tuberculosis hospital and during the war a school for air-raid wardens. In the garden were half a dozen Russian graves with their red stars of wood.

His goal was the great radio-transmitter building a hundred meters beyond the compound proper. Built of pallid concrete diseased with green-and-black camouflage splashes, the structure bulked four floors tall, was as long as high, as deep as long, and had no windows. To a median groove in its rear face rose a pile of rusting Wehrmacht helmets, taken off German heads by Russian hands. Also in the environs were: cartridges and shells, both unexploded and used, all calibers; hand grenades, both as loose eggs and, with the wooden handles attached, potato mashers; bayonets; *Panzerfaust* bazookas; elements of the imitation Luger called P-38; corrugated gas-mask canisters; gray-green tunics with a thread of red decoration through a middle buttonhole—the rusted and patinaed and mildewed and rotten, already forgotten, material particularities of an obliterated army. Which meant nothing to Schatzi—he remained.

As he entered, Schatzi took a noseful of the unique odor of the interior, a blend of urine, feces, damp, fire, and electrical effluvium from a transmitter that through it all—last stand, Russian plunderers, American snoopers—retained a deep, visceral stream of life. Its inexorable hum, issuing from the second floor but audible throughout, with the odor and, where the bulbs remained, the dim lights still burning in the halls from which humanity had fled and yet remained in the characteristic carpet of litter and excrement, had spent its force on Schatzi. Once inside he passed into a calm, and picking his way down a concrete stairway clogged with junk, which two steps before its bottom connection surrendered and itself melted into waste, he descended to the basement. Where, since he had earlier extinguished the ceiling lamps and smashed their sockets, he worked his passage with the hand torch that had once disturbed Schild.

Already he thought of Schild in the past tense, no feat for him who had but lately served in that enclosure where the present was so difficult to establish and all Jews looked alike. There had in fact been a uniform diminution of indentities as one went down through the categories of prisoners, from the green breast-triangle of the professional criminals to the yellow and black superimposed to form the Star of David. On his morning work gang the faces were the same for three years, yet a good five thousand individuals, by the record, had come into that lineup and shortly gone, without distinguishing themselves in transit. . . . It was most unlikely that Schild was a fairy; to be a Jew was enough, and a Communist to boot. (In Auschwitz his breast patch would have been superimposed yellow and red, to show his double affiliation.) Therefore all the less was his keeping the Russian understandable. After Schild and the preposterous Sankt George had carried the Russian, all bloody, upstairs, a piece of chocolate oiled the woman's tongue: the fellow was a deserter, of course.

The Red Army had dismantled the dynamos and shipped them off to the Soviet Union—this made all the more mysterious the live transmitter on the floor above; its power supply was gone—but in their great haste to complete the job before the Americans took over the sector, they built huge crates that couldn't clear the basement door, then had to take them down and start again. The detritus from their work—boards, tarpaper, peels of metal housing—Schatzi had assembled wantonly to fill a shallow corridor off the end of the main cellar-hall. Which barred the nosey without teasing them to burrow through it, and also caused Schatzi himself some trouble in his arrivals and departures. For this reason he placed a rigid limitation on the latter, and returned now, breaking his own rules, only to fetch some Meissen china for the last deal with Lieutenant Lovett. That worthy, who had been as the Americans said "framed," was flying out of Tempelhof tomorrow in the direction of the U.S.A. and wanted a souvenir for his mother.

It took both time and care to pass through the barrier, since one had to close in the tunnel behind, and before he could draw after him the last length of coat tail, above the noise of his entrance he heard quick paw-sounds on the stairway and in the hall and, unseen but heard, his dog announced itself without the blind. Nothing to do but grasp rearward to its collar and pull it in, and forestall in oneself the impulse towards congratulation, which was what, with idiot tongue and rolling eyes, it sought and getting would store up as merit against future failures.

Back of the debris, a door unlocked directly into Schatzi's quarters. For earlier tenants it had served as storeroom; its walls were continuous metal shelves from floor to ceiling. They now were heavy with stores of another nature, the materials of Schatzi's major trade: cigarettes, confections, cosmetics, and the mechanical instruments of utility-pleasure: fountain pens, watches, lighters. And also: china from Meissen; Black Forest cuckoo clocks; uinque beer steins, hand-crafted and -colored, each with a history; Hitleriana: signatures of the Man, photos of same with notable associates, counterfeit currycomb scrapings of his dog Blondi's coat, and two books from his personal library: a sob-sister romance by Hedwig Courts-Mahler and one volume of Ranke's *History of the Popes,* the latter with marginal annotations in the Führer's hand, often simply *Scheisse!:* souvenirs from a broader range of Nazidom; and finally a sheaf of small paintings on cardboard by an old man who lived under a heap of rubble in the Soviet Sector, whose wife had been killed in the bombings, whose daughter was raped and VDed by the Russians, and whose pictures—calendar landscapes painted in saccharine and molasses—were moving slowly even with Ami soldiers.

Schatzi took some teacups and saucers and wrapped them in pages of the Red Army paper *Tägliche Rundschau.* Although his collection held twenty-four, he had chosen only five sets and, moreover, had in a sharp, glancing blow against the edge of a shelf chipped the rim of one saucer. It was just those persons who claimed sophistication in *objets d'art,* like Lovett, who were the easiest marks, who could be relied on to call it "Dresden" and be suspicious only of the price.

Warehouse, yes, but the place was also home; there was a cot for Schatzi and a length of chain for the dog (where, having enough foolishness for the day, he now secured it), and a little iron stove whose pipe issued through a chink in the wall, emerging outside beneath the cairn of helmets. Even so, he did not dare to keep a fire in the daytime—giving precedence of mind over body, for he was always cold notwithstanding summer. Cold always, a feeling to which one never adjusts, the history of which is the history of the person and in his case almost a history of the times.

The first, the only, personal comment the man had ever made him, and he could not recall it without its full complement: 1919, seven idealists in the private room of a cheap café in München. The sour and insidious stench of beer, not only in the air, one's own mouth, and the breath of the others, but in clothing dropped on the foot of the flophouse bed and donned again the next day (one could not go naked while they were washed), and doubtless also in Harrer's briefcase, which along with the cigar box for funds made up the Party office.

Harrer was president; had he remained so, it must be admitted that events would have been less interesting. For one thing, Schatzi's clothes would likely have stunk of beer to this very day! He enjoyed such reflections, trifling with times past and irrefrangible; they were the only feasible control—which surely even that other early member, he who drank no beer, would admit now, granting for the moment that he could be assembled from the ashpit in the *Kanzleigarten*.

But the cold. . . . This fellow, about thirty, voice roughened by poison gas in the war, clothes neat but knot of tie off center, capable of incredible fury in abstract argument, but when the *Ober* splashed beer (which he would not suffer in his mouth) on the green fedora upon light raincoat on the adjacent chair, unruffled and gracious. In the discussion he moved that invitations to meetings be printed on the gelatine-duplicating machine and, further, that the cigar box be opened to buy three rubber stamps. On this matter Schatzi cautiously stood with the majority, thinking it over till next week; he had understood the group's aim was to put a little money in his pocket, rather than take it out—the latter, however, being only academic at the time, for he was a month in arrears in dues and on the point of ejection from the "Home for Men" for nonpayment of rent. No, it wasn't true that he had joined to make his fortune in the narrow sense—unless one is a German bourgeois or an American of any class, money is an obsession only when one is poor—but a country is putrid and needs airing when it gives no justice to him who still carries enemy shrapnel in the meat of his thigh.

He, Schatzi, seldom spoke at meetings. He was never strong on ideology, and for that reason his associates treated him with a certain condescension. But earlier in the year when the premier of Bavaria, the Red Jew Eisner, was shot in the street and the ensuing proletarian revolution caught Schatzi's friends of the Thule Society momentarily planless, he had got a chance to show his talent. The Reds hung a picture of Eisner on the wall against which he fell and mounted a guard nearby to force passersby to salute. Schatzi bought a sack of flour, soaked it in the urine of a bitch in rut, accidentally dropped it while passing the portrait. The bag burst, and the stuff powdered the base of the wall: soon all the male dogs in Munich were congregated there to whine and sprinkle their eulogy.

In crushing the revolution there was some loss of blood. The Thule Society—a different order from that of the seven café-gatherers, though with like sympathies; the fellow of the rubber stamps, for one, had been elsewhere—fought as underground shock troops within the city, while the Whites besieged it from without, and in a matter of weeks the revolutionary forces had dwindled to a rabble of left-wing soldiers in the 19th Infantry barracks, of whom the Whites executed every tenth man, and a swinish lot of prisoners in the courtyard of the Munich slaughter-house, some hundreds of whom were formally shot and the rest battered, pierced, crushed, mutilated, and otherwise coaxed to enter the land of the shadows. Having won some merit in this action, Schatzi came to the attention of Captain Ernst Röhm, who was always on the lookout for young men—for more purposes than one, as it turned out—and was recruited for one after another of Röhm's private armies, some disbanded the day they were formed, by the Jew-Socialist traitors in the government, the same that had betrayed Germany in the last days of the war. Schatzi had been very young in that time, twenty-two and three, and a prisoner of the feverish passions of the callow: for example, when he thought of the government he saw a single face, wan, spectacled, hooknosed, showing sly sanctimony that broke quickly into womanish fear as a good fist smashed into it.

But the cold. . . . After this meeting, when the cigar box had been replaced in the briefcase and the briefcase snapped and the reckoning paid, Röhm paying Schatzi's, the seven rose to leave. Even as he buttoned his poor outer clothing—he had no overcoat—Schatzi trembled before the thought of the late-fall wind in the street; and the man beside him, getting into the raincoat, stared from the deepset eyes since famous.

"I don't know why, I am always cold," Schatzi apologized, and didn't know why he did that, either, for it was honest enough, but the man without opening his mouth seemed to demand it.

In answer Adolf Hitler said: "You no doubt eat meat, which oxidizes too fast in the stomach and the warmth is dissipated. The German nation as a whole consumes meat in the manner of a pack of hogs at their swill, and can never be strong until all that is at an end—not to mention that, as Schopenhauer observed, it smokes instead of thinks. I oppose all that." He pulled the hat very low over his brow and left the cafe with quick steps as Röhm, smiling with his mutilated nose, took Schatzi's arm.

It was a tablecloth of many colors, handwoven, fringed, and according to Lovett, who folded it briskly and placed it in the wooden crate, an article of Holland. Although the old lady of the house swore that she had bought it once on holiday in that country, he had pronounced it contraband of war, first for her and now for himself. And now, in the incredibly solipsist way that only Americans can do well, he related the details to Schatzi, as if expecting congratulations.

After a cursory inspection of the china, he drew five hundred Occupation marks from a fat wallet and thrust them at Schatzi, for all the world as if he, Lovett, had got the better. For who feels he has got it, has it—added to which, by the look of the billfold, if when Lovett arrived in the States his purchase was exposed, the expenditure had been small and the swindle might even give him an aura of adventure. Standing there before him, Schatzi could conjure up a little narrative two months hence in which his own image would appear as a quaint, Old World rascal. And its force was sufficient to alter, for a moment, the long, straight direction of his life.

"No, no," he said, returning to Lovett half the sheaf of bills. "The price that we agreed upon was two hundred and fifty marks. You are so careless of your money!"

In Lovett delight and dismay contested, with the latter ultimately victorious. For, while he took the money, he now for the first time studied Schatzi and then applied the same inspection to the china.

"This chip," he said. "Oh! It isn't old at all—"

"But," Schatzi broke in happily, "it is not the age of the chip that must trouble one, but instead the age of the china. As it does happen, I know the late history of these pieces. They were on the estate of the Graf von Halsbach zu Willmark in East Prussia for decades of many years. Unfortunately for him, the count remained until the last hour in the face of the Russian advance, and is it necessary to relate further of his outcome? His daughter alone escaped, with means of certain compromises—" He slowed down, watching Lovett's doubt metamorphose into a sexless, vicarious lust—whether fastened to the count, the Russians, the daughter, the china, or the unspecified violence, he could not say—and continued: "But one can never be for long uncertain in these cases." He turned over the saucer in question, and pointed to the moldmark of a factory in southeast Berlin: "You see, unmistakable. Every piece of genuine Dresden ware carries that age-old stamp."

"Yes," said Lovett, "unmistakable. I hope I didn't offend you, but the price, well frankly it's so modest. You see—" laughing girlishly—"I'm not one to usually complain about something costing too little, but some things you just *know* you have to put out a good price for, or they're no good and there's no use in puttin' out your money . . ."

Looking through the living-room curtains, Schatzi saw Nader, whom he feared, on the other side of the street and about to cross.

"The price," he said hurriedly, "is set at that level because I cannot in all decency take a commission on this selling. The count's daughter is in a bad state of life, ill and needs the money for drugs and food."

"You must take the rest of this." Lovett, who had also seen his roommate, thrust the bills into his hand, and they had disappeared into Schatzi's shaggy pocket before Nader entered.

Nader scraped about dispiritedly in the hall for some moments—time enough for Lovett to conceal his purchase beneath the tablecloth in the box—before he came into the room with a sad look for his friend and a hard one for Schatzi, who prepared to leave.

"It's no dice, Dewey. The Old Man's had it in for you for a long time. He told me frankly that he has been looking for an excuse to ride you out ever since you joined the outfit. And he also said he always thought—he said—I don't want to hurt your feelings, Dewey, but he said, 'Nader, I soldiered with you for ten years. I'd hate to think you turned queer when you got your commission.'"

"Well, Wally, you tried, and I am very grateful," said Lovett.

He flipped away like a doffed glove and began to stuff the crate with his enormous stock of extra underwear. "I told you before that I'm quite actually happy to be going. By the time I get back to the States I'll be up for discharge, and I'm so anxious to get out of this horrid uniform and back to the shop. Mother's been going it alone there for three years and just hasn't been able to cope. The *qui vive* is what one must always be on in antiques."

"That prick!" said Nader. "His trouble is he just hates culture. You know his idea of fun? Throwing down glass after glass of booze and telling stories about toilets. Hour after hour. I used to have to listen to all that trash without opening my mouth in the old days when I was top for the station-hospital company at Bliss. One time I signed up for a correspondence course on how to improve my English. When he saw it he said: 'Now, Nader, you can't make a silk purse out of a piece of sowbelly.' How I used to ache to get that dirty muff diver in an alley and slam the poison outen him—why can't a man improve himself?"

Nader's body took on the temper of the grievance; the trapezius muscle at the base of his neck threatened to burst from the shirt.

Lovett fussed the rough top onto the crate. "It's all right, Wally," he said. "One can't right all the world's wrongs—Ouch!" He had got a splinter in his pinkie.

"The point is," answered Nader, taking over the job, nailing down the top with sixteen nails, precisely one hammerblow for each, and without a break in rhythm getting after a nose-itch with his left hand, "the point is, a guy does all he can for a friend." He manhandled the great carton to his shoulder and fought it to the porch, being at the door the recipient of Schatzi's courtesy.

Rid of his burden, and having no gratitude, he blocked Schatzi's exit. "What the hell are you doing here?"

Schatzi's arms flew up to guard his face.

"You know why I don't like you?" Nader continued, glaring. "You always look like you want somebody to kick your ass."

"But I have authority to come now to this house," said Schatzi "The Lieutenant—"

"Well, if you're finished, screw."

Schatzi glanced up and down the street and moved closer. "My dear Captain"—his upgrading Nader had a gross purpose for what he assumed to be a gross person—"I have been told that the Lieutenant Lofatt's difficulty can be traced to a Russian officer, is it true, and perhaps if this Russian can be discovered, your friend will not suffer for it."

Nader was not attracted. "I said blow." He offered Schatzi assistance in negotiating the stair.

At the same moment, however, and before Schatzi had begun to move—looking at Nader with an odd smile that the lieutenant did not understand was admiration—he saw the old housekeeper issue from the door and hail him with her fingers.

"The blond officer has stolen my tablecloth and I don't know what to do," she cried. "You are their friend? Then you can help me."

She was breathless, fat, and wheezing, and what was left of her reason and passion obviously had its locus in the thick and tasteless furnishings of her home. It was precisely this kind of person that the movement in its early days had been pledged to get rid of; Hitler had instead purged Röhm and dispensed with the Strassers, and Goebbels, degenerate, maimed opportunist that he was, had submitted to the policies under which the bourgeoisie flourished.

"You are a widow, no?" he asked, noticing that on her second sentence Nader went within.

"My husband was office manager of a fine company, small but fine. It was a direct hit. Afterwards we couldn't even find his body. Please, I have no one to help!"

"My good lady—" he drew back as she clutched at his sleeve.

Anybody with a brain in his head would have anticipated Lovett by offering to sell the cloth before he had ever touched it. "—the Americans are honest enough. There has no doubt been a misunderstanding. You must speak with him again."

He was already on the bottom step, but the woman followed him down and, unless he broke away immediately, would surely weep, and that he must be spared.

"With their parties they already have destroyed everything else," she wailed. "Did you see, the living room is empty, and I have not yet been paid. The ceiling—the ceiling was shot away for no reason."

Now that it was called to his attention, he remembered a certain damage in the room—yet still not enough for his tastes; they would have had to burn off the roof and knock out at least one wall for it to seem anything like a home to him.

"But of course, this is why the officer is being sent away. You do not go unrevenged."

The silly bitch listened to nothing he said. "Please speak to him," she cried. "I have no English."

"Ah, my good lady, neither have I, you see."

He had left his bicycle in a clump of bushes around the corner—not from fear of theft, for in spite of all it was still an honest land, but out of caution; avoiding the neighbor Schild, who might have seen an unconcealed vehicle.

On the long trip to the Soviet Sector, Schatzi had to show a different combination of papers at each checkpoint, American, British, and Russian, and there was always the possibility that some illiterate of the last type might shoot him. Sergeyev would of course spring him from an arrest, but, in his own words, could "grant no immunity from a bullet." However, he once again without incident went through the waste of Potsdamer Platz and the barricade on its east side, and although the crowds delayed him—where did they all come from, and why?—it was far better than to chance a remote and less-peopled entrance, with guards accordingly more primitive.

From here on he found it more politic to walk much of the way, wheeling the bike beside him: it was unwisdom in this area to distinguish oneself on a wheeled possession. Even so, he was stopped once by a Russian private, not a guard but one of the many roaming at large, who would have confiscated the vehicle had not Schatzi thrust in his face the pass from Sergeyev that read: "The bearer, L. K. Burmeister, German national, registration number 2XL-1897340-C, is on special business for the Army of the Union of Soviet Socialist Republics. —V. Sobko, 10th Section, Hdqrs., Red Army." At which the fool saluted as smartly as a Russian could, and went on.

Arriving before a relatively sound four-story building off Alexander Platz, Schatzi parked his bike in the iron rack, and this time snapped a small lock around two spokes and an upright of the frame, and with still another pass issued him by Sergeyev, with data as false as the other, persuaded the soldier on door-duty to lower his machine pistol, and entered under the long red banner that said: "The unity of all Antifascists is the guarantee for the construction of a democratic Germany."

"Yes, do that," Sergeyev was saying into the telephone as Schatzi entered the smallest room, at the farthest end, on the last floor. "Show him no more mercy than you would a fly that had fallen into your soup, and at the same time deal with care, just as you would with the fly, for if you crushed him then and there you might have to empty the entire bowl."

To one who on first meeting Hitler had seen an eccentric small-town sissy, there had come in ensuing years a disbelief in anything but the unlikely. However, it must be faced that Sergeyev differed from the commissar of legend only in his wearing mufti rather than the high, tight collar that was wanted to set off his bullet head. But then, even the civilian clothes were regulation for the type: the paradoxical jacket, both too tight and too baggy; dark-green tie and blue-striped shirt, both clean but looking dirty; and on a folding chair in the corner, a black felt hat with a little pond of light dust in its crown-dent and the brim lowered all the way round.

Replacing the instrument in its cradle and without giving Schatzi any sign that he was received, Sergeyev revolved his squat weight, the ancient swivel chair croaking like a frog, to a low wooden shelf on the wall behind the desk, where, as usual, the articles from his pocket were scattered: crushed packet of Russian cigarettes, cheap brass lighter that took forever to catch, mean collection of zinc small money, and a nail file in a mock-leather case frayed here and there to its subcutaneous paper. On his own initiative—for he wished to give Sergeyev no more than he already had, and the best strategy to that end was no unrequested sound—Schatzi had assumed this foible owed to a stout man's difficulty in getting to his pockets while seated. As to the drawers of the desk: Sergeyev had no more considerable paunch than a keg, which is to say from shoulders to thighs he was one thick swell with no protuberance, but he sat so tight against the furniture before him as to join it to his person. Thus the shelf. Facing which he now stayed and, to it, said in German: "This is not your day."

The diameter of his cropped skull widened as head gave way invisibly to neck, and both head and neck, and face, as he now made his return revolution, and the thick, hairless hands that grasped the cigarette and smashed at the lighter's wheel, were crimson as an angry baby. Sergeyev, however, was never angry. If anyone threatened to make him so, he had him destroyed. As, anyway, he had once told Schatzi, who was disinclined to demand proof.

"You have no answer to that? Ah well, in the east country you'll have years to talk all you wish to the ice and snow, unless a guard puts you out of your madman's misery with a rifle butt."

Schatzi waited through the inevitable joke about Siberia, as one does for the amenities. "Yes, quite true, it's not my regular time, but I have something you should want to know."

"And you've come here last of all, not having been able to sell it elsewhere. You think you can fool me, you piece of filth? You still do not believe that I can fling you down the stairs at my pleasure?"

Sergeyev arose and pounded to the door, opened it and thrust half of himself into the hall. "Yes, that stair down there, the one you came up," this part of his speech itself being flung in that direction and thus scarcely audible to Schatzi. Who nevertheless had heard the threat clearly enough in the past to know it was habitually delivered in a voice devoid of all emotion; but not that he believed it empty—somehow one knew without evidence that Sergeyev was the type to say it a hundred times and do it on the hundred and first, or the thousand and twelfth, or not at all, for he had no rhythm and no limit and, indeed, beyond the pocket articles, no discernible self. These on the return trip he cleared from the shelf with one hand as sweep and one as scoop and buried in his clothing, as if in anachronistic worry that Schatzi might swipe them while his head was out of the room.

"*Also!*" He threw himself into the chair and grasped either end of the desk. "Proceed!"

"Lieutenant Schild—"

"*Are you insane?*" shrieked Sergeyev. He sprang up again, went again to the door, looked out, came back on a circuitous route of examination—his office was small as a private washroom, with no window, the streaked beige walls marred by no ornament, and no furniture beyond the desk and the lone extra chair that Schatzi occupied—and disengaged the telephone's handpiece from its berth.

"Do you think me so naïve that you can inform to American Intelligence before my face?" he screamed, still with no emotion, stamping out his cigarette in a little glass bowl evil with tobacco tar.

"Fritz, then," said Schatzi. "*A Russian deserter is living at Fritz's billet.*" He stirred in his chair, smiling ill in fright and pride. "Also: Fritz is going to marry an American nurse."

He was met with an open mouth of short teeth, which appeared to be a smile. "Tell me," said Sergeyev, his voice liquid with unction, "confess to me—you were Ernst Röhm's very favorite fairy-boy of all, *nicht wahr?* This is the sole reason why you were present on that famous 30 June 1933 when your lover and his faction were purged. We know all this already, so I can tell you it is useless to continue your mad resistance!"

A half year before, in the middle of January, when the Russian forces were rolling through Poland, the SS closed the Auschwitz camp and herded the dangerous prisoners—mainly such Jews as were left, and politicals—on a long death march to the enclosure at Mauthausen, in Germany. Schatzi was permitted to escape. Right off, he was almost murdered by Polish vigilantes who came in to fill the vacuum. For the uniform he had continued to wear as protection against just such a hazard, snipping the green triangle off the breast, was precisely what identified him to a Polish tradesman who had made deliveries to the camp and seen Schatzi in his privileged role as "professional criminal" leading work gangs to dig their own mass graves. This Pole, until two weeks before a collaborator, was now applying the same industry to preserve Number One in the new arrangements; in which he was as unsuccessful as a man can be: the guerillas shortly knocked *him* off, but saved Schatzi for the oncoming Soviet authorities. Who in turn not long after arrival dispensed with the vigilantes themselves, so neatly that no trace of the bodies was found by three Swiss Red Cross delegates searching for eighteen days, *but saved Schatzi.*

In neither case were the Russians wanton: the Polish guerillas, having shown enterprise once, would likely have proved troublesome in the Soviet occupation, and Schatzi, being officially an unperson and by personal history an advocate of no live cause, a friend of no man, totally dependent upon his captors and nicely shaped by years of captivity—it would be almost indecent to get rid of a man who could be used, and for no payment, beyond not taking that which had no absolute value: his life.

He was taken to Berlin and assigned to Sergeyev, who notwithstanding the mufti, was apparently an officer in an Intelligence section of the Red Army: *apparently*, because this was never mentioned, Sergeyev's office being this shabby, airless cube in a building tenanted otherwise by the German Communist Party.

"And we know, believe me, that you make daily reports to American Espionage," Sergeyev continued in his genial way. "Must I remind you once more that you are no safer in that sector than this one? How much sufferance would the Americans show if we informed them of your past, *Misterrrr* 'Burmeister,' *sirrr*." On the English words he did a humorous imitation of the American *r*, which at the same time was very accurate.

"The only American agent I deal with is Fritz."

"Never mind about that!" Nevertheless, Schatzi saw him write FRITZ on the back of a used envelope—which he pulled from a wastebasket; there was nothing on the desktop but the glass bowl for ashes and a pile of paperclips artfully arranged to appear loose but really joined into a two-foot chain, as he had discovered on an earlier visit when Sergeyev suddenly hurled it at him—FRITZ, he wrote it a second time and began to elaborate its lines with the pencil as he started again on Röhm.

Röhm, Röhm! From Sergeyev's badgering at every visit, each time with a different angle of attack—the last time, of all things, he had been accused of being a spy in Röhm's camp *for Hitler*— one could see that beneath the surface foolishness they knew everything already. And if they knew everything, they must surely know he had not been with Röhm's personal party on the terrible night of June 30, 1933, when Hitler and company burst into the Bavarian hideaway and carted them off to the slaughter.

And, to boot, Sergeyev had once asked him for an account of the executions at the Lichterfelde Cadet School in Berlin. But surely they knew that if he had been with Röhm he would have been taken to Munich, if not killed on the spot, as some were, in the sanatorium at Wiessee.

As to his erotic associations with Röhm—it was impossible to explain to anyone who had never know him the dynamism of the man, the virility which made denying him his pleasure almost shameful. Schatzi had not been given to the practice before he met him, and did not continue it extensively after the purge— indeed, although he had tried most of them, he had yet to find a kind of sex that was not tedious.

His not having been with Röhm's party on that historical night was a piece of the strange kind of luck that blessed him his life long—or plagued him, for with his leader's death perished a purity that he had found neither before nor since in the walks of men, a hard, clean, uncompromising resolution, honor, and bravery that the foul little Austrian upstart had betrayed to a moral leper like Goering, a weak-minded fanatic like Himmler, the antediluvian cowards of the Reichswehr, and the reaction-aries of the Ruhr who had given niggardly money to the Party with the sole aim of getting more in return.

What was there to tell? Schatzi stayed in Berlin at headquar-ters, keeping a finger on developments, while Röhm and the other SA leaders conferred in the Bavarian retreat. Aware that they were incessantly calumniated by the evil voices at Hitler's ear, sensing that they, the private army of the National Socialist revolution, the oldest fighters, the idealists, the conscience of the movement, had already been made superfluous in the general corruption, they were yet unprepared for the ferocity of their blood-brothers. Röhm was expecting a visit from Hitler on July 1, at which he intended to plead again to his old comrade-in-arms the case for the SA. He had a touching little gift for the Führer, a handsome bookplate. He waited in trust, with no guards; he was after all the only man in the Party who called Hitler by his first name, not to mention that he had been a Nazi even before Adolf. But when Hitler arrived, it was with a band of thugs and in the dead of night.

Simultaneous with the raid in Bavaria, Himmler and Goering took the headquarters in Berlin, capturing a hundred and fifty officers, whom they imprisoned in the Cadet School coal cellar in Lichterfelde and shot in quartets throughout the next twenty-four hours. The condemned men kept precise count of the executions; guessing whose turn came next was insurance against despair. They sang the song named for Horst Wessel. And, in innocent trust, heiled Hitler and went to their deaths faithful to his memory, for they supposed him also to have been a victim of the reactionary plot to crush the revolution.

In the twenty-seventh group-of-four Schatzi's name was called —not, of course, "Schatzi," but "Ernst, Friedrich Paul, *Obersturmbannführer*," and even at that moment he thrilled to the crisp drumroll of his title: he had been a poor lance-corporal in the army for three years of the war, owing to the petty jealousy of a sergeant who consistently blocked his promotion. As he was marched with three others out into the mild morning and across the yard to the execution-wall, he saw some of the faces of his remaining comrades pressed against the cellar window, those old veterans of the Putsch, of a thousand café and street fights, of the Freikorps, and, before that, spotted here and there in the army of the Western Front. They had been fighting somewhere for almost twenty years, against impossible odds, for much of it ill fed and ill clothed, and always betrayed. Not one had broken down in the cellar. That was pretty good for the "pack of fairies" that so revolted Goering.

The wall was a dripping stucco of human flesh; fired from six yards away, the bullets blew the heart through a man's back. An SS guard opened their clothing at the breast. Having difficulty

with Schatzi's woolen undershirt, he parted it with the cere-
monial dagger from his belt and, inadvertently nicking the skin,
excused himself. On Schatzi's right hand was Appel, whom he
had never liked. He caught his eye now as the guard went down
the line drawing charcoal target-circles around their left nipples,
and said softly, "Ahoy!" the old Freikorps greeting. Appel had
been one of Röhm's especial favorites; he smiled now over the
gravity of his girlish face.

"By order of the Führer, FIRE!" The four prisoners stiff-armed
the salute to Hitler and cried his name so loud they did not hear
the order, and their chests were blasted through their backs. Or
rather, three died not hearing—or if they did, were in a second
beyond knowledge. Schatzi, falling with the others, heard, and
knew that Röhm was dead, that Hitler had betrayed them, and
that from then on he would give credence and fealty to no
movement but that of his own pulse—which he heard now
in the wrist crumpled beneath his ear, for he was not dead, had
not indeed been hit, but rather was pulled down by the unity
with his fellows. Lying with slit-eye at the level of the concrete,
he saw the approach of the sole of a boot, was turned over and
tested by it. A pistol slug fractured the pavement near his nose,
the sharp chips whipping his face, already bloody from the
liquid of Appel's heart.

Schatzi preferred later, with his last ration of sentimentality,
to believe that the officer had missed on purpose—it was said
the executioners' squad had to be changed frequently because
of nerve failure—but he dared not see who it was. Shortly the
disposal wagon, borrowed from a local butcher, returned from
its last trip, and he along with the lifeless others was sacked into
its tin bed. The rear doors were secured. The deliberate horse
wheeled it creaking to the gate, which, opening, had its own
sound. Fortunately, he had been thrown on top of the pile and
was not crushed by the other bodies. Giving fate five minutes, as
near as he could estimate, he tried the doors and found his hands

too weak to manipulate the catch. Treading back, the wagon swaying, Appel and two more soft underfoot, he hurled himself forward. The wagon stopped—he had been conscious of the awful silence only as something to flee, but of course his movement broke it for the guards up front. The blond face of a horrified SS private was a circle in the bursting doors. Gory and wild—he had come so far since that he could smile at the remembered terror of that young calf—Schatzi flung out, felling the boy. They were on a deserted side street near the Stich Canal. He knew the area well, and escaped unpursued.

"I can only repeat what I have told you before," he said to Sergeyev's smile, which was turning more grisly. "My associations with the Nazis ceased on June 30, 1933, except that for the next twelve years I was their victim like so many others. What we in the early SA wanted was much the same as the Communists; we were even called 'brown on the outside, red on the inside.' "

"Don't insult me with your filthy comparisons between the international workers' movement and a reactionary-mystico-homosexual cult," Sergeyev shouted. "That was the only intelligent thing that Hitler ever did, to crush that foulness without mercy. What I want from you is the truth about those intervening years. In reality, you all the time were working with the Hitlerites as underground agent, *nicht wahr?* Or were you even that early taking American money?"

Schatzi patiently went through it all once more: after his escape he had lived for two years under a variety of aliases, outside both civil and Nazi law, until discovered by the Gestapo; after which he was kept in places of confinement for ten years.

"Excellent, excellent," said Sergeyev. "Go right ahead with your resistance. But when you collapse into a quivering, boneless mound, remember it was your own doing. . . ." He put down the pencil and, with the difficulty Schatzi had foreseen, dug into his pocket and found the nail file, put it to work with minute attention on the fingers of the right hand. One by one; it seemed hours before he finished and started on the left. Finally, though, it was done, and he brushed off the fall of nail dust—only to go into his breast pocket for a toothpick and clean around the little pegs which served him for teeth.

Schatzi ever so slightly changed his position in the chair, which made a loud, splitting, flatulent sound. He was genuinely embarrassed. Sergeyev bit through the toothpick, chewed it up, in fact, and blanched.

"*Did you,*" he said, for once not acting, and thus showing that everything heretofore had been dramatics, and in a voice so mad with anguish that it seemed afraid, and Sergeyev afraid was so fearsome that in another moment Schatzi might have flung himself from the window, had there been one, "*did you have the audacity to fart?*"

Perhaps because this time he had really been moved, he accepted the explanation, took up his pencil again, and twitched it in dismissal.

"Report on your regular day."

# CHAPTER 18

Now to the saving of Veronica. Of all women for fertilization of the egg, a nurse; of all for illicit impregnation, a Catholic. Finally, a professional worker in the branch of healing to which problems of love were fundamental, herself love's dupe.

Since on her own terms her infraction was inexcusable, his job would not be simple. It was even possible she would resist being saved—as she had refused that first, hysterical offer of marriage —and absolutely certain she would not admit the mode he had determined on. To a Catholic the mere use of a Trojan, he understood, was the denial to a new soul of its right to incarnate, reach puberty, and disapprove of contraception. Either you suppressed lust at its first tingling or, embracing it, you were obliged to stay for the dénouement. Abortion, of course, was downright murder.

Therefore would his guile be summoned to sally forth from the imaginary fields where it had so often bested Machiavelli. And his ingenuity: not even in a military hospital with a hundred doctors could one hope easily to recruit an abortionist, another nurse was unthinkable, and although he could name as many unscrupulous enlisted technicians as there were wards he had little faith in their Army-learned craft.

In the last he was terribly confirmed by a story of Marsala's. Roy Savery, an enlisted assistant in the operating room, had just yesterday performed an abortion on his German girl friend and she bled to death.

"His trouble was," said Marsala in high disgust, "oh my aching back!, he loved her. If he didn't of, she would still be alive and he wouldn't be up for court-martial. Any girls I knock up I do them a favor and don't see them again." He chuckled and screwed his gangster's face around the stump of cigar on which his large incisors were clamped, smoke and speech intermingling from the side alleys of his mouth: "Why not? I never raped anybody long as I lived. Am I right?"

They sat *en famille* in their living room, at the round table beneath a chandelier of five dead bulbs and one live. Marsala took off his undershirt, revealing a natural vest of hair, from deep in the tangles of which glinted a silver religious medal as might a fragment of broken airplane within the jungles of the Mato Grosso. He had too extravagantly stoked the corner stove an hour before, and the air was at that temperature in which the skin weeps and philosophy proliferates.

"Poor girl." Reinhart groaned, in part because he was miserable with perspiration.

"Yeah, he held a gun on her to make her haul his ashes," Marsala growled disingenuously, suspending from his index fingers the dancing, ghostlike undershirt, which he inspected for cleanliness and finding insufficient balled and cast under the sideboard. "He should of done it, see? Then he woona owed her nothing at all, if you get my meaning."

"It's burning in here. I'd better open the window."

"No, whadduh yuh crazy? I take pneumonia with no shirt on, you dumb dong. . . . So get yaself a American girl like you got, huh you big dummy Carlo? Knows how to take care of her humping self, huh? Now don't tell your old buddy you don—"

"You got any extra money, buddy?"

Marsala snatched from a back pocket and propelled across the table his old brown billfold fat as a squab and said, while drawing on the stogie: "Take whadduhyuh want."

Reinhart chose a sheaf of one thousand marks from a store of twice that much. "Can I have this?" He fanned the bills so Marsala could count them.

"*What* is this?" his friend answered, outraged, and bending over, seized the wallet's remaining notes and threw them in his face. "*What* is this, fuck-your-buddy week? *La putana Maria!* You won't take my money, I give you a shot inna head."

"I can probably pay you back next month—"

"Okay, say one more word and I go rub shit in your sack," shouted Marsala, dilating his hirsute nostrils. "Don't hump me with them college insults, Carlo Kraut. My cash's not good enough for you, okay, okay, OKAY!" He paced furiously around the room, having his great noisy pleasure.

In a moment he marched into the hall, flung wide the outer portal, and bellowed Riley's old call up the stairwell, hearing which Jack Eberhard came out upon the top-floor landing and cried in riposte: "You like cake? Take this, it's raisin." Then more doors opened and some of the other good old boys popped out shouting all the grand old irreverences on the genito-urinary tract, the oestrous cycle, the gastro-intestinal system, and their heresies, and when someone mock-flatulated with a hand in bare armpit, someone else whooped: "Kiss me again, sweet lips!"

"Where's Reinhart?" called the guys from the third floor, and the cry was taken up by throats on all levels to the roof: "Reinhart! Reinhart!" Inside, Reinhart listened, a kind of warm cramp in his stomach, and then rose, went into the hall, and looked up through the spiral of shining comrade-faces whom one day it would be a death to leave.

"Short arm!" he shouted. "Marsala, get the flashlight!" And everywhere sounded the cheers and catcalls and boisterous generosity, and the third-floor guys fetched a pitcher of water and poured it down in a great quivering sheet, really funny because they really aimed to hit them and only narrowly failed. Marsala got angry and had to be held back by real force from climbing up and kicking the bowels out of the whole bunch. To soothe him Reinhart recited everybody's favorite poem:

> When the nights are hot and sultry
> Is no time to commit adultery.

But when the frost is on the punkin,
That's the time for Peter Duncan.

A society grounded on common inconvenience, where friendship was innocent of opportunism and tolerance flourished without manifesto: no crime could outlaw you from this company; no
merit beyond the grossest went recognized; where sensitivity
was soon reduced to coarseness and ambition stifled; where leth-
argy was rewarded and disenchantment celebrated; this cul-de-
sac off the superhighway to the glorious Houyhnhnm of the
future where a chicken would stew in every pot and each man
be his own poet, unarmed, owing allegiance to one world—this
splendid, dear, degrading society, here as nowhere else Reinhart
felt at home and loved.

An invitation from an *ad hoc* party headed for the noncoms'
club, there to swallow strong German beer, cuss, spit, smoke, and
perhaps, about closing time, to plunge into a sharp dispute on a
subject of no permanent importance (such as Marrying a Virgin)
and nearly come to fracas, poignantly tempted him—as in college when a gang formed in the recreation room, he had never
been. At the moment, having a role, he saw his mission to save
Veronica as only arbitrary, but manhood's job could be defined
as that which replaced the known and comfortable with the
difficult and unpleasant.

Being a man, he went inside to the bathroom and spread his
available money in series along the washstand lip, which being
European did not seek to stint on marble and extended flat and
wide for ten inches on either side of the basin. Last week, unsuspecting next week's extremity, he had mailed home a money
order for his maximum allowance, corporal's pay plus ten per
cent, roughly eighty bucks. Remaining were three thousand
marks, to which were now added Marsala's twenty-two hundred,
totaling the equivalent of five hundred twenty American dollars.
Vis-à-vis such a sum, a German physician of the present day

could ill afford to stand upon his ethics. How Reinhart would lure Veronica to a foreign operating table, unsuspecting, he had not as yet studied. But the means by which the doctor would be gained were as close as belowstairs in Very's very billet.

Lori Bach—Lori and Bach, who in their combination, in their cellar, in his conscience, localized a grief which, unable to admit, he for a month had pretended was not there. Also manly was his resolve to go, on the strength of a concrete purpose, and look it in the eye.

"Ah!" said Bach from the sofa. "So kind of you to bring a friend, Mr. Corporal Reinhart, and if I am not deceived by my failing vision—although the cooked carrots brought almost nightly by my good wife from the American mess, if indeed stewing does not destroy their sight-giving properties, are restoring it—he is an officer; and where but among you excellent Yanks could be possible such a friendship: corporal and lieutenant, splendid, splendid."

Falling from Reinhart's hand, his cow-teat fingers in a feat of levitation floated to the lieutenant. "Bach. So good to know you."

"Schild," answered the officer who bore that name. "*Es freut mich.*" And then his eyes, pained, confused, bugged at Reinhart and seemed to ask approval for himself.

Instead, Reinhart recommended Bach. "He is a good man, Lieutenant, he is a better man than I can say. I am very proud to know him."

Schild stared dully, said plaintively: "Yes." Without waiting for the invitation Bach already prepared upon soundless, moving lips, he fell into the nearest chair and put a grim surveillance on his own feet.

"My wife," said Bach, beaming on Schild but speaking to Reinhart, "has not yet returned with him you require. Let us then, over three of the cigarettes you so kindly sent along to me, commingle our thoughts. The packet is just there upon the table. Please serve Mr. Lieutenant Schild—which of course means 'shield'; and one is happy to see, ha!, that he has come *with* rather than *upon* it; every American, how singular!, seems to be of German descent—and yourself, and then I shall be so bold as to ask one."

And there was all of it again, like the landscape of a recurrent nightmare: the concrete tomb, the sweet smell of garbage, the white monster; all awful and yet familiar, like Xmas with the relatives, or for that matter, life, simply life in general, from whose calculated ills we do not fly to seek others known not of but surely worse, because unchosen.

Choice: make this one and you must also make the next, and once begun you have the habit. A mere hour ago he had sought out Lori as she came from the mess tent, given her, right there on the plain thronged with her colleagues making for the trucks, his problem, bald and coarse; and so forthright was his temper that he left uncorrected the implication Veronica was his mistress.

Certainly she knew a German doctor, and her wise-weary eyes took no stock of him at all, seeing him as end, not means, yet were fond in recognition, attended on him specially and without demand. Yes, that very evening, if he liked, she could bring the physician to her cellar for a meeting, Bach's and her cellar on Nürnberger Strasse, which since he could never have found it again she placed in relation to the Kurfürstendamm and the ruin of the Kaiser Wilhelm Church. She would see him there at eight o'clock, as simple as that. He shook her fine-boned hand, her small, dynamic hand, and saw her hair again could use a soaping, that her beret was frayed, that her stockings of rough brown cotton sagged at the ankle and the gray coat wanted its central button; and each deficiency was another focus for his sudden love.

Having chosen action, then, having chosen love, clothed in the

warmth of his volitions he had wandered through the slowly
chilling late-afternoon light, in the time of day for gentle melancholy, the hour when perhaps even devil and saint are briefly,
postprandially imperfect; when colors, which had been subdued
by its noontime flare, spring defiantly at the sun in its decline,
radiantly false as Kodachromes; when Reinhart in his earlier self
had been wont to dream of being ruthless Tamerlaine, or Don
Giovanni severing a maidenhead, or a poet with flashing eyes
and floating hair.

Now, however, in the realization that he had, in the only
sense harsh actuality permits, done these, been these, or didn't
wish to be, he forgave himself and plunged into the palpable
present. Schild. He would go upon this moment to Lieutenant
Schild and squeeze from him Schatzi's money. Moreover, since
morally speaking it was beside the point and tactically an ob-
stacle, he dispensed with the identification of Schild as Jew, thin,
dark, sharp, arrogant, and deceitful as the man incontestably
was. To dispense with it he had first to make it; and then must
congratulate himself on its not making a difference, and then say
a thanks to fate for at last coughing up a Jew who had trespassed
against gentiles.

But the first-lieutenant's bar was quite another thing. To beard
an officer, a corporal armed only with right's might was ill
weaponed, and the technique of obsequious insolence which in
three years' service Reinhart had made his own was a device
rather more for survival than dominance.

He moved along the street of officers' billets, a short block of
the little toy houses of Zehlendorf with terracotta-tiled tentroofs,
tight fences, and playing-card lawns. How queer it must be for
Schild to live in such a house and look out upon a provincial
street through white curtains; whereas Reinhart himself had
done it for years; how contemptible to Schild's keen senses. How
could Schild forgive the neat-meshing casements and the correct
dun stones in the walk? A spreading evergreen bush flanked his

stoop, from the lintel above his door sprouted a night light like a globed mushroom. Had a Jew ever lived in such a house, and had he been ripped screaming from it by pink-and-blond young men?

As, asking, he lingered at the gate, the answer opened the door and stood uncertainly upon the threshold, *ecco homo*, Lieutenant Schild, and the response of Reinhart's heart, in the same vocabulary lately used for loving Lori, said: even had he raped Veronica and murdered Schatzi, I could never raise my hand against him.

Man, man, one cannot live without pity. What Reinhart proposed to feel was the general emotion, but as he watched Schild come pitiably down the walk in his forlorn movements and crummy uniform, wiry hair bushing his cap, opaque spectacles, blousefront a home for lint, splay-shoed, wrinkle-pocketed, choking on a necktie with a dirty knot, insignia corroded and awry, haddock-faced—as he made these sorrowful entries in the ledger, Reinhart's sympathies became particular. Whatever pity Schild deserved for simply being a Jew, he required more for merely being Schild. The decent thing to do was leave.

But before sluggish Reinhart could get under way, Schild had reached the gate and, with its faded pales between them, said stoically, for all the world as if he knew of the mission which Reinhart had just abandoned: "Yes, Corporal, you came for me?"

"I was taking a walk," Reinhart answered shamefully. "And I saw this house and remembered the crazy Russian we took upstairs last month—" he broke off and in concern came back: "Did you get all the files from the office?"

"You did me a kind service that night," said Schild, cloudily, fingering the gate's catch; but though it was a simple rod and slot he could not work it, stopped trying and capped his hands on the picket-points. "I wish I could do something about repayment, but you see I am not in your company."

To Reinhart, too, it seemed a tragedy; he felt his cheeks lose their blood and fall in, to match Schild's; like Schild's his voice sounded as if it crossed a body of water: "I'm sorry, very sorry. . . . That German kid hasn't bothered you any more, has she, when I'm not there? Dirty little whore, she makes me sick."

Without trying the exterior handle, without hands he applied his hip against the gate and pressed inexorably in: the hardware ground, bent, was sprung free, shooting its several parts and screws tinkling to the walk; and Schild came through to the pavement, unheeding what had been necessary for his egress—which, done, struck Reinhart as regrettable and clarified his mind. He gathered the fragments of the lock and after a quick determination that they could never be reassembled, at least left them available on the cap of the gatepost.

"Since I can't repay your favor," said Schild, perhaps, in the public air, a breath or two less mad—for mad is what he was, or had just been; as clear a, as well as the only, case of depressive mania Reinhart had ever seen and which, now thank God it had begun to pass away, he was able to identify and reflect that he had answered it correctly—"since I can't repay your favor, may I ask another one?"

A formidable non sequitur, yet suggesting an idea not at all lunatic; irony, rather, and one had only to look at Schild, in whatever condition, to understand the authority with which he manipulated that instrument. Half-dead from some despondent cancer, he yet in one short question, in a failing voice, exposed the skeleton of charity: he who takes a favor returns it by asking another; he who gives one is repaid by the commission to do a second; and the score is even throughout, unless, indeed, the giver has the better.

"Of course," granted Reinhart, foreseeing the little drama without passion in which he would deliver to Very a billet-doux from Schild, foretasting his own humiliation and perversely enjoying its savor.

"May I come along with you on your walk?"

So. Again he had persuaded another to play him for a fool, for, make no mistake, people use us as we ask them to: this is life's fundamental, and often the only, justice. If he understood that, on the other hand he saw that to Schild it was not a mocking, ass-making request. The lieutenant actually waited on his approval, head down, his cap points echoing the general wilt of his body.

Did his grief owe to Veronica's, of which he had been agent? Surely no man, whatever his responsibility and whatever the upshot, would lose his nerve by this. It was rather Schatzi's money; but again, would a bad debt to a *German,* even a good one, so resound in the sane conscience?

"Would you like to borrow some money?" asked Reinhart, without a warning to himself. "I have an awful lot." He drew his wallet as if it were a gat and with one finger triggered it open. "See, over five hundred."

Interminably Schild stared into the note-clogged leather breech, and so near Reinhart could have snapped it to and clipped off the end of his nose. When at last his eyes lifted, their fright was giving way to the old, cold certainty that they, and no one else's, owned all truth and virtue.

Superiorly turning his head towards the house, he said to the yard: "Now I know how a whore feels. Everybody offers me money."

Oh, he was a fellow who could be rubbed the wrong way, and certainly he had his reasons; society had slipped him the shaft, he had doubtless been diddled by the dangling digit of destiny; there was some extenuation for his own failings, but none for those who trespassed against him—and for once to all this Reinhart, rebuffed, said *balls,* and with as much offensive familiarity as he could summon from dead start, clapped him smartly on the shoulder and announced:

"Why sure, come along. I'm going to see a man about an abortion. A broad I know, as they say, has bread in the oven. How do you like the size of this wad? If that won't buy the job, nothing will."

Not waiting for Schild's reaction, he businesslike stored the wallet and marched down the sidewalk. At the corner he was pleased to hear the hurrying footsteps behind, but still he gave no quarter, and who knew how far his calves might have propelled him unaccompanied—for in contrast to Schild's they were muscled as an oak root, tireless as pistons, and at the moment the body they supported was, inflated with purpose, a lighter-than-air craft—in reality, he was detained at the curb by the passing trucks of Lori's caravan.

Reaching him, Schild spoke breathlessly above the roar: "You can't be serious! That's against the law; besides, it's dangerous. You could be tried for murder."

His concern, if innocent, was madly out of proportion to their acquaintance; if disingenuous, nonsensical—if he knew Very was the object of the plan, why should he, who already had fled from his own responsibility, complain? Anyway, God damn the man for his officiousness.

"But you see," said Reinhart. "I'm not doing the job myself. I'm going to hire a German doctor."

"So." Schild gave him a face of regretful sadism—a smile of malice taking pleasure in itself Reinhart had seen, but never a *frown*. "So, the little blonde got to you even though you were warned."

Now here, where Reinhart should have felt anger, he did not. His reply was simple sullenness: "You're not even an officer in my company."

Hard upon the tailgate of the last truck he stepped into the street, into a cloud of blue exhaust, choking. Thus, with his eyes closed, he did not see the jeep which turned the corner and, also blinded by oil smoke and carbon monoxide, might have injured him, or he it, had not his persistent saviour this time succeeded. Schild's thin fingers, he felt with smarting arm, were strong.

"Nate!" shouted the man behind the wheel, a fattening captain who wore a knitted OD tie, "I thought I might *run* into you, a-ha-ho, mpf, mpf! Give you a ride?"

Hand still hooked into Reinhart's swelling forearm, and applying a force whose aim was the other side of the street, Schild answered curtly: "I have some private business with this corporal."

"So be it," spoke the captain, reaching for the gearshift, gathering in at the mouth the drawstrings of his barracks-bag face. "Nowadays you're always arresting someone."

"If you can't use that ride, I can," Reinhart told Schild, shaking him off. "Going towards the Ku-damm, Captain?"

"Could be, if you'll tell me where it is, unless that's in the Russky sector. Brr, I wouldn't chance it there, and do you know, Nate, I still can't get that poor devil out of my—"

Schild interrupted: "We've changed our minds." He produced the kind of smile, with much evidence of teeth, that one shows when his underwear is torturing his privates. "I'll confess to you, St. George, if you won't tell my C.O., the corporal and I have something cooking on the black market." He lowered the back of the front seat so Reinhart could hop in back.

"I know your commanding officer—a real son of a bitch," replied St. George, going into uproarious mirth. "A dirty son of a bitch! Corporal," he said, gagging on the *r*'s, "in case you didn't know, I'm cussing out myself. You got that kind of C.O.?"

Reinhart grunted icily at the silly slob. Tyrannical officers, who were candid about their power, were preferable to jovial ones in love with their own decency. As to Lieutenant Schild, whose head snapped back on his fragile neck as St. George jerked the car into forward movement, he defied classification: who was doing what for whom and how was one to feel about it?

So started they towards the enormous cairn of rubble underneath which lay Nürnberger Strasse, in whose name Reinhart for the first time recognized a memorial to his old city of legend and determined to lay the symbolism before Bach, the specialist in things undreamt of by other philosophers.

However, now that he faced Bach, with Schild in the adjacent chair, Reinhart could worry over nothing but that Bach would begin where they had last left off, on the Jews; or, before an audience half of which was virgin to his dramaturgy, repeat the farce so successful at its opening, while Reinhart sat paralyzed by the ethics of entertainment: *please do not tell your friends the surprise ending*. Hastily he began to collect the differences between this visit and his last, as the man lying down to rest adds up and tries to cherish the details which differentiate this night from last, the nightmare-ridden: tonight I am lying on my other side, the pillow slip is fresh, the moonlight does not shine upon the window—oh, but God, I have the same head and I am scared.

First he noted an increase in illumination. The oil lamps were in their old positions but unfired. From the center of the stained ceiling, the nucleus of a web of hairline fissures, hung a hot electric bulb. Augmenting whose glare Bach's reflecting, porcelain head irradiated his immediate area. His sofa, at the principal surfaces worn to the bare hemp of warp and woof, in the hitherto obscure corners shone now in a pattern of emerald, turquoise, white, and scarlet: a scene, a world, the edge of some equatorial swamp profuse with hot flowers and curving flamingos and reed-green water, and, on the lip of the depression behind Bach's shoulder, the great throat-cup, here in ruby, of the bird whose beak can hold more than his bellican.

Bach himself wore a green suit, a moss-colored huntsman's suit with oval bone buttons and odd straps and trimmed in gray beading; in the lapel slot, a spray of edelweiss, fake, showing its wire stem. His trousers were cuffless, bell-bottomed, seam-striped like a uniform, and between them and the floor lay ankle-high shoes of reversed leather, pine-cone brown, fastened with tasselled cords threading through a series of bright chromium clips.

"You are feeling better now," said Reinhart.

"Oh thank you, thank you," Bach replied, the inside of his mouth red as the flesh of a blood-orange, here and there the yellow seeds of teeth. "But the clothing produces an illusion at odds with reality. In truth, I believe that I am dying"—he threw his hands at Reinhart to dispose of a reaction which had not come—"please do not grieve: 'by my troth, I care not; a man can die but once; we owe God a death and let it go which way it will he that dies this year is quit for the next.'" He looked slyly towards Schild and returned, fingering the blossoms in his lapel. "This flower, by the way, is quite false."

"It is very nice, anyway," Reinhart replied.

"You are always kind," said Bach, coyly raising his right trouserleg to reveal an inch of brace, as a Victorian coquette might have exposed her ankle, "but the chiefest consideration will always be: where could a man with my infirmity get the real thing? Mountains, my good Corporal, one must climb the highest peaks to reach this noble plant, which is as difficult to come by as an honest man." Having exhausted his air on the speech, Bach took more through the tube of his cigarette, in a long and intense suction which burned back an inch of ash. "The same characterization that applies to me does as well for the so-called building under which we sit at this moment"—swinging his head over the sofa arm, he spat the smoke at the floor, as if it were a mouthful of milk—"despite its apparent improvement—the laying on of electricity—it is quite likely, I am led by all my senses to believe, to collapse without warning."

Reinhart, who would never again be taken in, said in swaggering irony: "Not while I am here, at any rate; because I have a charmed life."

"*Is* that true!" exclaimed Bach, fanatically interested, seeking to rise unaided, in the violence of his attempt giving the illusion that he had almost made it and lost by a hair; whereas in fact he had not moved a centimeter.

"Indeed it is. May I sit down?"

"Ohhhh—" Bach began a long gasp at his own poor manners, not waiting for the completion of which Reinhart fell beside him at the end of the couch and ground out a space with his hips, at Bach's yielding expense.

He plucked at the threads of upholstery on the sofa arm. "Handsome, very tasteful."

"Gobelin," said Bach, with difficulty twisting his neck, upon a static body, to face him.

"I certainly know his name," Reinhart replied, crossing his legs and inadvertently fetching Schild, whose chair was a good four feet away, a kick in the shins, smiling absolution for himself for that, smiling then at Bach in self-admiration which quickly shaded into joke as he saw upon the great grapefruit a polite confusion that told him he had guessed wrong. "Don't mind me," he said rakishly. "I told a Catholic friend last week that I had never read Father Douai's translation of the Bible."

"Yes," Bach answered, still perplexed. "May I ask, however, of the charm upon your life?"

"Oh of course." He glanced covertly at Schild, who had, as late as a Stanley Laurel, just begun to rub his injured shin. "Well, I think I felt it first when we were pinned down along a hedgerow in Normandy. There was the enemy a bare hundred yards away in the next hedge, laying down a withering machine-gun fire. Well, they were bottling up the whole American advance; somebody had to do something. And I must confess, our leaders had failed us completely. The company commander, the platoon lieutenants, the NCOs, they all proved to be perfect cowards. You see, this was our baptism of fire—"

"You were infantry?" asked Bach, a hand against his left cheek, as if he restrained his head from swinging back to the frontal position. Despite the evidence of a similar, internal attempt to control his eyeballs, they were their own masters and veered continually towards Schild, until at last they fixed in that direction as a lecher's will upon a maiden.

"Glider infantry," Reinhart corrected, "a unit in the 101st Airborne Division, later to become the so-called 'Battling Bastards of Bastogne.'"

"How terrible!" interjected Bach.

"And I don't mean to say that at first I wasn't scared myself. But then, crouching there, staring across that new field of rye through the hedge, towards that line of green blooming like roses with gun flashes, I suddenly looked down and saw my trousers were open. I put down my submachine gun to button them—and then I thought: 'What a wretched little swine I am to care about this when I might be killed in two minutes!' And then, just as quickly, I *knew* I would not be killed, got this absolute certainty that I could stand up and walk slowly across the field and never be hit. So I did just that, climbed up over the top and began to walk slowly towards the German line. After I had got about ten meters out, slugs whizzing all around me but never hitting, the Krauts stopped firing! Stopped cold. I think now they thought I was coming to surrender; and it is true that the end of a white handkerchief was showing from the breast pocket of my field jacket. Anyhow, when they stopped I gave a big holler and discharging my Thompson advanced on them as fast as I could run. Behind me the rest of the company came whooping forward, not shooting, though, because I was in their line of fire. And do you know—" he slapped his hand upon Bach's green knee and felt, rather than the expected quivering of aspic, a hard and sharp junction of almost naked bone and metal brace—"do you know, those Germans sat paralyzed behind their guns and did not shoot once more, and when I looked over the hedge, down into their trench, all fifty-three of them threw up their hands and yelled '*Kamerad*'! And of all things they turned out to be a crack unit of the SS, you know, the SS, fiercest fighters of all, who never surrender."

"Oh yes," Bach answered, lowering his hand; his head, as promised, instantly swung away like some half-door between a kitchen and dinette. "I surely know of the SS and can only say that the fact must have been as you suggest, that they anticipated the surrender would be vice versa. For to them fear meant as little as does memory to an ingrate. In the Warsaw Ghetto the SS fought on until the last schoolboy put down his penknife and the last little housewife dropped her paving brick."

So of course there it was, Schild raised his eyes, the curve of Bach's fat cheek glistened with triumphant sweat, and Reinhart's big feet began to punish each other for the humiliating failure. "Ghetto," that beastly ugly word the pronunciation of which began in the deepest throat and worked forward like a piece of phlegm—he had heard nothing else. The loathsome Germans and the damnable Jews: the plague that had befallen both their houses was kind beside the one he now wished upon them. He also wished for nerve to direct Schild to the booby hatch and for courage to tell Bach he intended to carry off his wife, with whom he was in earnest love.

Yes, spiting all his wishes, he forced himself to say: "Were you in the SS at that time?"

Bach again pushed round his head, but before he made a word Schild rose and spoke ferociously to Reinhart: "I'm not going to let you do it, you understand? If anything goes wrong they'll put you in Leavenworth for twenty years. According to your stupid middle-class morals, I suppose, better to take a chance on ruin rather than beget a child out of wedlock. You are an idiot!"

There was no longer a question that he had gone nutty as a fruitcake: with hard steps he strode to the end of the cellar and leaned against the wall and gravely examined its waterstains.

Bach began to speak in a low, grating, regular tone, like an electric drill needing oil: "The SS? My friend, I—"

"What business is it of yours what I do?" Reinhart screamed at Schild, notwithstanding the poor fellow was mad. "I can get through life without your help!" And notwithstanding that Bach, poor chap, was an invalid, he turned on him viciously: "For Christ's sake can't you talk of something other than the Jews?"

"Curious," said Bach, smiling mildly, "the manner in which a member of the other ranks may speak to an officer, in the American Army."

"He's not in my unit," Reinhart answered, lowering his voice. In the corner of his eye he saw Schild return.

But the words were kind; the face, gentle: "Because I am your friend. Isn't that reason enough?"

"Sure it is, sure it is." Reinhart swallowed. "I suppose it is the only good one for doing anything in the world." He dared not admit to himself how deeply he was touched, how much sense lay in madness, how heroic was decency's response to brutality's negation. For this he could repay Schild only with candor.

"Things have got all complex," he said, "simply because I let them slide." Schild, standing, hovered before him blankly, nervously. Beside him Bach breathed with a slight moan. Perhaps, after all, now that truth was having its day, he *was* about to die. The winding stain which Schild had traced on the wall was not, he could see now, a decoration of seeping water but rather a weakening division in the concrete which seemed to widen as he looked and perhaps *would* bring down the house—there had been sense in that, to him, lunatic action as well.

"I should have told you before. But maybe it wasn't eccentric to think you might know. Veronica Leary is pregnant."

"That big nurse?" Schild shrugged, splayed his hands in impatient despair.

"Why put it that way?" Reinhart was angry all over again and himself despaired that relations with his newly found friend could ever be on the unswerving line of constant respect. "Can't you even call her by her name?"

Bach snorted as if he, too, had never witnessed an outrage of that magnitude, but turning to him in alliance one saw him chatteringly blow his snout into an aquamarine handkerchief.

Schild's feet, too, were splayed, and his head forward and depressed below the level of his shoulders; sitting before him Reinhart could look down the back of his head to where the collar, too large, yawned out from the hairy neck.

"So," said Schild, "that's worse yet than the German girl, isn't it? How could you get in such a predicament?" Fierce yet charged with loving concern, like that sonorous old actor who always played the father of an East Side boy torn between the life of the spirit and the life of matter, when that theme was à la mode.

"Ah God!" sighed Reinhart. "Finally, I see. I didn't knock her up, if that's what you mean. I'm just trying to help Veronica out of it."

"Why?" Schild again chose his chair.

"On the basis of friendship. She was never my girl. She didn't 'betray' me. But I might do the same if she had. Common humanity is more important than sex. What matters is, she's in trouble—just as, a moment ago, you thought I was. I'd rather aid than be aided any day, just like you."

"Then I am out of order," Schild replied, "and there's no help for that." After the briefest illness, his face lay down and died.

But why take so hard a simple error that in the end had done no harm? In his statement was implied a personal doom, unpeopled, glacial, bone-white, so much more terrible than Bach's presages of a technicolor disaster. Was he serious? Reinhart looked at Bach, the absurd man, the absolutely useless man, who even if he were restored to health, if he had ever been there, would only stand and gawk at Oriental art, crap like that, and rant foolishly. But was he frivolous? And finally, did it matter?

He asked the last question only to make sense of his ready answer—for that was truth: first the answer and then the question, so that while we wonder we can continue to live—did it matter?, oh hell yes, for all we have in this great ruined Berlin of existence, this damp cellar of life, this constant damage in need of repair, is single, lonely, absurd-and-serious selves; and the only villainy is to let them pass beyond earshot.

"Do you know what we could use right now?" he said unwaveringly to Bach.

That huge fellow swung round his enormous head, his pale eyebrows climbing in inquiry, his second chin reluctantly altering its seat in his collar, which was white and overlaid with peasant embroidery in red thread.

"A good laugh. Say something funny."

"Very well." And Bach was as good as his word in that at least he tried. He told a story of two friends, Palmström and Korf. Who, finding a mouse in their house, built a cage of latticework, into which Palmström climbed at twilight and began to play the violin. As night fell, the mouse was lured in by the music. Palmström went to sleep, then so did the mouse. In the morning Korf put the cage into a furniture wagon and hauled it out to the country. The mouse was there released. He loved his new home. Korf and Palmström, delighted, returned to town.

"That's the end?" asked Reinhart.

"Of course," said Bach, wincing in amusement, suffused with rose color. "What more could we wish? Consummate art, which I can assert only because it is certainly not of my own creation— needless to say, for what is?"

For Christ's sake what a story. Then he heard Schild snicker, and saw him laugh with a naïve mouth of which the upper lip flattened and glistened tightly midway across his upper teeth, and his ears protruded like a schoolboy's.

Through water-brimming eyes—his spectacles were tiny fishbowls—Schild finally looked at Bach.

"That is Christian Morgenstern."

"Exactly," answered Bach. "How exciting that you also know his work!"

"Do you remember this one?" Eagerly he moved to the edge of his chair and rapidly, in an accent which to Reinhart sounded perfect, quoted in a German of which Reinhart understood nothing.

"All right," said Reinhart testily, watching them howl at each other, "what does that mean?"

Bach began: "This gentleman named Korf—"

But Schild, impatient in his high levity, broke in: "He has invented a kind of joke, you see, that works by delayed action. The people he tells it to are horribly bored. But later that night, when they are in bed, they suddenly wake up and laugh like babies."

All very German and although remote from Reinhart's old medieval visions, somehow not alien to them. At least he was gratified by the alliance of Schild and Bach, Jew and German, in a common cause.

At this point he heard a distant, cavernous sound, as one in the bottom of a sewer would hear a person scratching at the manhole. Lori approached through the passageway.

## CHAPTER 19

By the sleeve, Lori ushered in a man wearing dark glasses and carrying a cane, a meager man concealed within an enormous overcoat. This doctor, if such he was, would be splendid for the job. He was blind.

Reinhart heard and felt the slow removal of Bach's weight from the couch and, staring up the rising underbelly of the green Zeppelin, towards the gondola, discerned that respect drew him up. Schild, too, had risen, was already, being nearest the door, in an introduction.

"Sir," said Lori in her to Reinhart always lucid German, "I am Frau Bach. I should like to have you meet my brother, Dr. Otto Knebel."

"*Herr Doktor, es freut mich*," said Schild, shaking the hand which groped for his, showing an unsuspected command of the gracious forms, even slightly bowing. "Oberleutnant Schild. *Ich bin ein Amerikaner.*"

"*Ich bin dessen gewiss.*" The reply was in a high, aspirant voice, not ugly or unpleasant but strangely lingering within the innermost channel of the ear, as if a bug had crawled in there to die and, caught, changed its mind. "I am certain of that."

For the second time in his life Reinhart had heard "certainly" as answer to an American's self-definition. It no longer seemed strange, but because he had already got his he did not wish another. Therefore when the doctor was moved to meet him, he, mimicking Schild's handshake and suspicion of a bow, rumbled low and uvular, authentically, "*Sehr angenehm!*"

"This surely," said the doctor to Lori, "is your Ami corporal."

Compared to his, Schatzi's hand had been full-fleshed, ham-like; one thought not of bare bones: one held tendons and a complex of thin vessels through which slow and miserly came corpuscles one by one. Behind the glasses, in front of the tall back collar of the coat, was a real head: small, stark, but real, and so marked with life, so marking life, that the memory of other faces was rank on rank of dummies. The lenses were too black to see through, in compensation for which they themselves were animate. Finely amused now, they dramatized the implications of the breathy voice which rendered stout German as if it were the tongue of dragonflies.

"Yes," said the doctor. "But you should have seen me six months ago!" Bach made a giddy noise. "What, Bach, my good fellow! You have held captive these Americans? Then there is still a chance that we may win the war! Very well, my dear Lenore. Now that I have located Bach I can manage alone."

"Ah Doctor, you come right to me and take this seat, *my* seat, *bitte, bitte*. May I help you? Please, please."

In the strength of his schoolgirl agitation Bach took two quavering steps and grasped for the doctor's arms, which that gentleman, moving efficiently behind a probing cane, ignored with a blind man's insouciance. On his left sleeve he wore a yellow armband carrying the rubric, three black balls, of a vicious, violent, antidemocratic cause. (Reinhart remembered his colleague Cronin's description of such an insigne, such a movement, the week before on Cronin's boarding an airplane which would fly him back to France as a case of chronic athlete's foot. "Open your eyes," Cronin said, upon no provocation whatever, "the same old thing's starting up all over again." The boring ass; why had one come along on the truck to say goodbye? But then Cronin hit him lightly on the shoulder and said, "So long, Reinhart. You're the only one I could ever talk to." Very simple: one had come along because one, all in all, had liked and would miss him.)

Sitting down in Bach's corner of the sofa, the doctor said:

"Lenore, have you some of those excellent American pastilles? The anticipation of talking dries my throat."

"Oh, here," said Reinhart, who happened to be carrying a cylinder of Lifesavers. "Take these . . . and keep them."

The eyeglasses widened their circles. "*Vielen dank—sprechen Sie Deutsch?*"

"A little. *Ich verstehe besser als ich spreche.*" He grinned in self-deprecation, though his auditor could not see it.

"Your accent is very good." The doctor's mouth was a pale pink cave, toothless; moreover, showing no evidence that teeth had ever been.

"Not good enough to fool you."

"Why you should wish that, especially nowadays . . ." A Life-saver tumbled over the doctor's tongue, glinting orangely. "But I knew you from your hand, not your speech. . . . Now Bach, are you still standing there with your misplaced courtesy? Kindly be seated. And Lenore and the Lieutenant, and you, Corporal, please. As to the Lieutenant, now, I should think that though he has been in the U.S.A. some years, he was born in Germany, no?"

Since seeing the armband Reinhart had been occupied with nothing but worry for Schild. From the data of his first visit to the cellar he could hardly suppose Bach and Lori were the doctor's fellows in a neo-Nazi faction. Who then was the doctor but the blackmailer that had preyed on them during the Hitler years and still today somehow retained his evil power? And how compelling he was: Reinhart had brought forth the Lifesavers like an automaton. Schild, the eternal do-gooder, was already captured by the man's infirmity; Schild, the Intelligence officer, did not see the armband; Schild, the Jew, already was impaled on the doctor's fascist needle.

Schild, the innocent fool, looked sadly pleased. "Is my accent so good?" He sat down, as he had been ordered to. "I am a native American, doctor. I am one of the lucky Jews."

"I too am lucky, but I have not been able to decide whether my luck owes to my Aryan mother or my Jewish father," said the doctor. "This is the kind of thing which confuses everybody but the Nazis." He closed on his candy, swallowed it, and took another from the pack. "Why do your countrymen waste so much paper, Mr. Corporal? Really, these fruit drops would not grow stale exposed to the air. Really, what are they but crystallized sugar-water? But won't you, all of you, join me? Bach, you must! I prescribe sweets as a substitute for that abominable ersatz-schnapps with which you are destroying your liver."

"Doctor, I have sincerely tried to stop drinking," Bach said, his face a quivering sack of shame as he lowered himself onto a folding camp chair which he overhung in every dimension. "I will conquer it, I will, you shall see."

"May your reformation not wait upon my seeing," replied the doctor, lightly. And Bach's despair was as if a truck passed overhead.

Of course, if the doctor was Lori's brother he was but half a gentile, had but half the aptitude for corruption. Of course, Reinhart had not forgotten that so much as ignored it in his quest for a villain to save someone from. Yet why the brazen badge?

"Now Corporal, I think you and I have a private matter to discuss," said the doctor, placing his cane on the floor and in so doing offering a view of his full profile in the various perspectives of slow movement. His right eye, seen in the harsh knife of light which, as he bent, thrust in from the side, behind the dark glasses—my God, an eye? A navel, rather, a belly-button of the head, baby-new and pink within the old foxed leather which bound the skull.

One's own eyes indrew behind the barrier of cheekbones, hid in scarlet darkness, as nevertheless one's more courageous mouth asked: "Doctor, what is the meaning of your armband?"

"It means"—the black circles swung round and established

order—that if you drive an automobile French fashion, use it, that is to say, as a projectile with which to aim at pedestrians, I am your perfect target. I cannot see you come."

"*Wie bitte?*"

"*Es tut mir leid.* I was having a bit of a joke, most unfairly. The sleeveband is of course the sign of the disabled person. Unfortunately I do not have Bach's gift for foreign languages. Bach, could you perhaps—"

"No, it is not necessary," said Reinhart. "I understand. It is an excellent thing—"

"They do not have it in America," Bach cried eagerly. "Never, nowhere have I seen it."

Lori, still standing, chided: "Now Bach, if you do not permit Otto to have some privacy, he will not talk with you later."

"Quite so, quite so," Bach mumbled, turned laboriously, and to Schild instituted a speech which began: "However—"

"Lenore," the doctor said, "There is no reason why you should not sit here and assist us with your good sense. Also, working for the Americans you should have learned some English by now, unless Father's old claim was true, that we were the champion dunces of Dahlem."

Although, because of the difference between the doctor's and Bach's girths, there was now a good seat and a half to the left of Reinhart's port hip, Lori sat down so close against him that, for the comfort of both, he had to lay his arm along the back ridge of the sofa. His love for her was just in the degree to which it remained intactile. Introduce desire and you would soon have the same old two-backed animal scuffling in the dirt, into which he and Trudchen transformed themselves daily, destructive, nightmarish, impermanent, having nothing to recommend it but necessity. With Lori he mixed spirits, was embarrassed by the flesh . . . but she rested, almost lay, within his arm-hollow, her hard, thin bones piquing him, the shoulder of her thick old prickly-wool sweater, carrying a scent of spice, touching his cheek. And he, who involuntarily rose at a woman's smell—as a sleeping cat erects its ears at every sound—almost any woman, any smell, sometimes, in the street, at pure cloud of odor, the woman having long gone by, was shortly, or longly, risen.

"Now," said the doctor, to see whom Reinhart had to clasp Lori more closely in looking round her blondeswept head, "this young woman you have got in trouble—"

"Ah no, Otto, it was not he," Lori broke in far too eagerly for the pride of the fellow she had made her cave.

"How do you know that?" asked Reinhart, arrested in his drawing away by the sofa arm in the small of his back; because of this his irritation became briefly paranoid: how dare he be boxed in?

"Because maids, like concierges, know everything," said Lori, mock-mysteriously, without trying to turn. "The Gestapo of belowstairs . . ."

The doctor disintegrated another Lifesaver and swallowed its rubble. He chose a third, perhaps a fourth, since the pack appeared to stand currently at three-quarter size. His thin lips, opaque glasses, and traces of eyebrow expressed satisfaction. His hair was a thick bush, one finally noticed as one continued to creep so tightly against Lori that when she spoke he heard the vibrations in his own chest. Bach, remote in a spirited monologue to Schild, Reinhart worried over not, nor did he despise him.

"There, there," said Lori, patting his nearer knee with a twinkle in her hand, "everybody knows you could have."

The doctor stared exhaustively, sightlessly, at Reinhart. Finally he spoke in his loud whisper: "Let me for a change be honest. Obviously I cannot perform the operation. I could find a colleague to do it, of course. But I intend not to. I have come here and taken your time, and your pastilles, under false colors. My motive was simply to 'see' an American. Are you angry with me?"

"No," Reinhart answered. "Surely not."

"But you should be." The doctor was impatient. "I can solve your problem, yet I will not. And as far as you know, for a capricious reason."

Reinhart smiled tolerance and dropped his cupped left hand on Lori's shoulder. "I can't force you, can I?"

"Then you are not serious?" asked the doctor in dramatic astonishment. "Disgrace for the lady, shame for you—for although you may not be the other principal in the catastrophe, your honor is somehow involved, yes?, or you wouldn't be here. Come now, at least try to bribe me."

Smiling again, Reinhart answered, conscious that when he had to speak without preparation his damnable German was certainly ungrammatical and, despite his "good accent" Americanized in pronunciation—you cannot take care of everything simultaneously—so that to these Germans he was ludicrous for another reason. *In their reality* he sounded:

"I donnt tink dot so easy to corrupt you are."

"On the contrary, I am supremely corruptible. I have no honor whatsoever. For example, I would do anything to save my life."

Reinhart felt Lori stir against him, and he released her sweater-shaggy shoulder. "Oh well, wouldn't anybody do that?"

For the first time, but briefly, the doctor lost what had all this while been more nearly ebullience than anything else. And then, taking another, a purple, Lifesaver, he said, with the old aplomb and in the voiceless voice Reinhart had come to hear as oddly beautiful, "On the other hand, if by necessity you have learned this fact about yourself, it is nice to know. Some American writer —have you read him?—wrote a verse about seeing a man eat of his own heart. 'Is it good?' he asked. 'Well,' said the man, 'it is bitter—but I like it. First, because it is bitter, and second, because it is mine.'"

Reinhart did not understand. And Lori had *not* learned much English, therefore could only repeat the words more slowly, in her low-pitched music.

He shook his head. "The funny thing is that I know all the words; it must be the combination."

"Bach!" cried the doctor. "Excuse me for a moment. Please give us the English for this."

Bach did, with an attitude of excessive expectation; sought to explicate, was halted.

"*Danke sehr.* Now just return to your lieutenant. We did not wish to disturb you."

Reinhart determined to read, when he went home, this author whom a non-English-speaking German knew better than he. However, the doctor had turned out to be the usual lunatic, in love with his own rhetoric. He returned to the subject which had become a great bore to Reinhart, who had decided at the first resistance to seek another physician through Schatzi.

"I have no scruples against abortion in itself—"

His speech came within an interval of breath-taking on the part of Bach, who heard it and answered: "*Die meisten meiner Mitmenschen sind traurige Folgen einer unterlassenen Fruchtabtreibung.*"

"Bach, don't you realize you are interrupting?" chided Lori, seizing the hand with which Reinhart, bending forward, traced his trouser crease in the area of the shin. "I assure you that if you persist Otto will avoid you. . . . Please do not do that," she said to Reinhart. "A hard object in your breast pocket jabs into my back."

A pencil, which he removed to the other side. Nevertheless, he disliked a carping woman.

Bach desisted, and when Schild spoke, cautioned him with wrinkled forehead.

"Did you get that?" Schild sadly asked Reinhart. "Most men are the sad results of abortions never undertaken."

But by now, having adjusted to German, Reinhart heard English as somewhat dull upon the ear and difficult to follow. He believed that Schild was repeating his old objections to the plan for Very's salvation, and assured him resignedly that it was all off. "You can stop worrying." He should, in the first place, have hired Schatzi and thus given no one an opportunity for humanitarianism, friendship, theory, oratory, and so forth: that was the way with intellectuals; from his old uneasiness towards them, for which he had blamed himself, he was at last liberated; worse than boring, they were of absolutely no utility; if you want a barrel built, hire a cooper.

"You have changed my mind," said Reinhart to the doctor. "Forget it. I was foolish. I don't want to get into trouble."

Bach, still actively desisting from interruption, wrestling with himself, gave up suddenly on an interval of losing and said, with hysterical bravery: "Tell him, Doctor, tell him about the Russian concentration camps! They were worse than the German ones!"

Lori wrenched angrily within Reinhart's surround, Schild recoiled sickly upon himself, as if someone had hurled towards him a bucket of filth, and the doctor sighed.

His weary answer: "Ah Bach, you take what you choose. But so be it, we shall leave it at that."

Reinhart somewhat rudely thrust Lori from his line of vision. She pushed back with unusual strength for so small a body, crumpling his outstretched fingers, and if in that second of pain he had been asked, do you still love her?, he would have said, sorely, because she is as tough as a root. Gently this time he raised himself from the slump and looked over her head.

"Are the Communists as bad as the Nazis? Were you in a Russian camp? I didn't even know the Russians had concentration camps." Saying which he looked haughtily at Schild, whom he had gauged as a pro-Russian liberal, and saw thereupon what he should have known from experience was more to be pitied than defied. He would never be able to match his moods, to meet aggression with the same, and humility in kind.

"Bach provides a much more effective torture than either," said the doctor genially. "Whatever theories of coercion are developed in the future, they must take account of his method:

admiration of the nonadmirable. He believes that because I was a prisoner I have a special and heroic wisdom. He is wrong, but my vanity insists otherwise; therefore, in my sense, which is nobody else's business, he is right. Why, however, should you permit me, or him, to inflict this nonsense on you? . . . Now tell me, is it true that one can enter an American cinema while the motion picture is in progress? Isn't it queer to see middle, end, and then the beginning?"

"Yes," Reinhart answered, "yes, one can enter at any time. But American movies are made for an audience whose average mental age is twelve years old. You should have seen the pictures they made on Nazism. Such trash is almost criminal."

"The Nazis were presented as good men?"

"Oh no, but either they were monsters who did not resemble human beings or they were ridiculous buffoons." He was making out all right with his primitive, do-it-yourself German, for the doctor seemed to understand.

"*Also*, this was an error: too realistic. I agree with you, this theme should be dealt with as fantasy. Lenore, do the privileges of your job include Ami films?"

"Not exactly, Otto," Lori answered brightly. "But do you recall the old joke of Father's about the man who was asked if he had ever eaten hare? 'Not exactly,' he said. 'But yesterday I shook hands with a fellow whose cousin's brother-in-law lives next door to a widow whose late husband once saw someone eating hare.' It's not as bad as that with me. I make the beds of persons who see the pictures every night."

The reference to Veronica could not have been more obvious. Reinhart intended his response to be equally obvious in disregard.

"Your father has a good sense of humor?" he asked. How strange for a German! But then he remembered that her father was a Jew.

"Well, yes," answered Lori, looking at him from the corner

of her eye, he thrusting himself to the side so that she could do it, "I have never thought about it so seriously, but I suppose he had."

*Had?* Yes, dumb Reinhart, not everyone is always young and American enough to have two living parents. Besides, he was a Jew. Yet he had to speak, he, Reinhart, one in five in this subterranean, brightly lighted urinal—monstrosity, Jew, half-Jew, half-Jew, Siegfried.

"He was killed—"

"He is dead," said Lori.

"—by the Nazis."

"He is dead."

"And who else, who else?" If in all his life he had reached no goals, he would take this one.

From his implacable face she turned away in embarrassment and towards the doctor gave her dirge: *"Vater, zwei Brüder, Schwägerin, Neffe, Nichte."*

In English, thus excluding his wife and brother-in-law, Bach cried: "There is no wit like that of Berlin, of which since I am not a native I can assure you without immodesty. Hitler and his damned barbarians hated this city because they could never break its spirit, because they could not transform it into a Nürnberg. I confess to you that I am a separatist. I fervently hope we remain forever isolated from the Fatherland." He slapped his knee—too hard, and winced.

"I wish I could do something," Reinhart said. "I wish I could say something—"

"You can indeed," the doctor answered, impatiently stripping the paper tube from the remainder of the fruit drops, catching five of the six in the wire whisk of his left hand: one fell to the concrete and broke into three golden arcs and a modicum of sugar dust. "A lemon, *ja?* I can smell it now it is crushed."

Either Schild or Bach made a sound like the winding of a watch.

"You can," the doctor repeated, and whatever else he said wound through the holes of the five candies in his mouth and expired before finding the orifice of speech.

*"Ich habe ihn nicht verstanden,"* Reinhart whispered into Lori's hair.

" 'You can say something,' " Lori answered loudly. " 'You can tell us what you will make of yourself now the war is over.' "

He raised his meditation to point at the ceiling, to macerate his vision on the fierce lightbulb: father, two brothers, sister-in-law, nephew, niece, like the roster of a holiday reunion.

"Well, I cannot bring them back, whatever I do," he shouted quietly. "But in my own small way I can fight all hatreds based on race, color, or creed. In my own small way I can say: we must love one another or die!" When he was moved, words came from nowhere, inspired; yet he was conscious of the falsity of those which had just arrived. It was fairly certain that of the six victims in Lori's roll he could not have loved at least one, so goes the world. And how did a fellow go about loving any of those who killed them? For a principle means either what it says or nothing; if we love one another, we love the murderers, every one. And finally, was love really the sole alternative to massacre?

"One must love himself," said the doctor. "The men who killed my family did not. What are totalitarians but people who have no self-love and self-respect, who believe that the humanity into which they are born is contemptible?, who believe a thing is preferable to a person, because a thing is absolute."

"But a thing," said Bach, "has a sense of its thingness. The Will works in inanimate as well as animate objects. That sofa may know very little, but it knows that it is a sofa."

"Of course I agree, Bach, that this sofa has a self: I have heard it most painfully groan when you sat upon it and chuckle when you arose, but we shall wait forever if we expect it to will itself into a chair. This poor couch is so predictable." He actually looked sad and patted its arm. "If you prick it, will it not bleed? But that is not necessarily true of a man, who may spit in your eye, or, having a taste for pain, beg you to prick him again, only harder. And what might he not make of it as a moral act? That by taking his life you have confirmed his conviction that you are inferior to him, and for some men life is a small price to pay for such reward. Or that by causing him to die well you have relieved him of the need to live well, for any victim is willy-nilly a success. Or that by divesting him of everything but the naked self you have made it possible for him to accept that self. In the end he may have used you as you believed you were using him, and who can say who was the victor?"

"Oh no," cried Reinhart, even though he thought it likely he had misunderstood, "you cannot build some elaborate theory that in the end Nazism did good. That sounds like the idea of those old fellows in Neuengland—the northern U.S.A.—Rolf Valdo Emerson, *und so weiter,* who wore frock coats and walked in the woods and never cared about women, and therefore had this dry belief that evil was only the servant of a greater good."

During this—how fluent?—speech Lori twisted round and studied him, trying, he supposed, to be unnerving: a person without experience should sit silent as a vegetable. Well that, last time with Bach, he had done. He felt now as if *he* were drunk, and finishing his representations to the doctor, he stared defiantly at her strong, straight nose.

"Otto can say anything he likes. You see, he has paid for the right."

"There you have the corruptive results of working for the Amis," laughed the doctor. "If I paid for the privilege to be theoretical, then I was cheated, my dear Lenore. All other German males are born with that right and obligation. But how true if you imply that this chap from over the sea should not be permitted to speak further without paying tribute! Come, Herr Unteroffizier, surely you have some more candy about you." The doctor retrieved his stick from the floor and brandished it. "Here comes some English—you did not know I had some? *Komm on you dirty rat hand ovuh zuh goods.* This is what the racketeers order, no? Bach has a detective novel which he reads aloud to me—"

"*Ja, ja,* I have it just here," Bach said eagerly, struggling to rise. "I read with simultaneous translation—"

Reinhart grandly waved him down. "That won't be necessary at present." He did, of course, have in his clothing another piece of sweet: a chocolate bar foolishly stored in his shirt pocket, over the heart. It was now limp. He gave it to the doctor and apologized.

"*Sehr gut,*" the doctor responded. He smelled it. "*Schokolade!* I will not eat this. I shall present it to the widow who lives across the hall from me." He placed his cane on the concrete, giving Reinhart another sight of the umbilicus of his right eye. "I am trying to seduce her."

Reinhart grinned anxiously and withdrew an inch from Lori, as if it were a mistaken but justified statement of his own aims, but when the doctor's glasses were turned on him again he saw their terrible wistfulness.

"Oh God, Doctor, eat it, eat it," he said, his voice ragged in pity. "Next time I can bring you a carton for your widow."

"If your motive is kindness, please do not. Such largesse, if I gave it to her, would earn me only contempt. And if I kept it for myself I would eat it all immediately and fall ill. In either case I should curse you. But why do you now wish to bribe me without profit for yourself when earlier you refused to do it for gain?"

"Because he is a good man." It was Schild who spoke, and pleadingly, and Reinhart suffered for him in anticipation, for the doctor *was* a kind of demon, after all; in revenge for his having been tortured by evil and falsity he would torture goodness and truth.

"And I suppose you are, too," sharply replied the doctor. "I don't trust a man who would rather give than receive. I can't stand his damned pretense that he is too good for the world. He is mad. I disapprove of lunacy, illness, disability, and failure."

Reinhart could no longer contain himself. The mad doctor's ranting left him personally untouched, but poor Schild gulped it all down, sounding again and again that watch-winding noise in his throat, and poor Lori was limp against his shoulder, used, no doubt, to the habitual insane rhetoric of the cellar; she had, as before, gone to sleep, but the constant strain!; he would rescue her from it before the hour was out; if need be, kick Trudchen's cheap little ass into the street and give Lori her room. Meanwhile he must catch Schild before he disappeared round the bend.

He shouted: "*Das ist National-sozialismus!* I don't know what you are trying to do, Doctor—I sympathize with you, I would give my own eyes to get yours back, believe me, I would give my life if your family could come back again, I have never done anything—I couldn't even hold a gun because of the Geneva Convention—but don't say the Nazis were right. If that is true, then it was all useless; your loved ones died for nothing. All those corpses—I saw them in the photographs. Those beloved people, they were too good for the world. The rest of us are too bad for it . . ." His voice had broken, broken, as he knew ever more poignantly that with whatever motive he had begun his defense of general reason, he continued it for the sake of his own.

Therefore was the doctor right, even as he sought to repudiate him; therefore was he cramped with guilt for a crime he had not perpetrated and agonized by a suffering he had not had to endure. To be vicarious always is always to be base.

"Why do healthy people believe there is wisdom in a wound? *Mumble, mumble . . .*" The doctor slipped the envelopes from the Hershey bar, which in his stark handbones had lost its borrowed warmth-of-Reinhart and returned to brittleness, and segment on segment inserted it into slit-mouth quick-lips, munched,

munched, munched. Soon was the lower third of his face child-ishly smeared with brown. His hair, dark-blond, high, luxuriant-grown as a Zulu's, had burst forth from the cropped skull of the camps. Against Schild his whisper had gone hard, cruel; to-wards Reinhart, Reinhart now decided, it had always been a snicker.

On he went in the idiom of masticating chocolate, with a ne-cessarily greater show of gesture than when he spoke audibly, which nevertheless stayed Greek. Schild, who had been slumped, wired up his spine and sat straight, neurasthenic. Lori slept, heavy for so light a girl.

Bach, however, listened eagerly and when the doctor, the last bit of candy down the hatch, gave off, the giant bobbed his peeled egg at Reinhart and said in English: "There you have the doctor's world-outlook in a nutshell!"

Then it was that Reinhart realized the doctor was fake from the word go; that he was no more an alumnus of a concentration camp than Schild was a hangman.

The latter suddenly glared at him and snapped: "Very well! Russian 'concentration camps.' *Sehr gut,* ask the doctor about them! Simply the Buchenwalds of another fascism . . ."

The doctor wiped his mouth on a handkerchief as holey as a net dishrag, to get which he had opened his coat and revealed the necklines of, at quick count, four gray sweaters and a shirt collar of brown.

"Certainly they are not," he said good-naturedly. "If you won't let me avoid the subject—it is not offensive to me, since it is mine, but it should be, I insist, to you. If I must talk on this theme, I'll take my stand on precision. Young Corporal, you talk of love. But perhaps love is for boys and girls and old ladies who love their dogs. For us professionals, consider precision. Love one another or die? But we die anyway, *ja?*"

" 'The subject is not offensive to me,' " Reinhart suspiciously repeated.

"I did not say pleasant or without pain. I said not offensive,"

said the doctor, impatient. "Now you interpret it as you wish."
He resumed: "The Soviet camps: as you must know, Lieutenant,
they have quite another purpose than the Nazis', which latter
were in their most extreme form mere extermination-places. The
aim of the Soviet camps is to change people. Sometimes, inadvertently, live men are there changed into corpses; well, at least
they are no longer counterrevolutionaries.

"Each kind of camp has a favorite kind of prisoner. The Nazis
preferred the man who by existence was a criminal, that is, the
Jew. Good Jews, bad Jews, Jews who as individuals *were* criminals by the usual definition, even those Jews who would have
agreed with everything in the code of fascism but that all Jews
should be exterminated—no, this is not yet enough: even those
Jews who might have helped the Nazi cause—were murdered in-
discriminately. There was some early plan for 'useful Jews,' but
it was soon abandoned. An Einstein perhaps could have been
forced or tricked into giving Hitler the atomic bomb. Nevertheless he would not have been saved from the gas chamber.

"Where in all history can we find another idealism comparable
to this? Hitler did what we have always been told is the supreme
glory of man, and apparently impossible to a god—for what
chance did Jesus of Nazareth take if he was immortal?—Hitler
sacrificed himself for that which is greater than the self, for he
stuck to his guns and he is dead now. I think a name for that
is Love.

"With the Soviets, however, no man is judged by what he is
but rather by what he can become. Their favorite prisoner is the
man capable of learning the error of his ways. He must do this
through hard labor on projects useful to the state, and hence to
mankind, and thus there is no waste. The penal system of a faith
as inclusive as the Nazis' was exclusive, and for that reason psychologically superior to the latter. Here at last the Jew, for
example, is not a second-class citizen: he can be as great a
swine as a gentile. Did you know, until that desert tribe of
Hebrews found the one authentic God and that they were His

chosen, an exclusive religion had never been invented? Ever since, the gentiles, who never could take a joke, have been punishing the Jews for being so damned clever. To the Communists, however, this old strife is a great bore. A man's a man, and is capable of anything. And of course when you believe that, you are loving one another."

"Excuse me, Doctor," said Reinhart, adjusting a prickling shoulder under Lori's weight, "when you opened your coat I saw your shirt. It looks like part of a uniform, but not quite the color of a U.S. Army shirt—"

"I should not suppose it does." The doctor's whisper lost strength in extended speech; Reinhart really helped him by interrupting. He cleared his throat with the soft yet dynamic sound one might make shaking out a floormop. "You are wrong if you think the average German feels no guilt; he simply will not dance it to the tune of you people who were not involved. My widow gave me this shirt. I suspect it is a storm-trooper's garment, but naturally I cannot see it. . . .

"*Also*, Lieutenant, we have looked precisely at the differences. My brother-in-law insists, however—since he cannot forgive himself for being a gentile German [Bach flushed and looked at his legs]—on their similarities. His interest lies in proving Communism worse. Because I was once a Communist I am inclined to agree. The conscience is a Himmler as demented as the real one. Remorse, whose seat is in the memory, has a purpose. Guilt, the product of the conscience, is always useless, the wrong kind of self-concern, cheating, cowardly, immoral."

Since the doctor's comments on his shirt, which had proved him as false as anything could, Reinhart had been rather nursing his shock than listening. He came back now to strike another blow for virtue.

"It isn't hard to be a murderer. The tough thing is to be a victim." He smiled so bitterly that Lori woke up on his shoulder, saying "*Wie bitte?*" to which he answered, "*Nichts, schlafen Sie noch.*"

For the first time, Bach, who had been frozen in wonder and delight, noticed her.

"Rude!" he cried in outrage. "Your brother is speaking!"

"*Ach,*" she said, "*was kann man tun?* He hasn't stopped since I was a little girl." Her head sank again.

The doctor laughed and laughed at the awful thing—if he *was* an authentic ex-prisoner—she had said to him. "When we were small she used to punch me if I talked too much. In the solar plexus. Very effective when struck just right: I couldn't speak for half an hour. Therefore would I take revenge by playing the Leonore Overture on the gramaphone, which, because I insisted she was named for it, she detested. Then in would come brother Leo, who couldn't study mathematics for the din, and he would shout in his shrill voice: 'Twins have only half a brain each.' But if the altercation continued until Father had to come upstairs, we were all for it. Father had a face like a weapon. He was a very severe man. I can recall nothing loving about him but much that was precise.

"Once when at table I spoke without permission he afterwards beat me so strenuously he sprained his arm. Feeling guilty, as I usually did upon such an event, but not remorseful, I offered to fit him out with a sling—already, you see, the future physician. 'Do you want another whipping?' he asked. 'This time for being a fool? From your point of view my sprain is richly deserved.' That is to say, he was a self-respecting man. I hated him for years. But now I think he must have died well."

"That old Prussian authoritarianism," said Reinhart, remembering an argument of Cronin's. "There you have the origin of Nazism."

"Except that my father was a Jew," said the doctor.

"Jews can be tyrants, too." Reinhart was earnest, no longer baited or tested the doctor. "Isn't that what we mean when we say racism is a lie? Everybody gets his chance to be a bastard."

"Yes, and we should not deny it even to, especially to, a victim. For there are victims and there are victims. If you read *Mein Kampf* you will find Hitler believed himself a victim, and because when he became a master he failed to do his job well, I am still able to agree with him in that early appraisal of himself."

"Haha," jeered Reinhart. "Victim of what?"

"Of indifference. The German people never understood what he wanted of them. Being normal people, they were always interested principally in themselves."

"While the innocent were being murdered all around them . . . to you this is right?"

"If you think I shall tell you what is right or wrong, my friend, you are mistaken. That is your own affair. I care only for practical matters."

Reinhart rubbed his head. Fresh from yesterday's close haircut, it felt to his hand small, hard, monkeylike, and shiny as a convict's.

"I give up," he said, without knowing whether the idiom was feasible in German. "The trouble is, Doctor, I just don't know what you want. If everything we have always thought is decent, is wrong, false, misguided, or useless, what alternative is there? The only thing I can see is the contradiction of decency; Nazism is as good a name as any, so long as we understand that Nazism in this sense is not just a German but a human thing. The Russians, then, if they have concentration camps, are Nazis. Perhaps there was some Nazism in dropping the atomic bomb on Japan, which must have killed a lot of women and children and at least some Japanese who never wanted to go to war in the first place.

"The British, someone once told me, invented the concentration camp during the Boer War. The French, so I heard, put German refugees in concentration camps at the beginning of this war. In democracies there are white people who lynch Negroes; there is anti-Semitism. *I* have been guilty of Nazism when I used force or threatened to on someone weaker than I or outnumbered, or when I had bad thoughts about Jews and other defenseless people—because I have done these things." He looked proudly guilty.

"I should hope so," said the doctor. "What's good enough for everybody else should be good enough for you."

"But isn't selfishness the terrible crime of the modern era, selfishly being concerned with oneself and therefore thinking the other fellow is garbage?" He took his arm off Lori's shoulder so that he could rub his head with both hands. "*I* want power, *I* want money, *I* want to be superior to a man with a colored skin or with a hooked nose"—from his tumult he was able to call time, to say "Excuse me, it was just an example" to Schild, who, in the reverse of Schatzi's habit, was looking at him but not seeing— "therefore I tell myself he does not matter, is not even human. Then I can go on to do what I wish with him, slavery, torture, murder."

"Imagine yourself a citizen of the American South," said the doctor, "a person who is in daily contact with Negroes and thus must come to terms with the fact of their existence. Would you mistreat them?"

"God, I should try not to."

"You might occasionally fail, *ja?*"

"I am just a human being."

"No question of that, and so was Julius Streicher, as Hitler, who was no man's fool, said so well: 'He may have his faults, but well, probably none of us is entirely normal, and no great man would pass.' Yes. But why would you try not to mistreat Negroes? Is there profit in it?"

"It would mean something to me," said Reinhart.

"So there is a profit after all." The doctor spoke as if he, himself, were making the discovery. To be sure, his manner throughout had been rather seeker than owner of fact; did he lack the courage of his confusions? "You cannot get respect for yourself by robbing it from another man. As to the Negroes, they might not know or understand what you were doing and therefore show no gratitude, *ja?* But to a healthy man this would make no difference. The self is not a gallery with a claque. And it would not be necessary for him to love the Negroes or hate the brutal whites, or worship a god or history, or be a radical or conservative. Just to be a man were sufficient, *ja?*"

"Your example is too easy. Excuse me for trying to tell *you* about life, but is it not more complicated than that? I am not likely to live where Negroes are mistreated. I did not live in Germany in Hitler's time or in Russia. I am not a Jew, my father is not an oppressed worker or sharecropper. On the other hand, neither am I a fascist or a boss—well, let's face it, *I* am nothing in particular, but you know what I mean. What would I do in a situation where an Auschwitz is possible? . . . I have not told you—somewhere in Berlin, if they are still alive, I have some relatives. I hired a man to find them, but just now I realized I have always hoped he never could. What if they were Nazis?"

As a further twist of the knife, the doctor removed his glasses and began to clean them with breath and handkerchief. Reinhart averted his eyes.

"Since I can't see through these things," said the doctor, "I clean them from a motive of pure vanity. I do not wish to be thought a sloven." He replaced his spectacles and took up his cane. "I should like to meet your relatives if you find them. By various accidents and choices, I have a foot in everybody's camp. I am a halfbreed of every persuasion. You claim to have done nothing. I have done everything. Every individual life is a questioning of the validity of all others."

"And also a confirmation of it?" asked Schild.

"Ah now," answered the doctor, "that is irrelevant, for why should I need you, or you need me, or either of us need, say, Hitler or Stalin to tell us what we are? *Ich bin kein Weltverbesserer und lasse Sie liegen.*"

"Then you should be satisfied with your lot," said Reinhart, "neither were the Germans who were not Nazis world-reformers, and they let you lie."

"True," said the doctor cruelly, "and they were not the ones who killed my family and took away my freedom, were they? They heard the cries and turned away, but at least they did not come and help fire the ovens."

Reinhart had chewed his gum too long. It disintegrated. He tried to reassemble it with his tongue. He failed. Ashtrays here were unknown; the smokers had crushed out their butts on the floor. He swallowed his fragmented Spearmint and said—

But the doctor had not waited for him: "There is but one demand we can make on others: that they let us alone. Anything beyond that is a corruption or will be one within the hour." He rose easily and hunched over his cane, which his fingers grasped as an owl a branch. "Do you think I say this because of what the others did to me? The others, I tell you, are irrelevant.

"I was a Communist. The day after Hitler came to power I fled to the Soviet Union with my family. Thanks to the tactics imposed on it by Stalin, the German Party was shortly wiped out by the Nazis. But we all knew that history was using the Nazis for our ends, so we—those of us who got out in time, that is— did not despair. The Jews? A kind of vermiform appendix on the body of history. An illusion. Science knows no definition of Jew or gentile. . . . In Moscow I had a good job in the Medical Institute, doing research on skin cancer. I won two decorations for my work and soon rose to head my section. My family and I, four of us, lived in a modern apartment of four rooms—had four times the space, that is, of the average Russian family. After the required time, we became citizens.

"My chief assistant, at whose cost I had been promoted, for he had worked there since its founding, was an old Russian Jew with, like so many of them, a German name: Kupstein. He was the sort who would always be an underling. He did nothing well, but what was worse he knew and admitted it. He broke slides, he misread calibrations, once he managed to fracture the lens in a microscope—rather a difficult thing to do under ordinary conditions.

"But we human beings were not so ready to exploit our power over him. Obviously he could not help it, and his constant contrition! He could, naturally, not only have been discharged but also imprisoned for his failures. Indeed, in the Soviet view he should have been; insofar as I made allowances for his good intent I was a bad Communist and perhaps an outright traitor —and when I say this I do not refer to the disguised GPU informer on our staff. I speak of my Communist conscience. The secret police are given too much credit; for the important things we never need them."

Crazed old man, leaning on a cane, rasping in *Deutsch*. Why had Reinhart almost flunked German 2? He understood every word, every nuance. The doctor condemned guilt in others but loved his own. He suffered retroactively for being sloppy years ago in Russia. . . . If he had been in Russia how could the Nazis have got at him? Lori stirred. Without prior planning he whispered in her ear: "I love you." She smiled sleepily and closed her lashes again, muttering *"Knorke mit Ei."* Something with an egg. Total misunderstanding.

". . . after that episode I had no choice but to relieve him of his duties. We could all have been killed. Yet I still could not report him, sentimentalist that I was. And quite rightly was I punished for that weakness. With nothing to do he hung about my elbows all day and interfered with my own work. Titration tube in mouth, I would hear his squeaky voice and almost swallow some septic liquid. Bending over the microscope I would suddenly smell his breath, vile from some horrible cheese, as he bent alongside.

"And what did he speak of? Palestine, which he called Israel. He had been there for two weeks in the 1920's with a Soviet scientific team and was terribly impressed by everything from communal farms to climate. 'Believe me, my dear Doctor,' he would squeak, 'working on the *kibutzim* seems a pleasure for these strange Jews. Imagine Jews as farmers! The sun turns their skin black as Africans' and has bleached the hair of some as blond as a Pole's—or, as your own. Sabotage is unknown, yet one never sees a policeman. Is this possible? I doubt it. But it is the witness of my own eyes. And oranges! As many as you can eat. And the young people. Imagine happy Jews!'

" 'Hirsch Davidovitch,' said I, 'your satires are very clever but they may be misunderstood. Besides, you are interfering with the experiment. Really, this sort of time-wasting is more appropriate to a bourgeois-capitalist laboratory'—I spoke that way in those days, and not simply for the GPU informer—'we work here for the health of the international working classes and have not a moment to spare, please.' But next day he would start in again: 'My dear Doctor, the olives! I have seen them large as this.' Pointing to the bulb of a Florence flask, he would knock over a rack of test tubes and then, sponging up the mess, strike the flask from table to floor.

"Kupstein, Kupstein, of course you were winning," said the doctor, sinking an inch into the orifice of his coat collar; he had once been a tall man, but that too was now a memory. "From the first time I had tolerated his statements without an effective rebuttal, I was a fellow conspirator. It was 1938. In Germany the Nürnberg Laws had sealed the fate of the Jews—foolish Jews, one beats another and shouts 'help,' as the saying goes. My father, the lifelong reactionary who ordered me from his house when he found my copy of Marx, loses his department store to the Nazis, brings suit in the bourgeois courts he trusts so much, leaving the Nazis no choice but to send him to Buchenwald. Almost did I ask: well, what does he expect? With my brothers Leo and Viktor, who had given neurotic importance to their Jewish halves and turned active Zionists, they had been doomed by their stupidity and cowardice. Marxism, they agreed, was 'no answer.'

"In the Soviet Union, meanwhile, the great purges which had begun in 1936 were now in full fury; among the high Government and Party officials only Stalin seemed secure. Could our entire leadership, except Stalin, be corrupt? Yes, no question that it *could be*. Communism, as I said before, admits unlimited possibility. A man can be anything history needs him to be. No chosen people here, either for good or evil. For example, among the condemned officials were many Jews, and of course the commander-in-chief of the whole plot was Trotsky, born Lev Bronstein. He had conspired with Nazi Germany to destroy the Soviet state. Impossible? *But nothing is!* By definition a state built and maintained by the proletariat is just, and whom it charges with a crime is guilty.

"When the rosters of the eminent were depleted, the purge began to claim the malefactors among the technicians and managerial workers. I at last discovered who had been the police informer in my department—Rostov, a biochemist—for he disappeared soon after Yezhov, the head of the GPU, was purged. The director of the institute had not survived through 1937; three successors, with only a month or two between turns, followed him to the wall or to Siberia. Dr. Narovkin, in effect my chief assistant, though Kupstein still held the title, was called to a corridor telephone one afternoon and never came back. His replacement, a simian type by the name of Gorky, sent by the personnel section without consulting me, did not bother even to imitate a scientist. All day long he sat in a corner of the laboratory, behind two carboys of acid, watching the rest of us.

"Dr. Narovkin's work had been essential to the experiment. He had done months of research on malignancies in lymphoidal tissues. If I could at least have had his notes! But they too had vanished, the day after his own disappearance. The project was hopeless? You must remember that this was a Soviet laboratory. We had been *ordered* to discover, first, a preventive against sarcoma and, second, a cure for it. I reinstated Kupstein in his old post. What difference could it make now? None but for the better. Kupstein had worked in Soviet laboratories since 1919, and one thing he could do well was write reports. On his own initiative and with a perfectly straight face he now composed a manuscript of fifty thousand words reporting the successful achievement of our goal: we had found both a preventive and a cure for fleshy malignancies, and in one year less than our allotted time. I solemnly read and appended my signature to this handsomely written nonsense and forwarded it to the newest director of the institute. Not long afterward I received another decoration."

"Doctor," said Reinhart. "Aren't you uncomfortable standing up?"

"*Schweigen Sie!*" Schild ordered in an offensive, Prussian manner, so startling Reinhart that he answered, as Prussianly, "*Jawohl!*" and did shut up most smartly. Bach smothered a giggle behind a trembling hand.

"Now there was no restraining Kupstein," the doctor went on. "Defying Gorky's unwavering surveillance, he no longer whispered. Now he spoke his heresies in the tone of normal conversation. 'Do not despair over your loved ones back in Germany, Doctor, every death there is a life for Israel. The Jews one day will leave the cities and return to the land. Olives, lemons, palm trees!' I could not admit that he was mad, you see, because then I should have had to accept that I also was a lunatic—for from the first his rantings had taken malignant growth in my imagination, like that very sarcoma which he and I so successfully defeated in our report. Damn the Jews—my relation to them had always been an embarrassment; now it became a poison. 'The Law,' Kupstein would sometimes say, 'the immutable Law. The Jews have little else, but they have the Law and it does not change.'

"One day, speaking so, he followed me into a storage room at the other end of the laboratory from Gorky, who as usual sat at his table, but would come after us if we did not soon reappear.

I took quick advantage of the situation. I seized Kupstein and said: 'What would you have had me do? Stay in Germany and die like a fool? You know how Nazis deal with Communists!'

"Brushing my hands away, he answered in a loud voice: 'Just yesterday there was an unopened crate of new test tubes right there. Now where could they be?' His eyes were innocent behind their pince-nez.

"I seized him again. 'Kupstein, have mercy, I beg of you. We here in this country, in this very laboratory, are working for not only the Jews but the entire human race.'

" 'I don't understand,' he said, again very loud, 'since the end of the sarcoma project one can't find a thing here. How can we proceed to defeat carcinoma without test tubes?'

"He referred to our new assignment: a preventive for bone cancer. At any moment Gorky would come snooping. 'I warn you, Kupstein,' I whispered. 'I have heard enough to have you sent away for twenty years, if not executed, as a foreign agent. Have you forgotten that Palestine is a British colony?'

"In astonishment he answered: 'I? Have you forgotten'—there was the slightest pause, perhaps not really in Kupstein's speech but rather in my hearing—'that central supply holds you responsible for every piece of equipment?'

"Gorky stood in the doorway, his thick eyebrows gathered in upon the root of his nose. 'Doctors,' he said, 'I must confess I have those test tubes in back of my table. I have been taking them out one by one from the straw and shining them with a bit of cloth, being ever so careful. They are now ready to go into the sterilizer—may I operate the sterilizer, Doctor? You will see I can do a good job.' His face, menacing until a moment ago, was a cretin's.

"Two days later, at three o'clock in the morning, I was arrested by the NKVD and taken to 22 Lubianka Street. I never saw my family again. For what I estimate to be seventy-two hours— there was no window in the room—I was interrogated without pause. I received no food, and water was administered—a glass-ful was dashed against my face—only when I attempted to collapse. For at least forty-eight of those hours I was given no idea of the charges against me. The NKVD officer—he was replaced by another from time to time, but they all looked the same—insisted again and again that I confess, that my crimes were known to him but, consonant with the just laws of the Soviet Union, he must hear the details from me. By turns he addressed me as villain, child, poor idiot, honorable but misguided patriot, personal friend. At the idiot level I had an opportunity to think . . . that devil Kupstein! Obviously he, and not Gorky, had been the police spy. Being a loyal and convinced Communist, I knew too well I had no hope this side of a full admission, but of what? Kupstein had surely turned me in on a charge of Jewish chauvinism. I could not confess to that, of all things. In an access of shame and hatred I asked for pen and ink. I wrote a statement which in style, if not quite in length, rivaled the sarcoma report. I revealed myself as an espionage agent for the National Socialist government of Germany.

"My interrogator read it with satisfaction. 'Excellent,' he said. 'I'm sure you feel better for having got this off your chest.' He flipped through the pages. 'You see, you cannot fool us, although you are a most clever man. As a half-Jew you did not think we would suspect you of working for the Nazis, eh? And marrying a Jewish wife was also shrewd, eh? But we are shrewder yet, eh? Now name your accomplices and we will be finished with this unpleasant business.'

"My accomplices. To be sure, I had neglected this all-important matter. I wrote fifteen pages more, implicating Kupstein. This was a grim joke for which I was prepared to pay: since he worked for the NKVD, I had no doubt they would reject it. But here I intended to take my stand if it killed me, as well it might.

"'Splendid.' The interrogator smiled. 'Now your conscience is clean. You understand that we already knew everything about the entire conspiracy. Your fellow agents in Leningrad and Kiev were arrested last week. Kupstein is also certainly no news to us; for years we have known of his fascist, Zionist intrigues as an agent of Trotsky.'

"Which in the language of the NKVD meant precisely the opposite. Somehow Kupstein the *Verderber,* the spoiler, had blundered through two decades in his own kind of peace—until I betrayed him.

"I was sentenced to fifteen years of hard labor—a mild sentence considering my grave crimes—and sent to the Kotlas camp in the region of Arkhangelsk. The details of that servitude are not as relevant as Bach maintains. The Nazi camps were worse. To make a comparison of the two, Lieutenant, is pointless. A single principle applies to both: in both the prisoners properly are innocent. I represented a grievous error on the part of the Soviet authorities. As you have heard, I was guilty."

"And Kupstein?" asked Schild.

"And," said Reinhart, "will you kindly explain how you got to Germany from Siberia?"

The doctor pulled a blue muffler from inside his coat and draped it around his head as a woman would; but when he brought down his hands Reinhart saw he looked rather like Mahatma Ghandi.

"Through the camp intelligence, I heard that Kupstein was executed. My wife and children were not arrested, but they had to leave the apartment and it was made difficult for my wife to find work. I don't know how they survived. Before long the question was academic. I was arrested in July, 1938. A year later, when Stalin and Hitler signed their pact and divided Poland, I was brought back from the camp and deported to Germany."

"Oh *no,*" Reinhart gasped, a sound applicable to whichever judgment he would finally make on the doctor's tale.

"My Soviet citizenship was revoked upon my conviction for the crime of espionage. In the pact each side agreed to return the other's nationals it held prisoner. The Gestapo met us at the border between German and Russian Poland. My wife and children were included in the transport, I understand. I was not allowed to see them. . . . They died, I believe, at Buchenwald, where my father and brothers had earlier.

"The Nazi methods of interrogation were second-rate—exclusively physical brutality; there has really been nothing new in that line since the ancient Chinese." He shook his head almost regretfully. "The Nazis were a mediocre lot with only one idea: audacity succeeds; the *idée fixe* of the suicide. Where, other than poor stupid Germany, could they have got twelve years to discredit it? . . . To the Nazis I was the same kind of embarrassment that the Jews had been to me. I repudiated my Communist affiliation, citing as evidence my treason to the Soviet Union, and demanded to be held as a Jew. If I had been interested in preserving my life, I chose the correct strategy. For here was another point of difference between the two systems.

"In the USSR one is given just what he asks for: at the end of my confession I asked for punishment. My request was honored. Not so with the Nazis. In their Neanderthal psychology a man asks for one thing to conceal his aim in another direction. Besides, they thought, who being something better would ask to be a Jew? I went into their dossier as Communist first, Jew second; and that took my eyes—convinced I could give them information on the Communist underground, they tortured me—but saved my life."

Plucking at the floor with his cane, the doctor walked to the door. They all rose. Reinhart reached him first and took his arm. The doctor shook him off irritably, then repented, saying with a smile: "*Es geht allein schon schwer genug!*, it is hard enough alone."

Tough old cuss, said Reinhart sotto voce, and then he saw him pass a skeleton hand across the dark glasses, as if to verify he was indeed sightless, but the very movement was evidence of an unextinguished hope that he was not.

"Twins have but half a brain each." The doctor grinned and pointed in Lori's direction. "She still sleeps. *Knorke*, I go."

Twins, he and Lori. Which meant the doctor looked twenty years older than he was and Lori was twenty years older than she looked. Unless it was another lie.

The doctor shook Reinhart's hand, and then Schild's, and finally that of Bach, who had just reached them.

"Gentlemen, I say good night. You no doubt agree with me that an inconvenient means to self-respect is to undergo punishment for a crime you have not committed—as you tonight have been punished. What a lunatic way for two young men to spend an evening! Have we nothing here in our Germany with which to entertain you? Especially you, old chap." He punched at Reinhart with his cane. "Why so solemn? Doesn't it bore you?"

Reinhart had imperfectly understood the doctor's story (his mark in German 2 had, after all, approached justice), but on the basis of the experience with Bach, he smelled the self-hatred in it and understood, anyway, that people in their most serious monologues depreciate rather than celebrate themselves, and are given to exaggeration besides.

"Well," he said. "Do you expect me to laugh at life in our time?"

Instead of answering—he should have known better than to expect him to—the doctor said: "Perhaps it will be as well if your relatives turn out to be Nazis; they have nothing further to lose."

Reinhart said: "I personally don't think Schatzi will find them."

"What was that name?" asked the doctor.

"Clever fellow," said Bach. "He gives a job to his sweetheart. But she won't try very hard if it means the food you give her must be shared with them."

"No, 'Sweetheart' is this man's name. Don't ask me why."

Reinhart raised his nose nobly. "And who cares? He was three years in Auschwitz."

"There could be only one," the doctor murmured, as if to himself, and then he gave a succinct reminiscence of Schatzi. Which, Reinhart observed as he fell through space, yet clubbed Schild harder.

"I will kill him," he said quietly. The great cables in his biceps expanded and split both sleeves at the seam.

"Good," said the doctor. "But I hope not in ignorance. Kill him because he, as much as any of us, is a victim."

He insisted that Bach not disturb Lori: he knew the contour of every broken brick between this cellar and his own, which was close by. Again he said *es geht allein schon schwer genug,* and went out.

# CHAPTER 20

SCHILD thought: how awful for Reinhart, now he knows how it feels to be a Jew. He himself was weary of trust and mistrust, weary of hatred, of victims, especially weary of Jews, as, he thought, only a Jew can be. His predominant emotion towards Schatzi still was envy, now unconditional: the freedom he had seen in him was no illusion.

When the door banged behind the departing doctor, Bach's wife woke up. A plain girl, but Reinhart, as unrepresentative an American GI as you could wish, seemed taken with her. He was not as innocent as he had seemed. Perhaps he was even sinister, now that Schatzi no longer was. What did he want of Schild? asked Schild unfairly, for it was he who had pressed himself on Reinhart, but unfairness is also a freedom. Schild liked Bach, therefore he must keep Reinhart from seducing his wife. But illicit love is also love, which must not be opposed. *Ah, but we die anyway, ja?* said the doctor, forgetting to add: *alone.*

Who weeps for a Jew? he had asked with respect to Lichenko, one of the little men, symbolic Jews, for the love of whom we—they—control experience. Lichenko did not, but Reinhart and Bach did. Perhaps even Schatzi did. *Give to a man a chance,* he had said so plaintively. He also was a victim, a kind of Trotskyite of Nazism, and though privileged—for the Nazis were more tolerant of their heretics than were these others—though a labor supervisor, also a prisoner. Schatzi's present allegiance signalized his reformation. Communism excludes no one, denies nobody his opportunity to alter, recognizes no people intrinsically chosen or condemned.

Standing large and slumped before the sofa, Reinhart spoke low to the girl. So as not to jinx him, Schild made his congé to

Bach, whose great kindly face looked down like a benevolent Buddha's, and opened the door—or tried to. Five minutes ago a blind skeleton had flung it back as easily as if it were a curtain; for him, Schild, the door was frozen. The knob, a European type, a curved lever, broke off in his hand. And no putative seduction stayed Reinhart's, Mr. Fixit's, prompt assistance.

Using his elbows like Schild's father commandeering the telephone, Reinhart forced the *Brecher* to give ground, examined the damage, described it as negligible, made temporary repairs.

"It will come off again if it is pulled too hard," he said to Bach, in German. "Now if you had a bit of wire—"

Bach answered in English: "My dear fellow, do not concern yourself about that. We live beneath a heap of ironmongery. Tomorrow, in the full sun, I shall grub in it for wires. What gauge is to be recommended for this purpose?"

"*Bach hat kein Draht*," said Mrs. Bach, who had a certain animation, but Schild decided Reinhart's interest in her owed to the incapacity of her husband; thus it was a sinister thing, the sexual excitement of betrayal, in which she herself at least connived: "Bach has no wire."

Lichenko's way had been wholesome, to take the German woman by force. Last night when in sleepless midnight clarity he labored on the pillow, adding sums, he believed he had denied her to Lichenko because he wanted her for himself. Holy as a monk dreaming of the Virgin, he crept down to the kitchen and sacrificed himself upon the altar between her hard legs, she soundless except for piston hips upon the mattress. At seven o'clock, tame, she knocked upon his bedroom door and entered bearing breakfast on the last tray with which he served Lichenko and had no stomach to return for the last time to the messhall. In another land it would have been touching: bread, jam, coffee, from her own meager rations—her pantry was no Army larder— but the old hatred, now compounded, moved him rather to strike it to the floor.

"Bach has no wire," Frau Bach repeated, and now Schild heard the contempt fall on Reinhart, not the giant. "If you wish something in this place, you must ask *me*."

A flush of embarrassed lust suffused Reinhart's skin, although she proceeded to define the precise limits of her statement. She drew a pin from her hair and threaded it through the lever's empty screwhole. "*Also*." Tense with pride, she opened the door.

Reinhart shook Bach's hand. "We must go. Did I tell you that I like your suit?"

Bach perspired with gratitude. As high above Reinhart as the latter towered over Schild, as Schild himself loomed over Schatzi—but there ended the stairway of heads, whose lower steps would bear most weight, carrying as they did the others. But he had excluded Lichenko, smaller than he, larger than Schatzi, a truly free man who would fit in no progression.

"A gift," said Bach, "of my kind wife. She adorns me rather than herself, probably because I am good for nothing else. But that, too, one learns to accept. The mystery remains, for whom was such a garment made? For it is my perfect size, and no tailor came to call with his tape measure. Singular!"

Reinhart, lifting away up, felt a lapel, and Schild remembered an old anti-Semitic routine: 'Sam, the customer wants a green suit. Toin on the green light!' Bach's horn buttons were his proper interest: how much the gross, less the usual two percent for cash?

He supposed he saw in Frau Bach's smile, which was entitled to it by half, the Hebraic celebration of a shrewd purchase as she spoke to Reinhart: "*Mögen Sie den Anzug,* do you like the suit? I bought it from this 'Schatzi,' little Trudchen's friend."

Reinhart gave her his large, gentile blandness: "It is beautiful." Schild shook hands with everyone.

"You are always welcome here," said Bach from the heart. "Next time perhaps things will be better and we can serve coffee!"

Schild permitted himself briefly to see that vision of Schild to which Bach had given, and offered to give again, hospitality; it was not unloving and it was not unloved, it was not institutional. Perhaps it also was free—but it passed too quickly into the dark cloaca of the cellar hall, and he had time only to call, in simulated enthusiasm: *"Knorke mit Ei!"*

"Berlin slang, meaning 'Splendid.' " He answered Reinhart's question as they clung, Alpinists, to the summit of Monte Klamotte, Mount Rubble, and searched in darkness for the coomb so marked in daylight.

" 'Splendid,' " Reinhart repeated, " 'splendid with an egg.' There's something about Berlin that gets you, isn't there?"

"Me?" asked Schild.

"That gets a person, I mean." Reinhart turned his ankle on a broken brick, starting a minor avalanche. "It always used to have an evil ring—also awesome and faraway, like 'Mars,' or 'Jupiter.' But here it is, and it is real. Strange to say, I just realized I love it."

"Because it is broken," said Schild.

"I guess so. All the crap has been blasted away, leaving something honest, and I think what the doctor meant was that honesty really does win out in the end. That is horrible and at the same time funny. . . . Funnier yet because I believe the doctor himself is a fake." By the poor, cloud-filtered light of an introvert moon he checked Schild's face. "You see, I have been to that cellar before. The other time Bach told me a long story which turned out to be a lie."

"A lie?"

"The whole cloth. Imagine him in the SS!"

"I can't imagine anyone in the SS," Schild lied. "Maybe that was a fake, too." He did not understand why he could not speak straight to Reinhart; the good intent was there.

"Would to God it had been," Reinhart answered fervently, and tripped himself up on a naked concrete-reinforcing rod, fell, kept talking: "Like the murder of the Belgian babies in World War I —give me a hand please?, I feel a hollow under here that I'll break into if I make a commotion myself. . . . Thanks—which was a propaganda lie. Dirty Nazis! They made it impossible to lie about the Germans. Thus Martin Luther and Frederick the Great and Johann Wolfgang von Goethe are swine, too, because they helped to make all this. Nürnberg, were you ever in Nürnberg? I used to think there was something fine there—" He crashed through the intervals of a grounded metal bedstead.

Schild took a lower way, through a shallow trough which yielded underfoot as if he walked across a human body. "When?" he asked.

"Never," said Reinhart. "I was never there, *naturally*. I saw a book once. Albrecht Dürer's house stands to this day, Albrecht Dürer, the old artist of the Middle Ages. He made one etching called 'Ritter, Tod, und Teufel.' When I first saw it I couldn't read German, I didn't know what that name meant, I knew only *Teufel*, and he was easy to spot: a face like a wolf, with mad eyes and one crescent-shaped horn in the back of his head and two like a ram's curving out from under his ears. His ears were donkey's. On the other side of the picture is Death, on a crummy, melancholy old horse. He has a long white beard, a hole for a nose, and wears a crown full of snakes, holds an hourglass. The scene takes place in a gully full of junk, lizards, skulls, tree-roots, etc.; it looks something like Berlin today. A sneaky-looking hound runs along the bottom, and there is Dürer's trademark and the date on a little sort of tombstone."

They had reached the bottom of their own declivity, which egressed to nowhere, and attacked the next smoking slope, Reinhart continuing to walk point.

"But in the distance you can see the towers of a great castle. Death and the Devil may have entree everywhere, but they are not in that castle, which I believe must represent a heaven. And

**neither** is the Knight, who I'm coming to in a minute. Because
he would not be a knight unless he served his time in the gully
of death and the devil. Well, the Knight—there he is in the foreground, on his splendid charger walking stately through the
crap, the Devil leering over the horse's rump, old Death wheezing
at him in front, the dog *schleichend* along below, the castle far
away—they could do him in and nobody in those towers would
know it until too late, but even if they did, what good would
it be? What help can anybody else give you against Death and
the Devil?

"The castle is not relevant, as the doctor would say." Reinhart
passed through a doorway and was immediately again in the
free air, for the wall stood alone in the world with no building
as relative; Schild followed.

"Welcome to mine house," said Reinhart. "I wish I knew where
the hell we are, I think we're coming back to Bach's cellar."

He stopped abruptly and Schild bumped into him and excused
himself and said: "If you'd wait a minute I could show you." He
knew the way and wondered why he did not seize the leadership from Reinhart.

But Reinhart pistoled a hand and shot at a great concrete box
on the dim horizon, an entire basement blown intact from the
earth. "No, I see what I've been looking for. . . . Neither are the
Death and Devil relevant. The Knight rides through the gully as
if he doesn't see them. Of course he does—the style Dürer draws
in, there's not room for the enormous horse let alone anything
else; they are packed in that lousy gulch like a frankfurter in its
skin. Therefore the Knight sees them—but he walks on. And I
tell you, they look pretty squalid. If you glance quickly at the
picture you won't see anything but the Knight, with his long
straight spear, a bit of fur towards the tip, the splendid armor
with which he is, as they say, caparisoned, but most of all that
wonderful tough face, sure of itself, looking not at the airy castle
or horseshit Death or the mangy Devil, because they'll all three

get him soon enough, but he doesn't care. He is complete in himself—isn't that what integrity means?—and he is proud of it, because he is smiling a little."

Reinhart reached the caisson, where he waited till Schild climbed the rise and stood puffing beside him.

"And he is not en route to do combat with an unarmed enemy. He is a man and needs no helpless victim to give him respect. When I think of him there, walking forever across the pages of a moldy old book—and I guess not even there now, since my father burned it—I could . . . I could smile, I suppose, because I do not feel sorry for him."

Schild smiled wryly and said: "You never saw the serf who had to help him into that heavy armor and take care of the splendid horse, or the bonded peasants who tilled his field, so that the knight could strut about as he pleased while the underlings did the work." Perversely he clung to his loyalties while still older ones besieged him: stifling summer on the ramparts above Manhattan, windows sealed and blinds lowered as antithermal charm, faint sounds of street serfs playing stickball, Sir Nathan riding the rug, charging through a bowdlerized Malory in which Launcelot and King Arthur's wife exchanged ethereal admiration. *For the French book saith that Sir Servause had never courage nor lust to do battle against no man, but if it were against giants, and against dragons, and wild beasts.*

"No," said Reinhart. He tore off a chunk of loose mortar from the wholesale cellar—astonishing that such strength was accompanied by any mind at all—and pitched it like a baseball, although it must have weighed fifteen pounds, far across the rubble range and down night's black throat without a murmur.

"No," Reinhart repeated, "you don't get the idea. There were no serfs or vassals in this picture. This Knight was real, but not real. How can I say it? I just thought, he was not necessarily even a German. He is just a drawing—just art, is all—a lie, if you like. He belongs as much to a serf as he would to a real knight. A picture belongs to anybody who looks at it. It can even be burned, and somebody will still have it in his mind. Besides, you admit anyway that Death and the Devil are free to all—why not then the Knight?"

Because Jews were never knights, even though they had lived in Germany since long before the Middle Ages; was it in Heine that one read of the ancient Jewish communities along the Rhine?, who said: Don't blame us for the killing of Christ, we were living here at that time! But riding the rug, working at the exalted old language to which he then had not yet realized he was historically a newcomer (but so, in his day, was Reinhart), neither did Sir Nathan admit his native disqualification for the quest of the Holy Grail. *Sir Launcelot let them say what they would, and straight he went into the castle, and tied his horse to a ring in the wall; and there he saw a fair green court, and thither he dressed himself, for there him thought was a fair place to fight in. So he looked about, and saw much people in doors and windows, that said, Fair knight thou art unhappy.*

"But," Reinhart said unhappily, "if you want to say they don't make them like that nowadays, I agree with you. That's progress for you: get rid of the whole works, serfs, peasants, castles—and knights, not to mention *Tod* and *Teufel*. Where do these kinds of Death and Devil fit in the doctor's story—even if he is a fake?"

"He was real, all right," Schild snapped. "I'm not sure about you and me, but he was real."

"Nobody in that cellar ever shows you any evidence."

Schild laughed in sharp anger and answered in his birthright idiom: "So whadduh you, district attorney?" It sounded authentic; he had not come so far; his temper softened. "You just said it is impossible to lie about the Nazis—"

Reinhart had found a chairleg and now slowly, inexorably bruised it against the concrete wall, until its end was fibrous as a brush.

"The Germans, I said, but I am glad to hear *you* think there is a difference."

Quite right, the error was his, but why the special punishment? And why should Reinhart bring it, whom he trusted, to whom he was in a unique relationship of owing nothing and vice versa, his friend. . . . The moon had eluded its cloud but was still niggardly, showing Reinhart as a large pale blob belonging to the powdered landscape. The gentile is everywhere at home. Reinhart leaned against the basement as if he owned it, waiting for the Jewish opinion.

"Why *me?*" Schild shouted in fear and loathing.

Reinhart was hurt, but calm. "Because you're the only other German-American I've got to talk to. We have a common interest in those potato pancakes we were fed as boys." His irony surprised him; he grinned and wrinkled his brow low, like an ape.

"For Christ's sake," said Schild, "don't tell me you don't know I'm a Jew."

He had been wrong about Reinhart's face; its contempt was as acute as its good feeling had been blunt.

"All right," said Reinhart. "You're better than I am, you know everything without having to try, and you can stick it up your ass."

He shuffled along the basement wall, kicking up brick dust, which filtered through the hairs of the inner nose smelling like cordite. He now looked rather more resigned than angry, and at the corner of the concrete he threw up his head, pointed, and called: "The path is here!"

He had known where it was all the while. Why had he led them to wander? He was sinister, but he was also good. He descended an excavation, his round head falling evenly from sight.

"Wait!" Schild shouted, pelting after, through the crying, broken turf. When he reached the bombhole Reinhart's broad back was laboring across the other rim. "I gave you an order!" He suffered fear that the man would deny him again, this time in insubordination—the first irregularity had been merely personal —and he would be required to turn him in for arrest. 'You are always arresting someone,' St. George, whose Army it was and not Schild's, had complained.

He scrambled across the chasm as Reinhart, obeying, waited. He had trouble, too, at the rim, and not being as tall as Reinhart, could not have made it without help. Which he received, unrequested. Reinhart's hand was cold and dirty.

Reaching the upper level, he began to speak his amends, which, as always, altered during their travel from source to mouth. Hysteria was, finally, the only cause he had ever served, but at least he was loyal to that. He accepted his uniqueness, and remembered an old story told him by a fellow traveler undergoing the transition to simple liberal and eventually no doubt to worse—the typical American politics of *pis aller*—and that was his respects to Reinhart.

"When Trotsky and Stalin first fell out, the Politburo met to resolve their differences. Since Stalin controlled a majority of its members, it soon decided in his favor and demanded that Trotsky recant. 'You are ordered,' the decision read, 'to stand up and say: "Comrade Stalin, you are right. I am wrong. I apologize."' 'Very well,' Trotsky answered, 'I accept the decision.' He stood up and said in a heavy Yiddish rhythm: 'You are *right?* I am *wrong?* I *apologize?*'"

Reinhart grinned. "Neither do I, sir. . . . Since we are speaking freely, I can say I knew that whatever else might be said of you, you weren't chicken-shit. Jewish officers never are. They have too much pride to be. They are free."

"No," Schild answered quietly. "If you believe that you believe in a lie and you make it too hard on the Jews."

"But I have seen it. I have three years' service—I enlisted," said Reinhart in pride. "If you don't mind my saying it, Jews are sometimes know-it-alls and their manners could stand improvement, but that doesn't have anything to do with decency and is anyway a proof of their freedom—" He checked on Schild's reaction with the defiant self-righteousness, nose slightly flared, of the man who by his general benevolence is sanctioned to be specifically offensive; he wished to hurt Schild, Schild could see, in the interests of some comprehensive good that would finally bankrupt him, Reinhart, but first he would take a small profit.

"—and don't tell me that is anti-Semitism," said Reinhart, cowering, for all his size. "I'm sick of being made to feel a swine because I'm of German descent. I'm sick of being in the privileged class that nothing ever happens to. I'm tired of being big and healthy, but I can't help it, I was born that way. If you would be a prisoner in any concentration camp ever made, I would be a guard. Now, you know everything—but do you know that? How that makes a person feel? Do you know what it is to be in debt to everybody? Not you, you are always right."

"I?" said Schild. He sat down on a ridge of waste. The sudden armistice within had relaxed his muscles. He repeated the grammatical fiction almost genially: *I*, the pronoun of rectitude: "I am a murderer."

Reinhart took seat beside him, and with the added weight the ridge of brick-halves squashed out about their ankles.

"Ah," said Reinhart, "you should have a pair of these boots. Now your shoes will be filled with that junk."

"That's all right," Schild said, although he too, with a sense of expansiveness, granted its tragedy; he, the rude *Besserwisser*, accepted this Middle Western, gentile horror of discomfort and unrespectability, opened his shoes and dumped them clean. His right sock had a large hole revealing his largest toe.

"Why don't you turn that in to salvage?" paternally asked Reinhart, pointing rudely.

"No salvage for officers," he answered, self-consciously pitiful. "We have to buy our own."

"I keep forgetting." Reinhart searched his pockets. "You got a butt?—wait, by God, here's that little pack of Fleetwoods you yourself gave me last month. Well, they're as good now as ever. They are made stale."

Schild took one and found he was quite right; Reinhart knew everything.

"Now don't you worry," Reinhart said, "all that was just talk. Berlin does something to everybody; makes one want to accuse himself." He blew a smoke-mustache from his nostrils. "In a war there's no such thing as murder. It's kill or be killed. I don't blame the regular German army, for example, for fighting against the Allies—even if their cause was wrong; that's a very different deal from the particular Nazi outrages. To be precise—when I said the doctor might be a fake, I meant in the unimportant things, such as whether or not he was in those camps, whether or not he was a Communist or a twin of Lori, and so on. I never for a minute doubted he was honest in the fundamental human things—you see he could be an ex-Nazi and still be straight on those. Did you ever think of Hitler as just a man eating jelly omelets, needing a haircut, clearing his throat, getting out of bed in the morning and yawning? Did you ever think of someone saying to him at such a time: 'Come on, Adolf, I see a bit of dandruff on your collar and I heard you belch, and I know you have your troubles. Come on now, you can't crap me, you're a man like any other.'

"But I started by wanting to be precise. Precisely, I can conceive of an honorable German hating Hitler yet fighting for his country in the Wehrmacht. I can also imagine a German Jew who in spite of what was done to him thinks of Germany as his own country, for he is a *German*, isn't he? And if he has permitted the Nazis to convince him he isn't, he has let them win—in a way they never did with all their bullies and gas ovens. *They* are the non-Aryans, *they* are the degenerate race who rotted and betrayed a great people, not the Jews. I can conceive of such a man, I don't mean I expect any particular individual to be one, you can't blame a man for *not* being a hero."

Despite his fervor Reinhart spoke slowly, and Schild for once was not impatient. Having confessed, he had awaited the question of a pure-hearted fool, which, the old legends promised, would heal his wound. Instead he found himself cured of Germanic whimsy. He, and not Reinhart, was the romantic; fools there are in abundance, but not one is innocent.

"Reinhart," he said evenly, "now listen to me. I forgive you. Do you understand? I forgive you."

"That is not what I want—"

"But that is what you get from me, nevertheless. And if you won't take it"—he grinned and shot his cigarette-end in a high rocket which no sooner exploded on the wasteland than two shadowy children filtered from behind a rubble hillock and claimed it as prize, quarreling on who should pinch its ember, whose ragged smock-pocket should tote it to their used-tobacco Shylock—"you can stick it up your ass."

"It doesn't do me any good," said Reinhart. "Now them—forgive those kids. They really had nothing to do with it, unless you believe with Hitler that a whole people can be degenerate."

But he would not let a gentile be sanctimonious with him. On the other hand, he again cleaned his shoes for Reinhart's sake and rose, saying: "Do you know we have to walk back to Zehlendorf?"

"Unless we can hitch a ride."

"This late?" asked Schild, looking at his bare wrist. In what bleaker field was his watch ticking now? To Reinhart, he knew all the answers, yet why was his every emotion another question? "Do those children stay awake all night on the chance an American will come by and throw away a butt?"

"What else have they got to do?" Reinhart asked toughly. He field-stripped his own cigarette and hooved it into the ground. "What do *you* have against them?"

"A private grudge," said Reinhart, "that's my own damned business. Well, if we have to walk, that makes it easy, no choice." He rebloused his pants, tightened his belt, adjusted the jacket, made his cap smart, and, ready for any D-Day, motioned Schild to take the lead.

Once they were out of the rubblefield and in the open gray

streets gulching the ruins, Schild fell back beside him in an aesthetic revulsion against captaining one man all the way to the Grunewald Forest. With no one before him to control the pace, Reinhart increased his stride, measuring off a yard per step. Schild fell behind. On the bicycle path of the Hohenzollern-damm, in Wilmersdorf—they were beyond the congestion and, hence, the worst damage, on a wide thoroughfare becoming sub-urban, with streetcar tracks, bounded by greenery and particular rather than mass ruins—Schild leaned against a poster-pillar and took air.

Marching with loud slaps of his rubber soles, head fixed as if he were in ranks, Reinhart went on unheeding. Schild watched him for a hundred yards in the light of Berlin's dawn, which came early in the small hours—therefore it was later than he had supposed. Reinhart would soon look back. On a childish im-pulse Schild stepped behind the pillar and waited. The footsteps rapidly tramped beyond earshot.

He found that inadvertently he had kept Reinhart's veteran Fleetwoods. Going in through the cellophane and limp paste-board, his fingers made inordinate noise, and had he still been a nervous man he might have mistaken the sounds for those of someone creeping out of ambush behind him. He fired his ciga-rette and took a lungful of corrosive smoke, toying with a para-dox: the one man he knew who was the ambush type had least need of concealment. In proof of this he saw Schatzi standing nearby on the sidewalk, hiding in the open air and light, a con-crete apparition.

"I have followed you like a sickly conscience," said his courier, who wore a motley of olive-drab clothing.

"You are out of uniform," Schild answered, laughing softly. "If the MPs come along I can have you arrested."

"I'm doing you no harm," Schatzi said in some worry. Then he smirked weakly. "Come Fritz, you make the joke with your old comrade with whom you have already deceived, so that I am in trouble across the boundary." He pointed over his shoulder. "The Russian is gone, *ja?*"

Schild asked: "Do I throw off an odor, that you can follow me with your nose?"

"Perhaps you will not believe, what can one do?" He shrugged. "Having some business on the Tauentzien Strasse—very well, being exact, in the basement of the KaDeWe—ah Fritz, what a pity that excellent compartment store must be bombed!" Tears coursed the runoffs on either side of his crag-nose. "Ah, Fritz, I must confess I have had a drop—I am in my glasses, as it were." He wove across the bicycle path and rested against the pillar. *"Verzeihung, Herr Litfass!* . . . Why should I care about this ugly place? What have they done to my Nürnberg? Because I am not *Saupreuss,* a Prussian pig, *beileibe nicht.* Pure Bavarian, *verfluchte Scheiss!"*

His American overseas cap was pulled low and round as a sailor's. His nose began to run; he cleared it onto the dark green of his new field jacket in two short swipes marking the chevrons of snot-corporal. "From the Ranke Platz I saw you creeping over the ruins with that oaf and I thought, this Fritz has lost his Russian fairy-boy and got him a nice young American in its stead. You have been foolish, Fritz, and they know about it—they know everything—you don't deal now wiss stupid Nazis."

He reached for Schild's sleeve and, missing, fell to the ground on his hands, yet caught himself arched, and backed spiderlike till his rump was against the pillar. From the point of contact he rose inch by inch along his spine, cleaving to the shaft.

Erect, coughing vacantly, he whined: "They killed my dear dog, Fritz, with a machine pistol shot him through the head. That is their kind of people! I loved that creature, to which they should not have done this harm. I gave to him food from out my own mouth."

Schild began to walk away, in peace.

"Come again here and listen, you bit of turd!" Schatzi

screamed. "In Auschwitz I liquidated better men as you by the thousands. *Du kannst mich im Arsche Lecken.*"

"No," said Schild, calmly smoking, "no, you did not. You only buried them. You were forced to, you yourself were a prisoner."

" 'Forced to,' " Schatzi repeated drunkenly. "I carried a club, Fritz, but one must be careful how hard one beats them, or the SS will rage with jealousy and take the post away. Then too, these thin bones were easily cracked, which meant the job would be nonsense because they must remain strong enough to dig—I always knew you were a double agent, didn't I always say so? You yourself are Intelligence! Pity me, Fritz, they have murdered my dog. Dirty Russians! It unsecured itself from the chain and came by my heels already, unknown to me until I was stopped by this sentry at Sergeyev's building. The dear dog has been thinking, 'Ah my master is attacked!' He sprang at the soldier and the Russian shot him."

"I am sorry. Really I am," said Schild.

"Brown on the outside, red on the inside like a beefsteak, we were in the early *Sturmabteilung*. We had many similarities to the Communists, Fritz. Idealism, we were idealists, and we died for it—like the Jews. We were the first Jews. Thus I can understand you. I too hate this filthy Germany." He wiped his nose again, promoting himself to snot-sergeant. "You are a soldier, but you were shrewd enough to get for yourself a safe position behind the lines of battles. Why should you not, if you are clever enough? I do not criticize. In the Great War I was not a shrewd fellow like you, but a simple foot-soldier. Just see this." He raised his trouser cuff and lowered the stocking. "Verdun, February 1916"—a blind, purple hole in his calf. He opened the jacket sleeve and that of the wool shirt beneath it, and drew back the arm of heavy, dirty underwear: "Verdun, September 1916" —a masticated chicken leg was his left forearm. "August 1918, mustard gas in the lungs, the forest of the Argonne. As you known, I still today cough. While I collected these thanks, I must not tell you what was occurring behind our back in Germany, you would believe me insulting to you and your peo—no, one does not say that, but there existed fat swine who profited by our blood. And when after the war we went to settle wiss them, these Nazis killed us instead. *Berufsverbrecher,* professional criminal, I am called in the camp—" The liquid discharges of the eyes and nose left prison-bar traces on his dusty face.

Schatzi continued the catalogue of wrongs done him, and Schild thought, they are as real as anyone's, as Reinhart's, as his own: *who among us is not a Jew?*

He said: "All right. Now you'd better get yourself together. Perhaps you can find another dog—"

"The only thing in years I wished to love!" Schatzi threw his head back against the pillar and unabashedly wailed.

Twice tonight Schild had been chosen to hear a candid heart; it was the old choice and fitted his old gift. For the first time he knew it as a tribute to what he was, or what they supposed him to be, and perhaps after all these were one and the same. If Hitler had not died in the Chancellery garden he would one day seek Schild out and tell him, weeping, of being twice denied a career in art by the academic examiners; rejected by his sweetheart niece who then blew out her life; a bum in a Vienna flophouse, befriended by a Jewish old-clothes dealer; gassed in the war; and, finally, of his last defeat as the Red Army swarmed over the Spree. And Schild would say, All right, Hitler, we shall weep together.

To Schatzi he repeated: "Collect yourself, man. Sergeyev will have your head if you are reported drunk."

Immediately Schatzi dried from within and became one hard instrument of suspicion. "Whom did you say?"

"Sergeyev. You just mentioned going to Sergeyev's building—"

"Ah, but did I mention why?" He fell into his usual semicrouch, which put his head four feet off ground, and Schild, who had always believed this the stance of attack, realized at last its purpose was rather to make Schatzi a small target.

With supreme distaste, but nothing else would serve, he grasped Schatzi's jacket and pulled him upright and vulnerable. "The next time you see him, report that Fritz is finished." He watched the red respect flood Schatzi's eyes. "Do you understand?" Schatzi trembled in admiring assent. "If you do not tell him, I shall let Corporal Reinhart beat you to death."

"This great beast?" whispered Schatzi.

"All I have to do is nod to him." Schild released his grip, requiring all his muscles to hold his face stern. "He also knows your story and, because he is a gentile, holds a grudge. Do you remember a Dr. Otto Knebel in Auschwitz?"

"They all looked alike to me," Schatzi answered without thought, then taking a sober one: "Perhaps he was in Monowitz, another section of the camp from mine."

"He remembers you."

"Maybe he lies. The SS marched them out to Germany when the Russians approached, and who would survive such an ordeal? Lucky, I escaped. Luckier yet, you were never there in any case." He was returning to his old self, with both relief and disappointment at Schild's apparent decision not to molest him further. "But accept from me this warning, Fritz. Serg—*they* do not recognize luck. And they have also their camps. You did better to transfer from Berlin, where they can easily get at you, before playing the renegahd."

Without feeling, Schild said: "I'm no renegade. You can also tell him I won't talk."

"Fritz,'" said Schatzi. He came close in a reek of liquor, eyes drifting: "I have some regret for mistakes in my life. Wiss my family was not the love you Jews have for each another. You can not understand how my father was beating me always. I have had another dog at ten years of age. My father struck that dog

to death when it slipped its chain and entered the house and fed
upon his slippers."

Behind him Schild heard the noise of a vehicle in Hohenzollern Platz.

"Was that in Nürnberg?" he asked.

Schatzi was caught up short, made his eyes keen, and answered: "Precisely. Do you know the city? In the Altstadt, below the cahstle wall."

"Near the *Dürerhaus?*"

"In fact, overlooking," Schatzi answered. "I have heard Dürer's
house is *kaputt* from the bombing. Is it so?"

"I don't know. I have never been there."

"*Dürerhaus, Scheisshaus,* what should we care, eh Fritz?"

Schild backstepped from his camaraderie, turned and saw the
jeep bumping over the streetcar tracks. It was now as light as an
overcast afternoon. The tall MP beside the driver saluted, and
Schild knew a moment's qualm. But it was not he who arrested
Lichenko.

"You want a ride, Lieutenant? Is that crumb bothering you?
Hey Hitler, spricken see English?" He smacked his billyclub into
his palm. "C'mere. I'll give you some democracy right in the
nuts."

"He's with me," said Schild, officerly factual, showing his ID
card. "If you drive on down this street you will see a corporal.
I want you to give him a lift if you are going that way. He too
was with me on official business, so don't bother him about a
pass."

The MP obsequiously lowered his club. Likely had he seen
Schatzi alone, he would not even have made the threat; he
wished merely to be appreciated.

"I hope," Schild continued nevertheless, "you don't speak in
that loose fashion to every German you meet. You might run
into an anti-Nazi."

Again the MP assented, careful in his policeman way to give

excuse without a show of confusion. "I didn't know there were any."

"Neither did I," said Schild. "But we can't let that make a difference."

The jeep snorted down the vacant Hohenzollerndamm.

"You Amis are strangest of the strange," said Schatzi. By means of the MP's menace he had regained full dignity. "This I first believed was a weakness of the mind, and next for me it was a sinister thing. Finally, I see, and it is harmless: you really believe that you are the master race." This time he wiped his nose on a handkerchief. "The Germans, you know, never did, and least of all when this crazy sissy Adolf, and this cripple Goebbels, and that fat Zeppelin with the large mouth Goering, told them they were. A German knows he is not anysing. Instead for a time he thinks that *they* are, Adolf *und Gesellschaft*. Never himself. A French waiter makes a German feel like an ox. An Englishman makes him feel ill dressed. His great philosophers either talk so he cannot understand them, like Hegel, or tell him what a disgusting lout he is, like Nietzsche. And then there are the Jews, always so clever and so successful. See the magnificent land where they run things, America! . . . Fritz, I am speaking earlier of my mistakes. I work for the Communists because they force me. When I am a young man I spilled much of their blood, but now I am old and weak. Unless I serve they will denounce me to the American police—this thing with Röhm and the early SA. I will be treated like a Nazi, *ja?* At least this way I am free. But can you get me to America, I shall not inform *them* you will go. Is it an honest arrangement?"

"Perfectly," said Schild, "except that I don't get a profit. Now I'll make you a deal. First, you report to Sergeyev that Fritz is done. Second, you make certain I never see you again. On my part I'll keep Corporal Reinhart from killing you. Now"—he seized Schatzi and turned him around—"that way is east. Go already, in peace and freedom."

Schatzi went, looking back from time to time with the re-proach and puzzlement of an exiled pet, but going. Schild watched him as far as the Platz and, reminded by his animal progress, pitied him again for the loss of his dog.

Reinhart was at Roseneck, Rose Corner, when he heard the jeep engine and, because his permanent pass was good not later than 0100 hours, he crept into an empty beer garden and hid behind a tree. The car made the turn and vanished into Rheinbaben-allee. Emerging, he saw the darkness of the Grunewald woods a couple more football-field lengths down the street. He had lead in his ass and his feet were aflame. Distances elsewhere stand-ard, in Berlin were triple; and he had taken no real exercise in years. As well he was a chair-medic, the Rangers and paratroop-ers were lucky not to have him. He regretted having pulled on ahead of Schild, for not only was he tired, he was lonely. But the Jews and their mad pride, he would never learn to cope with it.

Crossing Kronprinzenallee at last, he saw where someone had chopped down a tree in the Grunewald. He walked in and sat on the fallen trunk. He searched in vain for a cigarette, but the Pall Malls were at Bach's, the Fleetwoods with Schild. No mat-ter, his lungs were weak enough. He struck himself in the chest and coughed histrionically, feeling a certain softness in the pectorals. Weight lifters out of training develop breasts like women, look worse than the ninety-pound weaklings they origin-ally were, he remembered. Undoubtedly the same thing hap-pens to the muscles of the trained mind: in time intellectuals' heads grow flabby. The morality of Puritans becomes mushy. Life mocks those who try.

Now that he had found Kronprinzenallee he knew the way home: straight down it about fifty miles to Argentinische Allee, around that crescent about halfway, another twenty, until you reached a patch of trees and sandbags and excavations, travers-ing which you came finally upon the farthermost limbs of the detachment headquarters building. Trudchen would be long gone to the bosom of her family, obeying her parents' ukase against staying in bed with a man after ten o'clock at night. He had his joke; actually, she told them she had to work overtime at the office. They were, he supposed, a typical German familial unit, of which he should make a sociological investigation—except that he knew all about normal people, who are everywhere the same.

Rest in his condition only made it more difficult to return to movement. He checked the blouse of his trousers, that precise indicator of a soldier's smartness—Schild, for example, had he worn boots would have stuffed the cuffs crudely into their mouths and buckled the straps. The contraceptive around his right boot proved to be frayed. He took a new one from his watch pocket, peeled it, tied it in place. The Kraut who found the discarded rubber would never figure it out.

Ready to move, he saw in Hohenzollern's distance the insignificant form of Lieutenant Schild, walking steadily, nothing ambitious but with a certainty in his carriage that he would get there, wherever it was. A tough little guy, in his own way. If I could be like Schild, Reinhart believed, I would not complain. So he waited for him.

Arriving, Schild said: "The MPs didn't find you?"

Reinhart boasted: "I was too quick for them."

"They were going to give you a ride."

"I can make it all right. Why didn't you take one?"

"I have an aversion to the police."

"You and me both."

"I wanted to ask you," said Schild, "what are you going to do about your friend Nurse Leary?"

"That's a difficulty." He was getting nervous again at having to walk so slowly. "Let her go to hell, I guess. Except that I gave my word."

"What do you owe huh?" Schild asked, New Yorkly.

"Nothing whatsoever. That is exactly why I cannot go back on my word."

"I'd think it would be the other way around."

Reinhart felt the newly arranged cuff working loose with his stride. Screw it. He smiled down at Schild and said: "What you mean is you thought *I* would think so. But I don't. It would be letting the other fellow decide what you yourself should feel. I never have been able to stand that. That's what I like about the Army, where you are told what to do and eat and wear, but never what to think and feel. Everybody but me seems to hate it, on the grounds that it takes away their 'freedom.' When did you last see a free man in civilian life?" He pushed back his sweat-heavy cap and snorted. "Look at me. I alone am right. Ha! Join the Reinhart Party!"

Paired, the travel had improved; already they had crossed the sandy Pücklerstrasse and the apartment houses of Argentinische Allee lay in the field of vision.

Schild said: "The knights of Cornwall are no men of worship, as other knights are. And because of that, they hate all men of worship."

"What is that?"

"From King Arthur. You put me onto him with your 'Ritter, Tod, und Teufel.'" Schild slowed. "Here, let's have the last two of your Fleetwoods. . . . You think a lot, don't you?"

"Too much," Reinhart complained with a mouthful of smoke. "Indeed I am a drone. However, I don't usually do the talking. By nature I am a listener."

"Do you ever get any snatch?"

Astounded, Reinhart asked him to come again. The same, and this intellectual was not even grinning.

"Since you ask, Lieutenant, only that little Trudchen—just as you predicted. She was no virgin. She is depraved, in fact, was already, which makes me feel less badly about it."

"Well," said Schild, "if she's old enough to have it, she's old enough to use it."

"War is terrible when it corrupts a young kid like that," Reinhart said piously.

Cigarette in the side of his mouth, head cocked so the smoke could not catch in his glasses, Schild asked: "Are you serious?"

"No."

They joined in pragmatic, male laughter, the kind that would have stimulated the heroines of those movies Very loved to heat up their castrating irons.

Then it was only fair that Reinhart interrogate Schild. Who confessed to having been a teacher in civil life, specializing in English, in a private school that Reinhart suspected was "progressive," where the students did whatever they wished and called the instructors by their first names. Was it? In part, Schild admitted, laughing more than ever.

"Frankly, that's just the kind of thing I would have loathed as a kid. I always got a lot of satisfaction from believing I was more progressive than the school. Your place would take that away. Don't you think it is better for superiors not to understand the people under them too well? I like a rather stern authority that I can hate and feel morally better than."

"And overthrow?" Because he had done less talking, Schild's cigarette was down to a nub carrying a long, quivering ash. A sudden burst of fresh morning wind snowed it across his blouse.

"Sure, sure, but there will always be something else." Throat parched, Reinhart threw away his half-smoked smoke and said: "I accept life. Some things in it are by nature hateful."

"You are the most extreme reactionary I have ever met," said Schild, but pleasantly; almost, one could imagine, with approval.

As they turned into Argentinische they met a light, drifting film of rain, which was refreshing to the warm cheeks but also a douche on Reinhart's spirit. He had run off at the mouth, revealed the location of his defenses and their strength, while wise

Schild had really said nothing. Worse, he could not have faith in his own honesty: in action he had always proved to be the least independent of men, not reactionary at all. This evening, for example, he had needed Schild's open ear.

They cut through the little woods and came out by quiet detachment headquarters, passed the sleeping hospital, and in the now generous rain took each other's leave at the corner of officers' row. Schild dripped water from the end of his obvious nose and smelled of wet wool, even as Reinhart did himself, and had trouble with his spectacles.

"I'm supposed to wear glasses myself," Reinhart said. "For reading. I am farsighted. But I broke them in England. . . . Do you feel all right now, Lieutenant? Frankly, I thought you acted a bit odd early this evening."

Schild removed his cap and wrung it like a sponge, put it back all wrinkly. Then he saw Reinhart's frown, took it off again and smoothed it across his knee. "Okay now? Reinhart, you are a fop. Why yes, I feel good. But I thought you were interested only in yourself."

"Never did I say that," Reinhart answered dolefully. "You have any idea of how late it is? We must have walked ten or fifteen miles."

"Three-thirty perhaps, four, who knows? If you get in trouble at your outfit I'll fix it." He returned Reinhart's salute and said: "I never have anybody to talk to, either. Thank you for letting me come along."

Reinhart watched him all the way to the gate of his billet, thinking, I have done you a favor? His own waterladen cap weighed on his head like a sandbag; he removed and wrung it à la Schild. When he looked again through the rain his friend was stepping safely over the threshold.

Reinhart approached the rear of his apartment building on the alley that was but an unpaved continuation of the officers' street. He stifled an impulse to climb up and enter his flat through the balcony, which might have incited the half-awakened Marsala to witless mayhem. Similarly, before going around front he took a leak in the bushes lest toilet-flushing would wake his buddy. While in midstream he heard a door down the street and there, inexplicably, came out Schild again, walking to the corner at which they had parted, and then out of sight up Possweg. Cursing the capacity of his bladder, he at length finished. At the corner he saw Schild enter the dark grove where the mess tents were pitched. It's too early to get coffee! The guard there will shoot him! were among his angry self-expostulations. Reaching there himself, he saw the tents were farther to the left than he had remembered; besides, Schild was fifty yards into the trees and still going.

Like an Iroquois, Reinhart crept silently from pine to pine until there were few left and a plain like a soccer field showed light before him. At the edge of the grove Schild stood with two civilian persons, one of thickset middle height and the other a great lump of fellow larger than Reinhart by three inches in every dimension and, by the set of his massive shoulders, no Bach. Drawn up on the soccer field beyond, a black European sedan.

Perhaps because the wind was wrong—at that moment he realized the rain had stopped and the wind risen, cold against damp clothing—he heard nothing of their speech, knew only that they looked at Schild and Schild at the ground. But the evil voice sounded within him: *The black market, how like a Jew.* As if upon that signal, the two men seized his friend, each on an arm, and dragged him towards the car.

Fear's fat serpent squirmed down Reinhart's throat, circled the belly, and undulated through his intestines. Even the smaller guy looked as if he were built of bricks—the larger one was a monster; he could not have felled him with a baseball bat. They wore cloth caps and neckerchiefs and dark clothing, were some European kind of thugs, ranged against a little Jew and an oversized boy. Oh, unfair! he whimpered and had every intent to hide, but was too limp to stand still, too weak to walk away, so no choice was left for a coward but to run towards them.

He squished over the wet sand and was nowhere near when they heard him and turned. The large one released Schild and stalked forward.

"Go away, boy," he growled in German. "This is no affair of yours."

Reinhart slowed but kept coming, still too scared to stop.

"He means no harm," said Schild. "Let me talk to him."

Brick-built, maintaining his hold, answered: "All right, but not in English." And told Monster to stand aside.

"This is private business," Schild said harshly. "Intelligence work. I'll thank you to keep your nose out of it."

Reinhart stopped three feet from the giant. It was so strange to be addressed in German by his friend. Groping for vocabulary, he said: "What kind of Intelligence needs the capture of an American?"

"Damn you," Schild yelled furiously, shaking off Bricks's arm. "Don't come here with your naïve bungling. I give you a direct order to leave this minute if you value your stripes."

Planning something, an old trick of movie combat, Reinhart trembled in anticipation—for it never could be worked in real life, on this damp plain, in wet clothing, by a coward who was sure he had misjudged appearances. With relief he heard the threat to his rank. A man in authentic danger would hardly be so precise.

"All right." Shamefaced, he added: "I forgot to tell you earlier: I have never understood the Jews, but I'm not proud of it."

Schild answered: "Neither have I, neither am I." Yet his head rose in pride.

Monster mockingly repeated: *"Die Juden habe ich nie verstanden—"*

Knowing his fist would shatter, and caring desperately about it—he hated to be hurt—certain that as usual he was wrong and lost and impotent, he released what little reason he had accumulated in twenty-one years, wheeled badly, plunged slippingly, and weakly struck into the giant's armored belly. Wondrously he felt his hand prevail as if it had punched a cushion. The man's deep guts wormed against his knuckles. Monster buckled, retching. Reinhart kicked his face.

He turned towards Bricks, just in time to save Schild's blood, for the man exposed a paratrooper's gravity knife, dropped the blade, and waded in low.

He screamed: "Get away you fool!" Which brave little Schild ignored, waiting defenseless, calmly, Jewlike, for his fate.

Reinhart sprang, Bricks did quick footwork, Reinhart fell flat in muck and looking up saw Schild professionally elude the blade, simultaneously knee Brick's groin and chop his neck. Wilting, Bricks cried in pain, to which Schild's cruel answer was a hacking at his forearm, precision hands above and below, that snapped the bone.

But Monster, face of gore, had meanwhile lumbered over. With his hobnailed sole he opened Reinhart's cheek as you would boot a melon. On all fours, Reinhart took another, ill aimed; still, his cropped skull was grooved from fore to aft and red fluid flowed out and blinded him. A third and he would be dead. It was all very real.

Unseeing, he crabbed as Monster swung again; he tumbled over, cleared his eyes. His life's dear blood left gout on gout; his bare cheekbone sorely caught the wind; but he got up. He stalked Monster, who great as he was now retreated; who could not have been an ex-SSman, for they were not craven. He caught him, took the battering of the leaden fists, bore in inexorably, embraced him in murderous love. Monster's hands belabored his kidneys, tried for his neck, but he was now in too close; therefore they tightened around his own small-of-back and sought to break it.

His head within the hollow of Monster's neck, he bit for the jugular. The skin was tough as chain mail, and besides he could not close his jaws, having an obsession this would push his senses through that cranial wound which Monster was opening further with each chin-stab. Then did he turn his face sidewise, upon the good cheek, and join his hands—he could just barely, around that iron barrel—and compressed, and it was hopeless.

From his good eye he saw Schild leave the fallen, whining Bricks and come to punish Monster's back, futilely, without a weapon. The rabbit punches which felled Bricks bounced harmlessly from Monster's invulnerable nape. Slowly Reinhart's spine began to crack. But then within the clasp he believed so weak, so did Monster's ribs, fibrously, like celery, yet not in sufficient time. For there was Bricks rising from the ground, crippled, twisted, knife in a left hand sufficient for the job on Schild's unguarded back.

"Lieutenant . . . behind you," he panted, his voice loose air and too little of that. At the cost of his life he loosed the hold on Monster that curtailed his own breath, and Monster exploited it. Off his axis now he shouted: "Schild for the love of Christ—" Still was Schild deaf, the bastard; he would give his life for Reinhart's which was already gone. A last hope was to call the worst he could; to stir his friend, if only by hate, to preserve his own hide. And surely he hated him enough then to frame the cry, as one can only hate him who makes you beneficiary of his total sacrifice. *Jew, I want them to kill you.*

He never said it aloud; too authentically had it sounded through the chambers of his heart. Rather have him dead than hear that knell.

So, looking into his eyes, he saw Schild get it once, twice, thrice, in terrible thumps up to the knife's haft, and squint in agony and sink. His thick glasses slid down his thin nose. He fell behind Monster, sparing Reinhart further sight, but his feet were in view and writhing.

Now came Reinhart's turn. Monster was killing him as it was, but Brick's dagger were quicker. Yearning for peace he awaited its first nick; getting it, heard a queer noise which he supposed was his heart ticking out. Monster loosed him slightly, turned head to look at Bricks in the sedan, stripping gears, driving off.

Monster roared, and was cut short by the vise of Reinhart's arms. He pleaded, shedding tears and blood from his raw face, and Reinhart was moved but could not oppose his own awful will. Not even when he heard the tearing of the vertebral column beneath his wrists could he free poor Monster, who thus died in his embrace. Life all gone, he let him fall. He knelt by Schild and searched for a pulse. He found none. He retrieved the spectacles, which were unbroken, and mounted them on his friend: he recognized him again.

He stood up, victor, and surveyed the field. Then jealous Death, who wins all battles, wound him in its dark sheet.

# CHAPTER 21

EACH night after his error with the agent Fritz, Major Sergeyev went to bed in his street clothes. Nail file, lighter, toothpicks, etc., remained in the pockets. Checking their location was his first concern on arising, unarrested, in the morning. On the nearby camp table, a foxed and worn edition of *The Foundations of Leninism,* by J. V. Stalin, lay ready to be seized as one went to answer the knock upon the door. Beside it, a toothbrush, a bit of salt twisted in a paper, a safety razor, a sliver of soap, and a hand towel, in a small cloth bag.

Seven mornings he arose in a Soviet officers' billet in Lichtenberg, ate breakfast at a mess in the basement of a commandeered factory, was driven to his office in a confiscated German Opel sedan.

Emerging from the messhall on the eighth morning, he saw, ten yards away, that his driver not only had a different profile from his usual but wore a blue cap. The man got out and politely opened the rear door of the automobile. His trousers were piped in red and blue. Within were two more bluecaps. Silently they cleared a space for Sergeyev to sit between them. He said: "*Spasibo,* thanks."

They drove for a time on the wide thoroughfare which when he had first come to Berlin as an agent in the Thirties was called Frankfurter Allee, but now he understood was to be renamed for Stalin. It had been badly bombed. He tried to go to sleep, but whenever the bluecaps saw his eyelids droop they jolted him with their elbows, in silence and without malice. Thereafter he slept with his eyes open, a technique he had developed while interrogating Social Fascists, Trotskyists, members of the POUM, and other mad-dog wreckers and counterrevolutionary jackals in Spain.

He awoke as the car stopped before a prison in Pankow. The bluecaps accompanied him to the gate house, where they signed him over and he was searched. Two prison guards, also in blue caps, were his companions on a walk of moderate length inside the building, down a damp corridor, into a bare room with a boarded window. Before they gave him the order he had begun to disrobe. Naked, he pressed himself against the concrete wall. The guards examined the seams of his garments, looked between his toes, searched the hair of armpits and pubis, peered into his mouth, probed his anus. They confiscated the pocket articles.

He dressed. They conducted him to a small cell four floors above the ground. Its window was boarded; in its iron door, a spyhole and a letter-sized slot. After some time a pan of gruel was passed through the latter. He wished he had his packet of salt. To keep fit he strolled occasionally from the door to the slop bucket at the back wall of the cell, three steps, then from his bunk to the other wall, one step. He wished he had his *Foundations of Leninism.* The ceiling bulb burned all night.

Next day he got a boiled potato, and at another meal found a bubble of fat in his hot-water soup. He wished he had his manual for espionage agents, but it was at the office. The toilet articles he did not yearn for, not having been permitted to wash.

On what he estimated, by the number of times he had been fed, seven, to be the fourth day—not having seen the sky since he entered, he did not try to fix the hour—the guards took him to a room containing a desk, one empty chair and one filled one. In the latter, behind the desk, sat a uniformed man, lean and elegant, drinking from a china cup. He wore long hair, graying at the temples. He motioned Sergeyev to sit.

Having swallowed, he said pleasantly: "My name is Chepurnik. Of course you can see my rank."

"Yes, Comrade Major.'"

"You yourself were once a major, were you not? Of course you were!" He poured himself another cup of water from the glass carafe, drank it off, and said: "Now Sergeyev, tell me like a good fellow, have you been fed decently here?"

"Excellently, Comrade Major."

"And have you been given something to read, to put in the hours profitably?"

"I made no request, sir. My book was left at the billet."

Chepurnik opened a drawer. "I believe I have it just here. . . . Ah yes, *The Foundations of Leninism*. Splendid." He leafed through the pages. "I see you follow the practice of placing little brackets about certain passages that you should like to turn to again. Here is something: 'the proletariat cannot and ought not to seize power if it does not itself constitute a majority in the country.'"

"Yes, sir. But you have not read what comes just before: 'The opportunists assert that the proletariat, etc.'"

With no change in his expression of encouragement Chepurnik half-rose and threw the contents of the carafe in Sergeyev's face. "You see," he said, with fox-bark laughter, "it is not vodka, but pure water!"

Reaching for his handkerchief, Sergeyev remembered it had been taken from him in the search; no doubt, so that he could not knot it about his neck and hang himself. He wished he had his towel. He was surprised by Chepurnik's sudden offer.

"Go on, use it!" The major tossed a handkerchief at him, which floated just out of reach. As he bent to fetch it, Chepurnik rose again and, leaning across the desk, with an inexorable meterstick pushed the chair-edge slowly backward: Sergeyev fell to his rump. Chepurnik came around and helped him up.

"There," he said, returning, "is a lesson. Observe how lean and muscular fact upsets dull brutishness. And you a major in Red Army Intelligence! Poor fellow, you could not have been an officer's orderly in the NKVD. You, with your low grade of cunning. Use Stalin's *Foundations* as your codebook, leave it out where anybody can see, this will fool everyone! Poor chap, I would pity you were it not that I am nauseated by treason. . . . Your only hope is to convince me you were misled in your criminal ventures."

It was still too soon for Sergeyev to know how and what he must confess to, as experienced in the area, from his years on the other side of the desk, and willing as he was. He lowered his head and said nothing.

Chepurnick raged: "You upset my stomach. You look like a syphilitic chancre. Get out!"

The guards came in and took Sergeyev back to his cell. He asked for writing materials. They were provided. He composed a *mea culpa* referring to sins as far back as his residence in a seminary just before the Revolution. And admitted having at that time entered into a long-term conspiracy of priests and fellow novices to overthrow the rule of the proletariat in favor of a clerical dictatorship. As an agent in Hitler Germany he betrayed *sub rosa* Communists to the Gestapo. In Spain he took Franco money. Currently, at the time of his arrest, he had been employed by the Joint Distribution Committee, a Zionist branch of the American FBI. Yet his capture had revealed to him the overwhelming might and right of the International Workers' Movement and he expressed contrition. He asked that he be punished mercilessly.

Finally he again faced the examiner. Chepurnik now wore golden pince-nez. For some reason he seemed to cultivate the appearance of an Old Bolshevik. Sergeyev could not understand why, since they had all been put to death as traitors.

The major drank from his cup, but the carafe was missing. Wiping his mouth on a beige silk handkerchief, filmy as a cobweb, he said: "Ah yes. I have read your lies." This time it was vodka, and not water, that dashed against Sergeyev's cheeks and fierily into his eyes. "Your face reminds me of a pig's rectum."

Back in the cell, as soon as his sight returned, Sergeyev began to write a new confession. He admitted having been lured by the American Intelligence agent Schild ("Fritz") and the Fascist homosexual Ernst ("Schatzi") into a plot to restore the Nazi regime in Germany. The leader of the movement was Hitler's lieutenant Martin Bormann, whose whereabouts the Allies had sought unsuccessfully since the fall of Berlin. Sergeyev could reveal that Bormann had been flown out to Lisbon and there awaited recall.

At the next interview Chepurnik gave him a cigarette.

"My pitiable fellow," he said, "you have convinced me of one thing: that you are honestly trying to tell the truth. But it is most difficult when everything one has to work with is as corrupt as a boil. For example, your so-called information about Bormann. I can assure you that he was captured by the NKVD on the second day of the fall of Berlin and has long ago been executed. And while we are on the subject, you probably also do not know that Hitler did not die in the Kanzlei as is popularly supposed. The NKVD got him and he has since been held secretly in the Kremlin, pending Stalin's decision on how best to make use of him, which is to say, as prisoner or as corpse. Also the Braun woman." Removing his pince-nez, he winked. "She was imprisoned here for a week before being sent on to Moscow. French underwear. Too skinny. But . . . *où sont les neiges d'antan?* This is how the French say, all that is past." Chepurnik was indeed a good-looking man, with a high forehead and long jaw. Sergeyev could smell his cologne.

"But to your problem," said the major, "from what principal did you get orders to kill the agent Fritz?"

Sergeyev collected his forehead sweat on a bladed hand and rubbed it into his frayed, stained trousers. "A terrible error," he answered. "I sent my men, these Germans, to bring Fritz for an interview with me. He resisted. In the ensuing fight he and my man Hans were killed."

"If you insist on telling me what I already have, and lying to boot, the Soviet people will be merciless. Fritz was your agent, and yet you did not know he went everywhere with a bodyguard, a professional athlete named—"he brought a dossier from a drawer and leafed through it—"yes, named Reingart. This man is in the hire of the Counterintelligence Department of the United States Army. Before the war he lifted weights in the Radio Music Hall, which is a sports arena in New York, U.S.A."

"No, I did not suspect that, Comrade Major," Sergeyev answered in profound shame. "I did not know that the bringing in of Fritz would entail difficulties. Those two worthless Germans should have been able to take care of anything. Just as well for them they did not come back."

"And why did they not, Sergeyev?"

He could not meet the major's eye. "Well, as you know, the one was murdered by this weight lifter. The other, I am afraid, had fled to the British Zone."

Chepurnik shook his head in tragedy. "The Soviet people gave you great responsibility, high rank, absolute trust. And you cannot live up to the most primitive concept of honor: a superior never hangs the blame on his underlings. Aren't you ashamed of yourself? What do you suppose these unfortunate Germans thought of the Soviet Union when they looked at you, its representative, a heap of garbage. . . . No, I refuse to listen to any more." He put his hands over his ears and summoned the guards.

Again and again Sergeyev rewrote the confession. He admitted his complicity in every crime against the Soviet state since its founding. He begged to be sentenced to lifelong imprisonment at hard labor. He implicated his wife and children, who lived in Leningrad, and asked that they be arrested. In his eighth revision he requested the death penalty for himself.

All to no avail. Chepurnik took every admission as evidence of a greater concealment. On the other hand, Sergeyev's infrequent and weak protestations of a particular innocence—in the context of the established general crime—outraged the major.

"How dare you assert you did not trade in American cigarettes on the black market!" he would scream, hurling the contents of his cup and carafe, or when those were not at hand, his meter-stick, which was rather more dangerous. "We discovered a hundred packages in the stuffing of your mattress!" And Sergeyev would return to his cell and incorporate this new failing into his latest confession. Which meant: in detail, for Chepurnik cast an especially cold eye on his prisoner's use of anything, he, Chepurnik, had given him. He was, that is, a man who could not be defrauded. Sergeyev, who had never seen a packet of American cigarettes, had to invent a brand: "Tom Smith Variety"; and to be precise in his count: "At the period of my greatest activity in this illegal and treacherous commerce—the purpose of which was to sow the seeds of dissension among Red Army troops to whom I distributed the cigarettes—I kept on hand approximately 523 packets, which, at 24 the packet, would in sum amount to 12,552 cigarettes."

Chepurnik hurled it into his face. "What kind of trick is this? Everybody in the entire world knows Tom Smith Brand is sold only in packages of ten cigarettes each! . . . By the way, don't you ever wash? You give off the odor of horse urine."

Chepurnik was still reading the nineteenth confession when the guards brought Sergeyev into the room. He scowled, and Sergeyev's heart mounted like steam from a samovar. No matter how enraged, the major had never scowled. Therefore it could mean only that he approved.

He did. He turned the manuscript to face Sergeyev, who saw with delight that it had been typed in the official form, and presenting a fountain pen asked him to sign it.

"Now," said the major, with the pursed lips of a French dandy blowing the ink dry, "now that should take a great weight off you."

"Sir, may I ask one question?"

Chepurnik began an ominous half-smile. "Careful now . . . just make certain it is not some punishable folly, and yes, you may."

"Has the Fascist homosexual Ernst, alias 'Schatzi,' been arrested?"

Chepurnik laughed: "Alas, you force me to do it. Your rations will be reduced by half for one week. I warned you! Herr Ernst is a loyal Communist of impeccable character and I advise you to discontinue your persistent attempts to involve him in your criminal activities. Without Germans of his kind we should have a most grievous struggle to create a Socialist society here. I shall not tolerate your Great Russian chauvinism!"

The major grasped his cup as if he might throw it, but instead he took a drink of water or vodka and wiped his lips. He went on: "Had it not been for Ernst we might have taken longer to uncover your crimes." He brought the old dossier from a drawer and leafed through its early pages. "Do you recognize this? 'Hitler cleverly crushed without mercy that foulness.' "

"No, sir."

"NO?" Chepurnik screamed. "How dare you say no? *I* did not speak these words, Ernst did not say them. Who did?"

Sergeyev remembered. "I am sorry, sir. I did, to the agent Ernst, in reference to the Röhm movement."

"Now do you doubt our tolerance? Can you imagine what would happen to an American or an English officer who praised Adolf Hitler? . . . Secondly, Herr Ernst learns of the defection of the agent Schild. Immediately, in the prescribed manner, he comes to give his report—only he cannot find you. The great Sergeyev is not at his desk, as the Soviet people expect their officers to be every minute of the day. No, the megalomaniac Sergeyev has, totally uninformed as to the condition, the whereabouts, the state of mind, and the companions of the agent Schild, already sent his men to fetch him for a 'talk,' and then himself gone with a German whore and a liter of vodka to the billet. Where did you plan to interview the agent Schild, between the whore's legs?

"No, even that would have been more sensible. You were going to have him held all night for your 'talk' in the morning, so that he would be reported missing from his unit and the whole American nation, from President Truman down, would protest to Comrade Stalin about another so-called kidnapping."

"My crime grows ever larger," Sergeyev muttered. He held himself erect only with supreme effort; so skinny was he the chair wished to eject him.

"I see," Chepurnik said. He closed his green eyes for a moment. Before opening them again, he slowly tore the confession in half. "Then this, too, is false. *Il faudra toujours recommencer.* That is French for 'we must begin all over again.' When will you learn that you do not have the intelligence for a large crime?"

## CHAPTER 22

REINHART turned on his side in bed and played it cool, studying the little blue light at the end of the ward. He saw Very's large, maternal shadow in the darker cavity of the office doorway. She had been his first concern on awakening from that positive death on the bloody field—somewhere back, weeks, he supposed; part of his trouble was a derangement of the sense of time. . . . No, he would not lie. Be fair to yourself, the doctors told him, but surely that did not mean believing falsehoods. His first occupation had been resentment and self-pity, for Schild stayed dead.

He passed out again when his wounds were treated in the emergency clinic, not from pain but in another attempt to die. In vain. You could not beat the Jews at sacrifice; it was their profession. Next he had come conscious as a patient in the ward for Superficial Wounds and Contusions, of which he did not remember Marsala was master until he heard the buddy's raucous complaints issuing from the treatment room: an underling wardboy had loused up the bandage-count. But the evidence of normality in the world outside his head terrified him, and when Marsala came to the bedside Reinhart simulated coma.

Later, en route to the night shift on the psycho ward, Veronica stopped in. Marsala was goofing off someplace, so Reinhart showed life. Then it was that he thought of her troubles and forgot for a moment his own.

"I'm sorry, Very, I tried as I promised but ran into a snag."

He felt her pat his brush and wondered where the wound up there had gone. The gash in his cheek he still had; its bandage refracted the vision of his left eye.

"Honey . . ." Poor Very suffered tears. ". . . was this terrible fight because of me?" Yet she once again looked full-blown, her splendid flesh bursting, wherever it could, from the common-place seersucker uniform.

"No, I never fight for any purpose. If I had wanted something from those Germans I would have licked their boots." He now licked his lips and found the cuts towards the left corner and the bitter medication upon them.

"Don't be so fresh with yourself," she said. Later, in his need to tabulate things, he recalled this as the first of a series of such admonitions from practically everybody.

"Anyway, I'm stuck here and I don't know for how long." He reached for her hand and then, remembering the other patients, gave it up.

Bending, she displayed the partition of her breasts and whispered: "Don't worry about me any more—I'm O.K. now—false alarm."

He laughed in a hysterical, private place, for one reason, because he could not in public: his face was cracked. There you had a capsule history of human affairs, amidst the larger one in which they participated with everyone else, including the nearby patients who gawked innocently at Veronica's body: what began in birth ended in death. Except that this one was all a mistake.

"Schild—you know I thought for a while that Schild was your lover"—she caught at her mouth—"no, that had nothing to do with this trouble, believe me . . . and he thought I was, and now none of it matters. . . . Very, look at the top of my head and tell me what you see."

She did more, exploring with a finger. "I think it is a slight bruise and nothing worse. You'll be better in no time."

"Are you sure? He kicked me bad. I was certain my scalp was laid open."

"You know it's all bone, with only a thin layer of skin and hair—" Her big teeth glistened in fun. "Excuse me, well, everybody has a bonehead, me too."

"Only mine is solid—but are you sure?"

"Clear the way for added cargo!" She bounced-sat on the edge of the bed and waylaid her rising hem at the bulge of rolled nylon. "It's pretty hard to 'lay open' a scalp; there's not much to cut and it would take something awful to break the bone wide open. Though of course there's fractures, but you don't usually know they're there until you look at the x-ray. . . . Know who's ward nurse here? Eleanor Leek, the cute little plump girl from the party where we met. She danced with that Russian. Sure you do! I'll put in a good word for you. Now I have to go, the schizzes all start crying if I'm not on time. Oh, did you want to talk about the fight? But I don't think it's good yet. Rest awhile. Now kiddy, I'll say goodbye. I would kiss you but everybody's lookin'."

As the *Santa Maria* must have swept from the Bahaman harbor, past the awed little brown men in their crummy dugouts, proceeding westward still, so Veronica sailed in splendor up the ward aisle and out the door, flying the high standard of her winged cap, and the natives returned to their fishing and coconuts.

Soon afterwards Lieutenant Leek, whom when he saw her he remembered, the fat, homely, merry person, hurried in from the corridor.

"Good, you're conscious. Holy cow, you kept the brass waiting all day. Can you talk to them now?"

"Who?" With Very's departure he stepped on a merry-go-round which turned slowly to no music. "I don't feel so good."

"I'll give you a pain pill soon as they leave." She left his sight and in a moment or two he was ringed by many male uniforms.

For one, the commander of the 1209th General Hospital, Lieutenant Colonel Fester, whom in three years' service with the outfit he was seeing for the fourth time, despite the legend that Fester was ubiquitous.

"Now Steinhart, look sharp," the colonel said in a clarion tenor. He wore white gloves, like a doorman. "This is a terrible thing you are a party to, but I know any man of mine can defend his actions. Handpicked, every man Jack of you. Remember how we kept those niggers out of our latrine on the troopship coming over? Medics, maybe. They don't let us carry guns, but by Jesus we've got fists. I'd put my hand in the fire—if I didn't have this eczema—for any one of you and know you'd return the favor— say, are you awake? Here you, Teats, or whatever your name is. Nurse! Give this man a hypo of something. What do you use nowadays? You've got all the drugs in the world nowadays. It wasn't like that in the old days. By God, APC capsules, gentian violet, and you had it; after that, the pine box. Remember the old days, Major, or was that before your time?"

Reinhart opened his eyes. Next to the colonel stood a major with a young face, yet old gray sideburns.

"We'll talk about that later, sir," the major answered with short patience. "Here, the fellow is awake—"

"Coming around, Steinhart?" the colonel cried. "Good, now stay awake for a moment. This is Major Koenig from G-2, Berlin District. I don't have to tell you he is a Very Important Person so far as we are concerned here in our humble way. He wants to ask you about last night."

Reinhart also saw Captain St. George, lachrymose; an enlisted man, PFC Walter Walsh, swelled with gravity; Lieutenant Nader, resentfully watching the colonel; and finally, a brutish-faced captain who wore the crossed-pistols badge of the military police.

"Your name is *Rein*hart, correct?" asked Major Koenig. "How are you feeling, Corporal?"

"Carlo T., 15302320, and a little dizzy, sir."

"Well, who isn't? And I haven't just broken anybody's back, either," Koenig said. "By the way, how did you do that?"

"Only because he would have broken mine if I didn't."

"I asked *how*."

"Just caught him around the waist and bent him backwards."

"Good fellow!" broke in the colonel. "I used to watch you wrestle at Camp Pickett every Friday night, Reinkoenig. You made me lots of money. That's why I chose you for the 1209th. You still a corporal? Months ago I told that goddamned Lovett to put you on orders for a third stripe."

"Thank you, sir, but I had basic at Camp Barkeley—"

"Quite all right, my boy. Just answer these questions—"

The major asked: "Do you feel well enough to get up for a few minutes? It's difficult to talk here. The nurse said we may use the ward office."

Reinhart lay quiet for a moment, his right as a casualty, then indicated he would try. Blackness flooded his brain as he sat upright, and he heard their voices as if through the closed window of a ballroom. His wrist was seized.

"Come on, fellow," the colonel shouted.

In transit Reinhart slept awhile and when he came to, watching the red-black ocean recede, thought they all had gone.

"You need a pick-me-up!" the colonel roared. "Teats! Mix an ounce of medical alcohol with grapefruit juice and bring it to this soldier." But Lieutenant Leek had crept off to hide.

"It's all right, Major," Reinhart said to Koenig, who offered no aid nor sympathy. "I can make it."

The major walked smartly towards the office. Reinhart shook himself, feeling a twinge in his cheek, slipped into the dirty canvas slippers waiting below the bed, rose and followed. With all manner of noise the colonel dogged him but was denied at the door.

"This," said Koenig, standing just within, "is an Intelligence matter, sir. Captain St. George and I will have to speak privately with Corporal Reinhart. If you gentlemen can give us a few moments?"

"Me neither?" The MP officer's growl betrayed a fright at his exclusion. He put a broken cigarette into his mouth and tried to light it, getting only air. From the patients out in the ward arose an anonymous murmur of ridicule, which was tonic to the colonel.

He said: "As to me and Nader and PFC Walter, we'll mix here

with the men till you need us." Followed by his reluctant entourage he went back down the aisle between the beds and shortly, among his bursts of loud, merry scatology, came the obstreperous derision which he was famous for misunderstanding as popularity.

Making an effort, Reinhart indeed felt better and stronger. The major, however, who sat upon a white-enameled chair, directed him to lie upon the operating table.

There was no allowance for discussion, so he did. St. George— he saw the genuine sadness on the fat face, and pitied him, and liked him—slumped against the wall.

"Now, PFC Walsh," said Koenig, "who was mess guard last night, heard noises on the sports field and went to investigate. By the time he got there you were unconscious and the two other men were dead. He states he heard an automobile engine, and there were tire tracks in the sand. May we hear your account?"

On his back, unable to see his interrogator, Reinhart spouted perspiration and anticipated a nameless catastrophe. Unknown enemies held him supine and prepared to work upon him an obscene damage; he felt womanly, about to be raped. Yet all through this, his fluent voice romped on, as if it were rather the child of another man. The voice told of the chance, friendly encounter early in the evening between Reinhart and Schild, of a purposeless wander to the Tiergarten, since the black-market contact never appeared and they thus could not buy their Meissen china. Then they took a drink in a jerry-built cafe on the Kudamm, looked for a ride home and finding none began to walk. They lost their way temporarily. Finally they reached Zehlendorf. Then the straight story of seeing Schild enter the grove, and the fight.

"There must be more," said Koenig in his ominous, factual way.

St. George spoke for the first time: "Lieutenant Schild had some of his own contacts whom I knew nothing about. We worked in that manner. Perhaps it wasn't SOP—"

"You said all that."

But once begun, St. George was briefly invincible. He owed it to his late colleague. And Reinhart thought, Schild was closer to him than to me; he was never really my friend, yet I did what I could to save him; why do I tell myself I was his killer?

"Perhaps it wasn't SOP, but I respected his intelligence. Then he was a Jew, you know. I never thought about it before, but it could hardly have been pleasant service here where they did such horrible things to his people. . . . One of his German contacts was a little old fellow dressed like a workingman, who rode a bike. He came once to the billet when the Russian stayed with us. But perhaps he wasn't there for Nate. When I saw him he was talking with the landlady."

"Russian!" blurted Koenig. He reassumed self-control. "You can tell me all that later, Captain. At the moment we are interested in the corporal."

Koenig did not trust Reinhart, so much was clear. But Reinhart had changed since he killed a man. Earlier he would have hated Koenig. Now he was beholden to him; wished he would let him rise, but knew he deserved no favors.

The major asked: "This little old fellow that Captain St. George mentions—was he one of the two Germans on the sports field?"

Reinhart answered no. Schatzi—Schild knew him too. He remembered the doctor's revelation and his own bombastic threat to kill this complex person both victimizer and victim. Doubtless no one took it seriously. Could they have seen him a few hours later! But Schild had, and thought him inadequate, and come to help, and died.

"I take it then you know the man St. George means, if you are sure he was *not* there."

"I believe so," said Reinhart, "he hangs out around here. He is a big wheel in the black market."

"Could this have been a dispute over a black-market deal?"

St. George answered, scandalized: "Certainly not! I never knew a man less interested in money than Nate."

Koenig sighed. "The corporal has just testi—stated he and Lieutenant Schild went to the Tiergarten, were driven to that area by you, yourself, in which you concur, to meet someone who offered a set of Meissen china for sale."

"Sure," St. George laughed indignantly, "but that was for Reinhart!"

"That's right," said Reinhart to the major he could not see, endeavoring to meet St. George's eye with a message of loyalty. But the captain seemed to avoid him.

"A do-gooder, the late Lieutenant Schild."

St. George answered: "Always," and hung his head.

Koenig continued his keen probing, to which his immaculate and subtle contempt was an additional tool. Reinhart dissembled in the only way he could, by blondly, wholesomely baring all but his suspicions, which anyway was legally impeccable. Later, the MP officer was let in, and Nader and Walsh, and, perhaps with an idea to stop his noise, briefly, the colonel.

Koenig suddenly finished; whether for good and all, naturally he did not indicate. Nader and the MP, although they showed a personal distaste for Reinhart, seemed in the absence of contrary evidence to believe his story and agree he must stand a court-martial which would formally find him guilty of homicide in the line of duty, sentence one dollar. This to forestall an attempt by Monster's heirs, if they could be found—he remained unidentified—to bring charges.

Everybody having left, Reinhart assumed he could get up, and did so, and was frightened by the appearance of St. George, who lingered behind the operating table.

"Listen," said the captain, with suppressed dislike, "maybe you know. Does Lieutenant Schild have any family? We don't know who to inform. For some reason he gave as next-of-kin the name of a prostitute in Paris, Texas. I never had occasion to look at the record until this morning, and then I recalled her name from when we served together at Camp Maxey."

"I never knew him well," said Reinhart, whoozily standing.

"Who did? . . . He had a strange sense of humor, and this shows he would go all the way with it." Still with obvious unfriendliness, he came to Reinhart's support. "You see, we were in combat zones since D-Day. He could have been killed at any time. But for the joke he gave the name of this streetwalker."

Reinhart took the offered arm. They moved together into the ward. At his bed, first one on the right-hand line, he thanked the captain and shook hands, and saw astonished gratitude, and understood merely another error: St. George did not dislike, but rather fearing being disliked.

"Oh that's all right," said the captain, pumping his fingers. "If you don't mind, maybe I can drop in from time to time to see you. But you'll be better soon." He left anxiously. He returned and placed a just-opened package of Parliament cigarettes on the night table. "Have a luxury smoke." At the foot of the bed he turned and said: "He was a good fellow," and waited.

"Yes, he was," Reinhart answered and blacked out. He dreamed he was twelve years old; selling newspapers from door to door he accumulated money for a bicycle; someone stole the money but when he went outside there was the bike on the porch; a Negro applied Simonize to the fenders; *so you're a Negro*, he said, *isn't that fine!*; the black man rose in terror, great white eyeballs gleaming, and ran down the street. When Reinhart awakened, the same Negro, whom he had never before seen in life, carrying a tray of food walked past the bed and to his own, number five, where he sat near its head and ate rather insolently, winding spaghetti into a spoon.

Leek appeared with a tray for Reinhart containing various forms and colors of mush. He was suddenly horny; she was not so bad. He invited her to come sit upon the palm of his hand. She thought he waved her off, and went. He called her back and asked the time. Six-ten. He slept for an hour. Awakening, he asked the time of the fellow in the next bunk, who had a wart in the center of a bushy red eyebrow. Six-eleven. He denigrated the fellow's watch, cursed its owner. The fellow slyly turned his back, and Reinhart cried into the pillow because he could not hurt him.

When everybody had gone to sleep he wandered into the toilets and counting them again and again at last made his choice of one to sit upon and read a comic book. He had not finished a page when a wardboy whom he did not recognize entered and ordered him back to bed.

"You been in here two hours."

Reinhart snarled contempt. "I've been in the Army since Christ was a PFC, and don't you forget it, you prick of misery."

But he went. Someone kept putting a flashlight in his eyes and forced him to eat sulfa pills and drink four glasses of water.

One day Marsala, whom he was forced to admit knowing, sat on the edge of the bed and whispered, so that the bastard with the red eyebrows couldn't hear: "Carlo, whadduh yuh doin'? You been here three weeks, your cheek is almost healed. But you keep acting crazy, they send you to Psycho. I don't shit you, pal. I heard Captain Cage talk about it this morning."

Reinhart had all he could do to keep from spitting in his ugly face. "Here's what I say to you: go to hell."

"See what I mean. Whadduh yuh want to be sore for? Jesus, I'm distracted." He rubbed his thick and whorled temples. "So you took too much sulfa, but that don't stay on permanent. Your white-corpuscle count is okay—"

"You flunky, what do you know about medicine? You traitor, you make me puke." He stared fiercely at the quondam buddy, stared through him as if he were cellophane—a gift he had nowadays and would have done anything to get rid of.

"Okay," said Marsala. "Okay then. You and I are through.

Get it? As soon as I get back to the apartment your crap goes out inna street." He symbolically spat. "And the same goes for your lousy *putana*, that little kid who's young enough to be ya granddaughter, dirty guy."

The return on his aggression soothed Reinhart, convinced him that even wounded and mad he was potent. In delight, he said: "I hurt your feelings, didn't I?"

Marsala looked at him a long time, his ferocity melting into a kind of grief. "Nah, I consider the source. . . . Look, what for did you tell that kid Trudy she could have your extra OD shirt and pants? Don't you think you will ever get out of here?"

"Did you give them to her?" He saw the whole thing and was serene.

Marsala clicked his teeth in lascivious regret. "You didn't say she could have them, you ain't even seen her since you're here, am I right? She talked me into it, kid. I'm sorry. When we get through and are in there washing up she says she is thirteen. Jesus I'm a dirty guy." He slapped his wrist with two fingers.

Happily, Reinhart lied: "Of course I did. I sent her a note. I'm going home soon and don't need that extra stuff. Give it all to her and take her for yourself. She is really sixteen and if she's old enough to have it, that's old enough to use it. I apologize for being nasty. You're the best buddy I ever had, and when I get home I'll write you a letter once a month. . . ." He closed his eyes and kept on talking. When he opened them again Marsala was gone and Red Eyebrows, who he also noticed had red hair, was peering at him most curiously.

"Hey Red," he called. "I didn't mean what I said yesterday about your watch. I was still a little dizzy from this trouble I had the other night. Have a luxury cigarette." He picked up the Parliaments and handed them over. They were strangely dry and friable for a fresh pack.

"Yesterday?" asked Red. "That was almost a month ago." He laughed as if he were insane.

But when later in the day they transferred a patient to the Neuropsychiatric Ward, it was not Red.

Veronica's shadow flowed back into the black cavity of the office, meaning all was quiet on the ward. Reinhart himself certainly never made a sound. In the latrine he had even perfected a technique for micturating without noise. He wished to call no attention to himself, because he was altogether mad.

It owed to that kick in the head which couldn't be proved. The staff in Superficial Wounds assured him he suffered from a mild toxic psychosis, the effects of an overdose of sulfa, for which they took full responsibility. Having admitted their guilt, they insisted it make him free, especially since the technical manual, *Guides to Therapy for Medical Officers,* called the reaction rare. And as to Reinhart's confession that he habitually swung the pills into the deep socket of his jaw, drank the water, and spit them out when the nurse turned her back: in their view this illusion was rather an index to how many he had swallowed and been deranged by. Apologizing, they force-fed him gallons of water. Drowning, he was still mad.

The Psycho people, on the other hand, kept their convictions secret. Lieutenant Llewellyn walked on eggs from bed to bed on his morning tour of inspection, wearing the silky, untrimmed mustache to make himself look older and the plastic-rimmed eyeglasses for wisdom, carrying his mouth slack and moist in an advertisement of patience. He was rather leery of Reinhart; few indeed of his patients had killed a man with their bare hands.

Captain Millet, the chief, stayed always in the office and one went to see him at intervals. From crown to temple he shone bald as Bach; around the ears, a ballet tutu of salt-and-pepper hair. As Llewellyn was listener, Millet questioned, and had a talent for the irrelevant: Do you like girls, did you ever play with yourself, do you have headaches, did you dress up in your mother's clothes when a boy, what do you think other people think of you, what do you want to be?

To the last Reinhart invariably answered: "Able to tell time again." For this was the heart of the matter, but Millet, bored, toyed with his pen and never took a note.

His head he had stopped bothering to mention; if Superficial Wounds, in whose area of interest it lay, could not find that seepage of brain fluid, Psycho, devoted to the impalpable, would hardly. On the basis of many motion pictures about amnesiacs he drew up his own strategy of treatment: he could be cured by another raking blow on the skull. But owing to the queer angle, he could not slug himself sufficiently hard, and he was afraid to ask one of the nuts to do it, who might kill him. Which brought to mind an essential feature of his condition: a lack of interest in death as therapy.

Once he had tried strenuously to die, and again the next morning, when it had seemed necessary to the *Gestalt* of himself-Schild-and-Germany. Now it would be a simple missing of the point, for the self within him was already unearthly and losing the rest were impertinent. If someone sought to kill him he might not resist, but he would not raise his hand against himself.

His inner cautions to the contrary, in a burst of bravado he delivered this information to Captain Millet. Who blankly answered: "That is comforting." And Reinhart was ashamed of his vanity and of his suddenly revealed wish for Millet's affection, whom he didn't even like and to whom he had bragged only because, he thought, Millet didn't care.

The captain went on: "You mean, you will not commit suicide by violence. That is too easy, whereas what always attracts you is the difficult."

"No," Reinhart confessed. "The impossible."

An ear fringe grew as fast as a full head of hair; Millet needed a haircut, which deficiency, however, and now a vulnerable smile—his teeth were crooked—canceled the disapproval from his next remark: "Why do you think you are so important?"

"Because—" Reinhart groped for something smashing; in his bare cupboard was one bone; he seized it—"because I am insane."

Millet said seriously: "The Army may make errors in assignment, but they were right about me. I can show you my diplomas. I assure you, you are not insane and will not be."

"Then I am a fake."

Millet's pen scratched upon his notepad, but Reinhart saw only doodles, and not imaginative ones at that. "As late as the nineteenth century they used to chain patients to the wall and whip the disorders out of them. The treatment was oftentimes successful. It might be used today except that its good effects were, I believe, only temporary and it required enormous physical exertion on the therapists' part. Now we have the lazy man's method. When you decide whether or not you are a fake, come in and tell me."

Well, he guessed he *had* made a mark on Millet, if Millet talked to him in that ironical way. The captain was softer with the other patients, according to them—for Reinhart sometimes conversed with those who were articulate. The enuretic poseur of a paratrooper, for example, whom Very talked about back in August, had returned. Perhaps he falsified the one symptom, but he had plenty more, couldn't use a tableknife, thought people were after him, etc.

But having got his special notice from Millet, Reinhart went back to where he started. Because his case was irrelevant to the fundamental proposition by which lunatics and psychiatrists are one: Life goes on. And not only proceeds to the measure of the ticking second hand, but also abides in wondrous detail which perhaps one can only know when on furlough from the process.

Who ever before had opportunity to study the fabric of a pillowcase? The close and naked eye saw no two threads the same. And the canvas slippers: their weave black with dirt, rich with memories of various feet walking diverse floors in many lands; their old human smell, sour, interesting. Chipped was the white paint on the bedstead, revealing multiform corrosions, patina, wounds in ancient iron; whom had it supported and in the aftermath of what: Caesarean sections, irrigations of the maxillary sinus, removal of the vermiform appendix, mere hang-overs, some deaths. Blankets of wealthy white wool, shrunken gray pajamas gaping at the fly and over the heart USAMD embroidered in red; maroon robe of weary corduroy, too short; night table all one's own offering water in pitcher and glass, and beneath, on the low-slung shelf, colored books random and in shadow.

And through the window—lingering on the glass itself, marvelous substance almost invisible, metamorphosis of gritty sand, just as the butterfly comes from a worm and remembers it not —a view of this side of the grove on the other side of which, on the sand, some fellows murdered his only friend while he watched through another window, that glass bell under which he was wax fruit.

In this celebration of matter he got through his mornings, which were worst. From within came spontaneous improvement as the sun traveled towards America; afternoons were fair, he could sleep, and wake up in early evening, glad of life's refuge from dreams. As natural light failed and Edison's took over, he was better. Finally, each dark midnight, the absolute cure: bored with the soul's business he lay unsleeping, yet not sleepless, believing in these hours of exuberant health that everybody should have a goal. During such a period of clarity and courage he decided to take his discharge, when it came, in Berlin and marry Lori.

Or join with her in whatever other relationship external conditions would allow, the mode was irrelevant; internal coherence was all. Even *ménage à trois,* in thinking of which he signified his affection, respect, and pity for Bach, nay his downright love for this man who needed and had a nurse, not a wife. She would continue in that role, plus which he would gain a friend to listen interminably. Reinhart spoke frankly to himself of its romanticism: this boy from distant and simple Ohio oh beautiful for spacious skies and amber waves of grain, in a rathole under the rubble of a dark and evil idea, living in adultery and cuckoldry sanctioned by mutual love, talking art and philosophy: there at last was the old German idealism he had searched for so long.

On the third night of his planning, in the second week of his residence in Psycho, he believed it politic to leave the bed and steal to the office. The paratrooper, next to him, sobbed peacefully; from elsewhere sounded placid onanistic rustles; the coast was clear.

Veronica, back to doorway, sorted files. Before Reinhart could announce himself—because he meant no harm—he was seized from behind by two husky wardboys leaping out of ambush, who were lucky to remind him poignantly of Monster's dread embrace, and he offered no resistance.

"Oh that's okay, fellows," said Very when she saw, holding up parallel fingers—for some reason, all five instead of the standard two—"this kid and I are just like that." She directed them to the treatment room, to prepare wet cocoons against an expected need towards dawn. They left, grumbling fealty.

"I was wondering when you'd come, you ingrate. I got put on nights so you could."

She almost leered at him, and he thought: working here gets them all eventually. They sat on either side of the desk, which had kneeholes on both sides, so that his and her legs touched. Soon she squeezed one of his between both of hers and crooned: "I've been feeling rational guilt lately. I thought of all I owe you, Carlo, and I could just cry. You were my friend when I had nobody else to turn to, and the fact that it all came to nothing doesn't make any difference." She slapped on top of his the right hand of the high-scorer on St. Something's girls' basketball squad of 1940.

"Glad to do it, Very," he answered quickly, for she was in the mood for something and he had little time; at that cursed early first light of Berlin he would lose his wits again. "I—"

"And I thought regardless of what went on you've always been my best boy friend, right here." She indicated her left melon, underneath which lay the heart. "Because you stuck with me, and whether you ever said it or not, that is love." She winced in ecstasy and pile-drove her linked fists into the back of that same old hand of his, flat upon the table. "Oh darling, you won't regret it!"

He withdrew; another such love and he was crippled for life. "Look, Very, what I wanted to talk about was—"

"I've been a fool," she said. "All the other men I ever knew wanted only one thing, like, excuse my French, this son of a bitch—"

"I don't want to know who he was," Reinhart interrupted. "And I'll tell you something about me." He had to do this, it was the only means by which he would ever get to his business. "So do I. Whatta you think I am, a fairy? I just use a different strategy. Now this thing about the abortion. If I could have arranged that, then I would always have something over you, get it? You'd be forced to let me have what I want." He feared it was too strong: what business was so pressing that one must for its sake kick another human being in love's groin?

Her quick answer spared his recantation. Through tears of happiness she sang, "Darling, I knew you loved me. You will never get a job in Hollywood, you are a terrible actor! You're afraid your feelings will be hurt, poor dear. But I tell you it's all right, I dote on you. I don't care if you are an enlisted man!"

So. One should not always walk against the wind. He rose and called her to him. Checking the door, she came. She had found him out, he admitted. He must have her, for love, and *now*.

Oh, oh, oh.

*Now.*

No, no, no.

*Now.*

Impossible. Duty. No. Where?

Her bailiwick. He was only a visitor.

Maybe—but no.

*Now.*

Ohhh. Terrible. Yet love was good.

Tell Tweedledum and Tweedledee to watch the shop.

They'll know.

So? A couple of privates.

So while he waited in the corridor, Very stopped by the treatment room and gave her excuse for ten minutes' absence. Then, down the hall, they found an empty, moon-illuminated ward whose patients had been transferred to another on the first floor, but the beds remained.

Not in love, he made gentle approaches. In love, sitting on the bed-edge, she grew fiercely reluctant. He had to take every button of her uniform as it were a separate fort. In her white slip she cried for shame and changed her mind, and having no effect on his, slapped his face but left her hand there and coyly squashed his nose. Dead weight he must lift to draw slip skirt over bottom. Opposing her own divestiture, she nevertheless stripped off his pajama shirt. His cheek wound throbbed in each little red hole left by the stitches; the invisible scalp-ache ached as if it would have a separate orgasm. In the sexiest presentation she did not match: brassiere of pink, pants of blue. A coldness on his back foretold that the swelling former was a hoax of sponge rubber or wadded powder puffs, and he knew he could not perform. But as he retreated, so did she charge. She liberated the strained hammock and held it conquered and limp as an enemy flag. Real? By Magellan, if they were not real, there were no Eastern and Western Hemispheres, which had sat as their models. *En voyage,* his trousers were suddenly gone, and also the canvas slippers. He dove towards her sea-blue pants. Then did she bound, like the well-known main, and give him a struggle beside which poor Monster's had been as a schoolgirl's in a pillow fight. Trudchen's old lacerations, which had healed, were reopened in his earlobes, and Very's teeth were twice as large. His solar was plexed and his clavicle cleaved. She probed for that rib which Adam had given to make her. When they fell to the floor, he hit lowmost, heel-ass-head. His only purpose was tenderness. Under incessant punishment he got her again to the upper level, dropped her on the mattress, *goyng, goyng* said the springs as she bounced with flying members. She gathered herself and shuddered, blurted: "My God, the night supervisor is due any minute!" She crawled towards the footboard and her clothes. "Shh," said Reinhart, "I think I hear her now!" She closed her legs, ivory in the half-light, pillars of the world; stood up and listened with flowing hair and sensate, rose-marked, goddess breasts, with belly-swell of satin and velvet groin. On Olympus sounded ox-eyed Hera's jealous thunder and Aphrodite practiced *Selbstmord*. "Where?" She heard the silence of the corridor, and was caught *en face* to Reinhart and borne down through the wine-dark sea.

Later, beached and dripping, she kissed his ten fingers and remarked: "You didn't hear the supervisor at all." He grinned splendidly, Zeus-like, and with his godlike ear heard her all over again.

Next morning he arose without his symptoms and with a grand conviction they were no more. In hubris he dared them to appear, dared also to draw up their roster: the quivering wire in his bowels; the cold sweat and hot chill; the vacancy of a head yet heavy; the apprehension of attack; the sense he shared the skin of another man; a feeling of insupport towards the sacroiliac, as if two segments there were rather gristle than bone; the famous derangement of time; a horror over possible events: Would Trooper, writing a letter in the next bunk, ever finish that line? Would Lieutenant Llewellyn start his tour on right or left side? Would, next time he looked, a straight pin still gleam from the crack in the floor?

Hard as he tried, he stayed healthy. Llewellyn, when he came and heard, was happy in his innocent, brotherly way and advised him to counsel with Millet. Trooper, waiting with his own troubles, in his turn told the lieutenant of the old dream of jumping without a chute.

Reinhart dawdled for more self-tests. When finally he was ready to see the captain, he was last in line. Waiting, he felt his euphoria fall into a dull headache of resentment towards the other patients, leavened by a sharp distrust of Millet.

Millet turned his head and blew a large nose into an olive-drab handkerchief, very insulting. "Of course your problems are important," he said. "More important than any other patient's. And so are those of each one of them—when they sit before this desk. That is a fact. Do you know what a fact is?"

Reinhart looked defiant. "Yes, something that cannot be changed."

The captain had finally got a haircut, the ballet skirt was trimmed to a gray fuzz. He sloppily put away his handkerchief.

"Isn't it rather, something that should not be ignored?"

All right, he knew everything. But Reinhart had seen him blow his nose; he was omnipotent and all-knowing, but he also caught colds.

"Well, I'll tell you a fact," Reinhart said. "In this fight, which I got into to help my friend, I killed the big German. It is a terrible thing to kill a man with your bare hands. I regret it, I think from now on I'll turn the other cheek, but I didn't have a choice then. But I don't feel *guilty*, if you know what I mean. It was a good fight, a fair one, I mean, for him. He was bigger and stronger than me, and we all take our chances. This is a fact. Why then instead do I feel a guilt for Schild's death? I'll tell you. Because I could have saved him."

Millet drew some rectangles on his pad. Nothing touched him. He said indifferently: "Why didn't you?"

Reinhart's symptoms had returned, full flood. While his chest shivered, bloodless, his suffused head burned; he could not recall whether he had sat in this interview one minute or all day; his whole spine was superimposed rings of lard; he looked for Millet any moment now to draw a long, keen blade and leap upon him.

Still looking away, Millet suddenly ordered him, as captain, not doctor, to answer.

Reinhart shouted, in glorious hatred. "Because I wanted you to die, you bastard."

"Not me," said Millet. "I was not there. That is a fact."

Terrible, deep remorse for the error. Not Millet, certainly: Reinhart wished to kill the only man he could ever talk to, and that was Millet, who wasn't even a Jew.

"Well, I don't feel so good. I'm not even sure I'm sitting here right now. Maybe I died back there on the field. What living man always feels guilty of what he hasn't done?"

"Every single one of us," Millet answered, although it had not been a question. "You are not special in that regard. In the heat of combat, soldiers always wish their comrades would get hit, as a kind of charm against their being hit themselves, and then experience guilt if their wish comes true—but not till the battle is over and they have time and security enough to brood about, rather than preserve, themselves."

"But," cried Reinhart, "that is all just personal. What I am involved in is the murder of a whole continent of Jews by my people."

"Excuse me." Millet reddened his nose with the handkerchief.

"Do you know what is good for that?" Reinhart asked. "One of those benzedrine inhalers."

"Thank you," said the doctor. "I will try one."

"Only not just before you go to bed. It will keep you awake. The benzedrine, you know."

Millet again expressed gratitude, and said: "The personal thing is very interesting. In the three weeks of our talks—"

"Is it so long? I can't remember, you see."

"Oh you will, you will. . . . Not once have you spoken of Lieutenant Schild as a person. Was he really your friend?"

He understood Millet's technique well enough. It was always to oppose the freely given and dig for, what was on Millet's terms and not his own, the withheld. Simulating anger and hurt —for his true feeling was of challenge to a battle of wits—he concluded the interview.

Then, back in bed, which had new, icy sheets, he found as usual he could not organize his thinking. Instead he tasted, in fancy, Veronica's aphrodisiac body and felt relief that tonight was her night off. Too rich for the blood. There was another crime for which he knew no remorse: taking advantage of her love. And now he compounded it. He wrote a note to Lori, asking her to come see him after work, and had it delivered by a wardboy, PFC Remington, whom he had done a favor for in England. "And," he cautioned, while Remington studied him with the same uncomfortable eyes he had used since Reinhart became a patient, "the German girl, and for Christ's sake not Miss Leary."

Lori came to the ward door an hour after the patients' suppertime. Nurse Bronson, Very's substitute, would have turned her away, but fortunately Lieutenant Llewellyn, permissive, dreamy type, had lingered late over his reports.

"A girl," he said encouragingly to Reinhart. "A visitor. Well, isn't that kind."

"It is most important that I see her for at least five minutes. I believe, sir, it would be a kind of therapy for my disorder. Of course I know it is against the rules, and if you say so, I must get rid of her."

Pain, like a wave of heat, warped Llewellyn's plastic glasses. "Oh no, Reinhart, we are absolutely opposed to duress! I hope you think better of us than that. I tend to agree with your feeling that you should see this kind lady."

"You won't think I'm a malingerer?"

"Please free yourself of any such apprehension. Perhaps you

will let me prescribe a mild sedative?" He went, lankily nervous, to a glass-front cabinet.

"No thank you, Lieutenant, she is not upset! Hahaha," laughed Reinhart.

After a moment Llewellyn bewilderedly smiled. Then he worried: "Normal interpersonal relationships are too rare in this somewhat false environment. No, I agree with you in your feeling that you should see her. But may I ask, if you don't mind, it is better in my judgment, whatever that is worth, that you and she do not confer out in the ward. It would disturb the other poor fellows. I should be glad to have your opinion on that, however."

"That's quite right, sir, quite right."

"Oh good. Well then, I am sure Miss Bronson, who has a fine sense of these things, will be happy to let you borrow the treatment room."

"We could be in love for a while," said Lori, her strong, realistic face undisturbed by his proposal, the harsh light, or Miss Bronson's periodic doorchecks one of which still echoed in the metal furniture. "But nothing else is practical."

Suffering a partial aphasia for the German language, he asked her to repeat.

Ingenuously, she shook her hair and said in his own tongue: "Uh little surp-rise: I study English already. . . . Wiss one another we may to love for some time. But alvays is *untunlich.*"

In his anticipatory fancies he had alternated between smugly hearing an absolute acceptance and listening with shame to an unqualified turndown. Instead, he had the usual compromise. He must learn, damn him, that people out there in the universe beyond his head were real and unimaginable. Had Schild really been his friend? What more could he, Reinhart, have done to prove it? Did he really love Lori? If not, why was he willing to live in that abominable cellar?

"*Liebling*," he answered in German, "I don't understand what you mean."

"Then you never will if I try to explain, Unteroffizier Carlo Reinhart, because my talents are not in analysis. You have met my brother and my husband. They never have allowed me to do anything but listen."

Reinhart left his table-seat, went to her, and took her hand. "Nobody has ever appreciated you."

Laughing astonishment, she squeezed him back. "What a strange remark! But I assure you that I have nothing to say, I have no ideas, why should I want to speak of nothing?"

"That's the old Prussian nonsense, children, kitchen, church is all a woman's good for." He was made reckless by his indignation: "Then come to America! I will send for you as soon as I arrive." Till that moment he had never believed he would go there again himself, but the sensible man, the Rotarian, the Philistine, who resides in the liver, somehow survives all blows to head and heart.

"*Kinder, Küche, Kirche . . . ,*" she repeated. "I have none of them. However, you would think my idea of American women just as funny, no doubt, but I shall spare you. America! This will interest Bach. You surely did not suspect he has long dabbled in technology. *Also,* he now announces to me that he has invented some means to make a glass which withstands heat. He has done this without a laboratory, simply mathematical equations in a notebook. Is this possible?—no. But in America someone will give money for it, perhaps. Is that likely?—no. But—"

"I didn't mean you could bring Bach!" Reinhart thought: besides, we already have Pyrex.

She shaped her thin lips as if to pronounce *o* umlaut.

"You understand," he said. "I even like him, but be fair once to yourself. That is no kind of life for a young woman. It isn't right to sacrifice oneself for somebody else, no matter who."

Placing upon him her famous direct look—that for which he

loved her—she answered: "Certainly. So do not do it for me. I don't know what 'Teutonic efficiency' is, since I have lived in Berlin all my life, but here you have an imitation: one, I love Bach very much; two, think of your self-respect! I am old enough to be your mother."

In confusion's rage, he shouted: "Then what did you mean by all your hints? If you love Bach why do you say you and I can love each other for a little while? Either way it's a betrayal of something or other. . . . I hate things that are dishonest and secret."

Hearing the nurse at the door, he withdrew his hand. Miss Bronson's beet-face, pickled, cautioned against further noise and gave him five minutes to conclude.

"Then you must hate love," said Lori, "not to mention life— no, I don't mean that. It has been a long day for me. Fräulein Leary stayed home from duty and had numerous requests—to press her clothes and so on. I think she is in love again. Why not get yourself an American girl? People from different countries really don't understand each other, as Bach says."

With one or two other more important items to check off his list, Reinhart put them by, to insert here: "That is why we have these tragic wars."

Lori rose and gathered her old coat about her waist. "According to Otto, no. War is the one time when they really do understand one another. Therefore he champions obscurity in human affairs—no," she raised a hand, "I will not discuss it; they both say I never can get anything right."

He had not only recaptured his sense of time: he had got back a better one than he lost, with a precise second hand. Exactly four minutes of Bronson's ration remained.

"Lieutenant Leary is in love *again*. Who was it the first time?"

The candid eyes were now impure. "Yourself, of course."

"Don't do me any favors. I'm not really sick. I've been faking all the while. And by the way, does nothing affect you? If you remember, Schild and I were at your home only a few hours before he was killed."

"If you remember, I have lived in Berlin for twelve years of Hitler and five years of war."

"I'm sorry," he said truly. "I just want you to tell me who was Miss Leary's lover in August."

"Facts, always facts, what will you do with them? *Oh-kay, it's ah deal!* This captain who lives, lived, with Oberleutnant Schild."

He began loudly to laugh, then choked it off for fear of Bronson. In mirth he used his own language: "He is shorter than her!"

"Please? As yet I don't understand so much English."

"*Knorke*, it doesn't matter. . . . So you are old enough to be my mother. You really are a twin of the doctor? Which would make you sixty." He shook his head. Two minutes left.

"Sixteen February, 1905, for both of us. Otto was the younger-looking before he went to Russia. I did not see him again until after he had gone through the camps." She shook Reinhart's hand, once up, once down. "If at eighteen I had had a son like you, and he survived, I would not be disappointed now."

Bronson stuck her head in and called time, and Reinhart growled: "Go away or I'll tell Lieutenant Llewellyn you applied duress." She winced and left.

"However," Lori went on, "I didn't and I'm not disappointed either."

"You would say then, life goes on."

She pushed a sportive lock behind her ear; she stood in need of a washing and combing; in the center of a general relief which he could not explain, Reinhart felt a twinge which he could: he would never provide the brush and soap.

"I do not!" she answered fiercely. "Life can do as it pleases." Still feral, she leaping captured his neck, drew down his head, and kissed his mouth.

He concealed his momentary anguish of regret: "Thanks, anyway, for never caring about me."

"Have it your own way." Tough, small, unkempt, Lori marched modestly into the corridor, uneasy Bronson voiding the route. Once through the outer door, she returned to hovering, vacant, liberated Reinhart for her formal peroration.

"I have forgotten! Here comes some English: 'Ve mawrn zuh death of a man of honor, First Lieutenant Schild, zalute zuh gallant Corporal Reinhart, shall effer keep green zuh memory of the former, and await with affection and respect the . . . re-choining by the latter of our fellowship, Knebel, M.D., your dear Lenore, and yours truly Bach, Ph. D.' *Also,* I have remembered every word!"

Old Sad Sack St. George had topped Veronica. Now Reinhart understood why the captain had not tried to visit him on the psycho ward. He should notify St. George that Very worked nights, up to suppertime the coast was clear; except that this action was as much as to admit he was privy to their quondam goings-on. And he detested having the goods on anybody, which were always squalid. Besides, the captain, who physically favored his father, carried to Reinhart a suggestion of what he, himself, would be in twenty years: middle-aged, ingratiating, secretly prurient. He didn't try to get in touch.

With Marsala, too, contact had been broken, which he laid to a primitive, Italianate superstition towards bats in the belfry: extravagance was permitted only in the service of lust, drink, and anarchy. Well, it had been an accident anyway that he was quartered with the damn guy; he was never so close to Marsala as the fellow ginzos with their home packages of sausage and cherry peppers.

Veronica returned to duty the next evening and squirted him loving, guarded looks as she went about ward business, but not having taken his afternoon nap, he dropped off to sleep at lights-out and so did not get to the office. Next morning he suspected having been touched on the face sometime during the night, but it could have been just a dream. However, he did find under his pillow a note on unlined paper, which read: "I'm going to knock myself off—Jesus destroy this mesage."

He actually believed it was Veronica's until Trooper reached over a long, thin arm and tore it away, saying, "I changed my mind."

Reinhart looked at his bird-dog face and said: "That wouldn't have settled anything."

"You're wrong," Trooper answered. "It would so have, but I just realized I don't want anything settled. That's my trouble."

"Well, what do I care about you?" Reinhart said irritably.

"That's all right. Nobody does. That's why I used to piss the bed, to get somebody to. But they didn't." He pulled the sheets over his head and said, underneath: "I don't care any more."

Furious, Reinhart jumped across the aisle and re-exposed the forsaken face. "Knock off that crap, Trooper. Tell me, is it true you got the Silver Star in the Holland jump?"

"I didn't deserve it. The ones who did were all killed."

"Don't hand me that. The fact is I understand you were screwed. Anybody else who singlehanded bumped off ten Germans and captured fourteen more would have got the DSC. An officer would have got it."

"He would?" He crept up on the pillow but still disbelieved, and they argued, Reinhart temporarily winning. However, it would be a long fight to get Trooper to understand that the world, and not himself, was wrong.

He concealed his new mission from Millet when they talked, and observed the captain's techniques. Afterwards, with his own variations, since Trooper was not so sophisticated a case as he, he used them on Trooper. Trooper ate a good lunch for the first time since he had come on the ward. Another two days, Reinhart had him traducing the doctors.

He said, almost smiling: "Reinhart, you ought to take up this psycho stuff when you get out of the Army."

Reinhart winked. "Have you been reading my mind?"

True, like knighthood, this profession gave you a permanent upper hand; like the priesthood, it made everybody else feel guilty and also grateful; like the Jews it was much reviled yet indispensable and always right. For example, Millet as a person was probably not much—he looked as if in civil life his sport was golf; his tips to caddies, meager—here he sat as universal daddy.

He sensed a certain competition with Millet in succeeding interviews, but was forced to simulate his old quest for approbation.

Towards the end of the week he reported: "I am all right again, Captain. I am sure now. I sleep well and in the regular hours, I realize that wound in my head was just imaginary, time is again just as it used to be, and I am not suspicious of anybody. Your treatment has been successful."

"That's good," admitted Millet. "Why do you refuse the recreational therapy?"

"Because I don't like to weave baskets and I already have a billfold."

Millet said permissively: "Uh-huh. Nurse Reynolds tells me"— he found the place in a document—"you stated a wish to make a shoulder holster. Which she opposed. Were you—"

"Oh that was a kind of joke. I wanted to give it to my roommate Marsala. His brother's a hood in Murder, Incorporated."

"No, I don't question that. I merely wished to know if Reynolds' refusal made you angry."

"Yes—well goddammit, she said no in that sweet, tolerant manner used towards psychos, yet I know what she was thinking—don't let Reinhart do anything that suggests violence."

"What did you do then?"

"I walked away and didn't say anything." He stared at Millet's pale, bored eyes and shouted: "What in hell do you think I did, beat her up?"

"Did you want to?"

"If you don't mind my saying it, sir, you know about as much of a man's mind as a golfball." He glanced at Millet's desk, insultingly clear of letter openers, etc., even pencils, for obvious reasons. "If you mean deep down, I probably wanted to screw her. All men want to make love to every woman and kill every man. Man is a savage only partially tamed."

Millet smiled. "Is that your own theory?"

"I read it somewhere, and then consulted my own soul. I know you people don't think a man can help himself, but I have."

"Was Lieutenant Schild your friend?"

Reinhart sighed. "You want me to say no. But one thing I will not do to get out of here: lie. It seems very clever to look only for the deep secrets. What we see of a person is supposedly only the false exterior; what he *really* is, is underneath and hidden. Thus a man who appears generous is really selfish, great lovers are secretly queers, and heroes are really cowards covering up. A fellow who feels guilty about the Jews is actually the worst anti-Semite of all, and so on. No doubt this is true. But out in the world we have no time to check these things. If a bully comes towards you with a club, you have no chance to reflect that he is actually not frightening but pitiful, that if you gave him love and understanding he would be your friend.

"Because if the front is a lie, so are the depths when taken alone. For himself, a hero may be a coward. For you, if he is on your side in a battle you do not want to know what he is in some reality outside yours. A Don Juan may be a fairy, but in practice he will make love to your girl and not to you. Do you see what I mean? The façade, too, has a reality and truth. You sit here in front of me like a god, asking me questions which I cannot ask you. Why? For reasons of your own. Somewhere back no doubt you grew a guilt towards people with mental troubles because you really have contempt for them. But I don't want to hear about it and obviously you don't want to tell it.

"Now the Jews and me. My feelings about them are irrational. Actually the Jews bore me stiff. And so do the Germans. All I ever cared about was old medieval Nürnberg, and that is long gone. Italy, I think, is what I like, with sunshine and that melodic language. I also hate politics and sociology and all that crap that deals with people as groups. I hated those mobs of idiots screaming *Sieg Heil!* and who didn't?, but I also dislike those hordes of Russians in Red Square, who in spite of Communism are supposed to be generally good, and also the 'starving multitudes' of Asia and the 'laboring masses' everywhere. I name these examples in an effort to be honest. I don't like conventions of generals and bosses any better, but there everybody agrees with me.

"So with the Jews, who seem to be a persistent mob throughout history, only acting in the reverse of the usual mob; they storm nothing but are stormed. They are always around with their dull troubles and their rituals and their foods, feeling special everywhere and superior. I confess I used to think it was a trick for the Jews to always complain about mistreatment. They seemed a race of gripers.

"Then the Nazis came. Or rather, I finally noticed the Nazis. And they were something new. When you speak badly about the Nazis you cannot tell a lie. Maybe, secretly, every gentile wants to kill every Jew, but the Nazis did it in practice and the other Germans, or many of them, didn't care. But you see, *someone must care.*"

Millet raised his head, which had been lowered as if in sleep, and asked: "Why?"

"So that Germany will not perish."

"But you were concerned about the Jews."

"If you want to understand anything, you must listen," Reinhart chided. "I am concerned about myself."

Millet's head sank again.

"So I met Schild that night. He forces himself on me. The motives get all mixed up, who is doing what for whom. We listen to a man who is himself confused. It is a grotesque evening, like everything in Berlin turns out to be: giants, twins who are apparently twenty years apart, blind men, would-be abortionists, experts on art, turncoats, Communists, ex-prisoners of the concentration camp, good Germans who turn out to be bad, and vice versa, and Schild and I."

"How many people were there?"

"In addition to Schild and me, only three. I assure you it was fantastic and ridiculous. And all in this damp cellar, but we sat on a Goblin couch worth a thousand dollars. And afterwards we get in this mortal combat. But I'll tell you this: it all happened and is still easier to believe than the concentration camps— which, by the way, the Russians have, too.

"Now I'm ready to answer. Was Schild my friend? On one hand, yours, no. I used him. If he hadn't been a Jew I wouldn't have given him a minute, for he was a kind of creep. I felt this definite satisfaction when he got it in the back, and it wasn't the one you spoke of. More complex than that. I felt it because, fighting for him as I was, *nobody could blame me for his death*. Well, here comes a joke: no one does but myself.

"But was he my friend? In my sense, yes. He was someone I could talk to, and not the way I am talking to you, which is a sort of fraud since you are invulnerable and never talk back. And then for another reason. When you hear it you will never let me out of Psycho, because I guess it means I really am nuts. When Schild was a boy he read the King Arthur stories. And he still believed them up to the time he died."

Millet asked lazily: "What's 'nuts' about that?"

Reinhart groaned: "Because so do I. Really."

# CHAPTER 23

TEMPELHOF AIRPORT was still a mess of cracked-eggshell buildings, but the Air Force had policed up the field and laid its steel-mesh runways. Grounded craft sat dirty and rather larger than they looked in the sky, on what Reinhart believed was in the jargon of the trade called the "apron." Identification of airplanes was a prideful talent with some people, not him. The nearest fellow in the party, a tall thin T/5 with heavy eyebrows arched in perpetual curiosity, pointed out a Liberator, joked: "It looks like a pregnant dachshund."

Upon application the T/5 confessed to being a case of chronic dermatitis, showed a bandaged right hand, said with a smirk of self-hatred: "I guess you were wounded."

"No," said Reinhart, pointing to Trooper, who stood sickly at his left, "he and I are psychos." Succeeding that, Trooper dug him with an elbow of embarrassment; he turned to the gutless fellow and bawled him out; therefore he did not see the T/5's reaction.

But he heard him say: "Well, this skin trouble is supposed to be psychosomatic, so we're all in the same boat."

"It's nothing to brag about," Reinhart answered. Crushed, the T/5 monkeyed with his duffle bag.

Staff Sergeant Owens, in charge of the patient group from door of hospital to hatchway of plane, again called the roll and lost four names in the roar of revving engines and the braggadocio bellowing of mechanics.

"See that rusty heap over there behind the Liberator?" Trooper asked Reinhart. "I bet you beaucoup marks that's what we got to ride. And we won't get any chutes. Oh my busted back, I feel bad."

426

"Now Trooper, I'll tell you a thing. Know that Air Corps gunner down at the end of the ward? When I told him we were shipping out to Paris by plane, he said, 'Then I'll never get out of Berlin. I love to fly but one time two months ago I dreamed the engines conked and I had to jump.' That's why he ended up in Psycho—the dream has haunted him ever since. He says he would rather go down in flames than hit the silk. Everybody has his own horror. You don't mind the jump but are leery of the plane."

"That's on account of my training, Carlo. Those instructors never had any elasticity."

Instead of wondering what that meant, Reinhart hung himself up on his own term: he was very leery of Very Leary. Although as late as the evening before she had betrayed no knowledge of his leaving, he, the old victim of guile, now practitioner, would not feel safe until he soared the air. He looked towards the buildings and would not have been astonished had Veronica come sailing from them and taxied up the mesh, dwarfing the Liberator. What a piece to run away from!; he supposed again that he *was* nuts. The T/5 there, who stared hornily at the female member of a professional party heading towards them, would sell his country for a Veronica.

He was torn by a distant shout and in involuntary panic tried to hide behind emaciated Trooper, who, a blotter for anybody else's emotion, almost wept: "They after you, too?"

Reinhart regained his self-respect. "Don't get your balls in an uproar. I'm looking out for you."

"It's not," said Trooper, "that I'm afraid to get hurt. I just don't like the humiliation."

The shout was closer, and clearer, and in the two syllables of Reinhart's cognomen. He turned to face the firing squad and saw—Marsala. He ran to meet him, ignoring Sergeant Owens' howl.

Ten yards away, Marsala slowed to a measured, inexorable

pace, waded in, hosing his target with an abuse of great variety and color: scatophagous Reinhart, the traitor, the Oedipus Rex, the fornicator of infants, the defiler of graves, the double-barreled international bastard and revolving son of a bitch.

"Fuck you and fuck your friends," he at length concluded. He turned away. His eyes were wet.

"I was going to write you from Paris, buddy. They only told me yesterday I was on shipment, and wouldn't let me get out to say goodbye."

Marsala wiped his nose and fired up a big black cigar, throwing the match over a shoulder.

"Well whaddo I care where you go in Paris, huh? What's it to me you die like a turd? You goin' on a plane, huh? I don't mean what I said then, I take off the curse, you die and ya blood will be on my heart. Here, you wanna cigar? I ain't mad no more. Besides you're a poor dumb cuckoo. . . . You're shit, too. How'd you work it? I'll say this for you, you got a lot of guts and talent to fool that old Millet. I been wrong about you for years. I thought you was this college type. But for Christ in heaven, after looking at you I think we run my brother from Murder Inc. for chief of police. You make a whore out of this young kid, you knock off a guy with your bare hands, then you play nuts and get home before everybody else. What college you come from, I think it was reform school."

Reinhart modestly smiled at this somewhat inflated précis of his career, which however was sound in the essentials—including the last-named. Millet had been on the verge of sending him back to duty—believing in the actuality of King Arthur turned out to be quite O.K. mentally—when in the interests of a new scheme Reinhart relapsed into the old symptoms. Just as he had foreseen, the ward needing his bed for new arrivals, Millet got rid of him.

"I don't know if this is the best way. I might get hung up in Paris for months, but I have to take care of that paratrooper over there. Where do you think they'll send us?"

Marsala spit out a fragment of wet tobacco. "The 179th General. That's on the north side in a place called Clitchy."

"Stinks, I guess."

"Oh no." Marsala's eyebrows climbed. "I saw it. I ran down there when we was in Normandy. It ain't a sow pen like the 1209th, I tell you that much. And then you get a pass, you go to Pig Alley—and don't try to crap me any more you would go to this Loo museyum."

The party of flight nurse, co-, and full pilot had passed them, and sure enough, skirted the Liberator for the rusty cargo plane behind it. Reinhart felt imminent-departure gas in his stomach.

"Well, this is it, buddy. I'll write you a letter, tell you how it goes. You'll get home yourself any day now, you got more than enough points." He shook his hand.

Marsala diffidently picked his nose. "I never answer."

"Why not? You going to hold a grudge?"

"Whaaat grudge, you rummy?" He punched Reinhart's hand aside. "Give the Princess a smooch for me. . . . Now I guess with all your twat here you forgot her: you know, that married chicken with a husband in the paratroops."

Oh by God, Dianne Cooley. He owed her a letter for three months. And her husband Ernie, in the 82nd Airborne, the bright shoulder patch of which he saw, across the field, on the narrow shoulder of Trooper. It was an off chance.

"To tell you the truth," he said. "I'm not convinced that I ought to leave. I like the Army, as I always told you, and I like Berlin, but it seems to be a good time to get out of both. But I'll have to play it straight in Paris. I don't want a Section Eight discharge. That might affect my career."

Marsala shivered in his overcoat. "It's gonna be a cold winter here for Jesus sake. A week yet to Halloween and it's already like a witch's tit. They're cutting down trees in the Tier Garden. No coal. . . . Career? I got your career." He squeezed himself in the crotch. "You're gonna be a hood, that's what."

"A psychiatrist. How about that? Except for a couple of people, including you, everybody I see is sick, boy, and bad."

"Especially you," Marsala complained. "I take back what I said about you fakin'. I knew old Millet couldn't be fooled."

Reinhart shook the buddy's hand again and saw the black eyes swim. "So long, Jimmy, you were the best of them all. Have fun with Trudchen."

Holding his back stiff, he rejoined the group of patients. Time, where did old Time go, what were its mysteries? Not the narrow time towards which some weeks ago he was disordered, but that great gray fog behind us and before us, into which our lovers and friends vanish, events pass, and which claims even our old selves as we stand here in the limited clearing, nude in our newest one. Having learned from the Italians that crying is no reflection on a fellow's manliness, Reinhart dropped a tear or two for the summer of 1945, already gone; the war, long gone; the Army, soon to go; his twenty-first year, going drop by drop; and inventoried in water the dear people known and lost in this adventure, Schild, Lori, Bach, even including Veronica, whom he now believed he really did love but even so intended to remain adamant towards, and that was the sadness of it.

By the time he rejoined Trooper his face had dried. He anyway reached for his handkerchief. A tractor was towing the cargo crate to a clear vista on the landing strip.

"Yep, that's it," said Trooper. "Like I said, the old C-47. I'm gonna faint."

"Like hell you are," Reinhart muttered. "Wait a minute, anyway, I'm looking for something." No handkerchief in his pocket. He opened his duffle bag. On top lay a little Red Cross sack of dirty socks and pinned to it was a note which he could, and did, read without undoing.

Kiddy—thanks for not making a scene about leaving. You have always been decent about a person's feelings. I

will always think of you close to my heart but I can't get
in touch with you anymore like this or any other way,
*because*—well, I never did tell you the name of my real
boy friend and I better not now—ha! what I called him in
front of you was s.o.b.—nasty to laugh tho, because I do
love him very much and now we are back together. He has
to get a divorce from his wife but is not a Roman Catholic
so its O.K. I have sinned but true love conquers all. We
plan a double wedding with Ann Lightner & Lt. Pound
who is in the same fix as X. Don't know where we'll live
—all around, I expect, since X is Regular Army. Oops,
maybe I told you too much. Anyway, I send you all the
love I can without being disloyal to my Husband To Be.
Your intimate friend,

VERY

He got a handkerchief and blew his nose just as Owens called
the roll again and, conveniently, just at his own name, and the
sergeant took it as answer. They filed towards the open doors in
the plane's belly. Trooper didn't collapse, because Reinhart
threatened to forsake him in Paris if he did.

Reinhart was last in line. He took a final noseful of Berlin air,
which was cold and fresh and yet carried a faint dust of ruin.
German rubble-workers around the administration building conversed in their native argot, and by some acoustical principle he
could hear them.

"*Kommste imma erst so spät nach Hause?*"

"*Nee, nur wochentags. Der Sonntag jehört meiner Familie—da
schlafe ick'n janzen Tag.*"

He did not understand a word. From the air the city would
look like the crater-pocked, man-void moon. Finally one foot, and
then the other, stepped from Brandenburg sand-plain to echoing
metal floorboard.

The flight nurse, who wore a long green coverall, took the
roster from departing, sycophantic Owens and began her own

count. This time Reinhart watched for Trooper's response. It came on "Poteet, Hastings F., Jr.," a name Reinhart had heard as many times as the roll was called and never connected with his patient for the simple reason that Trooper did not answer properly but rather raised one finger and coughed.

Reinhart shouted "ho" at his own name, which came right after, and asked Trooper: "Did you know a guy in the 82nd named Ernie Cooley?"

And Hastings F. Poteet said instantly, with no sense whatsoever of the coincidence: "Oh you know him, too. They'll never get Cooley."

"I'll be damned. You really know him, Ernie Cooley, from Norwood, Ohio? I used to go out with his wife, if it's the same one." He expatiated on the theme of one small world.

Which made no impression on Trooper, whose delusion was that while the world is infinite, all things are simultaneous. He waited with his polite, beagle eyes until he had his chance to say that Cooley had deserted in Normandy in June, 1944, almost as soon as the chutes hit the ground in their first jump of the war, and that, again, they would never get him—because if they did it was curtains.

"Why?"

"Desertion in the face of the enemy. They shoot you in the heart for that—and for other things too," he added darkly.

The T/5, who sat on Reinhart's left and had been listening, struck his curious brows into their business: "That's almost as bad as what sometimes happens in the hospital: desertion in the face of an enema. When they catch you for that, you get shot in the ass."

Reinhart thought it very funny—he was near hysteria, anyway, at leaving Berlin to rejoin the earth-people; the doors were still open, the engine quiet, the pilot outside on the ground, lazily joking with a mechanic; he could still burst away and regain the great, ruined, dear city—but a single slight smile and the T/5 would own him for the rest of the flight.

He looked about for another victim on which to stick this adhesive fellow. Against the other wall, on the line of metal seats which paralleled his own, sat eight or nine types; on his side, eight or so more. In addition to Trooper and himself there were five other psychos, all quiet cases, whom he knew only by sight; one obvious traveler from the skin ward—a sergeant of limited dimensions, whose acned cheeks were relief maps of Berlin; beyond himself, nobody from the staff of the 1209th.

The pilot climbed in and sauntered forward. Ground crew without, and nurse inside, sealed the doors, and probability surrendered to necessity. His chance was forever gone. Only Trooper's whine saved Reinhart from claustrophobic frenzy.

"We won't need chutes, old buddy," he told him with a pat on the shoulder patch. "These machines never fail." He looked across to Sergeant Acne for confirmation and saw, in spite of the eruptions, the crewcut showing at one side of a cocked overseas cap, the OD overcoat—he saw—well, he saw, but sick in the gut from his hallucination he begged forgiveness of Jehovah Millet and would have given blood sacrifices to have Him there to say he did not see—Schatzi. "Do they, Sarge?" he nevertheless asked.

Sarge silently turned his head towards the pilot's cabin. Poor chap, if he wasn't Schatzi—in his profile, corrupted by the malady, there was little likeness—he was to be pitied, for a hideous boil lived in the very orifice of his left ear. He had not heard.

But why should he be Schatzi? How could he be? From the second button of his coat hung the medical tag with which they each had been labeled, like laundry sacks, at the hospital. Then there were dogtags, medical records, shipping orders, and duplicate copies of the roster for everybody from Eisenhower down. And what of the ludicrous, revealing accent? Of course, some GIs were refugees, and many native Americans went through the Army with never a public word but "sir."

"Y'all want some chewin' gum?" The nurse stood before them, offering Juicy Fruit. "Y'ears won' have diffi-culty with th'air preshah, you chew gum." Tall, serpentine, rather slack-titted in the coverall, wearing tawny hair a bit long for a servicewoman, she handed a slice to each—her fingers touched Reinhart's and did they not linger?—and turned to the other row.

Sarge accepted his piece, unwrapped it with enormous care, folded the paper and placed it in his breast pocket!, put the gum in his mouth, chewed—and the largest boil beneath his left eye loosened and fell to the floor, where it stuck like the actor's putty it was.

Now was Reinhart astonished at himself: despite this proof he could not believe sergeant and Schatzi were synonymous. In Berlin he had learned to doubt all appearances, which must also include a false one: that is, its falsity might consist in its being real. The world was strange—and interesting.

And difficult. For of course he recognized Schatzi and his problem was what to do about it, which he would rather avoid. Crucial times were not at an end with the simple killing of a Monster, the dying of a Schild, with an unrequited proposal, or with leave-taking of lovers and friends; nor even with personal *non compos mentis*.

But the gods, to whom he was dear, no matter how far they had permitted him to wander alone, finally furnished aid. Apollo resolved himself into a sunbeam, came down through the livid overcast and penetrated the Plexiglas window, striking the T/5 in the medulla oblongata, inspiring him to jar Reinhart with his elbow and add: "That's what the sentries say in the hospital: 'Halt. Who goes there, friend or enema?' "

"What did we do to deserve you!" Reinhart cried in burlesque despair. "Talk to Trooper. I see a guy I know." He rose and crossed the cabin.

The seat at Sarge's left had been used briefly by the nurse to sort her gear; now it was empty. Sarge turned the other way when Reinhart took it. Seen at six inches, the make-up was an outrageously poor job, the acne an obvious work of mucilage, eyebrow pencil, and lipstick (Trudchen's 'raddest of the rad').

Whom could it have taken in for a moment? Answer: Every typical person, who would no sooner see the disability than avert his eyes, so as not to embarrass the sufferer; so as for health's sake to suppress an interest in the corrupt; so as—but Reinhart, enough! The typical person simply would not imagine such a fake and therefore would not see one.

Under the cover of the other passengers' conversation, which was amplified in the metal tube, he asked into the sergeant's pseudo-foul ear: "What did you hope to gain?"

Schatzi faced front, seemingly watched the T/5 across the aisle, and answered, quietly venomous: "I vill get to America and you vill not try to stop me."

Reinhart checked: the nurse had gone into the cargo compartment in the rear; Trooper, the T/5, and a redheaded fellow were pooling complaints about the Army.

"You are mad," he whispered, "hopelessly, utterly mad, and I pity you."

Schatzi choked on his gum, which he had been chewing all wrong anyway—too consciously, like all Europeans, as if it were candy rather than a substitute for twitching—choked and responded in desolation and fear: "Let me alone or you'll be sorry."

Reinhart covertly withdrew a roll of Occupation marks from his pants pocket—they had been too many for the wallet—and without a glance at the denominations pulled off and retained two, and placed the rest under Schatzi's tight arm.

"I promised I would get your money from Schild. There it is."

Schatzi was truly overcome; among the patches of false acne grew areas of real emotion's rash, mottled, hot. He grappled with his American uniform, then with himself. He wiped his chin and drew away a palm of smeared cosmetic. His eyes sprinkled. Yet he managed to stay inconspicuous. They still had no one's notice.

"I do not understand your tricks," he whisperingly wailed. "Are you the new agent? But being an American still comes first—I cast myself upon your merciness. Oh God do not give me to

Chepurnik. You cannot know what they are like, they are not people as we are. They are objects without blood. See what happens to Schild. With this I had nothing to do, believe me." But towards the end he had forgotten and raised his voice. The T/5 heard and in a mock soprano began to sing "They Wouldn't Believe Me." Schatzi turned on him the old death-ray eyes and he shriveled in midnote.

"I don't care about your squalid black-market deals," said Reinhart.

Instantly Schatzi dried and hardened. "Oh yes, your lovely friend Schild, for whom you would, and did, kill. You saw none of his profits, ja? He used you as a sexual rubber." At last he gave him the whole hideous face. But it was more ludicrous than repulsive. He stank of Juicy Fruit. "Black market! Black market was my trade. This swine Schild sold his country. This fine land America that we poor victims of to-tah-li-tahrianism would die for, he died to betray. With good fortune I happen to learn of these facts in the course of my business. I report them to the Ami FBI, who are ready to seize him just when comes this well-known fight."

Calmly, Reinhart enjoyed the lies, a souvenir of Europe. They would be all too rare in America. But he must get to work before the engine started, the propellers revolved, and his initiative was gone. If he knew the pedantic ways of people who do such things as fly planes, the C-47 would not kill its motor, once started, for the end of the world. And just this time he did not want Schatzi to succed in an imposture. Those of the past he forgave him—yes, truly forgave, not like a god but like a man; he expected no reward—but this one was too vulgar.

"What shall we do about you?" he asked, preparing to rise.

"You harm me at your own cost!"

"My dear fellow," said Reinhart. "With all good will, I cannot understand you."

Schatzi began a sneer of victory—or, at any rate, what *he*

thought was one—but the Juicy Fruit clogged in his teeth. Humiliated, he plucked it out and held it in his right hand. Obviously it felt nasty there, and no better in the left. He brought the paper wrapper from his breast pocket and was on the point of rolling the little gum ball therein, when the nurse came out of the cargo chamber and, undulating bow-wards, saw his heresy and warned: "You don' chew, you gon' be dog-sick." He guiltily returned it to his mouth, where, according to his expression, it grew to baseball size.

"Why you grinnin'?" she pseudo-sternly asked Reinhart. She bent and read his tag. "What's this, an Eyetalian name? Carlo. Kind of cute, though. You a psycho? Well then what do the normal ones look like?"

When she left Schatzi threw in the towel. He gagged on the gum, finally swallowed it, and again begged for mercy in the name of the United States of America: "You people believe a man is what he will become rather than what he has been, *ja?* I tell you I have reformed. Just this minute, sitting here amidst your fine comrades who love one another. I do not ever belong to anysing. Loneliness! Lack of love! These can make a man to a criminal. Have I been a rascal?—no. Yet had impulses come to me which have been dangerously near. After I arrange with great difficulty and money to be included in this shipping-to-Paris I discover your name on the list thereof. Wal, I thought, this Reinhart causes trouble and I strike back. His German relatives! Yes, I have found them, Heinz Tischmacher, son of his grandfather's sister and second cousin to him. Tischmacher, Heinz: office worker, member of the Nazi Party. Tischmacher, Frau Emmi: likewise. Tischmacher, Reinhold: twenty-one years of age, graduate of Hitler Youth to the Waffen SS, killed on the Eastern Front in 1944. Tischmacher, Gertrud, Trudl, Trudchen: sixteen, member of the Jungmädel, girls' branch of Hitler Jugend.

"On the other side of his descent Tischmacher has a distant relation to this monstrosity Bach, whom he takes money from, for four years, not to reveal to his Nazi comrades that Bach, Lenore, *Mischling* Jew, has not gone to Switzerland so much as does she hide in a closet of her man's flat so as to avoid the Gestapo and subsequent killing."

"These then are my people," said Reinhart. But he worried only over whether he had committed incest with Trudchen. "You have done a good job. I'm afraid this is all I have left to pay you." He brought forth his last two notes.

Chuckling madly, Schatzi refused them. "No, these are not your kinsfolk, dear boy! Is not this evidence of my reform? This is my untruth with which I prepared to threaten you. Which now I reveal and confess. This evil impulse to destroy you which I have conquered. So Christ said, '*Die Wahrheit wird Euch frei machen.*'"

"Destroy *me?*" asked Reinhart. He banged his head back against the fuselage, denting it (the fuselage), and guffawed.

Schatzi smiled, frightened to death but also hopeful. "Ah then," he whispered, "mirth and good feeling. You will not expose me, *ja?* In the States we must make a partnership: you belong and have the handsomeness and the muscles—however did you break that great swine's back?—I provide the mental."

The nurse appeared at the door of the pilot's cabin, her hip reared to catch her sexy, sinous wrist. She said: "Y'all settle down and connect your seat belts. We go in two seconds. . . . Ah got my eye on you, laughin' Carlo!" She would be a different kind of piece.

Reinhart shook Schatzi's hand and winked elaborately. He whispered: "My friend, you have my word on it." Then he went to the nurse, and for another reason feeling her supple arm, betrayed him.

## AUTHOR'S NOTE

As many readers will have recognized, I am indebted to Konrad Heiden's classic work *Der Fuehrer* (tr. by Ralph Manheim, New York, 1944) for some of the events in the career of one of my imaginary people.